One foe of yours is human,
One foe of yours is not.
And everyone you love most dear
In their dark web is caught:
Your brother fights for freedom,
At perhaps a bloody cost.
But it's here in these dark streets tonight
That the war is won or lost.

King's Man and Thief

A spellbinding adventure of magic and intrigue
from acclaimed author Christie Golden

Praise for *Instrument of Fate*:

"This is a fantasy in which the fears are as real as the
beauties . . ."
—Susan Shwartz, author of *The Grail of Hearts*

"With this launch, may we see more of the universe
through Golden's eyes!"
—Katherine Kurtz

"Most impressive . . . One could continue singing the
praises of this stupendous novel, but far better that you
discover them for yourself."—*Starlog*

D1571104

Ace Books by Christie Golden

INSTRUMENT OF FATE
KING'S MAN AND THIEF

King's Man
and
Thief

Christie Golden

ACE BOOKS, NEW YORK

If you purchased this book without a cover, you should be aware that this book is stolen property. It was reported as "unsold and destroyed" to the publisher, and neither the author nor the publisher has received any payment for this "stripped book."

This book is an Ace original edition,
and has never been previously published.

KING'S MAN AND THIEF

An Ace Book / published by arrangement with
the author

PRINTING HISTORY
Ace edition / May 1997

All rights reserved.
Copyright © 1997 by Christie Golden.
Cover art by Jeff Barson.
This book may not be reproduced in whole or in part,
by mimeograph or any other means, without permission.
For information address: The Berkley Publishing Group,
200 Madison Avenue, New York, NY 10016.

The Putnam Berkley World Wide Web site address is
http://www.berkley.com

Make sure to check out *PB Plug*,
the science fiction/fantasy newsletter, at
http://www.pbplug.com

ISBN: 0-441-00440-7

ACE®
Ace Books are published by The Berkley Publishing Group,
200 Madison Avenue, New York, NY 10016.
ACE and the "A" design are trademarks
belonging to Charter Communications, Inc.

PRINTED IN THE UNITED STATES OF AMERICA

10 9 8 7 6 5 4 3 2 1

As, at its heart, this is a book about love of family,
I therefore dedicate it to mine:
My husband Michael,
my parents, James and Elizabeth Golden
and my siblings, Chip Golden and Liz Ann Reynolds

King's Man
and
Thief

PROLOGUE

1278

"You don't have very long to get ready," Kastara chided her husband gently.

"I told you, I'm not going." Deveren's voice sounded like a stubborn child's, even in his own ears. His physical strength, though not inconsiderable, came from lean, toned muscles rather than a bulky, powerful frame. That, combined with a friendly, open face, made him seem much younger than his twenty-seven years. That boyish face was presently set in a scowl. He sprawled in one of the beautifully carved chairs that decorated their solar. Horse muck clung to his fine leather boots and spattered his breeches. His tunic was permeated by the scent of sweaty Deveren and sweatier Flamedancer, his lively new horse, and Lord Deveren Larath took a perverse pleasure in knowing that he probably smelled worse than the lowliest stable hand in his employ. He crossed his arms and glared at his wife.

Kastara arched a raven-dark eyebrow. At that moment there came a knock on their solar door.

"Enter, Yalissa," called Kastara.

"Go away," barked Deveren at the same moment.

Yalissa, knowing full well who was master of the house in this instance, stepped inside. "I've brought the tub and hot water as you requested, milady," said the elderly servant, motioning two strong young boys inside. The three set about readying Deveren's bath, selectively deaf to their master's complaints.

"I told you, I'm not going. I haven't been to a performance here in Braedon without you since the night we met, and I refuse to start now."

From their bed, Kastara gazed at her husband, amusement quirking her full lips. She absently rubbed her abdomen, eight months swollen with their first child, as she replied.

"It's a premiere," she said. "You're expected to attend premieres, love. That's why you're called a *patron*." Her blue eyes sparkled with mischievous humor in her pallid face.

Deveren gazed at her, his sullenness fading as he took in her paleness, her thin hands moving with an ancient rhythm over the mound of her belly. He could see the blue veins clearly through her skin, and those dark circles under her eyes worried him. Kastara had always been fragile. Part of her beauty was the enchanting contrast between the delicate frame and the fiery spirit it housed. But this pregnancy had strained her more than it should have.

"I won't enjoy it without you," Deveren protested in all earnestness. While master and mistress argued, the bath had been filled. The boys placed a cake of soap and neatly folded towels on the rush mat beside the tub. Yalissa took a moment to scatter some herbs into the steaming water, then followed the two serving boys out of the room. She closed the door quietly behind her.

"The cast will be heartbroken if you're not there. You've nurtured this show since the beginning, Dev, and if you're not in the audience tonight—well, you're always telling me how sensitive actors are."

"But . . ." He searched for the words to continue his argument, even as he undressed, immersed himself in the fragrant hot water, and reached for the cake of soap. "But I don't like leaving you alone here while I'm off enjoying myself. It doesn't seem fair."

Kastara rose with the singular combination of awkwardness and grace that marked a pregnant woman, and eased herself down onto a stool beside the tub. She took the cake from his hands and began to scrub his back with it.

"We'll be fine," she assured him. "Cassim and Yalissa will be here, and in case Baby decides he wants to come early they'll call in Health's Blesser right away. Besides, you leave me alone all the time while you conduct business during the day."

"That's different," countered Deveren, taking the soap back and finishing the job Kastara had begun. "That's not fun."

"If it's a good play," Kastara continued, her fingers playing with her husband's sandy brown hair, "it'll still be running when Baby comes. And if it's a bad play—well, then you've saved me from a dreadful evening."

He grinned at her, his hazel eyes laughing. They both knew he'd go, now, and Deveren was not one to hang on to a bad mood. Kastara answered his smile with one of her own, then heaved her bulk off the stool and back into the bed.

Deveren finished bathing, dried himself, and dressed in garb appropriate to the theater: a full-length, parti-colored tunic, a jeweled belt that accentuated his trim waist, hose, fine slippers, and a hat with a sweeping feather.

Kastara sighed in mock appreciation. "If I weren't with

child," she teased, "I might not let you go to the theater, handsome husband of mine."

He sat down beside her on the bed. "If you weren't with child," he rejoined, "I just might *get* you with one tonight, beautiful wife of mine."

Deveren lowered his head and kissed her. He'd meant it to be gentle—Health's Blesser had warned that Kastara was having a difficult pregnancy and was not to be overly excited by anything, including her husband's attention—but she snaked her hand up behind his head and crushed his lips to hers, hungry, seeking. She wanted him to go, yes, but like Deveren, Kastara would not enjoy the hours apart.

Ending the kiss, Deveren gazed down at his wife. He suddenly felt that he shouldn't go, that he should stay here tonight, but that was foolish . . . wasn't it? Kastara had reminded him that she would be well looked after for the, what, only four hours that he would be gone.

Gently he placed a hand on her enormous stomach, making a father's contact with the small being housed within. Kastara placed her hand over his. He smiled down at her, thinking that her black hair spread across the goose-down pillow looked like a dark halo, and went to the play.

It was good, better than earlier rehearsals had indicated. The weather cooperated, and the amphitheater just outside the Braedon city limits that was home to the city's dramatic productions during the summer months was filled to capacity.

Deveren had just settled into the second act, thoroughly engrossed, when he felt a light tap on his shoulder. He glanced up, dragging his eyes away from the most exciting scene in the whole play, to gaze into the concerned face of Captain Telian Jaranis, head of the local guardsmen of Braedon, and a personal friend.

Deveren's first thought was that the child had indeed come early. But Cassim would have come for him, not a guardsman, and there would be joy mixed with worry on the elderly servant's face—not this strange expression that sat upon Telian's handsome features.

"The baby," Deveren cried, not caring that he disturbed his fellow audience members. "Oh, gods, she's lost the baby."

"Lord Larath," and the formal title chilled Deveren's soul, "I'm afraid there's been . . ." Telian swallowed hard, could not complete the news he had been sent to deliver. To Deveren's horror he saw tears in the guard's eyes.

Growling deep in his throat, Deveren sprang at the captain, clutched his tunic. Telian's men moved, but a gesture from their commander stayed their swords. The crowd gasped, watching the real tragedy unfolding instead of that being performed by the actors.

"What happened?" demanded Deveren, his teeth clenched.

"There was an intruder," began Telian. "He broke in— we think he assumed that you had both gone to the performance—and Kastara—"

Deveren let Telian go and raced for the stables, taking the stone stairs that wound between the seats two at a time. He heard the sergeant crying his name, shouting something about how Deveren didn't want to see it, but Deveren paid no heed. He mounted Flamedancer swiftly and rode the gelding hard, denying the words of the guardsman as he frantically raced home and burst into his house.

Yalissa and Cassim held one another and wept. Several guards were talking to them, inspecting the first-story floor.

"Lord Larath—" one of them said, but Deveren ignored him and raced up the stairs.

Kastara. Kastara. Oh, gods, please, please . . .

The bedchamber was crawling with guardsmen. The place had been ransacked. Chairs were overturned. Drawers were open. The pillows had been slit and their feathery contents lay over everything like a bizarre dusting of snow. The guardsmen glanced up at his entrance, and upon recognizing him moved to block his view.

But not soon enough. Oh, dear gods, not soon enough.

She lay where the evil intruder had left her, sprawled on the bed. Her chemise was no longer white but red, and the wet redness clung to her breasts and full belly in an obscene caress. The redness came from the terrible hole between her breasts, the hole created no doubt by the same knife that had slashed open the pillows and . . .

Deveren, his knees buckling, stumbled to the bed. He felt concerned hands closing on his shoulders and arms, trying to pull him away, but he tore loose and fell upon his wife's corpse, sobbing hoarsely. Dimly he realized that her flesh was cold. Any chance Health's Blesser might have had of saving the child, if not the mother, had long since passed.

They had been married only a year and a half. They were expecting a child. They were supposed to have years left, decades together . . . and one stranger's greed and evil had destroyed it all.

"Kastara . . . I'm so sorry . . . I should have stayed . . ." She was stiff and cold in his arms as he clutched her to him, and hard on the heels of his wild grief was a hot, scorching rage.

One thought hammered at his brain, and would sustain him through years to come. Deveren Larath would find the man who had done this. He would find him, and then, he would kill him. It was that simple.

And among the crimes most loathed by Light's
faithful shall be the deeds done away from his face:
murder, treachery, and theft.

—from Laws of the Great God, Light

CHAPTER ONE

1285

Night is the thief's friend. It enfolds him in its blanket of anonymity, hides the glitter of the lethal blade, the gleam of stolen gold. Darkness is his sanctuary, as certain a refuge for him as a temple is to the followers of its faith. Folk who conduct their business in the daylight hours sleep in the illusion of peace, as ignorant of the burglars who steal their coins as of the blades that steal their lives.

Allika sauntered carelessly down Ocean's View, the main street of Braedon, with only the moon to light her path. Cool silver light gleamed on the dark cobblestones, slick with the early morning dampness common to all seashore towns. Allika was a child of the friendly night and had no fear of what might be lurking in the shadows in the predawn hours. It was the day, with its dozens of sharp-eyed vendors and, perhaps, city guards, that harbored danger. Her doll, Miss Lally, made no protest as she bumped her rag-filled head against the cobblestones. Allika tended to drag Miss Lally by one limb, usually a leg.

Allika hummed to herself as she turned left, then right, then left again, entering the labyrinth of back alleys that were the seedier areas of Braedon. Her stomach rumbled, providing a bass counterpoint to the girl's wordless voice. She patted it absently. There would be food waiting at the Whale's Tail, more food than she'd seen in a week. The group had made a wonderful haul two nights ago, and Allika wanted to arrive before all the good things were gone.

The Whale's Tail, a third-rate tavern on a narrow, claustrophobic street that didn't even have a name, was the only building with its lights on. Allika stood on her toes to reach the knob, turned it with some effort, and entered.

The cramped, shabby tavern was not exactly a place for a seven-year-old girl, but to Allika, it was the closest thing to a home she had ever found. She felt utterly welcome here.

" 'Lo," she said cheerfully, grinning at the curious collection of nobles and slum rats that considered her part of their family. "What can I have?"

"Anything you want, Little Squirrel," invited a laughing barmaid, stepping carefully around Allika as the girl, not really waiting for an answer, headed straight for the nearest table. The wine-stained wooden table was piled high with bread, cheese, meats, and most enticing of all, sweetcakes.

Even among themselves, the thieves of the city of Braedon called one another by special names. Allika was Little Squirrel. The barmaid/thief who greeted her was Dove, and the bearded, heavy-set man who lifted Allika high enough so that she could reach the beckoning sweetcakes was Bear.

Bear now watched with amusement as Allika grew frustrated that her small hands could hold only a limited amount of food. Attempting to grab one more item, she dropped two.

"That'll do you for now!" Bear laughed. "Come back when you want more."

Allika nodded. "Is Fox coming tonight?"

"He's been invited. But he's probably too busy with his rich friends for the likes of us."

"Oh." Some of the enthusiasm went out of the girl's face. She ambled behind the bar to eat her treats safely away from adult conversation and feet.

Bear watched her go with a gaze growing speculative. Little Squirrel was a good little pickpocket. She had a pretty face, a sweet face that deceived her victims. In a few more years, she'd have a figure to go with that face. Men would pay a lot for her. He wondered why he hadn't considered prostitution before. After all, his group didn't need to limit themselves to theft. Hadn't they just proved that?

Bear had held his post for a record twelve years, and the recent robberies and murders of no fewer than three Braedon councilmen in one swift, sure highway attack would do nothing but strengthen his position as chief wolf of a savage pack.

The thought of the money Allika would earn him in a few years brought a smile to his thick lips.

"Another round," the Bear told the tavern keeper, a balding older man called Badger. "I see a few hardworking men whose glasses aren't full." He laughed and drained his own mug, which was promptly refilled by the equally genial Badger. As the *"barmaids"* set about the task of refilling the empty glasses, a not terribly sober, bone-thin man stumbled to his feet.

"A toast t' Bear! Today the city councilmen—tomorrow, the city isself!"

As a cheer went up, the door to the Whale's Tale splintered with a thunderous crack. The thieves, utterly shocked, hesitated just an instant too long. Then there was little time to act as armed men dressed in black clothing, their faces smeared with soot, suddenly swarmed into the tavern.

Bear overturned his table and dove behind it. A knife whistled through the air and landed with a *thunk* in the wood, inches from his head. Seizing two of the many daggers he always carried with him, Bear took aim and hurled them at the silent, black-clad attackers. One fell, the blade in his throat. His comrade turned coolly around and lunged for Bear.

Bear had expected more thrown daggers, not a suicidal charge, and he had only just reached for another knife when the killer was upon him. Though he outweighed the intruder by about fifty pounds, Bear fell beneath him. He felt cool metal touch his throat, then a brief, searing flash of white-hot agony. Then he felt nothing at all.

By the time the unknown killer had dispatched the leader of the thieves, seventeen of Bear's followers lay dead in pools of their own blood. A few had escaped, but not many. The men in black glanced around, their breathing heavy, searching for any who might have escaped their notice. In a corner, Dove groaned as she clutched her abdomen. Blood pumped through her fingers. The man who had murdered Bear knelt beside her and, with a quick, strong movement, snapped her neck. The gesture was professionally executed, and might have been considered a mercy.

The men listened, tense. Silence.

No, not quite. From behind the bar came a soft, faint whimpering sound. The men snapped to attention, and two of them swiftly went to the source of the noise.

Allika stared up at them, her eyes enormous with terror and her face moon-pale. She clutched Miss Lally to her chest and mewled helplessly.

One of the Black Men raised his knife. Allika remained frozen, enthralled with horror, unable to move, to flee, or to defend herself.

"No," came a voice. "She's just a child."

"Children grow up to be thieves."

"We don't know that she *is* a thief." A second man, taller than the others, stepped into Allika's view. "She could be just the brat of one of the women."

"We have our orders," the first man protested.

"And I'm giving you yours. Let her alone." The tall man knelt. Allika stared at him, unable to stop trembling. The man's blue eyes seemed to bore straight into her brain.

"Listen to me, little girl. I want you to tell your friends something. Tell them that the city will not tolerate what they did on Travsdae. Any more incidents, and we'll come for the ones we didn't get tonight. Understand?"

Allika nodded. The man rose and left without another word, motioning to his fellows. She heard their retreating footsteps, then silence.

For a long time, Allika cowered behind the bar. No guards came to investigate the shrill screams that had filled the Whale's Tail. No concerned citizen, roused from his slumber, came to rescue her. Finally, she realized that she would somehow have to walk, alone, through the carnage that littered the tavern floor. She picked up the doll and sat her on her knee.

"No one's going to come get me," she whispered to Miss Lally.

Then it was Miss Lally's turn to "talk" and the words came easier, crept past the lump in her throat, when Allika was speaking for her cloth playmate.

"Come on, Allika," she said in a high, squeaky voice, moving Miss Lally's head as if the doll were speaking. "We have to go see Fox. Fox will know exactly what to do!"

"But, Miss Lally, I'm scared to go out there," she whispered in her own small voice.

"I'll be with you, Allika. They can't hurt me, and I'll be brave enough for the both of us!" Her voice cracked a little, and she laughed at herself. Rising unsteadily, the girl tried to brace herself for the scene, but her young mind was incapable of visualizing so brutal and bloody a horror. The bodies of people she had considered family were sprawled across the floor. Blood was everywhere. Allika choked back a sob.

They look just like dolls, she told herself fiercely. *That's all. Just like broken dolls.*

She took one step, then another. Her poorly shod feet squelched in blood, and she swallowed hard. Allika did not look down, but kept her eyes on what was left of the tavern door. *Step carefully, over the limp arms, between the sprawled legs, next to the bloody heads . . . broken dolls. Just broken dolls.*

The thought got her through the seemingly endless walk to the smashed door. Once out in the cool, safe emptiness of the streets, Allika gasped the brine-scented air as if it were the sweetest fragrance in the world. Then, no longer dragging Miss Lally but clutching her tightly, she broke into a run.

She would deliver the Black Man's message to Fox, and Fox would know exactly what to do.

Fox, known to everyone but the thieves of Braedon as Lord Deveren Larath, patron of the arts, connoisseur of the finer things in life, and incidentally possessor of a slight bit of hand magic, did not know exactly what to do. But he had a good idea.

Thirty-four years old, he had no crow's feet and only a touch of gray in his light brown hair. His hands were the hands of a musician, a surgeon, or a thief—slim, delicate, and clever. The fact that he had the gift of hand magic, magic that allowed him to manipulate objects to a certain degree, accentuated his dexterousness. Tonight, Venedae, only one night after the massacre, he wore an unembellished, royal blue tunic and comfortable black breeches—clothes that would allow for swift, unencumbered movement should the need arise.

Allika huddled in his lap, her small face nestled against

his broad chest as if she could absorb his strength. Absently Deveren stroked her short black hair, his eyes flickering over the assembled company as they waited for the emergency meeting to begin.

Rabbit, a local apothecary and herbalist, had volunteered his shop for the meeting. Once, such a gesture had been commonplace, even expected. Now, in light of the murders, the offer was an act of quiet courage. The back room was where the herbs used in his medicines dried, and those who entered had to brush aside fragile, fragrant bunches of basil, marjoram, fennel, and other plants that hung from the ceiling. The warm, friendly scent of cinnamon vied with the strong odor of garlic and the tang of some kind of citrus. Rabbit had done what he could to clear the floor so people would have places to sit, but the quarters were still cramped. A few encased candles provided flickering illumination.

Deveren noticed that, to a man, the thieves all wore the same strained, wary expression that he himself bore. Everyone here knew that it was simple luck that he or she hadn't been in the Whale's Tail Desdae night, quaffing a toast to the soon-to-be-deceased Bear. As they entered, the men and women, some clad in finery, some in functional, working clothing, and some in rags, spoke soft, somber greetings.

Deveren knew them all: Clia, "Sparrow," the fortune-teller whose sultry charms diverted attention from her quick fingers; the noble-born Pedric, known as Otter, who delighted in audacious plans and narrow escapes, and his current woman Marrika, "Raven;" Freylis, "Wolf," whose bullying manner and greed would have embarrassed any pack of real wolves; Hawk, Mouse, Cat, Hound . . . tonight, all their voices would be heard as they selected a new leader.

After all the surviving thieves were assembled, a pitiful twenty or so, the low conversation ceased. With their leader dead, no one was sure who would conduct the meeting. The thieves raised eyes that mirrored their inner apprehension and turmoil. Only black-haired Marrika, seated cross-legged on the floor with her ubiquitous chunk of wood and her carving knife, seemed at ease. Save for the *scritch-scritch* sound of her whittling, the room was filled with an awkward silence. At last, Deveren gently pushed Allika off his lap and rose.

"If I remember correctly," he began, "anyone may volun-teer to be leader, and then we pare it down from there." He raised his own hand. "I'm willing. Anyone else care to put his neck in the noose?"

Freylis's big hand shot up at once, as Deveren could have predicted. Freylis had been close to Bear and was certainly that man's equal in strength and viciousness, though he lacked the late leader's cunning. Of course, Freylis would covet the position. And he was popular enough that he just might get it. Deveren sincerely hoped not.

A slight movement attracted his attention, and he saw Marrika elbowing Pedric. The young man, his fine velvet doublet and hose clashing with his woman's manlike working clothes, rolled his eyes and stuck his own thin, aristocrat's hand in the air. Marrika had paused in her whittling and her dark eyes snapped fire. Deveren knew that, had tradition not forbidden women to become leader, she would have raised her own hand.

He waited a few more moments, but no one else seemed to be interested in either the great honor or the great dan-ger that came with the position.

"We three, then," he said, leaning up against the wooden wall of the room. He gestured to Rabbit. "We'll need three colors of pebbles." Rabbit, who had spent the better part of the afternoon sorting a variety of colors of beads and peb-bles, nodded and slipped out into the front room. Deveren returned his attention to the gathering. "Who would like to speak first?"

Freylis rose. His bulk loomed large in the tight, packed

room, and the flickering flame of the candlelight made his bearded, scarred face look even more sinister than usual.

"Bear was my friend," he said quietly. Deveren raised an eyebrow. He hadn't expected a mournful Freylis.

"I been in this group for a long time, and there wasn't never a better leader than Bear. He gave us back our pride. He had plans for us, plans so that we wouldn't have to skulk around like cowards, jumping at our own damn shadows. We went out and we *took* what we wanted, *when* we wanted, and all of Braedon was afraid of us!"

"That's for certain, Wolf," said Clia, her lilting voice now dripping scorn. "So afraid that they slaughtered unarmed men, women, and children!"

"*So we fight back!*" roared Freylis. His eyes were bright, burning with fervor. The small hairs on the back of Deveren's neck rose, a primal response to present fear. This was the Freylis he'd been expecting to see emerge tonight: a fanatic.

"Don't you see?" Freylis continued when the group did not immediately respond. "Either we're the hunters, the killers, or we're what they eat! Bear was right—I want to follow where he tried to lead us. We have all the power because we're the ones who break the laws! I say, let's let Braedon know that we won't be intimidated!"

The spirits of more than a few thieves revived under Freylis's tirade. Fear and helplessness gave way to eagerness and arrogance, and some cheers went up.

Deveren's heart sank. "Thank you, Wolf. Otter, it's your turn."

The Otter, Pedric, had just turned twenty-four but he was a veteran thief. Deveren had been witness to his coolness under pressure before, and this time was no exception. In fact, if anything, Pedric seemed bored by the whole proceedings.

"I've been in this organization for quite a few years now, and I think it's been improved by my participation in it." Murmurs went around the room. Deveren suspected that, while Pedric's statement was undeniably true, his superior attitude wasn't going to win him many votes. "I've got some pretty good social contacts—" here a few people actually burst out laughing at the understatement; like Deveren, Pedric traveled in the very best circles possible, "—and sometimes that comes in pretty handy."

His casual pose bespoke his utter lack of interest. Marrika gazed up at her lover with thinly concealed fury, her expression darkening with every word Pedric uttered in his soft, disinterested voice. Her hand tightened on her knife, and for a moment it looked as if she would like to stab Pedric's leg with the little weapon. Deveren assumed that Pedric was going to be alone in his bed tonight when this was all over.

"Anyway," Pedric continued, "if I'm chosen leader, I'd do my best to fulfill my duties."

He sank down beside Marrika. She stared at him with eyes that sparkled with anger, her lovely face hard and unforgiving. "What?" Pedric asked. *"What?"*

The other two had spoken, and now all eyes turned to Deveren. He crossed his arms in front of his chest in an unconscious gesture of defense. What he was going to say was, he was certain, not going to be well received.

"I don't think that we as a group call ourselves loyal templegoers." He grinned, and the crowd chuckled. "We know well enough what the gods have to say about us. Light, in particular, couples us with traitors and murderers. I don't know about you, but I'm neither of those. There's a saying, that there is no honor among thieves. *I* say, that's a lie, and I want you all to help me prove it.

"What I would do as leader is to prove that there is honor, that there *is* fair play and some kind of decency— that the title of thief doesn't have to taste like filth in our own mouths. Wolf speaks of unity, of reclaiming lost pride, and I'm all for that. But where is the pride in butchery? Last week's . . . haul . . . got us some trinkets, yes. But the three councilmen we ambushed last Travsdae were unarmed, trapped in their carriage. I don't think there's too damn much to be proud of in running a blade through men as if they were rabbits in a hutch."

Freylis frowned, his rough face made more malevolent than ever with the slow flush of anger. Now he bellowed, "By Lady Death, you want to castrate us!"

Others joined the outburst, crying "Make us weak!" "We're criminals, not king's men!" "Quit slumming and go back where you belong!" Some of the catcalls came from people that Deveren had considered friends, and the insults stung. But he had known that his idea, revolutionary and alien, would not be understood—at least not at first.

"You don't understand!" he shouted, his strong, clear voice barely heard above the din. "Don't you know what went on at the Whale's Tail? Those weren't our own city guards, you fools, *those were hired assassins!*"

The single, dreadful word "assassins" was heard above the growing clamor, and the group fell silent, shocked. In the sudden quiet, Deveren continued.

"I know the guards. I'm friends with the captain. Don't you think I'd have warned you if anything like this was going to happen?"

"Maybe they didn't want anyone to know," said Clia uneasily.

"Even so, think for a moment. We all know Vandaris. Does anyone here seriously believe that he would have given the order for that kind of a bloodbath? And the constabulary—do you really think they'd be able to carry out something like that so quickly—and so successfully?" No one replied. Deveren began to feel, for the first time that evening, that maybe he might win.

"Besides, Allika, who's got as sharp an eye as anyone I know, tells me they were all in black. Had soot smeared on their faces." He lifted his hands and mimed the gesture, underscoring the point. "Now, as Otter said, there are advantages to social position. My brother's an ambassador, and thanks to him I know assassin technique and costume when I hear about it. We had gone too far when we killed those councilmen, and someone high up—*very* high up—wanted it stopped." He grinned without humor. "There's a balance, my friends, between crime and honest labor, and whoever did this knows the politics of such a situation very well indeed. This wasn't an outraged citizenry trying to quash a few cutpurses. Whoever did this doesn't care if we steal. They want us to know our place. The murders in the Whale's Tail were a message, and by the gods, we're going to either listen to it or be destroyed. Next time, they won't spare Allika—or you—" he pointed at Rabbit, who paled visibly, "—or *you*," and Clia glanced down at her tightly laced fingers. "It's simple. Change, or die. I know how we can change. I know techniques, tricks, other things I can teach you. Now, either you choose me and let me help—let me lead you—or I'm leaving the group. This out-and-out war with assassins is too risky a game even for a gambling man like me."

His appeal to their noble sensibilities had failed, but his harsh, truthful assessment of their current danger had given his colleagues pause. There was a long silence, as the thieves digested the new information. At last Rabbit, who had been sitting in a corner quietly observing everything, stepped forward.

"Are we ready to vote?" The thieves nodded and a few voiced affirmatives. "Then let's be about it. It's been a long time since we've had to do this, so let me explain the process. I've collected pebbles and beads in three different colors—gray, black, and white. Everyone gets one of each."

He began handing out the pebbles as he continued to explain the voting system. "Wolf is gray, Otter is black, and Fox is white. Think hard about your choice, and when you've made your decision, drop the appropriate pebble in the box in the corner."

He peered back at Deveren, then glanced over at Pedric

and Freylis. "The candidates will please cast their own votes first, so they don't know who's voting for or against them."

Freylis went first. He tossed his gray pebble in with undue force, glowering back at Deveren. Pedric then dropped his own bead into the box. When Deveren reached to deposit his own vote, he was surprised and moved to see a white bead, not a black, next to Freylis's gray.

He cast his own vote and went back to his place, watching the eyes of the thieves as, one by one, they stepped forward to make the decision that would have a vital impact on their lives. Deveren tried to read their faces. It was no easy task in the dim lighting, and thieves, more than most folk, learned early on how to cloak their expressions. Not for the first time, Deveren wished he had his brother's gift of mind magic. There were times when it would definitely be useful to be able to read thoughts. When it was done, Rabbit rose.

"I'm going to count the votes. Um, Cat, Sparrow, would you come with me? No one can accuse me of cheating then," he added grumpily. Cat and Sparrow nodded and accompanied him to the front room.

No one spoke. Freylis shifted uncomfortably. Pedric and Marrika argued in sharp, sibilant whispers. Many turned their gazes upon the candidates, though their votes had already been cast, and Deveren met each pair of eyes with evenness.

Rabbit opened the door. Cat and Sparrow followed. Every person in the room tensed. The slim, older man cast a nervous glance at Freylis, gave a smile to Pedric. Then his squinty blue eyes met Deveren's.

"Congratulations, Leader Fox."

Deveren let out the breath he'd been holding with an audible whoosh. Suddenly he found himself in the middle of a throng of well-wishers. Everyone, it seemed, wanted to congratulate their new leader and shake his hand.

No, not quite everyone. The door banged shut, and he

looked up to see that Marrika and Pedric had gone. Freylis, looking angrier than Deveren had ever seen him, was following suit, shadowed by a few of his loyal devotees. Their expressions were sullen and their eyes glittered with a smoldering hatred. Deveren knew that, while he had a host of new, probably false, friends, he had also made a few true enemies.

Through the press of people eager to ingratiate themselves with him, he felt the pressure of small arms going around his waist. He glanced down to see Allika beaming up at him, and an unexpected lump rose in his throat. To the Nightlands with Freylis and his group of malcontents. The child grinning up at him with delight shining in her eyes was the reason he had wanted the position. She was the future of the thieves' group, and more than he wanted to enrich the thieves, he wanted to protect them.

"As you know, Fox, you've got a job to do before the election's official." Rabbit's voice managed to float to Deveren's ears over the babbling of the crowd, but Deveren didn't quite catch the words.

"Quiet, everyone, please," he urged, and the chattering fell silent. "What did you say, Rabbit?"

"There's still the Grand Theft," explained Rabbit patiently. Deveren's brow furrowed. He wasn't familiar with the term. "The Grand Theft is your proof that you're worthy. Not," he added hastily, "that we think otherwise. Tradition, you know. We'll all meet sometime in the near future and decide on an item for you to steal."

"What kind of item?"

"Could be anything—the bell from the Godstower, perhaps, or a woman's brooch while she's wearing it, something like that. We'll inform you of our decision. In the meantime," he looked apologetic, "until we can put Leader Fox's plan of reformation into effect, I'll have to urge everyone to be going. We've been here a while now, and . . ." his voice trailed off and he shrugged his thin shoulders.

"Of course," replied Deveren swiftly. "By ones and

twos, everyone. I'll go first, just in case we've been spotted and someone's planning an ambush."

He didn't think so. The assassins had come, done their job, and left. If they had meant to eliminate every thief in Braedon, they would have already done it. Nonetheless, his offer, as he had intended, was regarded as a sign of his courage. He heard the murmur of approval and half hid a smile.

The night street was empty. Cool, moist air ruffled his light brown hair. He breathed deeply, tasting the slight tang of salt on the breeze. His ebullience stayed with him during the long walk home. He hadn't dared ride to the meeting, as the sight of a horse tethered outside the store would have drawn unwanted attention, and Flamedancer was unmistakable. The walk, though, was pleasant. The streets were deserted, the night still. Deveren enjoyed this hour, when the normally bustling port city was resting.

He passed a few of the temples as he took the road that led up to the hills and the better part of town. The temple to Light was, of course, brilliantly illuminated. Made of wood and stone, it was set apart by its many expensive windows of real glass. Some segments were stained, and Deveren had to admit that the rainbow of illumination was beautiful and appealing. The temple of Light was the only lit building in the area. At this hour, even the lamps that lined the city streets had been permitted to burn out.

He passed a guard post stationed on the road and saw the armed men standing over a makeshift brazier, for the bite of the sea wind could turn even summer nights chilly. One of them raised his hand and cried a halloo. It was more than a simple greeting; though polite, it was a challenge. Should Deveren not respond, not have a good reason to be out at this hour, the guards would be on him in a minute.

"Good evening, gentlemen," Deveren called back.

"Late night, m'lord Larath?" the guard who had hailed him asked.

Deveren chuckled, easy in their company. "Very late. I'm getting too old for midnight card games, I'm afraid."

The guardsmen, completely reassured, laughed comfortably. "Need an escort home, Deveren?" came a voice, deeper and more direct than the others. Deveren recognized the guard commander, Telian Jaranis. Things were serious indeed if the commander was taking to dropping by the guard posts at this hour.

"Well, good evening, Captain—or, good morning, rather. No, thank you, the walk'll help sober me up. Besides, my luck wasn't good at the tables tonight—I'd make a poor target for a thief."

"As you wish, sir."

Deveren continued on, humming a little to himself as the temples gave way to long stretches of flat, unused land. The wind shifted, bringing a sudden blessing of fragrance to Deveren's nostrils. He smiled. He knew he was close to home when he could smell the Garden.

Planted by and paid for by all the residents of the Square, as the most fashionable area of Braedon was known, the wall-encircled Garden was an enormous plot of land filled to bursting with the most beautiful and fragrant of flowers. There were many varieties of trees and shrubs as well, even a complex maze in which it was very easy to get lost—if one didn't know the secret. Deveren thought it a terrible shame that it wasn't open to the public; apparently, the richer folk of the city felt that the enjoyment of such beauty, bought and paid for by them, should be limited to them.

His own house, a comparatively modest stone-and-wood construction with only two stories and a tiny stable, was the first one on the right. The small patch of ground surrounding it boasted a wrought iron fence that bore the Larath family crest, and those who had visited Deveren knew that the deceptively humble home was furnished in a most tasteful and gracious manner. And Deveren's home had windows—thick, wavy-glassed windows. That alone marked him as a man of means.

Deveren's brisk stride faltered, stopped.

One of the first-floor windows had light streaming through it. He had left the house dark. One of the servants? Deveren quickly dismissed that thought. They'd have left for their own domiciles hours ago.

A sudden dewing of cold sweat dotted his forehead. He'd been wrong. It seemed as though the assassins hadn't finished their job, after all.

"How art thou my brother?" asked the Sun. "Thy light is not like mine, nor thy magics."

"Ah," replied the Moon, "yet we both rule the skies, and shine our lights upon Mankind, do we not?"

—from *Tales of the Sun and Moon*

CHAPTER TWO

For a long moment, Deveren simply stood, staring foolishly. One hand tightly gripped the cold metal of the wrought iron fence. Reason seeped back into his paralyzed limbs and he sprinted around the side, heading for the back of his house, away from the room with the lighted candle. Quickly he climbed the fence and jumped down, landing as quietly as possible in the soft grass. Hidden in the shadows now, he hastened for the shelter of the building's walls, flattening himself against the cold stone, listening, his body taut as a bowstring. Perspiration dampened his face. There was no sound, no evidence that he had been noticed.

The room to his immediate left was his library. It was dark, and far enough back from the lighted window so that even if he made sounds, he wouldn't be heard. But Deveren intended to make no noise. He crouched beneath the wooden sill and reached his hand up, pressing two fin-

gers against the window. Deveren concentrated on stilling
his racing thoughts, and visualized the window unlocking.
He did not have to raise his head to know that his meager
hand magic hadn't worked. Had he been able to lay even a
single finger on the lock itself, he could have managed it.
As it was, the additional barrier of the glass, frail as it
was, was an obstacle that prevented him from opening the
window.

He dropped down again and pressed his back flat against
the stone. Sometimes, Deveren thought with a hint of disgust, plain old burglary was more efficient than magic. He
fumbled in his pouch. Deveren had a bad habit of never
emptying his pouch from night to night or theft to theft.
Had he not already been a thief, he would, contrary to what
he had told the guards, have been a prime candidate for
robbery; the deceptively simple pouch he wore at his side
was crammed full of valuables.

Now his bad habit had become an unexpected blessing.
Fumbling blindly in the pouch, his questing fingers found a
ring whose stone was not embedded in its golden circle but
rather jutted up proudly. He closed his eyes in relief. Stones
set in such a manner, Deveren knew, were most usually di-
amonds. He pulled the ring out, then turned to the window.

Working by touch, he pressed back the soft gold prongs
that held the gem in place and removed it. Cupping the dia-
mond in his palm, he felt for its sharpest edge. He held the
ring in his left hand and, holding the small jewel carefully
between his right thumb and forefinger, reinserted the dia-
mond into its setting so that the sharp edge faced out. Then
he pressed closed the golden prongs. Grasping the ring,
Deveren cut a small hole in the glass, just large enough to
put his two fingers through. He pushed gently, and the
small circle of cut glass dropped soundlessly to the rushes
beneath.

Deveren bent forward and placed his ear to the hole, listening. Silence. He smiled, his confidence returning. If he,
a skilled thief, couldn't even break into his own house

without being detected, he had no right to be leader. He reached in, unlocked the window in a totally nonmagical manner, and eased it open.

He was halfway inside the room when the voice nearly stopped his heart.

"If only our mother were here to see this."

Deveren knew that voice. Relief flooded him, replaced almost immediately by a combination of delight and irritation.

"Damn you, Damir," he growled, grinning, as he swung his other leg into the room, "I have cats that are noisier than you!"

Damir had already lit a candle, and by its flickering light Deveren saw that his older brother was laughing at the trick he'd played. The two embraced with real warmth, although Deveren did land a good-natured punch to Damir's thin arm.

There was little about their appearances to alert the casual stranger that there was so intimate a bond between the two men. Deveren, boyish and well built, stood a good four inches taller than his "big" brother. His hair was a light brown, only slightly touched with gray, while Damir's thinning locks were a deep, rich mink color. Damir was slight and elegant; Deveren, muscular and athletic. Only their hands, with their long, thin fingers, and their eyes, a bright, knowing hazel, were the same. That, and their quick minds.

"Do you know how much a pane of glass costs?" said Deveren.

"I'll pay for it," Damir offered. "It's worth every penny just to have watched you sneaking about like that. You're slipping, Dev. If I had been waiting to kill you, I'd hardly have lit a candle to announce my presence."

Deveren was so embarrassed he actually blushed. Of course. Any other night, he would have realized that at once. But so soon after the massacre, he was understandably on edge.

"Pray tell, Ambassador Larath, what brings you to the fair city of Braedon?" he asked Damir, changing the subject as he led his brother out from the library into the dining area. "I'd heard that King Emrys wasn't doing so well, and thought you wouldn't be too far from his side. Come on, let's get something to eat. Sudden fear followed by intense pleasure always makes me hungry."

He reached for a bowl of fruit on the table in the dining room, seizing a fragrant peach and biting into it. Deveren's dining room would more appropriately be called a hall. The table at which he plopped himself so casually would easily sit twenty-four, and it stretched grandly into the superbly decorated room. Despite the fine old furniture, the lovely statues of elf-maidens and noble warriors, and the high, vaulted ceiling, the place, like its owner, was friendly rather than overwhelming. Damir, used to even more sumptuous surroundings than his brother's abode, followed his sibling's relaxed example. He eased into a plush chair, studied the bowl of fruit, and helped himself to a bunch of grapes.

"Actually," Damir began slowly, fingering the fruit rather than plucking it, "*you* bring me here."

Deveren nearly choked on his peach. "Me?" he mumbled. "Sweet Health, don't tell me your spies know about the election already!" Damir's position was, officially, that of an ambassador. Deveren knew that his brother's actual role in the function of government was far more important and far more dangerous. Damir had at his command a vast network of spies—though he liked to use the term "information gatherers."

Damir arched a thin, aristocratic eyebrow. "Election? Why, no. You'll have to tell me all about it later. No, I came to make sure that you were . . . all right." His eyes, bright as a sparrow's, met his brother's evenly.

All traces of mirth and welcome vanished from Deveren's countenance. He was silent for a long, tense moment, and when he at last spoke his voice was like ice.

"If you ordered that raid on the Whale's Tail Desdae night," he said slowly, "then you are not welcome in my home."

"Of course not, Dev!" The undisguised hurt and anger in Damir's normally modulated voice was proof enough for Deveren, and his posture relaxed. "You know I have no say in matters of that nature."

"But you knew it was going to happen, didn't you?"

His thin face still tense, Damir nodded. Deveren swore.

"I have no control over . . . that branch of the government," Damir continued. "I didn't even know who was . . . who had survived and who hadn't. I wanted to send you a mind-warning, but—"

"Braedon is too far away," Deveren finished his brother's sentence. He knew the limits of Damir's mind magic. Damir nodded, his eyes searching Deveren's.

"Gods, Dev, I couldn't even sense if you were still alive! I left home the minute I knew what they were planning. Maybe I shouldn't have bothered!"

Deveren looked down at his reflection in the highly polished wood of the table. "Sorry. But Damir—I lost friends that night."

The older man sighed and popped a grape into his mouth. "I realize that," he said in a calmer voice, after he had swallowed. "You wouldn't have if you'd stayed away from that group as I advised you to."

Deveren suddenly seemed to develop a great interest in finishing his peach and fell silent. Damir narrowed his eyes. Deveren could practically see wheels turning in his brother's head as realization dawned on Damir's face.

"Election," he said softly. "Please, Dev, tell me that what I'm thinking is wrong. Tell me you've been voted head of the local garden appreciation guild, or something like that."

"Sorry." He wasn't.

Damir sighed and rubbed his face for a long moment. "Deveren," he said gently, "it won't bring Kastara back."

The younger man flinched ever so slightly. Even now, seven years later, any mention of her name was painful to him. After Kastara's brutal murder, Deveren had gone slightly mad. The law officials could find nothing. Deveren became a constant fixture at the guard's offices, haranguing them daily, desperate for any sort of hope at which to grasp. Even Damir, with his vast network of spies and informants at hand, couldn't help.

When four months went by and they were still no closer to solving the crime, the law gradually began to cut back on the amount of time, money, and manpower it was pouring into the case.

So it was that Deveren had originally turned to the other side of the law for justice, seeking out and joining the thieves of the city. He had hoped to uncover Kastara's killer, and exact retribution.

"I know it won't bring her back," Deveren said after a moment. "I never did find her murderer, and I don't think I ever will. I'm reconciled to that."

Damir frowned, honestly puzzled. "Then why . . ."

"In my years of involvement with the thieves, I've learned something about them," Deveren continued. "Some who call themselves thieves are killers, but not all of them. While some look out only for themselves, others care about the group as a whole and as individuals. I've discovered that there's a sense of community, of, of—*family* in this group. Damir—among the people at the Whale's Tail was a little girl. Did you know that?"

Damir nodded. "I understand that the leader of the raid spared her life. His orders were to kill everyone in the building, but we hadn't expected to find children. When I heard, I was glad the man was wise enough not to follow those particular orders to the letter."

"So am I," said Deveren fervently. "She's a charming little thing—reminds me of your Talitha when she was that age. As leader, I have an enormous influence over how this group develops over the next few years."

A smile tugged at the diplomat's lips. "Ah, yes, the thieves of Braedon. They run a charity auction and orphanage—always donate to worthy causes. Did I mention the Fund for Wayward Kittens?"

The humor was misplaced, and a cloud came over Deveren's face. "A lot of people in that group are hungry. A lot of people are desperately poor. And you know as well as I do that if you really wanted to wipe out crime, you'd do it. One more 'purge' like the Whale's Tail and you'd have the rest of us. And speaking of crime," and Deveren's voice cracked like a whip, "I think the planned murder of seventeen people without benefit of trial isn't exactly *legal*!"

He rose and grabbed a bottle of wine that was on the sideboard. The bottle, an excellent vintage imported from Mhar, had been opened for a dinner earlier that month and the cork replaced. Deveren glanced about for something with which to extract the cork, found nothing immediately to hand, gripped the cork with his teeth and tugged. There was a slight pop. He poured himself a goblet of wine with a hand that trembled, and drained the glass.

Still angry, he placed the bottle on the table with a thump. Damir regarded it for a moment, arching a thin eyebrow. Then, to his brother's astonishment, he took the bottle, raised it to his lips, and drank directly from the neck.

Deveren stared, then broke into a loud, whooping laugh. The sight of formal, elegant Damir, who knew which eating implement went with which course and what side the wine was served on, guzzling like a sewer drunk was too ludicrous for any other reaction. Neatly, without spilling a drop, Damir finished his drink and set the bottle down on the table. He smiled slightly.

"I never liked for you to best me, not even in bad manners," he said drily.

They were friends again.

"Here," said Deveren, the bright bubble of mirth still in his voice, "let me get you a glass."

For a time, the talk turned to topics lighter, safer, than theft or murder or espionage. The brothers talked of children, and crops, and new plays, and bardic festivals. They finished each other's sentences, laughed at each other's jokes, and drank in fraternal closeness. At last, Damir glanced at the candle, now burning low, and then outside at the lightening sky.

"I'm going to stay here awhile, Dev, if I may," he said.

"Aha, I knew there was another reason for your visit. I didn't think it was simply brotherly concern that had you rushing all the way out here."

"It was, truly," said Damir. "But I . . . well, I'll be frank with you. Your . . . hobby might be useful. And while I'm not overly happy at your recent promotion to leader, I confess that I could use your help in that capacity."

Deveren's eyebrows shot up.

"If you mean what you say about helping the thieves of your city gain a little self-respect, here's an excellent chance to begin. Perhaps I shouldn't be telling you this, but . . ." Damir sighed. "You know of the planned marriage between our Princess Cimarys and the young prince of Mhar, Castyll?"

"Good gods, they've been betrothed since they were in their cradles!" snorted Deveren.

"Well, yes. But judging from the letters that have passed between them over the last year or so, it's developing into a love match."

"You read royal love letters?"

Damir looked slightly embarrassed. "It's one of my duties, yes. Anyway, Castyll sent a terse note a few days ago, terminating the betrothal."

Deveren shrugged. "Now that his father's dead, maybe he doesn't have to pretend he's fond of Cimarys anymore." He thought of the young Byrnian princess, barely fourteen but already graced with a womanly beauty. A smile tugged at his lips. "Send him a recent portrait of Cimmy. That should bring him to his senses."

Damir sighed. "Dev, could you be serious for once? Since King Shahil's death two months ago, a lot has happened in Mhar. A lot," he added, "that does not bode well for future relationships with Byrn."

Deveren was listening now. Mhar lay only a few leagues to the south, barely a day's travel by ship and only three days by horse. It was the nearest major city, closer even than the closest Byrnian city. War with Mhar would be a dangerous thing for Braedon.

"Such as?" he prompted. He leaned forward, his eyes narrowed. Had he indeed been the Fox that he was named for, his ears would have been pricked forward.

Pleased that he had gotten his brother's full attention, Damir launched into specifics. "First of all, they haven't had a coronation for young Castyll. He's fifteen, certainly of age to take the throne. Oh, they're calling him king, all right, but it's obvious that his power exists in name only. He and King Shahil went to Ilantha to stay at the traditional summer palace. Castyll ought to have returned to the capital city of Jarmair immediately upon the death of his father—but he's staying, finishing out the season, just as if nothing's wrong. That's hardly like the boy, from what I know of him. One of his father's counselors, a rather slimy fellow named Bhakir, is regent. It looks like he's the one in charge."

"What about the other advisors?" queried Deveren. Like Byrn, in Mhar the king's rule was tempered by a circle of "advisors" who wielded certain powers of their own.

Damir smiled without humor. "Such sad accidents," he said in a cool, polite tone that sent shivers up Deveren's spine. "Such dreadful illnesses. We've had trouble with Bhakir in the past, and now that he's in charge we expect more. This sudden end to an engagement that would bring the countries closer together would be suspicious at any

time—and it's made even more so by the, uh, clearly genuine interest these two young people seem to have in each
other."

"But Mhar would benefit by an alliance with us," said
Deveren, confused. "Why—"

"Mhar would," Damir clarified, "but *Bhakir* wouldn't."

Deveren nodded slowly. "So you've got a delayed coronation and a broken love match. What else?"

"Bhakir's been making changes in the top ranks of the
military, both land and sea," continued Damir. "It would
seem that many hitherto trusted generals and admirals
were traitors. How lucky that Bhakir discovered their
fiendish plots." If irony were a real substance, Damir's
would have burned holes through the beautiful table.

Deveren whistled. "The bastard wants war, doesn't
he?"

"Looks like it. I've been able to get a few messages to
and from the beleaguered young prince, though. He wants
to set up secret negotiations between his core group of
supporters and Byrn, as represented by me."

"And you want me to see that Braedon would be a safe
port," Deveren concluded.

"Well, you have to admit, having you as the leader of
the thieves just might insure that there would be no criminal incidents, should we host the meetings here."

Deveren nodded. "I don't think it'd be a problem."

"Then your thieves will take kindly to being told 'don't
touch'?" Damir teased.

Now it was Deveren's turn to be deadly serious. "They'll
take kindly to preventing war with Mhar. Sweet Lady
Death, Damir, Braedon would be their first target. If they
could get hold of our seaport . . ." He didn't even need to
finish the thought. He didn't really want to.

"These talks could be of great import," Damir warned.

"Obviously."

"Prince Castyll himself might come."

"Then he can stay at the King's Arms Inn," quipped

Deveren, reaching for the wine goblet and lifting it to his lips.

"He might want to pay . . . an extended visit. A *very* extended visit."

Deveren nearly choked on the ruby-red liquid.

Pedric was having a dreadful night.

Marrika had been stonily silent since she and Pedric had left the thieves' meeting. At first, the young man had respected her silence, but when it dragged on for a quarter of an hour he began to grow annoyed. He tried to take her arm, but she jerked it away. Annoyance blossomed into anger. He seized her arm, securely this time, propelled her over to a quiet alleyway, and demanded, "What in the Nightlands is wrong with you?"

It was dark, but by the moonlight that filtered its way down past the buildings he could see the rage on her beautiful face. She didn't answer with words, but snarled angrily. Pedric was thoroughly startled when he felt a stinging slap on his cheek. Automatically, his soft aristocrat's hand went to rub the painful area.

"You are such an *idiot*, Pedric Dunsan!"

"I'm not idiot enough to go shouting our true names in public!" he hissed back.

She sneered. "So it's Otter, huh? Well, for seven months I've been your woman, and I haven't seen you do a damned thing that a *trained* otter couldn't do. You humiliated me tonight!" She made a slack-jawed fool's face. "Uh, sometimes that comes in handy," she mimicked cruelly.

Pedric felt his face growing hot, and not just from the angry slap. "I'm not a very good public speaker," he said.

She laughed, a harsh, angry sound. "You're not very good at much, Pedric, except spending your papa's money."

"I've earned my place in the group," he began in a low, controlled voice.

"You *bought* your way in, rich boy, and everybody

knows it. Good gods, even Deveren's made a haul or two worth something. You just show up with that worthless art stuff—"

"—at any auction, that so-called worthless stuff would fetch—"

"We're not an auction house, Pedric, or haven't you noticed? We're *thieves*! We steal and we kill and that's what we do, that's what we *are*." Suddenly she laughed. "Well, I suppose I've got no one but myself to blame. Somehow I thought you'd do something with yourself. You had the perfect chance tonight. Everyone likes you, though I don't know why. If you'd been able to speak like a real man, you'd have won easily."

Pedric had gone beyond anger into open-mouthed shock. Marrika was a beautiful, sensuous woman. She had arrived in Braedon only a few months before, on a ship from Mhar. She'd been the first mate's woman then, but when the ship sailed back to its home port, Marrika had been in Pedric's bed, not on the vessel. Her hair was ebony, her skin tanned, and the movements of her body promised the ripeness of fruit newly plucked from the vine. She delivered on such a promise, and until this moment Pedric had assumed that he was the center of her universe. Despite her accusations, Pedric was far from being an idiot, and it was blindingly clear to him now that she did not desire him, had never desired him, and had attached herself to him only as the suckerfish to the shark. Had he won tonight, he wouldn't have been able to pry her off him. She would be all supple warmth and hot breath, sloe-eyed and eager for him. Now her fluid movements were stiff and frozen, and she was as cold as a breath of winter in the summertime, all the more chilling for its unexpectedness.

He hadn't loved her. Pedric didn't think he could love anybody; he was too frivolous, and he knew it. Losing the election tonight had been an enormous relief. He hadn't wanted the position in the first place, had only reluctantly volunteered because it seemed important to Marrika. No, he hadn't loved her, but he had liked and admired her. She was the first woman he had ever known who wasn't all aflutter with false courtesies and faintness. Marrika hadn't hidden her sharp intelligence nor her ambition from him, but had rather turned these attributes into ones to be admired. Now he realized that they were not virtues after all—not the way she used them.

His expression changed again, from shock to mild disgust. "Lucky thing I lost, isn't it," he said archly. "Not only would I have had to deal with responsibilities I didn't want and, as an *idiot*, couldn't have handled, but I'd have had to sleep with you again tonight. What a narrow escape."

He turned and walked back toward Ocean's View.

Marrika realized with a jolt that it really didn't matter to Pedric if she stayed or left. Her mouth dropped. She'd left men before, left them begging for her to come back. Less often, they had been the one to leave first, trying to salvage some shreds of pride, but she could always sense their bitterness and pain—and reveled in it.

Now that he knew there was no point in being around her anymore, Pedric had merely turned and walked away. The aristo bastard simply didn't *care*.

Recovering herself, she rushed out after him, intending to continue the fight and then, this time, conclude it with *her* walking away from *him*. She nearly collided with Freylis. "Oh!" she gasped, startled.

The big man grinned down at her. Marrika tried not to wrinkle her nose. Freylis obviously believed that in order to own the streets one had to smell like them.

"Overheard your conversation," he said. "Otter *is* an idiot, letting a pretty little fishy like you get away from him."

She gazed up at him, letting her lips smile sweetly. Behind the mask of her face her thoughts raced. Freylis was, if possible, a greater fool than Pedric. He also had his own group of followers. She knew that he was furious at his defeat tonight. If she was any judge of men, she guessed that he was in a mood for a bout of hot, primal copulation, followed by plans for revenge.

Both actions suited her just fine. "Would you mind walking me home?" she asked. "It seems I'm without escort tonight."

Freylis's ugly face split into an even uglier grin.

Who is our King? _____ is our King!
What can he do? Most anything!
He'll call the birds and make them sing,
And cause the bee to lose its sting,
Turn rocks into a wedding ring—
A wizard most wondrous is our King!

— Mharian children's rhyme

CHAPTER THREE

The summer day was beautiful, the breeze soft and fragrant as it caressed the down-covered cheeks of Castyll Alhaidri Shahil Derlian, king of the country of Mhar. The young royal's expression, though, was better suited to the harshness of the winter months. His face was pale and as hard as the flagstone path that led from the aptly named Castle Seacliff to its surrounding garden.

Behind Castyll, at a respectful distance, walked two men armed with swords. They were tall, though not as tall as the young giant of a king they guarded, and their faces were weatherworn and as hard as Castyll's. The two men were like dual shadows, and since his father's death Castyll had scarcely had a moment when they, or men like enough to them to be their doubles, were not with him. They were ostensibly his guards, posted out of concern by Counselor Bhakir, Castyll's regent.

"Since your dear father's untimely demise," Bhakir had moaned when Shahil was barely cool, "I fear for your life, Your Majesty. You should be guarded, at least until the crown is securely upon your head. Sweet Health alone knows what I would do should anything happen to you while you were in my care."

Like what happened to my father, when he was in your care? Castyll thought to himself bitterly. An accident, they called it; a bone stuck in the royal throat. But Castyll had been there when his father choked to death; had seen no bone in the soft pheasant meat upon which Shahil had dined. He had, though, been helpless witness to the dying convulsions of a great man, and had gotten a whiff of a bitter almond scent from Shahil's plate before it was whisked away.

He knew at that moment, with Bhakir sobbing loudly and falsely, that his own life was in danger. He and Shahil had come for a pleasant few months together at the summer palace, but the small, pretty castle had become a place of mourning and fear.

Castyll knew the men for what they were—guards indeed, but not for his protection. He was a prisoner here at Seacliff as surely as if Bhakir had clapped shackles on his arms and legs. His morning walk through the gardens and the occasional horseback ride—with his guards galloping at his side, of course—was all the freedom Bhakir would permit him.

The king's head ached with the tension in his back and shoulders, a constant tautness that would not leave him even in sleep. He tried to force himself to relax, but could not. He was not yet comfortable with his adult-sized body and did not know all its subtle secrets. At fifteen, Castyll had grown nearly a foot in the last year alone and had already attained six feet. He would grow more, he knew; Shahil had been a big man, and there was every indication that Castyll would follow in his footsteps. He was thin still, though, thin as a racing dog, and his guards outweighed him by at least fifty pounds. Besides, they were armed. Castyll had been taught a healthy respect for weapons and was not about to force a confrontation.

He had come to the culinary herb section of the garden, one of his favorite spots. Seacliff's garden, a modest name for an area that encompassed several dozen acres, was an elaborate creation. It was precise and ordered, with each section clearly defined either by a low stone wall or carefully cut shrubbery. There were several sections—culinary herbs; medicinal and magical herbs; herbs grown solely for their dried fragrances; small flowers; climbing flowers; fruit trees; and flowering trees; Each of Verold's gods had his or her own small statue, and there were gorgeous topiaries, sundials, and stone benches scattered throughout.

Castyll had had herbalism taught to him as part of his magical training—training for a gift that, he was certain, would never come. All the other Mharian kings who possessed the talent had shown it at their Testing, undertaken at age three. Castyll hadn't had the ability then, and had never manifested it since. Still, Shahil was nothing if not optimistic. He had ordered Jemma, current royal herbalist and former Blesser of the goddess Health, to instruct Castyll in the meanings of the herbs harvested at Seacliff.

Now Castyll, bereft of both father and tutor, knelt alone in the garden and reached for a sprig of mint on which to chew. He hadn't seen Jemma since Shahil's death. He hoped the old woman had come to no harm; probably she, like everyone else with whom Castyll was close, had been ordered to keep her distance. Early on, in the chaos that had surrounded Shahil's death, Castyll had been able to send and receive messages from those loyal to him, even to and from Byrn. Now, though, he was surrounded by silence as stony as the walls that encased him.

The cold freshness of the plant burst in his mouth, and a shade of a smile touched the youth's lips. Jemma had urged him to touch, sniff, taste everything in the culinary herb garden as he listened to "the lore of the plants." Such experimentation had encouraged learning in a child more efficiently than the normal adult response—"don't touch." *Oh, Jemma,* he thought, *if only things were as they had always been, and you were here, telling me that basil means love, and thyme means courage, and . . .*

He frowned slightly. Someone had been in the garden recently, and had damaged some of the herbs. He was about to raise his voice, call his guards' attention to the vandalism simply for something to do, when understanding broke in him with an almost physical shock.

The herbs that had been broken, their leaves plucked off and piled in small heaps around their roots, had not been selected at random. Castyll knelt, reaching for the small leaves of the thyme, forcing himself to move casually although his heart was thudding frantically.

Thyme—courage.

King's Lady—the "royal" plant.

Rosemary—remembrance.

Sage—salvation.

He read the message in his head: *Have courage, King, you are not forgotten and you will be saved.*

A lump welled in his throat. Jemma had not forsaken him! She was no longer in the honored position of Blesser, true, but she was still a wise and well-respected Healer. That she had the ear of many important people, Castyll knew. He blinked back quick tears and cleared the broken, bruised plants away. Turning his head slowly, the king glanced back at the two men. They were bored and talking casually to one another. Castyll puttering with the plants was something they saw every day.

Castyll closed his eyes and said a prayer to the positive aspect of the fickle god/dess, Hope/Despair. He also silently thanked the bountiful goddess Health, under whose dominion all healing plants came. Then, with apparent randomness, he selected herbs to leave his own message. He hoped that Jemma would be able to decipher the complex message.

He rose, brushing his dirtied hands against his fine linen shirt with the carelessness of his youth, and surveyed his handiwork. Obvious to a searcher; meaningless to one who was merely passing by. His task done, he decided to linger no longer and continued his stroll through the garden. But over the next half hour Castyll saw nothing of the beautifully landscaped trees and shrubberies. His mind's eye was filled with the small, short, wonderful plants of the herb garden.

At last a slight cough from one of the guards alerted him that it was time for the midday repast. Castyll glanced up at the castle and grimaced inwardly, but went with them obediently enough. Seacliff was perched almost precariously at the top of a winding road. It looked as if it might be vulnerable to a siege, but its builders had been wise, creating dozens of tunnels beneath Seacliff that led to secret exits. Most of them had fallen into disuse in these peaceful times. The castle itself was pretty, almost fragile in appearance from the ocean, built of white stone and adorned with many slender towers. It had been Shahil's and Castyll's favorite of the royal dwellings. Now Castyll wondered if he could ever look upon Seacliff without pain.

Bhakir insisted that the king take his meals with him in the formal feast hall. Without colorful decorations and a crowd of revelers, the feast hall seemed to Castyll gloomy and enormous. As he entered, blinking as his eyes adjusted to the dim lighting, dried rushes crunched under his booted feet. Torches burned smokily and the windows were open. Bhakir, still hypocritically clad in the long, flowing robe of sky blue that was worn only by counselors, awaited him at the laden table.

Bhakir did not look like a devious usurper. He looked more like someone's benevolent uncle. He was short and rotund, and his bright brown eyes seemed to always sparkle with laughter. He wore a beard, black and neatly trimmed, as if to compensate for the thinning hairs that barely covered his pate. Like the beautiful carnivorous flowers that were said to bloom in the Elvenlands, Bhakir lured the unwary with that doughy, defenseless exterior and a sweet, seductive laugh that encompassed everyone present. It was only when he had you, thought Castyll with a burst of impotent anger, when you had delicately put your oh-so-fragile insect legs on the shiny surface of the vile creature's mouth, that the teeth would appear. They would crunch down with a suddenness so swift that some were doomed even before they knew the instrument of their betrayal.

Castyll had never been taken in. Neither had his father. Both king and prince had mistrusted the man from the moment he had been elected to the Council, but they were powerless to dismiss him. Had Bhakir been convicted of a crime, he would have been removed from any position of power within the Mharian government. But not one breath of scandal touched him. And Castyll knew, with a heaviness that lay on his heart like something tangible, that there were those in Bhakir's inner circle who still held him blameless in the sudden death of the king.

"Ah!" boomed Bhakir, clapping his pudgy hands together in a facsimile of delight. "Good morning to you, Your Majesty. Did you enjoy your walk through the grounds?"

"Yes," replied Castyll curtly. He plopped into a hard, carved wooden chair and glared sullenly at Bhakir. He was the man's prisoner. That did not mean he had to show him courtesy.

Bhakir's dancing eyes narrowed, and for an instant, he bore a closer resemblance to a poisonous reptile than a jolly uncle. The king half expected the fat counselor to open his mouth and display a lolling, forked tongue.

Instead, Bhakir forced a smile. "Then you'll have worked up an appetite." Silk on satin was his voice. Strangers were charmed; Castyll felt a finger of fear prickle along the back of his neck. *For now*, Castyll thought, *he'll*

*take it from me. But not for much longer. How much time
do I have left?* he thought with a sudden stab of despair.
Breathing suddenly became difficult. *How many weeks,
days, hours will it be until I am no longer necessary?*

Bhakir gestured and unsmiling servants entered, bearing
plates heaped high with food. A cold soup, made with the
fresh fruits of the summer, was brought in a gorgeous ceramic bone tureen. The handles were modified lion's heads.
Three varieties of bread were served, along with cold and
hot roasts and fowl. Castyll watched the parade of food
with faint disgust. The midday meal in his father's time had
been, often as not, a crude repast of cold meat with a slice
of bread wrapped around it, eaten on horseback or while at
lessons. The spread before him was far more lavish than the
occasion warranted. Bhakir, he knew, would eat twice as
much as his king, who was a growing youth. Castyll said
nothing, sitting stonily as food that would choke a glutton
was piled high in front of him, obscuring the crest of Mhar
that was painted on all the plates and serving dishes.

"I know how dining with only me to keep you company
bores you, King Castyll," Bhakir said amiably as he spread
a thick slice of bread with herb butter. "So I've decided to
invite a few guests to join us over the next several weeks."

The constriction around Castyll's chest that had sprung
up without warning a few moments ago eased slightly. A
few weeks. He hoped that Bhakir would stick to his time-
table.

"I had thought," he ventured, "that we should be going
back to Jarmair for my coronation."

Bhakir appeared unruffled. "Soon enough, duties shall be
laid at your feet, Your Majesty. Enjoy the summer, while
you may."

Innocent tone of voice; sinister words. "Who will be
joining us, then?" he asked, as he bit into an apple. *A man
is known by the company he keeps*, he thought. *Who does
Bhakir consider suitable dinner company?*

"I thought you might like to meet your new Commander

of the Navy, Lord Carroc Zhael," said Bhakir. Butter clung in a greasy glob to his mustache for an instant before the pudgy, beringed hands lifted a linen napkin and delicately patted the offensive matter away. "He is so anxious to meet you."

The new Commander. Castyll had never had the dubious pleasure of meeting Lord Zhael, but he knew the name. Shahil had roared it angrily on more than a few nights. Zhael had marched swiftly up the ranks by legal but dishonorable means, stymied in his climbing only by the fact that the upper ranks of the military were staffed by men who were aware of Zhael's true nature. Now, with Shahil's death and the elimination of men who had been loyal to the crown, Zhael's way was clear. Castyll mentally filed the name away for information. How in Verold would he be able to tell Jemma about Zhael, using only herbs to convey the information?

"And Captain Porbrough is also invited." The brown eyes were intense, watching him with the coldness of a cat at a rat's hole. Castyll was instantly alert, though the name meant nothing to him.

"I'm afraid I'm not familiar with the good captain," he hazarded.

A fat red smile appeared in the center of the beard. "You might know him better as Captain Cutter."

Castyll's eyes opened wide, and he was unable to disguise the horror in his voice as he gasped, "The pirate?"

Bhakir shook his head reprovingly. "Captain Porbrough has been the victim of vicious gossip. His deeds, while admittedly illegal, are hardly enough to classify him as a pirate! No, he came to me for clemency, and upon observing he was truly repentant, I granted it. Now he is eager to serve in Your Majesty's navy. I accepted the offer on your behalf." He cut a small, tidy piece of meat with his knife, speared it, and inserted it into his mouth.

So, Captain Porbrough's crimes didn't classify him as a pirate? Castyll knew the man had gotten the name "Captain

Cutter" by his penchant for disfiguring anyone unlucky enough to fall into his hands. The prince himself had been present when one of his father's spies, his face a horrible, noseless revulsion, had reported on Captain Cutter's atrocities.

You bastard, thought Castyll. *You cunning old bastard. If I had my father's magical skills . . .* Furiously the king concentrated on an image in his head, a shockingly violent image for a youth usually so calm and controlled. He envisioned Bhakir exploding, his body parts igniting and burning away as they hurtled in various directions. He saw the image in his mind's eye and focused his energy on it.

Nothing. Castyll had no magic. His thoughts fell upon his dreaded enemy with as little effect as the sheepherder's black thoughts upon the wolf raiding his flock.

He licked lips suddenly gone dry and took a sip of the rose-flavored wine. "You're too kind, Bhakir," he said, making his voice sound as sincere as possible. "People will take advantage of you."

For an instant, the counselor seemed to see through Castyll's false flattery. But then, perhaps because Castyll was good at fooling people when he chose, or perhaps a pliant king was something he wanted to see, Bhakir smiled and cut another slice of the meltingly tender venison.

Castyll stared at his plate, certain that if he forced food down it would come right back up. He would be dining with traitors and pirates over the next few weeks. Desperately he hoped that Jemma would read the message—and somehow devise some means for Castyll's escape. He could not stay here. If he stayed, the Derlian line would assuredly end with him, and Mhar would have no one to stand between her and Bhakir's ravishment.

Jemma was permitted to harvest herbs from the garden twice daily—at daybreak and at dusk. As the sun sank slowly in the west, its magnificent departure uncontested

by even a single cloud, the old woman hobbled into Seacliff's garden.

For three days now, she had positioned the herbs in their
peculiar messages, arranging them at dawn. Each dusk had
brought disappointment. Castyll had either not noticed
them or had not deciphered their subtle code. Now, as she
walked, leaning heavily on the oak staff, she saw that the
herbs had been disturbed.

She lurched forward and knelt, trembling. "Oh, clever
boy!" she said softly. Castyll had received the message—
and left one of his own. Jemma examined the herbs.

Tarragon stood for ferocious strength. Horehound was a
known antidote for snakebite. Mugwort—protection.
King's Lady—the royal plant. Lad's Love—devotion. Pars-
ley—revelry and victory. And finally, a plant imported
from neighboring Byrn, the flowering borage.

*I am fighting the good fight, holding my own against the
Snake. But I need protection. I send love to Cimarys. We
will celebrate together—contact Byrn.*

At least, Jemma assumed that was the message. The sen-
timents were logical and typical of Castyll. Jemma raised
her gray head and peered about as best she could. She could
see no one, but that did not mean that there was no one
present. Guards were posted everywhere around Seacliff
these days. Jemma suppressed a shudder and began to carefully pick the herbs, cutting them with the small knife con-
secrated by Health for that express purpose, and placing
them in the small basket she carried. She was filled with
elation that her plan to communicate with the trapped
Castyll had worked, and harvesting the plants was the last
thing on the herbalist's mind. To have been to the garden
and not gathered herbs, however, would immediately
arouse suspicion in anyone who happened to see her.

When she had gathered enough to allay any doubts, she
left her own simple message: a large pile of sage and a
pinch of wormwood. She hoped that the amount of sage
would make Castyll recall a well-known quote: "Why

should a man die when sage flourishes in his garden?"
Wormwood was often used to fight off the effects of poison. In other words, as long as there was someone in contact with Castyll, the youth should continue to fight,
knowing he was not alone.

Jemma rose, slowly and with much wincing. She was
nearly eighty, and though her potions and frequent offer-
ings to Health had kept her mobile and healthy, the crippling pain in her joints served as sharp reminders that Lady
Death was also nearby.

"Wait awhile, Lady," she said softly as she walked out of
the garden into the deepening twilight. "I have tasks to do.
You know that as well as I. Come for me when I am done,
and I'll not refuse your embrace."

The evening that lay ahead of her would have tasked
even a younger woman, but the old Healer did not shirk her
duty. She walked the long distance, over a mile, from Seacliff to the port area of the town of Ilantha. It was a long
trek, but riding a horse, though she had done it often in her
youth, now proved too painful a means of transportation.
Better aching muscles from a walk than raging fire in her
joints from the horse's rolling, jolting gait. Besides, it was a
pretty view. The sun was nearly gone and Jemma was
headed due west, straight into the splendid vision of the
resting day.

She continued through the rest of the royal garden,
passed the guards of the encircling stone wall with a nod of
recognition, and continued down the hard-packed dirt road
toward the town and the dockyard. Most of the stores, with
the exception of hostelries and taverns, were closing for the
day. A baker, about to pull his shutters to, saw Jemma and
smiled a greeting.

Jemma's eyes were failing, but her nose was sharp, and
she breathed in the sea-scented air with a smile. She had
spent most of her life inland, and the ocean was still a
sweet pleasure to her. Once she had reached the dock, she
rented the use of a small, single-person dory and a lantern.

The fisherman knew Jemma, and the old woman's excuse that "there were certain seaweeds that I need to harvest after dark for my work" was accepted without question. Not for the first time, Jemma was glad that she had been born with the gift of Healing and had chosen to follow the goddess. Eccentricities went unquestioned in Blessers.

The sun was gone now, though the stars had yet to appear. The ships anchored in the harbor bore lit lamps, and for now it was enough for Jemma to see by. She rowed out onto the velvety black waters of the Ver ocean. There were always plenty of fishing boats crowding the harbor, and recently Jemma had noticed an increasing number of official military vessels.

The darkness grew, and the other ships dwindled as she left them behind, until the Healer's small lamp was the only real light at hand. The lanterns on the ships and the lights of the town were far away and looked like summer's glowflies. Finally, Jemma stopped when she felt she was a safe distance from the port. Then she fumbled for the anchor, tying a large bunch of sage securely around it. Grunting with the effort, Jemma heaved the anchor overboard. It splashed softly, then sank, the rope snaking into the water after it.

A few moments later, the rope moved, pulling taut. There came a sudden jerk, and then the little craft fairly skimmed along the water until it was a good half mile away from shore.

In the warm yellow light cast by the single candle in the lantern, the ocean rippled. A sleek, human-looking head broke the water's surface. Candlelight illuminated slanted eyes and pointed ears. In daylight, Jemma knew, the creature's hair would be dark green, like the color of seaweed, and his skin a pale blue. His eyes were emerald.

"You are lucky I am here," said the creature, in a voice as soft and soothing as the waves on the shore. "I was not expecting you tonight, my friend." He smiled, and the gesture lightened the solemnity of his wise face. He extended a strong, sleek arm and handed a bunch of seaweed to

Jemma. The Healer carefully placed the ocean gift in the bottom of the boat.

"I may need you every night from now on, Darshirin," apologized Jemma. "The king has deciphered the code, and we will be in daily contact. He's holding up well, but he's frightened."

"Of course," said Darshirin politely, though he knew little of the landspeople's politics.

"Give Damir this message, found at evening on Lisdae: 'I am fighting the good fight, holding my own against the Snake. But I need protection. I send love to Cimarys. We will celebrate together—contact Byrn.' "

Darshirin nodded his head and repeated the message verbatim. "Anything else?"

"Not for the present. Darshirin—I know it was unusual enough for you to trust Damir. I appreciate the trust you put in me, as well. I know the People of the Sea don't get involved with us land dwellers much—"

Darshirin, bobbing up and down on the waves, shook his head and gently lifted a webbed hand in a gesture of courteous denial. "I owe Damir my life. To help him where I can is nothing; and you share his good spirit. And to help bring about the downfall of the *pirates*," and his sea-soft voice now sounded like a crashing wave on the word he loathed, "we would do anything."

Jemma gazed at her friend with sympathy. The pirates, she knew, hunted the People of the Sea. Humans were almost as frightened of them as of the elves, these beautiful ocean inhabitants who could turn from human form to dolphin shape in a heartbeat. The pirates often sold the People of the Sea to greedy organizers of traveling shows. The pitiful creatures, floating listlessly in the still touring pools, would always die after a brief bout of grief at being separated from the ocean. Farther north, past Byrn, it was said the ratlike monsters called the Ghil enslaved the sea-people as well, forcing them to harvest the ocean's bounties for them.

"King Castyll will stop the pirates, won't he?" Concern was in Darshirin's voice.

"Castyll's a good lad. And when he learns of the service you've done him, I'm certain he'll do everything he can to put an end to the slavery of your people."

Again Darshirin smiled, and again Jemma's heart swelled with affection for the magnificent being. Without another word, Darshirin sank back into the arms of the ocean. There was a splash, and Jemma saw the flip of a dolphin's tail break the surface a few feet away. Then the rope was pulled taut, tugged by Darshirin's powerful dolphin's beak, and the little boat reversed course and skipped along the waves in the direction of the shore.

Sweet Health, thought Jemma to herself as she rowed the rest of the way to the dock, *I am getting too old for this*. She frowned to herself. Wasn't her stock of joint salve getting low? She would have to check.

Her mind still on her medicines, she retied the small boat in its proper place, picked up her basket, and began to walk down the now-deserted streets. Home was only a few minutes away. *This is good*, Jemma thought. *Not up to another long walk. When I get home—*

Her heart began to pound. She realized that now the streets were no longer deserted. Six armed guardsmen were waiting, concealed by shadows. Summoning her courage and straightening to her diminutive height, Jemma gazed at them in turn.

"Good evening, sirs. How may old Jemma the Healer help you?"

"There is sickness in Seacliff," said one. His voice hitched slightly. "The king is ill. Bhakir sent us to find you."

Fear coursed through Jemma's veins. Flight would be foolish. These men wanted her, and they would have her. That Bhakir sent them to find her, she had no doubt, but there was no sickness involved. Somehow she must have

been discovered. She only hoped that young Castyll was
still all right.

"If King Castyll is ill, of course I shall come." At least,
as long as she kept up the pretense, they would delay the
inevitable pain. Keeping her head high, her long gray braid
falling behind her to her knees, Jemma willingly went with
the guards who had been sent to imprison her.

Alone in the small room that was now his bedchamber,
Castyll lay in his bed. He was not asleep, but merely waiting for the dead time of night. When that hour came, he
quietly left his canopied bed, soundlessly pushing aside the
heavy draperies and moving with a deep grace that would
have surprised him had he noticed it. Bare feet sank into the
soft, thick fur of a mountain-cat rug. Naked, he walked
across the rug, steeled himself for the cold stone of the
floor, and went to the single candle that sat, unlit, on a
small table by the door.

Drawing up a chair, Castyll eased himself down. The old
piece of furniture did not creak in the slightest. He winced
but a little as the chill wood touched his buttocks. Placing
his broad palms on his thighs, Castyll stared at the candle,
and concentrated.

When he had been three years old, he had been given the
Test. Then, it had been simple: He had merely slipped his
small child's arms into an adult-sized pair of arm bracers.
Had he had the talent for magic, the bracers would have lit
up with a warm, red hue. But nothing had happened, and all
assumed that Castyll had, sadly, not been blessed with the
talent for magic that graced so many of the Derlian kings.

But King Shahil hadn't accepted the ruling of the bracers, and he had encouraged Castyll to keep working, to
keep learning, hoping that perhaps the talent would reveal
itself later. One of the simplest tricks, Castyll knew, was
lighting a candle using only the force of one's will. This
would reveal the talent for either hand or mind magic.
Mind magic would create the illusion of flame on the can-

dle; hand magic would make the candle actually burn. The bracers were locked far away from his reach now. Only the candle remained.

He stared at it, as he had every night of his captivity, willing its blackened wick to spark to new life. And in that warm, soft glow of a single candle, Castyll's life would change forever. He would free himself and avenge his father's murder, ease tensions with Byrn, claim his birthright, and wed the Byrnian princess he so loved.

But the candle stayed dark. At last, his eyes filled with grit and aching with want of sleep, Castyll returned to his bed as stealthily as he had left it. He laid his dark head on the feather pillow and slept the sleep of exhausted youth. As he slept he dreamed of Princess Cimarys, uncrowned, her hair falling in an ebony cascade about her slim shoulders. She wore a flowing robe of fragile gossamer, and she smiled at him as she walked barefoot through an herb garden with the scent of the sea surrounding her.

And Hope/Despair stood before him, but poor Tomai
did not know which one he faced. The little boy Hope
smiled reassuringly, but the old hag Despair leered. They
held out the dagger and said, "There is but one place
where you are sure to find the Tiger."

"Ah!" cried Tomai, his face pale. "So you would
have me hunt the Tiger in his own lair?"

—Byrnian folk tale, *Tomai and the Tiger*

CHAPTER FOUR

Braedon was an old city, one of the oldest in Byrn, existing by its present name and in similar incarnations for the better part of eight centuries. The name literally meant "place on the hill," and harkened back to a time when men had used the natural harbor and protective ring of surrounding mountains mainly as a defense against the Ghil. Trade had come later, after the more immediate struggle to eliminate the Ghil eventually drove the foul creatures ever northward, and humans rose in ascendancy.

Now the quiet natural harbor of centuries past was a bustling place of merchants and sailors, and those who made their living off of them. A few travelers, Damir among them, availed themselves of the perfectly serviceable road called Ocean's View that cut straight through Braedon and continued east through the mountains that pro-

tectively encircled the harbor city. The three ill-fated councilmen, brutally murdered by Bear and his cohorts, had
been traveling along this road. But by far the greatest traffic
in the city came by ship.

The worst parts of town were located "so near the water
as t' be wet theyselves," as some of the inhabitants boasted.
These were inns and taverns that catered to the needs of the
often harsh men who did the actual sailing of the vessels.
The farther east in Braedon one went, the better the envi-
rons grew. Continuing along Ocean's View, one passed the
temples erected to the seven deities of Byrn and Mhar:
Love, Light, Health, Hope/Despair, Traveler, Death, and
Vengeance. Here, too, on a raised dais, were the stocks and,
though not as often used, the gallows.

In the center of this area was a huge stone pillar called
the Godstower. A single iron bell, over two hundred years
old, hung from the top of the construct. The Godstower bell
was rung seven times each day by the Blessers of each
faith. Dawn was Light's time. Midmorning belonged to
Love. Health's bell rang at midday. Traveler's Blesser
pulled the rope in the afternoon. Twilight, that time of not
quite day or night, belonged to the twin-countenanced
Hope/Despair. Death sounded her knell when night was
well on its way, and the middle of the darkness was
Vengeance's domain. The gods lent their names, too, to the
days of the week: Lisdae, Losdae, Healsdae, Trvsdae
HoDesdae, Desdae, and Venedae.

Even farther down the road were the fine homes and
more exclusive inns, gambling houses, and other forms of
entertainment for the very well-to-do. Here, too, was the
beautiful Garden, the pride and joy of the rich.

As Death's knell rang out on Travsdae, a scant five
nights after the brutal murders of half the thieves of Braedon, the celebrants enjoying themselves in Deveren's
lovely home paid the sound no mind. Deveren sipped
honey wine from a gorgeous silver chalice and grinned to
himself.

He enjoyed entertaining, and the pleasure never faded. There was little else, besides his beloved plays, that satisfied him as completely as hosting a gathering. The gentle, unobtrusive sounds of harp, flute, lute, and lyre; the happy buzz of good conversation; the glow on the guests' faces; the lavish spread of fine foods; the shrill punctuation of pleasant laughter—these intoxicated the handsome Lord Larath. People still talked about some of the parties he and Kastara had hosted, in their joyful, agonizingly brief time as husband and wife.

Deveren took another sip of the sweet fluid to hide the momentary flash of sorrow that flitted across his face. *I still miss you so, my love,* he thought. Regaining his composure, Deveren moved smoothly, inconspicuously, through the crowd of guests, making quiet notes as to who had attended and who was chatting with whom. His entire home was open and filled with light. Guests could wander anywhere and often did, from the dining hall where dinner had been held a few hours ago to the small armory just off the hall, from Deveren's beautifully decorated bedchamber to the tiny, romantic room atop the faux turret that adorned the house.

"Absolutely wonderful honey wine, Deveren!" came Pedric's voice at his ear. "Imported?"

His host shook his head. "Only from down the street. When he's not pouring ale or making terrible food, old Jankiss at the Cat and Dog makes this."

"Dear gods, you're joking!" Pedric stared with wonder at the goblet in his manicured hand. "You can get this at the Cat and Dog?"

Deveren laughed. "No, Jankiss makes it, but he doesn't serve it there. I pay him far better than any of his customers would."

"Sweet Love, I shall have to do what I can to undercut you and get some of this nectar myself," replied Pedric.

Deveren laughed, took another sip of the superb wine from lowly origins, and continued to peruse the room.

Damir, looking elegant in black hose and a short houppe-lande of royal blue, was deep in conversation with Lord Vandaris. Deveren smiled to himself. Though the celebration was allegedly being held in Damir's honor, Deveren's brother had eyes only for the man who could help him most—the white-haired, good-natured head of the Braedon Council. Deveren estimated that it wouldn't be long before Damir steered Vandaris into a less public corner for some more private political conversation. He was right; less than a moment later, Vandaris leaned over to his daughter to excuse himself.

"Good gods!" yelped Pedric, startling Deveren. "Who is that lovely creature?"

Deveren smiled to himself. "Won't Marrika be jealous?"

Pedric's handsome mouth contorted in a sneer of disgust. "The unlamented Marrika has been consigned to the pages of history, old friend. Now, tell me about this vision talking so affectionately to our dear councilman—" he stopped abruptly. "And don't tell me that she's his daughter!"

"Alas," said Deveren, mimicking Pedric's affected banter, "I must say that indeed the fair Lorinda is the child of our good Vandaris." His voice dropped, and there was no laughter in it now. "I'd steer clear of her if I were you. The last thing one of us wants to do is get messed up with a councilman's family—especially Vandaris."

Clearly, Pedric had not heard him. He was staring, enraptured, at Vandaris's only child. And Deveren had to admit, there was much at which to stare. The young woman was tall, and her lustrous hair fell free about her shoulders. Most of her sisters in high society wore their hair either bound or piled atop their heads, laced with jewelry. Lorinda did not wear much jewelry at all, but her gown, though simple, draped her like the finest ornament. Her face was likewise bare, free of the often garish cosmetics that wealthy women used to color their lips, eyes, and mouth. Her skin was tanned, another departure from the current, milk-white fashion, and she seemed to like to laugh a great deal.

"I knew she'd been gone and had finally come home. Everybody knew that. But—" Pedric, for perhaps the first time in his life, was at a loss for words.

"She's been gone twelve years," Deveren explained. "Lorinda was sent at the age of eight to be one of the Tenders at Love's temple in Kasselton. When the former Blesser stepped down, she selected someone else to follow her as Blesser, so Lorinda returned home. This is the first time I've seen her make an appearance in public. Perhaps I should ask after her, see if she wants anything." He deadpanned this last line, and took a step toward the beautiful woman.

"Ah, no, Dev, I think I'll go convey your greetings for you." Pedric was moving before he had finished the sentence, and Deveren watched him go, worry in his hazel eyes.

So, thought Pedric as he stepped smoothly beside Lorinda, *she's fresh out of the temple, eh? Shouldn't be too hard . . .*

"Good evening, milady Lorinda. Welcome back to Braedon. I understand that you've just recently returned." He smiled charmingly. "Love's loss. I can tell just by looking at your fair face that you would have made a superb Blesser of Love."

He reached for her hand to kiss it, but somehow Lorinda managed to gracefully evade him. The look she shot him was decidedly cool. "Thank you for your welcome, milord . . . ?"

"Pedric Dunsan, Lord Asakinn. But I'd like it if you'd call me Pedric." Again he tried for her hand, snared it this time, and brought it to his lips. It was surprisingly callused, but not unattractive. He attempted to turn it over, to place a feathery kiss on the sensitive wrist, when suddenly the work-rough hand of the beauty of the hour wasn't there. He almost kissed his own hand, but recovered quickly.

"I'd prefer to keep things formal, Lord Asakinn."

Her voice was icy. If she was playing with him, she was

doing it well. Mockingly, Pedric shivered. "Trifle cold in here for early summer, don't you think? The winds usually blow," and he paused for effect, "warm and soft."

The brilliant dark eyes narrowed. "Excuse me."

She wasn't playing. She was serious. The realization unsettled him.

"No, wait!" The plea held none of the false calculation of his earlier chat, and Lorinda hesitated.

Pedric swallowed. Her fragrance, a mixture of rose and honeysuckle, was devastating.

"I'm afraid I've made a bit of a fool of myself," he stammered. Her full lips twitched. She did not contradict him.

He took a deep breath. All or nothing, then.

Out it came. "All right: I think you're the most beautiful woman I've ever seen, despite the fact that you're not wearing any of those horrible cosmetics, or, I don't know, maybe because you're not wearing them, and I mean that, and I'm fascinated by the fact that you spent twelve years in Love's temple, and I think I'd truly like to get to know you better." He finished, and looked at her pleadingly.

"You look like a puppy," she said, but not unkindly.

His heart lifted, just a little, and the old playfulness returned in some small measure. "If I had a tail, I'd be thumping it on the floor, but I don't. I must content myself with looking pathetic and hoping my mistress will toss me a crumb of her affection."

Mirth played about her face, and finally she surrendered to it. She laughed easily, like a child, and Pedric felt his heart speed up at what merriment did to her already lovely visage.

"I'm afraid I owe you an apology," she said. Her voice, when warmed with friendliness, was music. "Ever since I've been back, I've been . . . well . . . almost attacked by young men who think that simply because I served the goddess Love I'm ready to sexually oblige anyone who asks."

Pedric blushed at her frank language. Never had he heard a woman—well, at least a woman of quality—speak so bluntly before. He also blushed at his own guilt. That had, of course, been exactly what he had thought.

While all the gods were honored in Byrn, Love was perhaps the favorite. Depicted as a naked little girl playing with a fawn, Love was the gentlest and most forgiving of the divinities. Her Blesser had a unique, and powerful, role. When young men reached the age of thirteen, they were sometimes called to Love's Blesser. She would be their instructor in the art of physical loving; to be selected by her was an honor. Like all the priests, Love's Blesser had attendants, known as Tenders. These children were selected from the better families to serve for twelve years. When they reached the age of twenty, a Tender would either be chosen to replace the Blesser as the new Blesser of the temple, or else her time of servitude had ended and she returned home. Pedric had assumed that a child used to being around so much sexual activity would have matured into a woman with "loose morals."

"Just because the act is familiar to me doesn't mean I have no reverence for it. The Tenders, you know, don't participate in the Rite of Initiation, just the Blesser. And it makes me furious that people would think . . . !" Lorinda's tanned face flushed with anger and embarrassment. "It's—it's very difficult to come back to the world outside of the temple when you've been sheltered there so long, that's all. And I've probably offended you and I'll get a lecture from my father tonight."

Pedric shook his dark head. "No, you've not offended me," he said softly. "Far from it." He held up a finger, shook it, and in a lighter voice, he added, "Let me try this again."

He mockingly cleared his throat. "Welcome back to Braedon, milady Lorinda. My name is Pedric Dunsan. How may I help you enjoy your evening?"

Lorinda laughed, then matched Pedric's playful artifice with her own. "Ah, sirrah, I am quite parched. Might I have a sip of your wine?" She dropped the pretense and added

innocently, "Papa said it was awfully good, but I haven't
been able to get the server's attention."

"That I find hard to believe," said Pedric as he handed
her the glass. She placed her lips where his had been and
took a drink. In another woman, such a gesture would have
been deliberate flirtation. Lorinda merely wanted a sip of
wine.

The gesture was highly erotic, despite—no, because of—
its lack of contrivance. Somewhere in the back of his mind,
he knew that this woman was, in her own innocent fashion,
far more dangerous than a thief with his knife, but he was
utterly captivated. He had a dreadful suspicion that he was
halfway in love with her already, and when she smiled and
handed the goblet back, he surrendered utterly, and willingly fell the rest of the way.

In Deveren's library, Damir quietly pulled the heavy oak
door closed behind him and turned to face Vandaris. A single lamp glowed on the small circular table. The table and
two chairs, simply carved but functional and sturdy, were
the only pieces of furniture, if one didn't include the massive bookcases that covered nearly every inch of bare wall.
Deveren loved the smell and feel of books, but Damir wondered how much time his brother actually spent reading the
books in his extensive library.

Vandaris seated himself and looked up expectantly.
"Well?"

Damir put a thin finger to his lips. He went to the window and cursed silently. Deveren hadn't had time to replace the window he had damaged when Damir had shown
up a few nights ago, and the small hole in the pane let in
the sweet scent of the blooming Garden. It also would
make it easy for an eavesdropper to have perfect access to
the conversation. Well, it couldn't be helped. Damir
glanced left and right into the darkness, trying to sense the
thoughts of anyone present. He saw, and sensed, nobody
and turned back to face the head councilman of Braedon.

"How much has Deveren told you about me?" he asked. He walked back to the other end of the room, so that in order to watch him Vandaris would have to face the door, not the window. Damir had no desire to explain how that window had gotten broken.

Vandaris looked puzzled. "Your reputation precedes you, my lord. Your good brother hasn't had to say much. I'd venture to say that every lawman and councilman in Byrn knows of His Lordship Damir Larath, ambassador of His Majesty. You've got a bit of a nickname in the diplomatic circles, you know." His old eyes twinkled with mirth. "They call you the Problem Solver."

Surprised and amused, Damir laughed aloud. "Do they really?"

"Mmmmm," affirmed Vandaris. "They say that if only the king would send you, and not his armies, to confront the Ghil, you'd have a treaty signed within a week."

"Quite the compliment. And do you say that, Lord Vandaris?"

"I'm an old man, and I've seen a great deal in my day. I don't take the measure of a man by his reputation alone," Vandaris replied. "I like to see, and converse with, someone before I'll credit him with miracle making."

"No miracles, alas, but I do indeed solve problems."

"And what problem do you intend to solve here in Braedon?" Vandaris leaned back comfortably in the chair, but his eyes never left Damir's. "What problem is too big, or delicate, or dangerous, that we simple councilmen here can't handle it?"

Tread gently, Damir thought. Of course, Vandaris was wary. He assumed that Damir was in Braedon because of the recent murders. What a shock that must have been. Damir wondered how they were explaining it; probably as a tavern brawl that had gotten out of hand. The populace might not question that—as long as the exact number of bodies hadn't been made public.

Damir hesitated, then decided to trust Vandaris. His spies

had reported nothing but positive things about the chief councilman of Braedon. And his own delicate mental probing of the man revealed nothing to contradict those reports.

"The problem to be solved involves Braedon only indirectly. The real problem—" a brief pause to sense once again for other minds; they were indeed alone "—originates in Mhar. That troubled country may very soon be in a state of war with Byrn. The young king wishes to conduct secret peace negotiations before things get to that point. In fact, he may come here seeking more than a place to negotiate—he may come to Braedon seeking asylum, at least temporarily. I can make the city safe to a certain degree, but I'll need cooperation from you and perhaps the entire Council. Do I have it?"

Vandaris had paled and his bright eyes had grown enormous. Damir wondered if the old man might have a seizure. Instead, he began laughing, and color flooded his pallid face. "You lay down all the cards, don't you?"

Damir remained unruffled, smiling slightly. "Hardly," he replied. "What kind of a gambler would I be if I did? And you haven't answered my question."

Suddenly Damir sensed a presence. Simultaneously, behind Vandaris, a small, pale face appeared in the window. No, it was two small faces—one that of a child, the other the grinning visage of the stuffed doll she carried. He knew who it had to be at once. *By Love's smile*, Damir thought to himself, *she does look like my Talitha*. Horror transformed the hunger-sharpened features of the girl as she realized that she was locking gazes not with Deveren, as she had clearly expected, but with Damir. She quickly ducked out of sight.

Damir's face moved not a muscle as, waiting for Vandaris's reply, he moved casually over to the window and leaned against it, his hands linked loosely behind his back. "Can we count on your cooperation—and discretion?"

"I'd need to see some sort of proof that this will occur,"

Vandaris hedged. "And I'd need to be able to speak to a few of my men—the ones I'd trust with my own life."

Damir hesitated. He was used to ordering, not asking, but the situation was delicate and risky. "Very well. I have documents in my room, signed by His Majesty. I'm sure that you recognize the royal seal. As for your men, I'd like the names of those whom you feel you can trust before you speak with them. I have to make certain that I can trust them, too. I'm sure you understand."

Damir kept his voice level as he opened one palm toward the window. He felt a small piece of parchment scratch along his hand and he closed his fingers around the note. It crinkled audibly, and Damir spoke to cover the sound.

"If you would accompany me, I'm sure I can assuage your doubts."

"Not that I don't believe you," began Vandaris, concern crossing his still handsome, honest face. "It's merely that I cannot commit the Council or the town of Braedon without being absolutely certain."

"I understand perfectly. I'd expect the same myself. Caution has saved many a life—and reputation." He moved away from the window and extended his empty hand toward the door. Vandaris nodded and moved ahead of him. Damir followed after, casting a swift glance back toward the window. The little ghost-girl was gone. Quickly he unfolded the note and read it rapidly, crumpling it back into his palm when he had finished.

He walked alongside Vandaris as they re-entered the throng. Before they went to the spare room that served as Damir's chambers, Damir paused to talk to his brother, who raised an eyebrow curiously.

"Vandaris and I will be in my room if you need me." Casually he touched Deveren's hand as he spoke. His face as nonchalant as his brother's, Deveren took the note. No one noticed the transaction. Deveren waited a few moments, excused himself from his guests and stepped outside. When he was certain he was alone, he unfolded the missive.

Fox—

> *The Fox is clever, the Fox is wise;*
> *The Fox is getting a big surprise—*
> *Because your Theft is not one, but three*
> *If truly our Leader you wish to be.*
>
> *We leave to you the how and when,*
> *But the where must be the councilman's den.*
>
> *The Fox gives Fox a taste quite fine,*
> *When out of his head you drink your wine.*
>
> *The hounds will chase, the hounds will tear*
> *Your flesh, unless their teeth you bear.*
>
> *And last, the Fox of his brush is proud—*
> *But Vixen and Vandaris might not allow*
> *The Fox to acquire his one, two, three*
> *But if you fail, a mere thief you'll be.*

Deveren cursed softly to himself. He recognized the ornate, flowing script of his friend Pedric, and was willing to bet money that the feckless young man had been the one to both compose the poem and name the items. A few things about the note he would need to puzzle out later, but he'd guessed two things immediately. All the items were obviously in Vandaris's home—the words "councilman's den" made that clear. The phrase "might not allow" indicated to him that the objects had to be taken while the family was present. He reread the note, memorizing it, and shook his head. "His" thieves were clearly not going to let him off easily. He reached up to one of the lamps that hung outside the door and placed the parchment inside. A sudden voice at his ear caused him to start violently, almost burning his fingers as the paper caught and flamed.

"Well, Tomai," Damir said with a hint of humor in his smooth, cultured voice, "enjoy slaying the tiger in his own lair. I, of course, expect you to return the items as soon as you can." As Deveren sputtered his annoyance, Damir grinned wickedly and ducked back inside. As soon as the door had closed, Allika poked her head round a corner.

"He knew what to do, Fox!" she apologized as he glared at her. "He went right up to the window and stuck his hand out, and I knew your brother was in town, and I thought . . ." Her voice grew thick. She gazed up at him, remorse all over her face, Miss Lally trailing in the dirt.

Deveren squatted down to her level and smiled reassuringly. "It's all right, Little Squirrel. No harm done this time. But in the future, if you have notes for me, give them only to me, all right?"

She nodded, and smiled again. Like a shadow, she vanished from sight.

When Deveren returned to the bustle of the gala a few moments later, he saw that Pedric was deep in conversation with the radiant Lorinda. More than that, he'd managed to get the girl to hang on his words as much as Pedric hung on hers. Deveren maneuvered himself close enough to catch the drift of their conversation.

Pedric's normal expression at a social gathering was that of a slightly bored aristocrat who's heard everything worth listening to. Deveren noticed that the youth looked now as he did during particularly dangerous "outings," his eyes sparkling and his face flushed with excited color. His normally controlled movements were large and effusive as he gestured excitedly.

"And then the Queen, clutching both bloodied daggers, cries out, 'Ah, gods! They were not my enemy's children—*they were mine!*'"

Lorinda, enraptured, gasped sympathetically. "The Elf-King tricked her into killing her own children? Oh, how awful!"

Deveren was not disturbed by the blood-drenched conversation. He recognized it as a scene from *The Queen of All*, a play that had just opened at His Majesty's Theater.

Both he and Pedric were patrons of the show, and it was playing to a house that did not have a single empty seat for any of its performances.

"Yes!" Pedric yelped, thoroughly entrenched in his story. He plopped down beside Lorinda and continued. "And then there's a big flash and puff of smoke, and Lady Death appears. She's willing to make a bargain with the Queen for the lives of her two children, you see, and—"

"Pedric, Pedric!" Deveren admonished jokingly, laying a friendly hand on the younger man's shoulder. "It's one thing to give a play an enthusiastic review. It's quite another to spoil the plot for someone—you'll lose a sale that way, and that's bad for business!"

"On the contrary, Lord Larath," Lorinda responded. "I wish I could see *The Queen of All* more than ever! Do you know, I've never seen a theatrical performance in my life?"

"Goodness, how barbaric you servants of the gods are," said Pedric teasingly. Lorinda laughed. "Well, I will personally escort you to the next play that comes into town. Unfortunately for your theatrical edification, and not unfortunately for our purses, *The Queen of All* has no seats left for the rest of its run."

Deveren smiled. An idea had just come to him—a wonderful, perfect idea. "Well, at least not its public run," he said.

Lorinda turned her gorgeous eyes on him. "What do you mean?"

"Well, the Councilman's Seat has a large hall, doesn't it?" Deveren was referring to the honorary domicile of the Head Councilman, the beautiful, sprawling building that was home to Vandaris and, now, Lorinda.

Pedric's eyes lit up even brighter as he comprehended what Deveren was suggesting. "Of course it does! Oh, Deveren, you clever fellow!"

"What?" Lorinda, the novice theatergoer, was confused.

"A command performance," Deveren explained. "Your father, as Head Councilman, has the right to invite any

thespian or musician to perform exclusively at the Councilman's Seat. He could ask the cast of *The Queen of All* to do
the play on Lisdae, a night they traditionally have off."

"That sounds wonderful!" Lorinda clapped her hands together in an unconsciously childlike gesture. "Would they
mind? I mean, they might be looking forward to a night to
relax . . ."

"We'll make it a celebration," suggested Pedric. Deveren
grinned to himself. Only Pedric would have had the audac-
ity to volunteer someone else's home—and a councilman's
home at that—for a celebration. "It won't be as nice as
Dev's, of course, but then, no one's festivities compare to
Deveren's."

"I'd be inclined to agree," said Lorinda, gazing warmly
at the young man. "After all, it's where you and I met."

Deveren glanced from one youthful face to the other. His
heart sank. Much as he enjoyed being around young lovers,
he knew that this was a bad match. Pedric might be the
younger son of a nobleman, and titled in his own right, but
his habits and temperament suited his true occupation—that
of professional thief. And Lorinda was grounded in the
highest morals, thanks to her time as a Tender, and was a
councilman's daughter as well. No, it was bound to end
badly. He only hoped it wouldn't end with Pedric's slim,
aristocratic neck in a noose.

Lorinda's eyes left Pedric's long enough to register that
her father and Damir were returning. "There he is! Let me
go ask him right now. Oh, I do hope he'll say yes!" With
the carefree enthusiasm of an adolescent, she gathered up
the long, floor-length folds of her gown and literally ran to
her father. Deveren heard Pedric gasp, softly and poi-
gnantly, as the younger man caught a glimpse of long,
strong, tanned legs tapering to small, slipper-covered feet.

"You could break your heart over a girl like that," said
Pedric quietly.

"Well, damn it, don't," Deveren warned. The words
sounded hard; he changed the subject. "Thank you for giv-

ing me the idea about the play. The theater gathering will be a wonderful opportunity for me to complete my . . . job."

Vandaris and Lorinda were too far away for Deveren and Pedric to catch their conversation, but it appeared that the father couldn't resist his daughter's pleas. His face softened as he listened to her animated chatter, one gnarled, strong hand reaching to smooth a dark curl away from her high forehead in a gesture of paternal affection.

"You're welcome, though I hardly did it for your sake," Pedric replied. "And by the way, Dev, if you don't return her brush, I'll come looking for it on her behalf."

So that was what the cryptic rhyme about the "fox's brush" meant. He wondered if Pedric had deliberately given him the clue, glanced at the boy's face, and decided that the slip was unintentional.

"And how did you know about this?" yelped Deveren in mock outrage. Pedric turned his gaze back to his friend and grinned wickedly.

"Well," he said modestly, "I wrote the damn thing, didn't I?"

For my Chosen in this world walk a perilous path:
My Sword of Vengeance cuts both ways, protecting the
wrongly accused and destroying those who have trespassed.
Those who would be my Blessers must be strong men in-
deed, to wield so powerful a weapon as this.

—from the *Tenets of Vengeance*

CHAPTER FIVE

There were no windows in Jemma's cell. She was utterly cut off from the world outside, from the green things
of nature that for so long had been a daily part of her life.
She could not estimate the passage of the hours, nor the
rise and set of the sun. The guards, huge and silent, deliberately brought her meager meals at irregular intervals, to
further confuse her. As best the aged Healer could guess,
she had been in Seacliff's dungeon for five days.

The cell was tiny, with barely enough room for her to
stretch out. Old straw that smelled of rot served her for a
bed, though moments of sleep were few, as her inflamed
joints allowed her little rest. Torches burned in the hall-
way but not in her cell; the only light Jemma had was
what little managed to creep through the small, barred
window of the wooden door.

She clutched herself and shivered vainly against the

damp cold. The elderly Healer was almost beginning to look forward to the interrogation, which was, no doubt, exactly what her captors intended. Why were they postponing it? One man who had mind magic could have gotten everything from her. She wondered, with a faint burst of hope, if perhaps Bhakir was unaware of her communications with Castyll. *Please, gods, let it be so* . . . But that was false hope speaking. Bhakir would have no other reason to have taken her.

She heard the booted footfalls of the guards, and readied herself. The heavy bolt, ludicrously strong against so feeble an inmate, slammed back and the door opened. Jemma winced at the torchlight, even its faint illumination painful to eyes that had grown accustomed to the darkness.

"Come, old woman," one of the big men growled. Jemma tried to rise, but found that her knees would not let her. The guard, impatient, reached out a beefy hand and hauled her to her feet. Despite herself, Jemma cried out as the pain exploded in her knees and elbows.

"Shut your mouth, old bitch, or I'll shut it for you."

Jemma stifled her sounds of agony, for she had no doubt that the man was serious. The ungentle guard half led, half dragged her along the narrow corridor until he reached a much larger room. This door stood open, and several torches illuminated the interior. A brazier glowed invitingly. Jemma noticed that the stone floor was covered with sawdust, rather than the more common rushes, and the room was furnished with a rough-hewn wooden table and stools. Cloths covered items that hung from the walls and made odd-shaped bulges on the floor, but Jemma was not interested in the furnishings. A plate of bread, fruit, and cheese, and a pitcher of milk sat atop the table, and her mouth suddenly flooded with moisture in anticipation of real food.

"Bhakir says eat and get warm," stated the guard, shoving her inside. "Then he'll come talk to you." The door slammed shut behind her, and she heard the bolt being thrown.

Jemma stumbled toward the table. Trembling, she forced her aching hands to tear off a bit of bread and chewed it slowly, washing the bite down with a swallow of milk. It wouldn't do to gorge herself. She'd nursed the ill back to health far too often not to know that it was unwise to foist much food on a stomach unused to it. But oh, the bread was soft and fresh, and the glistening blackberries fairly begged to be devoured. She shifted her stool closer to the brazier, and stretched her empty hand toward it. The warmth calmed her joints, and she closed her eyes in pleasure.

She was about halfway through her repast, eating slowly and carefully, when Bhakir entered. Jemma paused, the food suddenly tasting foul in her mouth. The counselor bowed mockingly and smiled, showing even white teeth.

"Good day, my dear Healer. I'm so pleased you could join me."

Jemma finished chewing and swallowed. "If that is true, then your hospitality is lacking, Bhakir," she said drily.

The man laughed heartily and seated himself opposite the Healer. One soft, manicured hand hovered over the plate of half-eaten food and selected a peach. He bit, chewed.

"Delicious," he proclaimed as he swallowed the mouthful. "Now that you've had something to eat, let us proceed to business. I'm sure you're wondering why I've . . . er, brought you here."

"It had occurred to me. If you needed Healing work, you would have done better to talk to the present Blesser. I can do some, but—"

"It is not curing I'm after." And just that swiftly the pretense was gone. Jemma stared into the true face of Bhakir, a face that she assumed few seldom saw and fewer still wished to see. The dancing eyes had gone cold and piggish. No smile played about the red mouth, and the soft body suddenly seemed as hard and implacable as a boulder.

"Then . . . how may I be of service to my lord?" Jemma asked, fighting to keep her voice from shaking.

"Those who serve the goddess Health know a great many secrets," said Bhakir. "Secrets about healing, and curing, and restoration. Legend even mentions one or two Healers who brought the dead back to life."

Jemma felt a chill that even the warmth of the brazier could not dispel. "Legends are simply that," she said. "No Healer I have ever met could revive the dead. Only Health herself may do that. That is Lady Death's domain. We would not dare trespass there."

"No, no, you misunderstand me. Let the dead rot in peace." He leaned forward, his gaze boring into Jemma's. "Those who would heal must first understand what it is to harm. Those who can cure," he said slowly, "know how to curse."

You are mad! Jemma wanted to shriek, but the horrible truth was that the man was in fact quite sane. He knew what he was asking her to do. Her mouth, suddenly dry, formed voiceless words. At last, she stammered, "I will not."

Bhakir frowned, and Jemma shrank back slightly. "You know how, Healer. It's part of your training."

"We—we are shown these evils to know where not to tread!"

"And *I* order you, on pain of your life, to obey me! I need a curse, and you *will* give me one!"

Frantically, Jemma shook her head. "Kill me, then! I answer to a higher power, and I swear by she whom I serve that I shall never betray that trust!"

Bhakir's frown mutated into a smile just as cruel. "We'll see, old woman." He rose and tugged the concealing cloths from the walls.

Jemma's heart spasmed in terror. The room was filled with torture devices.

She recognized a few: the rack, the wheel, the cat-o'-nine. Others were foreign to her, but their cold metal and wood promised exquisite pain. Even as protest caught in her throat, the door opened and four guards entered. They moved deliberately but without haste, knowing that struggle as she would, she was incapable of escaping. Strong hands closed on her, ripping the robes from her thin, wrinkled body. The good food crashed to the floor as they slammed Jemma down on the table and secured her with iron bands that had hitherto been cleverly concealed.

"Lord Bhakir!" she cried, writhing against the strong flesh and stronger iron that held her. "Please, lord, what you ask is evil, and you must know it to be so!"

Bhakir had turned his attention to the brazier, and Jemma watched in horror as he extracted a pincer, the ends glowing orange-hot, from the depths of the coals.

"Oh, of course it's evil," he said in a conversational tone. "That's why it's going to work."

A thought pierced Jemma's haze of panicked terror. "My hands!" she screamed, thinking that Bhakir was going to burn her fingers off one by one—one of the more common tortures whispered about by those who were interested in such things. "You can't hurt them—I wouldn't be able to work the magic!"

"I know that," replied Bhakir, a sharp note of irritation creeping into his modulated voice. "I would never hurt your hands, Lady Healer. Or your tongue. Don't worry. But the rest of your body—" and his gaze swept her ancient, bony frame "—is fair game."

Before she realized what was happening, Jemma felt a sharp, stabbing pain in the big toe of her right foot. She jerked reflexively, but her knee banged against encircling metal. One of the guards had laid open her foot, the gash from ball to heel gaping open and dripping blood. With a curious calmness, she realized that the floor was covered with sawdust rather than rushes to make the task of soaking up blood that much simpler.

Then Bhakir cauterized the wound with the pincers, and her calmness fled.

Vervain cried out once, sharply, wordlessly, and the raw sound of her own scream brought her awake. She bolted upright, gasping and clutching the rumpled pillow protectively to her breasts. Her dark eyes flickered wildly, but nothing was amiss in her room.

All was as it should be. The door was closed and bolted. Moonlight, filtered through shutters, cast a pall over the many plants that filled the Blesser's private sleeping chamber. Vervain took a deep breath, the air fragrant with the scents of herbs and flowers, and calmed herself.

Though she now realized that her fear had come from a dream rather than an actual threat, she did not dismiss the nightmare as others might. Vervain knew better than that. The Healer who had trained her had taught her to respect her dreams.

"They are the messengers of the night," old Jemma had told her, back when Vervain was just a Tender studying in Mhar. "When you are awake, you trust your five senses for information. And when you sleep, you must trust your dreams in the same way. Pay attention to them!"

Vervain had been lucky to serve under Jemma. Her mother, a Healer herself, had been born in Mhar. It did not take too much effort to arrange for Vervain to study abroad, though it was not usual. Most Tenders were taught by Blessers in their own countries, usually their own cities or towns.

She reached down for the goblet of water she always kept at her side at night, and gulped at it. Her throat hurt from her scream. As she drank, Vervain examined her dream.

A red fox was running swiftly, but not in fear. Its brush

*was full and proud and its—his—movements strong and
bold. A bird—blackbird? Raven? Crow? Hard to tell—
dove at the running fox. Now the images blurred. A squirrel, small but full of chatter, scolded from a tree; a rat
poked its nose up from its hole—*

*—The image was swallowed by utter darkness. Then
Vervain was walking in the Prayer Room, kneeling before
the stone statue of Health, beseeching her aid. Without
warning, the plain but friendly features of the goddess
contorted, as if the divine being were in terrible agony.
Tears of blood streamed down Health's face, and the
stone head toppled to the floor—*

Vervain blinked. She clutched the empty goblet so hard
that her hands ached and her face was dewed with sweat.
She had no idea what any of the symbols meant, but if
Jemma had been right, the fear they had caused her sleeping self meant that they did not bode well at all.

She sighed, steadying herself. Putting the goblet down
on the stone floor, she swung her long legs out from under
the covers. Naked, she walked over to a table and poured
water in a basin. Vervain splashed her face, and the calming, chamomile-scented liquid drove the last residue of
terror from her mind. She reached for a cake of soap and a
sponge. Though dawn was several hours away, Vervain
knew that she had a difficult task ahead of her, and time
was running out. There would be no more sleep for her
tonight.

Her face set in an unaccustomed grimness, she un-
braided her long, thick, brown hair and began to brush it
out. *I only wish*, she thought wryly, *that I knew what it
was I was supposed to be preparing for.* As she brushed,
she heard the Godstower bell ring for Vengeance's service.

Freylis's snoring sounded like the growl of a mountain
cat, and Marrika bit down hard on an urge to kick the loud
sleeper in a delicate area. At last, she wriggled free of the

stain-stiff bedding, smelling Freylis's scent on her like a
noxious second skin. *At least Pedric bathed every day*,
she thought sourly as she reached for her clothes.

Pedric. The one man she had misjudged in her entire
life. Not only had he refused to be upset when she left
him, he had taken up with a lady of manners very shortly
thereafter. And not just a lady, but the daughter of the
Head Councilman! Marrika snorted in disgust, and froze
as the sound quieted Freylis for an instant. If he awoke,
he'd want her back in bed beside him. And that, Marrika
knew, meant another unpleasant bout of sexual activity.
The big thief mumbled something, rolled over on his
back, and resumed his deafening rumble.

Marrika breathed freely again. Freylis was usually a
deep sleeper. Heavy drinking tended to assure that particular habit. Her plan to seduce Freylis and thus avail herself of his rather impressive group of hangers-on was
working perfectly, except that she found herself disliking
more and more to have to pay the necessary price for such
a position. For the last couple of nights, when she was
certain Freylis would not awaken, Marrika had taken to
slipping off and wandering by herself at night.

She finished tugging on her calf-high, well-worn
leather boots, tucked her oversized shirt into tight-fitting
black trousers, and walked quietly toward the paneless
window. She glanced back at the bed, at the lump that was
her present lover, and her gaze swept the small room with
intense dislike. Marrika knew better than to expect any
thief's dwelling—again, except of course for Pedric's—to
be beautiful, or even large. She did, though, wish that
Freylis's room wasn't quite so . . . filthy. The sweaty
clothes could almost stand by themselves. Freylis would
eat off crusted, day-old food rather than clean his dishes,
and the chamber pot hadn't been emptied for several days.

She hesitated just long enough to retrieve her leather-
covered grappling hook, and stepped boldly onto the window sill. She sat, swung her lithe torso around, and began

to ease herself down. Freylis lived in the small room above
a candle maker's shop. It wasn't too far off the ground,
only a single story, and Marrika had no trouble negotiating
toeholds until she could drop safely, silently, to the ground.
When her solitary walk was completed, she would return
the way she had come with the help of her grappling hook.
Such entrances and exits were familiar to Marrika, whose
specialty was climbing into the rooms of unsuspecting
second-story residents.

Her feet landed with a soft crunch on the gravelly
stone. Once down, she crouched, tense, her back flat on
the wall until she was confident she had not been observed. She dropped the hook into the sack she had made
for it and tied it securely to her belt. Then, tossing her
mane of curly black hair out of her eyes, she strolled into
the darkness.

Marrika never had a destination on these late-night
treks. Her only desire was to steal a few hours to herself, a
few precious moments when she wasn't "Freylis's woman."
Tonight Marrika's aimless wandering brought her to the
center of the sleeping town. The temples were closed and
dark at this hour, save for the ever-present illumination
that spilled from Light's temple and the two lamps that
flanked the Godstower.

A movement in the darkness caught her eye, and she
tensed, hand on her dagger. But the shape scurrying
across the cobblestones, the lantern it carried bobbing as it
went, showed no interest in Marrika. It scuttled to the
Godstower and was swallowed by shadow. A moment
later, the deep, resonant tolling of the bell echoed through
the square.

It took Marrika a moment to recall whose time of day it
was. Her eyes widened as she remembered, and a slow
smile spread across her lips. She sheathed her knife and
walked, hips swaying deliberately, over to the Godstower.

When the man emerged, she stepped out of the shadows. "Greetings, Blesser of Vengeance."

The little man gasped aloud. Then, his voice trembling, he replied, "And unto you, my good lady. Are you coming to the service, then?"

"Indeed I am, Blesser." She kept her voice soft, pleasantly modulated, as she sized up the Blesser of one of humankind's most feared gods. He wore the robes of his brotherhood, black cloth that almost enveloped him. The moon shining down on his face gave her a good view of his countenance. He was small and slight, a young man to have such sunken, angular features. She couldn't see his eyes clearly, but knew they darted about because the moonlight glittered as they moved.

He's nervous, she thought. *Good.*

Marrika followed him silently as he hastened back to the shelter of his god's temple. It was a moderate-sized, low stone building, void of the ornate decorations that often adorned other holy houses. Within, the Holy House was dark, and as the Blesser pulled open the massive door, the blackness seemed almost palpable. But Marrika was not afraid. Unlike most of the citizenry of Braedon, she regarded the cloak of darkness as her favorite garment.

The Blesser entered, fussing about as he lit the few torches that provided illumination. The flickering lights seemed to actively struggle with the shadows, which retreated but did not flee. The floor was hard-packed earth. A circle was drawn in the center, made, if Marrika remembered correctly, from the ground bones of Vengeance's animal sacrifices. It was not a complete enclosure, however. The circle would be sealed later, as part of the ceremony. Inside the sacred ring was Vengeance's altar. Marrika couldn't quite identify the items on the altar this far away from them, but could make a good guess as to what they might be.

There were no windows at all.

The Blesser followed her gaze to the altar and started abruptly.

"My apologies," he said, "but I . . . I truthfully wasn't expecting anyone to attend tonight. It's not one of the High Holy Days, you see, and . . . well . . ."

"Vengeance is not honored as he was in earlier times, is he, Blesser?" Marrika's voice was cool, and her dark gaze pierced him. He stared back, like a rabbit caught by a snake.

"No, lady. Sadly, he is not."

"That is a loss to Braedon, not to Vengeance."

The little priest flushed with pleasure, his eyes glowing. "You understand," he breathed. "Have you come to be taught, my dear?" The thought made him breathe harder, and he clutched the folds of his simple black robe so tightly that his knuckles whitened.

Marrika was on her guard at once, although she still felt in control of the game. Should this little man, in the grip of either religious or physical fervor, try to overwhelm her, he would not enjoy the welcome he received.

"Regretfully, no, Blesser," she said softly. "But I am looking forward to the ritual."

"Then by all means, let us proceed!" He turned and went back to the still open door, peering first right, then left. Grunting with the effort, he pulled the door to. "It would seem that you are the only one attending the service tonight, lady. I will be able to grant you my full attention." The words were calm, assured, but the quiver in the man's voice and his rapid breathing betrayed him. He stepped closer, his hands nervously playing with the tassels on his belt.

He indicated the circle. "If you would enter, we may begin." The ritual words seemed to calm him, and some of his high-strung mannerisms began to abate. He stood straighter, though he was still not as tall as his lone parishioner.

Nodding, Marrika stepped into the center of the circle. She could go through the motions well enough, and feigning devotion to a god was more to her liking than soiling sheets with Freylis. She sat down cross-legged on the hard-packed earth and gazed up at the Blesser, waiting.

He followed, moving with surety now. From a pouch that hung at his waist he withdrew a handful of white powder. Muttering words that Marrika could barely hear and could certainly not understand, he sprinkled the ground bone on the earth, closing the circle.

The temperature within the sacred ring plummeted. Marrika inhaled softly, startled. It was like stepping from summer into winter. Fear began to seep through her, ever so subtly. She hadn't bargained on this priest having true power.

For a brief, wild instant, she wondered at the wisdom of the course she had impulsively decided to pursue. Vengeance, like the beautiful Lady Death, was not a deity to be trifled with. *But I'm not trifling*, she thought, grinding her teeth in an effort to control the trembling engendered by mixed fear and cold. *My desire is true—and so is my offering!*

And what is that, lady?

Now Marrika did gasp aloud, her gaze flying from the floor to meet that of the Blesser. He was sitting across from her with a slight smile on his unattractive face. The bastard had mind magic! Hard on the heels of her startlement was the realization that the priest's talent didn't run very deep, or else he would have known her true thoughts.

Her eyes searched his face, and she relaxed. He enjoyed catching her off-guard, but he'd exhausted his bag of tricks. Marrika, though, was just beginning.

"Tell me what you want."

He spoke the words aloud. It was a lovely phrase to Marrika, and one she had heard often. Utterly cool, Marrika leaned forward. She emphasized her cleavage as she brought her face close to his.

"I want justice. Vengeance's justice."

"What is the offense?"

"Betrayal of my affections. And the usurping of power by one who does not deserve it."

The Blesser clucked his tongue sympathetically. Marrika could actually see sweat on his pale brow. She dared not let her contempt show. For all his training, all his magic, she still had the upper hand. If she played this right, success would be hers.

"Those are grave offenses indeed. How do you wish them to be punished?"

"Death," answered Marrika swiftly. The man went even paler.

"My dear lady, I cannot ask Vengeance to kill for you! That is Lady Death's domain, and she will not murder at a mortal's whim!"

"I know this is not an ordinary request. Therefore, I do not offer an ordinary sacrifice," said Marrika. She rose and moved purposefully toward the dark-enshrouded altar. She heard the Blesser hastening after her, but did not slow. Marrika stopped within a foot of the altar, looking at it coolly. A knife, encrusted with dark red fluid, lay on a black silk pillow. The corpse of a rabbit, recently killed, to judge by its appearance, was suspended from the ceiling. It dripped blood into a small bowl.

"M-my own offering to Lord Vengeance," stammered the priest. "As I said, I didn't really expect anyone . . ."

The feeble excuse trailed off. Marrika ignored him, her gaze on the rabbit. It hadn't been quickly and cleanly killed, as was the habit with every other sacrifice she'd seen offered to the god. Its ears, tail, and all four of its small legs had been sliced off and the creature had been permitted to bleed to death. There was blood on the floor a good distance away, mute evidence to its futile struggle.

Two shivers, neither born of the unnatural cold, shook her body. The first was caused by the realization that Vengeance's Blesser here in Braedon was a man who was excited by pain and suffering. The second was due to the understanding that this little, perverted wretch could perhaps give her absolutely everything she wanted.

She turned around. "I understand," she said gently. "Vengeance does not demand just the blood of his victims. He wants their pain as a sacrifice, too."

"When I was a young Tender, they thought I was wrong," the man said softly. "They didn't see—they didn't understand. But you understand. You must have been sent by Vengeance to me, to show that he approves of my worship of him!"

"Perhaps," Marrika agreed cautiously. "I believe we two think along the same lines, Blesser . . .?"

"Kannil," he said. "And your name, O favored one?"

"Marrika. And as I have said, I offer no ordinary sacrifice for my favor. I will bring you . . . a human sacrifice, Kannil."

The excited color drained from Blesser Kannil's face. "There has been no human sacrifice in Vengeance's temple for . . . for decades, *centuries!*" Mixed fear and anticipation was in his voice. "I, I cannot . . . the laws of Byrn . . . it would be murder!"

"Exactly," purred Marrika, moving even closer. She couldn't let him turn back now. If he did, well, she would have no compunctions about sending Vengeance an offer of his own Blesser.

"No!" wailed Kannil, whirling away from her, his hand outstretched as if to physically keep her back. "I cannot! They would kill me!"

"Only if they knew," persisted Marrika, laying her strong climber's hands on the man's narrow shoulders and turning him around to face her. "And I won't tell. I'm bringing the sacrifice, remember? I'd be just as guilty of murder as you would be!" She had no intention of telling him that she had performed murder many times before in her young life. "I want this. Vengeance wants it, too—you know he does. You hear the call in your sleep every night, don't you?"

Trapped in the snare of her dark gaze, the unfortunate Blesser could only nod.

She'd thought as much. A quick flash of loathing shot through Marrika. She wondered how many of the animals, wild or domestic, who went missing in Braedon had fallen prey to this pathetic, depraved man. She squelched the thought at once. Keeping her voice low and seductive, she murmured, "And I think you want this, too, Kannil. Don't you." It was not phrased as a question, and his answering nod was almost unnecessary.

"When?" he asked, his voice dreamy.

"Soon," Marrika promised. Soon enough to satisfy her anger, and this twisted man's lust for pain.

*And the Dark Knight turned over his cards, but
lo, they were not what they had been! And he knew
fear such as had not been his to know, as he looked
at She who smiled at him and said, "None shall cheat
Lady Death."*

—from the folktale, *Cheating Lady Death*

CHAPTER SIX

Deveren was in high spirits as he rode Flamedancer into the bustling crowd that glutted the marketplace. At age ten, the gelding was well into his adult years, but he still had the fiery spirit which had inspired the first half of his name.

The wind was coming from the west, bearing with it the strong, familiar scent of fish and seawater. The salty tang of the ocean mixed with the equally salty but not so pleasant tang of human sweat. Deveren grimaced slightly. Summer was indeed well on its way; he didn't like to imagine what Market Day would smell like two months from now.

From his elevated perch atop his steed's broad back, Deveren had a good view of all the market stalls. He found what he was looking for—a sign that stated "Griel's Apothecary," with smaller letters proclaiming "Herbs, Insense, Teas, Baths, Cures For All Manor of Ailmints."

Griel was intelligent, no doubt, but he couldn't spell worth a copper penny. Smothering a grin, Deveren urged his mount through the pressing crowd of people. The animal, uncomfortable around so many humans, laid his ears back resentfully but complied. The great chestnut horse picked his way through the throng, lifting and placing his powerful hooves down with the surprisingly delicate grace that had earned him the second part of his name.

Deveren dismounted, letting the animal's reins trail in the dust. No one would steal Flamedancer. Deveren was known in these parts, if only as Fox rather than Lord Deveren Larath, and that was enough to ensure the horse's safety. No thief in his group would touch the beast, and they were well aware that they would probably make more money reporting a theft to Deveren rather than aiding a would-be horse stealer. He gave Flamedancer an absent pat on his sweat-darkened neck and went inside the building.

"Good morning, Griel," he called, blinking as his eyes adjusted to the dimness. He saw the thin, elderly man assisting several customers. Griel turned at the sound of his name, and the expression on his face when he saw Deveren changed from slightly annoyed to apprehensive.

"Oh, good morning, Lord Larath. I'll be with you in a moment, sir." He turned directly back to his customers. "For your son's respiratory problem, I would suggest this tincture of sundew and hyssop. Mix one drop with ten parts water and have him drink it twice a day before he eats. It will ease his breathing." He glanced again at the boy, a thin, wheezing child with large dark eyes. The boy glared back sullenly, his little chest heaving. "Mix it with a little honey," Griel added. The boy brightened a bit.

The mother smiled warmly, fished a few coins out of her pouch and handed them to Griel. The older man's thin fingers closed over the money as he waved his patrons politely toward the door. He shut the door behind them and leaned against it.

"Fox, you know I can't do anything to help you. You

must complete the Grand Theft completely without aid from any the rest of us."

Deveren feigned innocence. "Sweet Health, Rabbit, can't I patronize a fellow thief without being accused of ulterior motives?"

"You've never bought from me before," Rabbit said, still suspicious.

Deveren shrugged his shoulders lazily. "I happened to be passing by. But, if you're convinced that I'm trying to enlist your aid in my Grand Theft—or Thefts, I should say—then I'll take my business elsewhere. There are certainly other apothecaries in Braedon." His voice wasn't angry, and in fact he was speaking the truth. If Rabbit proved recalcitrant, he could always go somewhere else. He took a step toward the door, and the herbalist's cupidity won the battle.

"All right, all right, but if you *are* going to use anything I sell to accomplish your task, I didn't know about it. So, what do you need?"

"First of all, some pine soap."

Rabbit raised a thin eyebrow. "Bit early for hunting season, isn't it? No, don't tell me—I don't want to know. 'Spensive, too. I suppose I should have known you'd prefer the best," he said. He trundled over to a shelf where a variety of soaps, sorted by scent, were piled. Pine did not grow well this far south and this close to the ocean. It had to be imported from the northern climes and was only occasionally made into soap. Its primary users were wealthy landowners who enjoyed hunting; the strong, natural odor of the pine completely obliterated human scent and gave them an edge over their prey. Few cities south of Kasselton had any pine at all, but Braedon was a major port city. Everything in Verold had passed through here at one time or another. If you looked hard enough in the town, you could find just about anything.

Finally Rabbit found a lone cake wrapped in dark green

cloth. "You're lucky. That's the last one, but I'll be getting more in toward the end of the summer."

"Excellent," Deveren approved. "Next, I've been having trouble sleeping lately."

Rabbit's thin lips twitched in a slight smile. "Guilty conscience?"

"Not in the slightest," Deveren responded, chuckling a little himself. "Seriously. I suppose I'm a bit tense, with the Grand Thefts coming up. What do you recommend?"

"I have a special tincture for sleeplessness already made up. It contains vervain, chamomile, mugwort, a few other similar herbs. Ah, here it is. Mind, this is an extremely strong preparation, so you don't need much. Just a spoonful about an hour before bed should work just fine. Don't increase the dosage."

"Why not?" Deveren uncorked the vial and sniffed gently. There was the faintest whiff of rum and the not-so-pleasant fragrance of the bitter, earthy herbs themselves.

"Because if you take more than I tell you to take, you'll be sleeping for a week. As I said, strong."

"Just what I need. How much?" Deveren reached into his bulging pouch, rummaging among the gems and gold kings for more common coinage. A few items tumbled to the hard-packed earth that served as a floor for the shop. Deveren knelt and hastily picked them up, glancing toward the door as he did so.

"Death's breath, Fox!" hissed Rabbit, his parsimonious nature offended by Deveren's cavalier treatment of valuables. "Empty the damned thing once in a while, will you? Our group isn't quite the noble robbers that you'd like us to be, at least not yet!"

Before the apothecary could blink, a slim, needle-sharp dagger had appeared in Deveren's hand. It seemed to have materialized from nowhere. A second later the weapon quivered in the wooden countertop a fraction of an inch from the startled Rabbit's left hand—exactly where the leader of the thieves had aimed it.

"I've got good reactions," drawled Deveren. "But don't think the friendly advice isn't appreciated. Now, how much?"

Shaking, Rabbit clutched his nearly missed hand with his right one. "Uh . . . two princes, Your Lordship."

The man's face was milk pale, and Deveren regretted his impulse to show off before Rabbit. After all, the apothecary was more or less on his side to begin with. He badly wanted to bring the price up to a king—a gold piece—by way of apology, but he knew such generosity would merely further damage his reputation in Rabbit's eyes. Thief leaders were expected to be fair, perhaps after a fine haul even generous, but they never overpaid.

So he contented himself with dropping the two silver princes on the counter, thanking Rabbit, and leaving the poor man alone for the day.

Alone in his solar, Deveren worked the fresh-scented pine soap into a lather and proceeded to bathe his entire body and hair. As his fingers scrubbed his scalp, his mind went back, as it did every time he sat in this tub, to the last night that Kastara was alive. Even after the passage of seven years, the pain always caught him by surprise. It was nowhere near as overwhelming as in the beginning, of course. Nor was it as constant a thread running through the fabric of his day-to-day activities. But occasionally an odd phrase, or image, or scent, would come to whisper her name to him, and Deveren would feel his heart actually ache, as though squeezed by an unseen hand.

And for some reason, this innocuous wooden tub seemed to be the one thing that always triggered her image in his mind.

You don't have very long to get ready.

I told you, I'm not going.

It's a premiere. You're expected to attend premieres, love. That's why you're called a patron.

I won't enjoy it without you. I don't like leaving you

alone here while I'm off enjoying myself. It doesn't seem fair.

We'll be fine.

Oh, but she hadn't been fine, had she, not she, not the child she carried. Gods, he could almost hear her, could almost feel her smooth little hands washing his back . . .

The soft *plop* of a teardrop landing in the soapy water jolted him out of his reverie. Deveren took a deep, shuddering breath and bathed his face with the soap.

Kastara was gone. He had mourned her, and would, he felt certain, continue mourning her for the rest of his life. But now he had other people who depended upon him. He had come to the thieves thinking to expose and kill a murderer. He had stayed to help them, and had made them a promise. If he failed at his Grand Thefts tonight, someone like Freylis would take over the group. Everyone, from Pedric to Clia to little Allika, would suffer then.

No. He rose, shook off his moodiness, and began to towel himself dry. Experimentally, he took a sniff at his forearm. "I feel like a forest in springtime," he quipped, the old sense of humor that had come to the rescue so often in the past returning to him now. He truly did smell like an evergreen forest, at least to his own nose. He only hoped the three large, rather unfriendly dogs that guarded the Vandaris home would agree.

The Councilman's Seat was located in the heart of the Garden. Deveren could see it from his window as he finished dressing—a beautiful, large building that was as much a landmark in Braedon as the Godstower. The upper level hosted the current Head Councilman and his family, complete with dining rooms, gaming rooms, wine cellar, and a huge hall that would, tonight, serve as the stage for *The Queen of All.* Well below the finery were the cells in which prisoners awaited judgement. Deveren had always though it ironic that the only time a commoner could see the Garden was if he were sentenced for a crime. On the other hand, it was terribly civilized that Braedon's criminals had such a pleasant view while they waited for sentencing.

He toyed with the idea of riding, and decided to walk. He might need to slip off without being noticed once the thefts were completed, and didn't want to have to worry about retrieving Flamedancer from Vandaris's stables. Besides, it was a lovely summer evening.

So Deveren selected breeches and boots rather than slippers and hose. Instead of clothing that he wore often, tonight Deveren chose a blousey red silk shirt and overtunic that he had tucked away in a chest of cedar wood for several weeks. It would be less likely to retain his scent.

He grinned a little. Cedar and pine, how refreshing.

There was nothing he could do about his walking boots, save hope that there was more of Flamedancer about them than Deveren Larath. As he adjusted his pouches, making sure that the false bottoms wouldn't reveal the second space beneath, he mentally reviewed his challenge. Part of the "test," he assumed, lay in deciphering the code and figuring out just exactly what it was "his" thieves wanted him to acquire. Or it could be simply a case of young Pedric having a little fun—well, a lot of fun—at his expense. Deveren hoped that he wouldn't be disqualified if he, for some reason, didn't steal the correct items. Freylis would be overjoyed.

The thought of the big man erased any hint of a smile from Deveren's lips. Others were attending the theatrical performance for pleasure. He was certain they would find it—*The Queen of All* was a fine play. He, however, had a job to do.

He was glad he had chosen to walk. The air was thick with the scents of the Garden, which bloomed almost all year round with one sort of plant or another. Only in the dead of winter was the Garden anything less than redolent with fragrance. Now, in summer, the scent was almost as intoxicating as wine.

The play wasn't due to start for a while yet, and Van-

daris's guests milled about, enjoying the balmy evening.
They stood on the magnificent stone steps, draped themselves across the finely carved wood-and-stone benches,
walked in groups or pairs through the paths. As Deveren
approached the entrance, he was met by one of Captain
Jaranis's men.

"Good even, Lord Larath," said the guard courteously.
"I'm afraid I have to ask you to submit to a search, sir.
What with the deaths of them three councilmen and all . . ."

"Of course," Deveren replied smoothly. The guard patted
him down gently, respectfully, and halfheartedly, clearly
not expecting to find anything. He glanced briefly into the
pouches and nodded, indicating that Deveren might proceed.

This boded well. He'd been able to smuggle in nearly all
of his tools—the larger tools, such as heavy metal crowbars
he had, of course, been forced to forgo—and hadn't
aroused the slightest suspicion.

The Councilman's Seat was surrounded by a stone wall.
Within was Vandaris's private garden, a section of the Garden allotted for his personal use. There was even a maze,
smaller and far easier to navigate than the main one in the
center of the larger Garden. The dogs weren't out yet; Vandaris would wait until all his guests were safely inside before loosing the beasts.

Time to move on to another item, then. He'd get the
dogs' "teeth" later in the evening.

As he moved through the lovely home, admiring the
Head Councilman's fine taste in art and furnishings, Deveren thought about the rhymes he'd memorized.

That first challenge, at least, was easy to figure out. The
trick was in getting Vandaris to take him there.

He turned a corner, following the murmur of voices, and
was rewarded by the sight of Lord Vandaris himself, chatting politely with his guests. Deveren felt a smile of satisfaction tug at his lips. The room was one of Vandaris's
favorites, a smaller, more intimate, and more personal

chamber than many in the Seat. The room was filled with the Head Councilman's hunting trophies. Like most of the landed nobility, Vandaris was an avid hunter. His one regret, he had told Deveren once, was that, now that he was Head Councilman, he couldn't escape from Braedon often enough to pursue his favorite hobby anymore.

The walls were covered with tapestries depicting hunting scenes. One, commissioned by Vandaris himself, showed the lord—a considerably younger, slimmer man—pursuing a unicorn. Not that such creatures existed, of course, but when the art was that lovely and dramatic, who could object?

Skulls of various creatures—deer, wolf, bear, and others—had been placed around the room. There was also a fine display of riding regalia and hunting bows, spears and other weaponry. Vandaris sat on a cushioned chair, chatting animatedly with two other members of the Council. Over in the corner, Damir, who had left earlier in order to have another private talk with Vandaris, was admiring a carving of a leaping stag. Pedric and Lorinda sat closely together on a cushioned bench. They had eyes only for each other, and found excuses to casually touch. Deveren had never seen Pedric like this before. He tried to brush aside his worry. In the end, when it counted, he knew Pedric to be a good man. And Lorinda, clearly, was a special woman indeed.

At last, Deveren found what he was looking for. He took a deep breath and prayed that his plan would work. If not, he would have tipped his hand.

Casually, he wandered over to what he had determined was the first "item" on his list for tonight. It sat on a small table, seeming to taunt him.

It was a riding cup, shaped like the slim, elegant head of a fox. Its purpose was to provide liquid refreshment to hunters on horseback. When so employed, it fitted neatly into a special place on the saddle, hooked in place by its slender muzzle. When the rider wanted a drink of wine, the head was turned upside down, revealing a hollow cup into which the beverage was poured. *The Fox gives Fox a taste quite fine, / When out of his head you drink your wine.*

This had to be it. Picking it up, he examined it, as if he hadn't seen dozens like this before.

"This is quite nice, Your Lordship. May I ask who the maker is?"

As he had hoped, Vandaris warmed to the subject. He rose and went to Deveren, taking the little stone shape from him. "That, Lord Larath, I purchased from an obscure stone carver in Kasselton a few years ago. Can't recall his name. It's a bit crude, here—" he pointed at the slightly uneven eyes "—and it's too small. Barely holds enough to moisten your throat. That's why I've consigned it to display rather than putting it to use."

"I like the crooked eyes," said Deveren. "Gives the little fellow personality, don't you think?" Jokingly, he mimed petting the fox between the ears.

Deveren could feel the gazes of Pedric and Damir boring into his back. He ignored them and continued.

"Flamedancer stepped on mine, and I'm without one at the present moment. I rather like this one—don't suppose you'd be willing to sell it?"

Vandaris shook his head, and Deveren's heart sank. Now he'd be forced to steal it, and everyone would remember that Deveren Larath had made much of the small object . . .

"Goodness, no, Deveren, take the thing if you like it so much. It's been sitting here collecting dust for—well, more years than I care to remember."

Triumph burned in Deveren's heart. "Thank you, sir! It's much appreciated, I assure you. I'll just leave it here and pick it up on my way out."

He had wanted to buy the thing outright. The rhyme had said "take," not "steal," and Deveren wanted to show his thieves that, on occasion, it wasn't necessary to filch something. Sometimes, all one had to do was ask. He heard a muffled cough from Pedric and successfully fought a grin.

A servant appeared at the door and cleared her throat.

She dropped a curtsey. "Beggin' your pardon, milord, but the performers have sent word that they're ready."

"Excellent!" exclaimed Vandaris. "Well then, let us go. When actors are ready, I'm told, making them wait sours the performance. Isn't that right, Deveren?"

They were big, the dogs that Vandaris kept to safeguard his private grounds. Alone in the darkness, Deveren stared over the stone wall at them. The wall was roughly ten feet high, but Deveren had been able to scramble up far enough to get a good look at the true deterrent to would-be burglars. Silvered by moonlight, the large, shaggy beasts stared back. The milky radiance caught their eyes, making them glow eerily. Black dewlaps drew back from powerful yellow teeth as one of them growled at the sight of Deveren.

There came another glint from the shadowy beasts—a glint of metal at the throats. Deveren recalled the second task he'd been set: *The hounds will chase, the hounds will tear/Your flesh, unless their teeth you bear.*

Leather collars, with sharp metal points embedded in them. Any intruder who thought to hold the beasts off by choking them would have been in for a painful surprise.

The would-be thief leader waited until the growling stopped as the beast tried to catch his scent and failed. His muscles quivered from the strain, but he held his position. The dog cocked its head to one side and made a crooning, puzzled sound. The pine soap had done its job. Satisfied, Deveren dropped quietly down to the earth.

Quickly, he glanced around. He was indeed alone; the guests were engrossed with the performance, and the guards were nowhere to be seen. No doubt they were busy dallying with the serving girls. He took a deep breath, and opened one of the pouches. Carefully removing the false bottom, he felt for the chunks of raw meat he'd smuggled in along with his thieves' tools.

Deveren had taken the sleeping tincture purchased from

Rabbit and had mixed the entire bottle with a cupful of lamb's blood. He'd cut up chunks of raw lamb and let them soak in the concoction. Now he fished one out, climbed back up, and tossed it over the wall.

One of the great dogs jumped up and caught the meat in midair, its teeth clicking. It dropped back to the earth, licked its chops, and cocked its head.

Heartened, Deveren shifted his position, found more meat chunks and began to feed the other two. They ate happily, and Deveren wondered if the rules required him to explain how he had accomplished his Grand Thefts. He didn't want to put the idea of poisoning into the head of someone less scrupulous than he.

At last, all the meat that Deveren had brought had been eaten. Grinning, Deveren again jumped down, replaced the false bottom, glanced around again to ensure that he was alone, and waited.

It didn't take long. When next he poked his head over the wall, he saw that the dogs' alert poses had begun to droop. They yawned, and their attempts to continue patrolling their master's ground became staggering shuffles. At last, one by one, they surrendered to the drug and sank down onto their bellies. They placed mammoth heads on large paws, whuffed a time or two, and fell asleep.

Deveren waited, wanting to be sure, then carefully, quietly, began to climb over the stone wall. A movement from the house caught his eye. It was one of the guards, leaving the private grounds, coming out for a perfunctory inspection of—

No, damn it, it was Captain Jaranis. Deveren mouthed an oath. He was seated astraddle the wall now, one leg already over into a trespasser's territory. Even if he jumped back down to the ground now, the movement would certainly catch the sharp eye of the captain of Braedon's guards, and Deveren would be forced to explain what he was doing out here. The dogs' lassitude would be noted, and—

Nothing else for it, Deveren decided. He hoped desperately that Rabbit's concoction had had enough time to render the dogs completely unconscious. If not, well, there might not be enough of him left for Telian Jaranis to put into prison. Slowly, so as not to attract attention, he eased himself down on the opposite side of the stone wall. He plastered himself against its smooth coldness, sought refuge in its shadow.

A low growl came by his right foot. Deveren froze, fear jolting through his system. He didn't even dare look down at the beast, for fear the eye contact would be regarded as a challenge. Instead, he closed his eyes and wished desperately that he'd brought a dagger with him tonight.

He felt one of the great canines snuffling at his knee, felt the warm breath and cold nose even through his breeches. From the other side of the wall, he heard the crisp, firm sound of booted footsteps approaching.

Deveren held his breath, afraid that his nervous, rapid breathing might give him away, both to the animal that sniffed him with drowsy confusion and the extremely efficient captain who was on patrol just a few yards away.

The dog's nose moved to the other leg, continued sniffing. The booted footsteps came closer, closer, until they were right where Deveren stood huddled in the cold embrace of the wall's shadow. They did not pause, but continued purposefully on, fading into the distance as Jaranis's route took him away from the thief who stood, heart pounding, on the other side of the wall.

The sniffing stopped. The big dog snorted, irritated and baffled by this thing that looked human but smelled like a tree. The warm breath went away. When Deveren chanced a look down at the beast, he found it flopped over on the grass, breathing deeply and regularly.

Deveren closed his eyes in relief, the tension flooding out of him. Then, taking a deep, steadying breath, he knelt down beside the unconscious animal and gently unfastened its collar. The other two were equally insensible and of-

fered no protest as he relieved them of their symbolic
"teeth."

Stuffing the three studded collars into his pouch, Deveren cautiously climbed up and peered over the wall. Re-
markably, his luck still held. No one was about. Quickly he
scrambled back over the wall, landing softly on the grass.

"Be careful, Deveren Larath," came a deep, musical,
feminine voice behind him.

Startled, Deveren whirled. He stood inches away from a
beautiful young woman who smiled enigmatically at him.
At once he knew who she must be; her clothing gave her
identity away immediately. She was dressed head to toe in
a figure-hugging gown of dark black. She carried a carved
staff, which he knew to be made out of rosewood, and the
jewels embedded in it glinted in the moon's light. Her head
was bare, and her long hair was parted in the middle and
fell in a cascade of white down her back.

White? Deveren thought for an instant. *Bleached,
clearly. She's taking this resemblance to her goddess a bit
far.* For of course he knew the woman to be the Blesser of
the goddess Death. All Blessers would have been invited; it
would have been an unforgivable breach of etiquette for
Vandaris not to have extended an invitation. But most
Blessers didn't take advantage of such social gatherings—
and he'd never before heard of Death's Blesser ever appearing at such an event.

He opened his mouth to greet her politely, telling himself
that it was her dark clothing that had enabled her to escape
his notice, but she held up a commanding hand. The words
died in his throat.

"Be careful," she repeated, "on this night of nights.
Sometimes mortals try to cheat Lady Death. I am the First
who comes. Be prepared for the others."

Without another word, and completely ignoring his half-
voiced query, the Blesser of Death turned her back on him
and strode into the shadows, which reached to hide her as if
she hadn't been there at all.

Deveren's throat was dry. His heart slammed against his chest and he found his hands were shaking. He leaned back against the wall. What had she seen? What did she know? Was she just trying to frighten him with her strange pronouncement? What was all that nonsense about "first" and "others?" One thing was for certain. He did need to be careful. Deveren couldn't believe he hadn't heard or seen her approach.

He calmed himself, took a deep, steadying breath, and composed his features. By the time he ran lightly up the steps to reenter the Councilman's Seat, he had an easy smile for the guards on duty. Deveren Larath had clearly gone for a stroll in the pleasant night air; nothing more.

He walked down the hall, keeping his movements loose and comfortable in case anyone was watching, and paused by the doors to the large hall. Within, he could hear the clear voice of the "Queen" railing against her enemy, hear the answering rumble of the Captain of the Guards as he protested his innocence. Halfway through the first act, then. Plenty of time.

Deveren's normal cocksurety began to return in some small measure. He'd been badly shaken, first by the dire combination of dogs and guard, and then later by the uncanny visitation of Death's earthly representative. Now he reminded himself that he had finished two of the three tasks that had been set to him, and the third—stealing a hairbrush!—was certain to be the easiest.

He ambled guilelessly through the halls, smiling at everyone he met, conducting himself as if he belonged. He was known and recognized, and encountered no difficulty.

He entered the wing that housed the private solars, and quietly began poking his head into room after room. At last he came to the one that must belong to Lorinda.

It was simple, almost austere, as befitted one who had lived most of her life in devotion to her deity. There was only a trunk, a small table with a pitcher and basin, and a

bed. The stone walls had been whitewashed, and though
Deveren did not dare light a candle that might signify his
presence, there was plenty of illumination pouring through
the opened door and striking those clean, unadorned white
walls.

No, not quite unadorned. A painting graced one of the
walls. Directly beneath it was a small rush mat, a basin full
of dried flowers, and an unlit candle. Curious, Deveren
stepped forward and peered at the painting. It was small
and crudely done, probably the work of Lorinda herself, but
the image was unmistakable. It was Love, the naked little
child, embracing her sacred beast, a fawn as young and innocent as herself. At once Deveren realized that the rush
mat and its attendant items were the girl's private altar, and
he stepped back hastily.

As his eyes adjusted to the dim light, he saw still more
flowers. Clearly, young Lorinda went to the Garden every
day and festooned her austere quarters with the one decora-
tion that most pleased her goddess. A smile touched Deveren's lips. This glimpse into her private room revealed a
great deal about the girl—no, the woman, he mentally cor-
rected himself. And he liked what he saw.

But time was passing, and the longer he dallied, the more
likely it was that he would get caught. The thought snapped
him out of his reverie, and at once Deveren's eye became
critical, exploratory, as he began to seek out Lorinda's hairbrush.

He did not find it. Deveren frowned to himself. In a
place this clean, this uncluttered, it ought to be a simple
matter. He placed his back to the door and began analyzing
the room, inch by inch. The bed. Its coverings were not tousled. The blankets lay neatly over the pallet, the single pillow hid nothing. He patted the bed down gently, careful not
to disturb anything.

He examined the top of the little table. Bare, save for the
empty basin and pitcher full of water. Where would a
young woman keep her personal items? Kastara had always

left hers lying about. She was rather bad about it, actually, and Deveren was always finding hairpins or combs or mirrors in the most unlikely places . . .

The trunk. He knelt beside it and opened it. It was not locked, to his surprise and pleasure. Inside were several winter furs, many of Lorinda's clothes, and a small, simple, wooden box. Beside the box, glittering in the dim light, was the girl's jewelry—a necklace, earrings, and some brooches.

Deveren frowned. Why would the jewels be out of the—

Deveren picked up the box and shook it gently. Something about the size and weight of a hairbrush clunked inside. Deveren's confusion turned to annoyance. Pedric, of course. To add just a bit more spice to the quest, it was clear that the younger thief must have taken the one box that Lorinda would have locked—her jewelry box—and put the brush inside. Naturally, it wouldn't have occurred to Pedric to worry about the baubles.

I'll have to think of something to do to Pedric in retaliation for this, Deveren thought darkly. In the meantime, he'd have to open the cursed thing. It wouldn't do to abscond with the box—too noticeable. He hadn't expected to have to use his tools, but he had thought it best to be prepared. Now he was grateful for his foresight.

Deveren squatted back, pulled out the little box, closed the trunk lid, and placed the box on the trunk. He found his lockpicking tools, leaned forward, and examined the jewelry box. It was a simple wooden box, not even decorated. The lock appeared to be equally straightforward. Deveren moved the box so the light shone full upon it, and positioned one slender metal tool inside, moving it about experimentally. Then he twisted.

Nothing.

Odd. The locking mechanism must be more complicated than he had first thought. Now Deveren took the second tool and inserted it into the lock as well. His concentration narrowed, and he focused his thoughts, reaching out with his hand magic skills to augment his slim, delicate fingers. Too much pressure and the lock would break; too little, it wouldn't open.

Scritch, scrape. Unaware that he did so, Deveren gnawed his lower lip. He extended his thoughts, making them an expansion of his fingers. Something was in there, blocking his tools. Grimly, he applied more pressure, increasing it until he was pressing down hard against the blockage.

In the back of his mind, far away from his intense focus, a warning bell sounded. There was something wrong with this, something very wrong indeed.

Be careful, Lord Larath . . .

Just as he pressed as hard as he could with his tools, Deveren realized what the wrongness was.

It was a trap.

There was a loud *snap* and Deveren, gasping, threw himself backward, acting more on gut instinct than on logical thought. Something sprang at his face with the angry sound of a buzzing insect. He felt a sharp sting and clapped his hand to his cheek. At that same instant he heard a click and the box opened.

What in the Nightlands was going on here?

Cautiously, Deveren glanced into the box. There it was, the simple boar bristle hairbrush that had cost him so much effort. He picked the box up, absently sticking the brush in his pouch, and turned it to the moon's light.

It was a simple box, padded with linen, clearly designed to hold a modest girl's meager collection of jewels. But there was another, smaller box inside it, made of metal. This had been crudely fastened to the locking mechanism and had clearly never been part of the original design.

He was more confused than before. Pedric might have put the brush inside a locked box to provide his friend with more of a "challenge," but he had no skills that would enable him to set a trap like this. Neither did anyone else in Deveren's rather ragtag little group. For now that it was sprung, Deveren could see that it was clever, for all its simplicity. No, not merely clever—professional. Inside was the broken bit of his lockpick, wedged in firmly. There was also a small sliver of metal that clearly had been held in place by a tiny latch. When he'd sprung it, it had snapped forward, and a sliver of something white had shot out.

Deveren peered closer. It was a thin needle—or part of one. The same movement that had broken his lockpicking tool had also snapped this long sliver of what looked to be carved bone. Deveren remembered the small thing that had shot at his face, scratching it. Had he not broken the needle, it would have jabbed deeply into his fingers; had he not jerked back in time, it would have embedded itself in the soft flesh of his face.

Again, his hand went to his cheek, felt the already drying blood. Placing the box down, he turned and knelt, groping oh so carefully for the broken needle amid the rushes on the floor. He remembered where it had fallen and soon found it. Gingerly, he placed it in his palm and carried it to the open window for closer inspection.

It was a carved bone needle, all right. And there was something on it, something viscous and dark in the moon's silvery glow. Deveren brought it to his nose and sniffed. His eyes widened in horror.

Poison. Readily available from one of the translucent sea creatures that sometimes washed up on Braedon's shores, this poison was sent to the north, where soldiers augmented their weapons with it when fighting the Ghil. And it had scratched his cheek . . .

Deveren's legs gave way and he sat down hard. His heart pounded in fear. The poison would act quickly, within seconds. He swallowed, his mouth dry as sand, waiting for the pain to hit as he stared at the needle fragment.

It didn't come. After a long moment, Deveren realized he was probably the luckiest man in Braedon right now, perhaps in all of Byrn. He had been scratched with the broken end of the needle, not the poisoned end. He began to shake as the full meaning of this strange little trap sank in.

Only his thieves knew about the theft of the hairbrush. There was a traitor in his midst with murder on his mind.

Know Love, when she comes to find you.

—Love's motto

CHAPTER SEVEN

Pedric Dunsan knew a perfect night for romance when he saw one, and tonight was the most perfect such evening he had ever experienced.

Everything had gone beautifully. From the dinner of venison in pepper sauce, braised greens, and rose pudding, all complemented by lush Mharian wine, to the pleasant wandering hand-in-hand through her father's house, to the tears that dampened Lorinda's soft cheeks during the powerful first act of *The Queen of All*, there hadn't been an awkward pause or a misspoken word.

There were only two things that threatened to cast shadows on this most wonderful of nights as far as Pedric was concerned. The first was worry that Deveren might not achieve all three of his thefts, but that had been laid aside when Pedric witnessed the transaction over the hunting cup. If Deveren could manage that one, he could probably handle the rest.

The second was the tremendous, unlikely, indeed almost unthinkable act that Pedric was planning to commit during intermission. He kept turning over his decision in his mind, and coming up with plenty of reasons not to pursue such a dire plan of action.

But every time he decided against it, Lorinda would squeeze his hand, or laugh, or say something startlingly insightful, or simply look up at him with that serene half smile that seemed to be her constant expression and he would know, bone deep, that his plan was the right one.

During the intermission, alone with the adored and adorable Lorinda, with the exotic scents of night-blooming summer flowers surrounding them, Pedric Dunsan planned to propose.

Then, faster than he had imagined possible, the first act was over. The Queen's husband lay in a pool of blood, slain by the treachery of the Elf-King. She vowed a terrible revenge, and the lights were suddenly extinguished.

There was a hushed pause, then the sound of furious clapping. Pedric joined in, though his heart was pounding almost more loudly than the applause. The lights were lit, and the audience rose to their seats to mingle and discuss the play thus far.

Lorinda's face was blotchy red and her nose and eyes were swollen. She glanced up at Pedric, then away. "I'm sure I must look dreadful," she murmured, wiping at her wet face. "It's just—oh, Pedric, I never dreamed that this was what the theater was like! The actors—they had me completely convinced. Especially—what was his name? The one who plays the Elf-King?" The tears had dried, but her face remained red. Pedric gazed down at her, thinking of Marrika's scornful comments about the "playacting" that Pedric so loved, and thought Lorinda even lovelier now than when he had first met her.

She looked at him expectantly and he gathered his

thoughts. "Oh, yes, Kyle Kierdan. He's new to Braedon, but he's just wonderful. He can play anything." He extended his arm. "Would you care to join me for a walk outside? The Garden is lovely this time of the evening, and," he winked conspiratorially, "I can show you how to get through the maze."

Lorinda's reddened eyes narrowed as she regarded him. Innocent as she was, even she knew that walks in the Garden alone with a man—especially a walk in the maze!—were an invitation to dalliance. For a long moment, Pedric feared that she would refuse him. His heart lurched, and he wondered if she would also refuse his proposal. He realized that he hadn't the slightest idea what he would do with himself if she said no.

The half smile that melted him returned to her full lips. "Good gracious me, and how many ladies have you taken through the maze, Lord Asakinn?"

Her voice was warm, teasing. Pedric felt the cold dread seep away and he replied, "Oh, dozens, Milady Vandaris. But most of them have left me to find my own way out."

Something softened on her face, and when Lorinda spoke her voice was low and throaty with emotion. "I would never abandon you to find your own way out of such a tangle, Pedric." Her hand slipped into his, feather-light, warm.

Something crashed over Pedric with all the force of a hurricane wave. He began to tremble, felt the blood rush to his face, hands, and elsewhere. It was desire, certainly, but with a tenderness to its edge that he'd never felt before. The room suddenly seemed a whirlwind of humanity, a crowded jungle of people when all he wanted, craved, needed, was for the world to be reduced to himself and Lorinda.

His own voice betrayed him with a quiver as he replied in what was meant to be a jaunty tone, "Then by all means, my most beautiful Lorinda, let us tackle the maze."

Lorinda's hand was warm, her soft fingers curling trust-ingly around his. Pedric steered his way through the throng, out the wide, opened doors and into the Garden. The breeze was soft and cool on his blood-heated face, and when they entered the maze, surrounded on almost all sides by the tall, silent, deep-green shrubbery, he almost broke into a run in his eagerness to get Lorinda into the heart of the confusing labyrinth.

Then they were there, in Pedric's favorite spot for romantic liaisons, and he halted. It was harder than he thought to turn and face Lorinda, face the possibility that her blood might not be as inflamed as his, her heart as full and aching with unsatisfied want.

He needn't have worried, for the moment he turned around she was in his arms. She trembled violently, pressing the length of her slender body against his, burying her face in the soft velvet of his doublet.

Almost fiercely he crushed her to him, his arms encircling her protectively, possessively. He felt her breasts on his chest, felt the heart housed within beating swiftly. Pedric, almost overcome with emotion, laid his cheek on her silky reddish-brown hair, and pressed no further.

They stood so for a long time, then Lorinda moved within the circle of his embrace. He let her go—Pedric was ever the gentleman, and the thought of forcing himself on any woman, let alone this one, was abhorrent to him—but she moved away only a little. One small hand lingered on his chest, moving gently, feeling the softness of the velvet and the warmth of him through it. She did not meet his gaze.

"I knew," she began at last, "that if I became the Blesser of Love, I would share my body with many men, all strangers. I knew this to be a sacred thing, and had I been chosen, I would have gone to such a duty joyfully, in the service of my beloved goddess. But there was part of me that didn't want that, that wanted to—to wait, to—*be* with one man, and that my body would follow only after my heart had been given first. I think the Blesser sensed this in me, and that was why she selected another."

Now her lashes lifted, and Pedric gazed into her eyes. They were dark and full of mystery in the moonlight, but they gleamed like stars. His throat tightened and he knew she must feel his arousal through the thick folds of her gown.

"No one has ever made me feel like you have, Pedric. The hours away from you are years, and the time spent with you flies as if it were no time at all. I do not . . . I do not ever wish those times to end."

Through the tightness in his throat, he found words. "They don't have to, Lorinda. Not—" ah, gods, what would she say? "—not if you marry me."

She gasped, and jerked away, startled. "Pedric, I—" Even in the dim moonlight he could see color suffuse her cheeks. Suddenly she started laughing. Pedric felt as though she'd tossed icy water on him, and his passion vanished. Oh, what a fool he'd been, what a—

"That wasn't a ploy for marriage, my love," she said through her mirth. "I would have—I was offering myself without any promises!"

Part of Pedric, the rakish, devil-may-care bachelor part, figuratively seized him and shook him with an angry, "Are you crazy? You could have had her *without* a commitment!"

The other part of the young Lord Asakinn, the part wanted this lovely woman as a life mate, spoke and said, "I wasn't expecting to lie with you until the wedding night, but if you insist—"

His sally was cut off abruptly by the unexpected but welcomed pressure of her rose-petal lips pressing against his. She was clearly inexperienced, but equally clearly, Lorinda wished to learn this art of the kiss, and Pedric was an able and willing teacher. His hands went up to cup her face, stroking the soft cheeks as his lips brushed, explored. The kiss deepened, and Pedric was only dimly aware that they had moved to the damp grass and Lorinda lay willingly beneath him.

Sanity returned, definitely not welcomed, but needed. With effort, Pedric broke the kiss and leaned back, catching his breath.

"Oh, curse it," he swore, "you've got grass stains all over your gown. Your father will have my hide."

The humor was back in her voice as she replied, "What, and lose such a fine son-in-law?"

He gripped her hands tightly, all suavity gone, and asked pleadingly, "You do mean it, then? You will have me? Lorinda, I will love you until the day I die, I swear I will."

"Pray Love that won't be soon," she admonished. Her face crinkled into a smile. "I will have you, Pedric Dunsan, in as many ways as I can think of."

Her husky voice and hinted promise were almost unbearable. Pedric had to restrain himself from taking her right then, on the cool earth inside the maze. But that wouldn't be right. He wanted to romance Lorinda, pleasure her, not ravish her like a plowhand a milk-girl. He would wait.

Besides, there was something else, and that thought forced desire almost, but not completely, from his thoughts. He looked down at her hands, her small, strong hands, hands that with a few innocent touches had aroused him almost to a frenzy. He lifted them and pressed a long, lingering kiss on her fingers.

"You say yes now, love," he said softly, stroking her hands. "But there are things you don't know about me, things that you must know if we are to have any hope of happiness. I'm . . . I'm not what you think I am."

"Don't tell me. You're an elf-lord, under an illusion spell, who—"

"Damn it, Lorinda, this is important!" He regretted the harsh tone at once, seeing its force reflected in her almost imperceptible flinch. "I'm sorry. It's just . . ." and the words came tumbling out. "I'm afraid that once you know, you'll despise me, and dear gods, I think I'd rather be dead then have you look at me with hate!"

"Pedric," she soothed, reaching to touch his face. "Love, it can't be that bad. Whatever it is, it can't be that bad."

"I hope not. You don't know how badly I hope not." He paused, gathering his thoughts. How to begin. *Lorinda, I'm a thief. Lorinda, sometimes things that aren't mine find their way into my pouch. Lorinda, I'm a criminal.*

They all sounded dreadful.

He took a deep breath, opened his mouth. He wasn't sure what he would say.

Whatever it was, it would remain unsaid. Pedric saw Lorinda's eyes widen in horror as she stared at something behind him. He saw her lips start to form words, her hand begin to disentangle itself from his deathgrip on her fingers, lifting as if to point. At that moment Pedric knew a crashing, devastating pain at the base of his skull. Lorinda's face, filled with fear, mutated into a red flash. And then, darkness.

He awoke alone, to agony. The night had grown chilly, and the dew had risen. He lay, facedown, on the damp earth. For a long, disoriented moment, Pedric wasn't even sure where he was. He tried to lift his head but the movement threatened to make him scream aloud and lose consciousness again, so he simply surrendered to it while his mind began to clear.

The maze. He was in the maze. Why? With . . . with . . .

"Lorinda!" he cried, but the call emerged as a barely audible croak. He spasmed, trying to find the wherewithal to rise, but the gesture did now what it had promised to do earlier. Blackness descended again.

When Pedric woke again, he knew where he was, and the shrieking torment in his head had subsided to the point where it was merely excruciating. He tried to rise a third time, slowly, and his abused body permitted him. Pedric staggered, stumbling into the prickly solidity of the maze wall, and leaned against it.

"Lorinda!" he cried, louder this time. There was no answer. "Ah, gods, please, no," he murmured, but it was clear what had happened. Someone had set upon them both, had knocked him unconscious and fled with Lorinda. Who? Why?

One thing was clear. He had to find help. He pressed a hand to the back of his head, hoping to ease the pain with pressure. He hissed through his teeth at the initial sharp pain of contact, and knew the sticky wetness that covered his hand was his own blood. There was an enormous lump that had not been part of Pedric's physiognomy hitherto, and he grimly endured the pain until it began to subside.

For a dreadful moment, Pedric was still so disoriented he couldn't remember which way he had come. He glanced about frantically, fighting the panic that rose within him and almost reduced him to tears, helpless tears that wouldn't help to find Lorinda. He fought down the hysteria and concentrated. Yes, this way . . . and then take a left here . . .

It felt like hours. Several times he had to stop, fight against the gray cloudiness that threatened to reclaim him. He hated these necessary pauses with a brutal intensity. They kept him from getting out, from finding Lorinda.

At last, he stumbled out and promptly fell without the support of the maze's hedge walls. He hit the ground hard, too dazed with grief and pain even to put his arms out to stop his fall. His breath was knocked out of him and he gasped, his mouth opening and closing as if he were a fish on the deck of a ship. *Lorinda, Lorinda . . . someone help me . . .*

As if in answer to his unvoiced plea, strong hands were suddenly there, helping him sit up. The movement, gentle though it was intended to be, sent waves of pain through him. Dimly Pedric realized that he had probably broken his nose. The only thing that upset him about this was the fact that the blood pouring down his face kept getting in his mouth, making speech difficult.

He gazed up at his rescuer and relief flooded him. It was

Deveren, who flashed him a reassuring smile before turning
and crying, "I've found Pedric!" Turning back to his friend,
Deveren said in a softer voice, "Where's Lorinda? What
happened? We've been searching for you since Death's
hour!"

"My daughter!" came Vandaris's voice, tense with fear
and anger. "What have you done with my—" The big man
came into Pedric's view and, seeing the young nobleman's
condition, somehow managed to tame his outrage. *That's
what makes him such a good diplomat*, Pedric thought dis-
jointedly. Other footsteps running, other voices shouting.
Grayness seeped into Pedric's vision as Damir came up and
knelt beside him.

"Lord Asakinn," said Vandaris, his etiquette not faltering
even under this extreme pressure, "what happened to you?
Was my daughter with you?"

Pedric opened his mouth, spat out blood. His lips moved,
but nothing came out. He cried out in protest as the gray haze
darkened, deepened, and the concerned face of Lorinda's father was replaced by blackness.

Deveren swore. "We've got to get him to a Healer," he
told his brother.

Damir nodded, his dark eyes on Pedric's slack, ghastly-
pale face. "I've sent for one already. I only wish we knew
what had happened."

Deveren thought that was clear enough, and he said so.
"They were assaulted!"

"I have deduced that, little brother," replied Damir tartly,
frowning with irritation. "But by whom?"

"Your Lordship," interrupted Vandaris, "I grieve for the
boy, but at least he is alive and will survive the night." His
beautifully resonant voice caught, but he forced himself to
continue. "I do not know the same to be true of my little
girl."

Deveren glanced back and forth, from the pudgy, ruddy,
yet commanding, visage of Braedon's Head Councilman to
the thin, ascetic face of his older brother. He hesitated, then

said, "You could find out, Damir." To Vandaris he said, "He's got mind magic. He could read Pedric's last thoughts."

The keen hawk's gaze of Damir turned upon Deveren. "Not without his consent. There are rules, you know."

"He'd tell us if he could," protested Deveren. "He—" he glanced over at Vandaris, and directed his words to the councilman. "He loved your daughter, Lord Vandaris. I'm sure that when he regains consciousness he'll thank us for probing his thoughts. Gods alone know when this occurred. Every minute is precious."

"Dev, I cannot simply—"

"I'll take the responsibility then," snapped Deveren. "Lord Vandaris, I call upon you to witness: if Pedric Dunsan deems this a violation rather than a blessing, he can blame me. I'll pay whatever he asks."

"You're that certain?" asked Damir.

Deveren nodded, his gaze dropping to Pedric's face. Dear gods, he looked dreadful, but Vandaris had the right of it—he would live. Lorinda might even yet be dead.

"Do it."

"So be it," acquiesced Damir. He moved closer to Pedric, who lay limply clasped in Deveren's arms. Gently, he brushed aside the blood-clotted hair and placed his long, thin fingers against the youth's temple. He closed his eyes to aid his concentration.

Deveren watched intently, hardly daring to breathe, his eyes flickering back and forth from Pedric's face to Damir's. He knew that, in reading another's thoughts, the reader would experience everything as if it were happening to him. A slight smile touched Damir's lips. Watching him, Deveren felt like a voyeur. What had happened between Lorinda and Pedric probably had been intimate. Maybe Pedric might be angry with him, in truth. But no, Deveren reasoned, if Pedric truly loved Lorinda—and he was certain that the hitherto feckless young man did—then he would be grateful for the intrusion if it helped them find her.

Now the older man's high brow furrowed, as if distressed. Suddenly he gasped and cried out. The little crowd of guards and concerned citizens that had formed gasped in sympathy. As if he were physically hurled backward, Damir lurched away, severing the contact. Vandaris went to him, steadied him. Damir blinked, then his gaze focused. His voice, when he spoke, was raw with pain.

"I was—Pedric was—assaulted from behind. He never saw who hit him. He believes they have abducted Lorinda." His eyes found Vandaris's. "Sir, one thing I do know—there was love between them, true and deep. Pedric had asked for Lorinda's hand, and she had consented."

Vandaris's throat worked. He glanced over at the youth, raised a hand as if to stoke his hair in a fatherly fashion, then clenched his fist. Righteous anger now replaced grief. He stumbled to his feet, and his words were filled with command. All traces of sorrow had been banished from that sonorous voice.

"Jaranis!" The captain of the guards appeared. One hand had automatically gone to the hilt of his sword, and anger darkened his own face.

"Aye, sir!"

Vandaris clapped a commanding hand on the other man's shoulder, walking him away from Pedric, Damir, and Deveren. "I want you to put your best men on this. Someone has kidnapped my daughter. I'm not sure who or why. Be prepared to deal with a ransom situation. As for when, we believe it occurred sometime after intermission . . ."

His voice faded. The crowd began to disperse, urged to do so none too gently by Jaranis's men. Deveren and Damir regarded each other.

"I'll see what my sources can determine about this," said Damir softly, for Deveren's ears alone.

"Good idea," approved Deveren. "I'll get my—" he glanced around, amended what he was about to say "—my people on it too."

Damir's expression turned dark. "Why bother? It was probably one of them!"

Deveren rose to the bait. "What makes you say that? Pedric was one of their number!"

"Gods, Deveren, you speak as though the rabble had integrity. For the ransom they'd just as likely kill you!"

Deveren froze. Sweat broke out on his forehead as a memory of the events of the night, forgotten in the urgency of finding and tending his friend, came back full force. He could find no words to answer his brother. One of "his" thieves had tried to murder him already tonight. One or more of them could have tried to do the same with Pedric.

"Excuse me," came a feminine voice. It was soft, gentle, but the tone was of one used to giving orders and having them obeyed. Both brothers looked up and saw a tall woman with composed, attractive features. Her garb was simple, a plain, unadorned dress of vivid scarlet. Her head was swathed in a red wimple.

"I am Vervain, come in service to my goddess." Without another word, Health's Blesser dropped down beside Pedric and began to examine him with a knowledgeable, gentle touch.

"What happened here?" she asked crisply. She opened Pedric's eyes, gazed into them, placed her fingers on his throat to determine the rate of the pulse.

"He was struck from behind by an unknown assailant," Deveren explained.

Damir rose. "Think you can move him inside yourself, Deveren?" The younger man nodded brusquely. "Then I leave him to your care—and yours, Milady Blesser." He bowed, shot Deveren another quick, angry look, and went to join Vandaris.

"The blood is dried," said Vervain. "When was he struck?"

Deveren shook his head. "We don't know. An hour, perhaps longer."

Efficiently but tenderly, the Blesser slipped one hand inside Pedric's doublet and shirt, pressing it, Deveren knew, directly on his heart. The other crept unhesitatingly behind the youth's head to cradle it directly on the injured area. Deveren sank back on his heels and watched. The Blesser closed her eyes and murmured something Deveren couldn't quite catch.

Hand magic was something Deveren had lived with almost all of his life. Mind magic was nothing strange to him, either; not with an older brother as accomplished in the art as Damir. But he had, thank the gods, little opportunity to witness heart magic—women's magic—in action. This was the third of the Four Magics, the final one being spirit magic, worked only by the gods themselves or their designated avatars. And to Deveren, heart magic was closer to spirit magic than the workaday sorceries of hand and mind magic.

Pedric moaned slightly under her ministrations, and his eyes opened. "Dev . . ." he whispered.

Deveren reached to seize Pedric's groping hand. "I'm here, Pedric."

"Found . . . Lorinda?"

"No," he said, wishing he could say otherwise, "but they're out looking for her. I'm certain they'll find her." It was a lie, but he couldn't bear to look at the agony in Pedric's face. It was too much like looking into a mirror seven years ago. He had to believe that Pedric would not lose his love to brutality as he, Deveren, had. Had to.

"Got to . . . find . . ." Pedric struggled to sit upright, but the Healer held him fast with a strong grip. She placed a hand on his temple.

"Rest," she commanded, and all the tension left Pedric's body. He collapsed limply into Vervain's arms. "He needs sleep. He will survive, but first, he must want to."

Deveren glanced at her sharply. She answered him with a tranquil, knowing smile. How old was she? She looked young, but she had a wisdom and a grace about her that made her appear older.

"I thank you, Lady Vervain. Pedric's a friend of mine. I wouldn't see him suffer if I could help it."

"Then help me get him to a bed, sir . . .?"

"Deveren, Lord Larath. But my friends call me Dev. I don't tend to stand much on ceremony," and he grimaced as he hefted Pedric as gently as he could, "especially when a friend's in pain."

"In that case, Dev, you can help me clean his wounds." She was already rummaging through the large sack she carried as she followed Deveren, bearing his sad burden, into the Councilman's Seat.

After conferring briefly with Vandaris and Jaranis, Damir excused himself. He mounted his horse and rode as swiftly as he could away from the crowd milling about the Councilman's Seat, away from the city of Braedon entirely. He followed the coastline, keeping the ocean on his left as he headed north, until he was a safe distance away.

Damir's horse, an intelligent little mare from Deveren's stables, was laboring. He regretted having pushed her, but it was necessary. The sooner he got here, the sooner he could begin searching for Lorinda. He reached the spot, a rocky section on a beach deserted save for the beasts that belonged here, and tied the mare to the withered, slim trunk of a tree that had somehow managed to endure the winds that blew in off the ocean.

Lorinda. Poor child. Pedric had not betrayed himself by word, look, or deed, but Damir had been in his mind tonight. He had tasted Lorinda's lips, had felt Pedric's love for the girl. And he had endured Pedric's fear of rejection when he was about to tell Lorinda that he was a thief. Slightly censorious, Damir thought that Pedric should have known better than to steal away so far from anyone else. Two young rich people, alone in a maze, were a tempting target for greedy thieves, and Pedric couldn't be sure that his "fellow" thieves would recognize him in time. But Pedric was young, and the blood in his veins sang sweet and hot, and Damir was not so old as to have forgotten what that song did to one's judgment.

He scrambled over the rocks, nearly twisting his ankle. Normally when he came here, he was dressed for the excursion. Soft boots and hose were hardly appropriate for scrambling over rocks late at night.

At last Damir reached the spot. Though it was summer, the breeze off the ocean was chilly, and he shivered. He hadn't even brought a cloak. He physically steadied himself on the rock as he mentally steadied himself to call on his finest spy.

The song he had been taught was not for the ears or voice. Damir thought the notes, extended his presence, felt the song shudder through the stone, the sand, into the waters of the sea itself.

And in his mind, he heard an answer.

A distance away, a dolphin broke the surface, leaped into the air, and crashed back down into the water. When it next emerged, it no longer looked like a sleek fish-mammal, but a man, albeit such a man as never walked the surface of Verold.

"This is not our night for meeting," said Darshirin, his voice soft and velvety, scarcely heard above the eternal lullaby of the ocean.

"This is not a night for common talk," rejoined Damir.

Darshirin's slanted eyes narrowed and he swam closer. Damir gingerly sat down on a rock.

"Your heart is sore troubled, my friend. You have called; I answer. What may I do to ease your pain?"

As always, Damir was touched by the sea-being's genuine concern. Many years ago, when Damir was but a lad, he had been on a fishing ship—one of his father's. The late Lord Larath had wanted both his sons to know from whence came their wealth; know and treat those who labored in their service with due respect. They had caught Darshirin, in his dolphin form, in their nets. The young Damir had insisted the creature be set free, even though it meant cutting and damaging the net. Later that night, while Damir was on deck, Darshirin sang a sea-song of gratitude, and was shocked that Damir could hear it. They had been friends ever since, and Darshirin had more than returned the original favor by providing Damir with vital information about the sailing habits of other countries.

"There is a girl who has been stolen from her people," Damir told his friend. "I hope you do not see her, for if you do, it will be in the ocean depths. She is tall, fair as we of the land reckon beauty, and full of laughter." This last, he knew, would count the most in the eyes of one of the People of the Sea. These wise, gentle beings knew mirth far better than humans. He described Lorinda in detail, as well as what happened to her. "If you see her or hear tell of her, come to me."

Darshirin's shape bobbed with the rhythm of the waves. When he spoke, his voice was sad. "Such violence among your own kind . . . I can hardly conceive. No wonder you do not live long." Like the mysterious, elusive elves, the People of the Sea seemed to humans to live forever. "I hope my search is fruitless, and you find your Lorinda safely among the land dwellers."

"I do, too. Thank you, Darshirin."

The being smiled, and disappeared beneath the glassy surface. From a distance he flicked his fluked tail in a farewell gesture, and Damir was alone.

He did not return at once to his waiting and no doubt chilled mare. He sat staring, and wondering at the peaceful natures of those who dwelt beneath the surface of the sea, and at the dark, bloodthirsty character of those he called his own people. At last he sighed and rose to his feet.

"Lorinda," he said to the sea and star-filled sky, "please come home safely."

*The lamb shall bleat, and cast up its eyes, but
you must harden your heart, for its blood shall buy you
favor in the eyes of the gods.*

—instructions on ritual sacrifice,
from Blessers to Tenders

CHAPTER EIGHT

"Why in the Nightlands didn't you let me kill him,
bitch?" grunted Freylis, shifting his burden as he spoke.

Marrika turned cold eyes upon her lover. *Wait*, she told
herself silently. *You need him. Wait just a little longer.
Then . . .*

"You do not understand vengeance," she said icily.
They walked alone in the night, their path paralleling the
winding road that would take them from the Square and
the Garden into the heart of the city. She'd feel safer
there, among the back streets and dark ways that they both
knew so intimately. This road was open, exposed, and although she and Freylis had scouted out a parallel path the
night before, it was too close to the main road for her liking. It would not do to be questioned or stopped, not even

by their fellow thieves, not with the unconscious body of the girl lying limply in Freylis's ox-strong arms.

They had wrapped her in a blanket, of course, and bound her hand and foot in case she awoke sooner than was convenient. A dirty rag shoved into her mouth made an effective gag. Still, Marrika's eyes flitted about nervously. This was what she had promised the Blesser, and that she could combine her own burning desire for vengeance with the sacrifice formed a pleasantly dark symmetry in her mind. But others would not see it so.

"What do you mean, I don't understand vengeance?" spluttered Freylis, panting a little at the rapid pace. "I wanted to kill the little slug."

"I don't want him dead," she snapped, her patience finally cracking. "I want him to suffer." A muscle in her face twitched. "He seemed fond of her. What we do with her will hurt him far more than a dagger in the gut. You have no subtlety about you, Freylis, none at all."

Freylis growled menacingly. Time was when that tone would have frightened her, but that time was gone. Ahead and slightly below them, the city opened up, the street system becoming more convoluted. Marrika's heart lifted. Almost there—almost to safety. Not for her the open sky and road. She felt far more comfortable in close quarters, where she could get her back against a wall, or where she could hide in the overlooked corner or shadow.

Khem, known as "Hound," would be waiting for them at the first intersection. The dim moonlight revealed nothing so far. She waved Freylis on, following the deserted road—deserted for how long, she wondered—and moved toward the rendezvous point.

Now they saw a darker shadow in the shadows. Khem raised an arm and waved.

"There he is," said Marrika. They were approaching safety now, albeit a safety that was unpleasant and arduous.

Khem was small and wiry, but the little muscles that

knotted his arms and legs were powerful. He had a scar from a recent knife fight that zigzagged across his already ugly face. He flashed Marrika a yellow grin.

"Not sight nor sound of guards so far," he assured her.

"Excellent," approved Marrika. "But let's not take any unnecessary risks."

None too gently, Freylis put the limp body on the ground and went to help the sinewy Khem move aside the iron grate that opened up into Braedon's sewer system.

Few cities could boast the fine sewage system that Braedon could, and fewer still had one a third as old. Two centuries ago it was discovered, as the result of a tragic cave-in, that the city of Braedon rested atop an extensive natural cave system. Beneath the city streets, the ocean reached its long fingers well into the land. After the cave-in, in which an enormous sinkhole opened up to swallow the first Council site, Braedon rebuilt with an eye toward using this natural gift.

Over the long years, tunnels were dug, continuing the existing caves far back toward the mainland and eventually linking up with the several freshwater runoffs that poured off the encircling mountains. It was a good century and a half in the making, and building the sewer system had taken the lives of not a few men. The work had been hard and simple—convicts and prisoners of war, many of them Mharians, had inched their way through stony earth with plain picks. Hard experience taught the architects that while the earth was solid, it did need some help now and then if it were not to cave in along the entire sewer route. Therefore, large beams, coated with pitch to resist water, were used to shore up the surface. Cobbled stones lined the bottom and crept well up the earthen sides to prevent erosion.

After the first few disasters, the system had worked wonderfully. Every merchant and landowner was responsible, by order of the Council, to attend to the waste around his area. Several interconnecting tunnels led up to dozens of holes in the streets, carefully covered by heavy grates, into which the citizens of Braedon diligently dumped their refuse. Richer folk even had drains specifically built to carry off waste from garderobes and kitchens into the sewers.

A feat of technical engineering perhaps it was, but as Marrika peered down into the depths, she thought only of the filth that awaited her and Freylis when they descended. Fortunately, it hadn't rained for several days. The sludgy waters that flowed sluggishly some twenty feet below the surface would at least be shallow.

She wrinkled her nose as the stench wafted up. Grunting and heaving, Khem and Freylis managed to shove aside the grate. Moving quickly, Marrika opened the pouch at her waist and withdrew the leather-covered grappling hook. Freylis and Khem had been able to push the grate far enough aside to admit the passage of a human body, but the grate still covered much of the hole. Marrika snagged the hook securely onto the grate, tugging and twisting it a little to make sure it would hold. She sat down, her legs dangling into the hole. Gripping the rope, she lowered herself hand over hand down into the sewer.

The smell grew worse, but she forced herself to endure it. She knew from experience that she would soon grow used to the stench. Marrika had traveled these dank, filthy, subterranean paths before, as had most of the thieves of Braedon. The tunnels made for wonderful ways of getting around guards and search parties, and more than a few corpses of those who had "disappeared" had found their way to these surroundings, to be washed out to sea and never heard from again.

Her boots squelched ankle-deep in filth; the dirty water reached to the middle of her calves. It was pitch dark, save for the faint square over her head. That would shortly be remedied, for no sooner had Marrika landed safely than Khem lowered a bundle. Marrika grasped it and unwrapped it. Thick beeswax candles—donated from the

temple of Vengeance—revealed themselves to her questing fingers. There was something else, too—a small box
carefully wrapped in fabric. Marrika tucked the candles in
her pouch to free her hands and, working by touch,
opened the little box. Nestled inside, a small ember
glowed steadily. She smiled to herself, then lit a single
candle.

She lifted the burning taper and moved it back and forth
across her face, signalling that she was ready for Freylis
to descend. She watched as the big man prepared himself,
shifting the unconscious young woman over one shoulder
and anchoring her with a meaty arm. With the other, he
grasped the rope in his leather-gloved hand and slid down.
Marrika steadied him as he hit, taking care that the girl
didn't fall into the muck. Marrika didn't want her injured—not yet.

There was a groaning, scraping sound as Khem, alone,
slowly forced the unwieldy grate back into its place. Marrika didn't wait for the familiar clang to indicate that he
had succeeded. In silence, she moved forward, lighting a
second candle to help them see better. Behind her, Freylis
followed.

They did not speak. From time to time, Marrika heard
voices on the surface. At such moments, they would
pause, shrinking back against the walls, shielding the
lights as best they could. When the voices faded, they
continued. Once, they heard the telltale jangle and clatter
of armed guards hastening overhead. They spoke quickly,
in low voices. Marrika strained to catch their words.

"Vandaris . . . search everywhere . . . reward."

Heat surged through Marrika, the heat of a triumph
about to be tasted. By now Pedric must have revived, have
told the sad, sad story of beauteous Lorinda's dreadful abduction. The pain was beginning. She glanced over at the
still bundle in Freylis's arms.

"Thank you, Lorinda. You've made this all possible."

The tunnels became labyrinthine, but Marrika knew

them well and pressed onward. By the smells and type of refuse they encountered, she could tell where she was. They passed between the red-stained, fetid walls of the butchers, the multicolored stained walls of the weavers' shops, and perhaps worst of all, trod carefully through the acidic puddles of fermented bran, lime, and animal dung that marked the tanner's workshop.

A soft moan came from behind Marrika. She whirled just in time to see the bundle borne by Freylis move. Marrika cursed softly. Lorinda was starting to awaken, and they were still far from the site.

"Hold her," she snapped, then turned and quickened her pace. Filth splashed up and stained her breeches, but she paid it no heed. Lorinda was really beginning to struggle now, and Freylis snapped angrily at the frightened girl.

The smell of the shops began to fade. More pleasant scents reached Marrika's nose—scented bathwater mixed with the ubiquitous odor of chamber pots, the last lingering bits of incense from a ritual. They were almost there.

Lorinda, gagged but vocal, was fighting. "Quiet, curse you!" came Freylis's voice. There was a muffled sound of fist on flesh.

"Don't hurt her," ordered Marrika, "we want her awake and aware."

There it was, up ahead, a dim square of light crisscrossed by the shadows cast by the iron bars. Marrika stumbled to a halt, waved the two candles she carried as a signal. She was rewarded by the sound of the grate being moved. Turning around, she gazed at Freylis.

"Put her down. Cut her bonds."

Freylis gawped. *"What?"*

"You can't climb up with her fighting you like that. We'll have to haul her up separately."

Freylis cocked his big, shaggy head to one side and considered. Marrika thought that a dog understood things faster than Freylis did, but eventually the big thief nodded. He dropped the girl down unceremoniously and began unwinding her from the blanket.

Lorinda kicked and struggled. "Quiet, girl, we're trying to untie you," snapped Marrika.

The blanket fell off and Lorinda shot a frightened gaze at Marrika. Even trussed up like a hare, sprawled in filth, Lorinda Vandaris was beautiful. She heard and understood, and suddenly ceased her struggles. Freylis took out his dagger and sliced the ropes that bound her. Seizing her upper arm, he hauled her to her feet. The dagger pressed at her throat. Lorinda froze, panting, her eyes wide with fear.

"Good girl," Marrika said sarcastically. Confident that Freylis had the situation well in hand—terrorizing was something that Freylis did exceptionally well—Marrika turned her attention to getting out.

The thieves above had moved the grate out of the way, and she could see the shadow of someone peering down. She squinted, trying to make out the shape, and again recognized Khem. Surprised pleasure filled her. Khem had only been assigned to help them get down. Others had agreed to meet her and Freylis near the temple, but apparently Khem was enjoying himself enough to show up here as well.

"Awake," she hissed, hoping her voice carried without being overly loud. They were all still in danger of discovery. Khem shook his head and put a hand to his ear, indicating that she should speak louder.

"She's awake!" Marrika repeated, pitching her voice louder. This time Khem nodded his comprehension and disappeared from her view. He returned a moment later with others, then waved his arm in a *send her up* gesture.

"How strong are you, girl?" asked Marrika, her lips pursed as her eyes roamed over the girl's slim body. "Can you climb up?"

Lorinda's large-eyed gaze flickered from Marrika's

hard face to the rope. "I'm strong, but I—I don't think I can climb up the rope."

Marrika swore casually, enjoying the fact that Lorinda winced at the crude word. "Come here, then. We'll tie it around your waist and haul you up."

When the girl hesitated, Freylis pushed her forward. She stumbled and fell face-first into the swirling, waste-clogged water. Marrika watched her coldly as she struggled to her feet. Oh, she was enjoying this. What would Pedric think of his aristocratic lady-love now, with dung on her face and urine in her hair? She felt a smile curve her lips and she reminded herself that the fun was only just beginning.

Lorinda straightened, and stepped forward with an unexpected dignity. Marrika's smile ebbed. The girl stood obediently as Marrika wound the sturdy rope about her waist and under the curve of her buttocks.

"My father will pay whatever you ask," said Lorinda quietly.

Unable to help herself, Marrika backhanded the young woman savagely across her small, dirty face. Lorinda's head jerked sideways with the force of the blow and bloody spittle flew. Slowly, impossibly remaining calm, Vandaris's daughter turned her head back toward Marrika. Tears clouded those large eyes, but they did not spill down her cheeks.

"This isn't about money, you whore," hissed Marrika. She knotted the rope with a savage jerk, and Lorinda gasped as the rope cinched painfully about her slim waist. Expertly Marrika tossed the grappling hook upward. It caught on the first try. Marrika tugged, assured that the grip was good, and motioned for them to lift the girl upward. As Khem and the others began to slowly draw her up toward the surface, Lorinda's hands automatically flew to the rope to steady herself.

Marrika watched as she was borne upward, breathing heavily with the force of her hatred. The bitch'd cry soon enough, all right. She waited while her compatriots untied the girl, then dropped the rope down again. Quickly, with the sinuous grace of a cat, Marrika grasped the rope herself and, using her hands and feet, quickly propelled herself up its length. She accepted Khem's strong hand and scrambled out, scooting backward.

Clia, the Sparrow, was in charge of watching Lorinda while Marrika and Freylis emerged from the tunnels. Her dagger was perfectly functional despite its ornaments, and Clia's beringed fingers had a solid grip on the girl.

"Councilman's daughter, hey, Raven?" A white grin flashed. "Gold and silver a-flowing. A better haul than Bear pulled off!" She laughed softly.

Marrika didn't bother to contradict the fortune-teller. Clia would find out soon enough what they really planned to do with Lorinda. And then the garish-garbed Sparrow would either be with them—or dead.

Freylis now emerged, grunting as he pulled his mammoth bulk up hand over hand. He plopped himself on the street surface with all the finesse of a whale beaching itself. Marrika's red lips curled with disgust. If all went well tonight, she might never have to endure that sweaty body moving over and in her again.

She listened with half an ear as the thieves heaved the grate back in place. They were very close to the temple now. She could see it across the flat cobblestone center of town. Candles burned, and even as she watched, she saw a black-robed shadow scurry across the square. It stopped at the Godstower, as it had a few nights ago, but did not ring the bell. Instead, the shape waited, pacing nervously.

"There he is," hissed Marrika. "Let's go."

Clia prodded Lorinda's throat with the tip of her dagger. A small bead of blood appeared. "Come on, little rich sister," smiled Sparrow. The thieves and their prisoner hurried across the square to where the Blesser of Vengeance waited.

"Did you—do you—" he asked breathlessly.

Marrika nodded her dark head. "Indeed we do," she replied, nodding her head in Lorinda's direction. "I keep my promises to my god and my friends, Kannil. Are you prepared for us?"

The little man closed his eyes briefly in a shudder of ecstatic anticipation, then licked his lips and replied, "All are assembled, ready to honor the god, Lady Marrika."

"Lady?" scoffed Freylis. Marrika didn't even bother giving him an angry glare. Like the tide, Freylis's importance to her was ebbing, its ultimate demise inevitable. He had already almost outlived his usefulness to her. And if things went the way they should tonight, well, his time might already have run. It pleased Marrika that he had no idea how fragile was the thread by which he hung.

All was in readiness when they reached the temple of Vengeance. The stone building, not large to begin with, seemed much smaller than it had the last time Marrika had been there; but then again, there were many more people gathered than there had been on that fateful night. And this time, all the torches and candles had been lit. The circle of bone powder was drawn, with one part of it left open for the main attraction of the night to enter. Within the circle sat and stood the thieves who had chosen to ally with Marrika and Freylis. She felt her heart lift at the sight of their tense, wary faces. So many. So many, who did not want to be milk-and-bread wholesome under the leadership of Deveren Larath. So many like her, who could never forget that crime could not be reigned in, that theft went hand in hand with murder, that life in the shadows could never, ever, be anything other than dark.

"What do you want?" A cry, shattering the still, tense moment. It was Lorinda, of course, her calm demeanor broken by the same faces that so heartened her captor. Marrika turned to regard the prisoner. Lorinda's face had gone white. She, more than most, knew what kind of a deity Vengeance was. The girl must, in some part of her soul, be guessing what was about to transpire, even as she fought to reject the dreadful knowledge. "My father will pay—"

"There is no money that can buy what your blood will buy, child," interrupted the Blesser. He reached with one thin hand to touch Lorinda's soft cheek. With a soft little cry, like the mewl of a barnyard kitten, Lorinda cringed from that caress.

"What?" came Clia's voice, startled. "Wolf, what's going on here?"

It was the moment Marrika had been waiting for, the moment she felt she'd been leading up to her whole life.

"Be quiet, Sparrow, or we'll silence your chirping for you," said Marrika. "Don't ask Freylis." Oh, the words were sweet. "Ask *me*."

Stunned silence greeted her words, then chatter broke out. *Now or never*, thought Marrika. She seized the moment and spontaneously leaped onto the blood-encrusted altar. Gasps came, and the Blesser rushed forward, anger on his face. She stopped him with one commanding hand.

"Who brings you your desire, Blesser?" cried Marrika. Her heart hammered in her chest and the blood in her veins sang. "Who has made this possible? Thieves of Braedon, rally with me tonight, and you work hand in hand with Vengeance himself! We will take what we want, and who's to stop us?" She pointed at Lorinda, who stared back enraptured, her eyes enormous. "This girl is Vandaris's daughter. Sparrow and others think only of money. I think of power—power to get whatever we want! Who among us has not been wronged? Who doesn't, deep in his heart, desire vengeance upon another? Well, now's your chance. Follow me—and drink deep!

Her passion was like fire; and the thieves who beheld her, like dried timber. Their expressions changed, and they all crowded around her, helped her down off the altar. Freylis alone hung back, visibly deflated. Bully and tyrant he might be, but he knew he couldn't stand against one who seemed in such accord with the dark god.

Kannil was beside himself. "Yes!" he squealed. He seized Lorinda, yanking her out of the grip of the startled Clia and propelling her into the center of the thieves. Lorinda cried out as hands reached to touch her. They were not hurtful, not yet; they merely wished to touch the living covenant between themselves and Vengeance before the deed was done.

Marrika watched, pleasure burning deep within her, as Lorinda was roped to the altar. The wooden platform had never been designed to accommodate a human sacrifice. Lorinda was forced to kneel in front of it. Rough hands grabbed her arms, pulled, secured her to the blood-covered table. Now she fought, now that it was too late, her lithe body thrashing and twisting, but to no avail.

Marrika's palms were wet with anticipation. Clearly restraining himself with difficulty, the Blesser moved to close the circle, murmuring the ritual words in a voice that trembled, and sprinkling more white powder on the earth. Marrika shivered as the temperature dropped, smiling at the discomfiture of some of "her" thieves who were experiencing this for the first time.

Now Kannil moved toward Lorinda. There was a flash of reflected light from the ceremonial dagger he withdrew. Inspiration struck Marrika.

"No, wait!" she cried. Kannil stared up at her, torn between carrying out the murder at once and listening to what Marrika had to say. "We are all in this together," she said, moving up beside the Blesser and extending a hand for the blade. "Let us all leave our marks on the girl."

Joy flooded the man's pale face. "Yes," he breathed. "Yes. Slowly." He handed her the knife, and placed one hand on Lorinda's back. "You may go first, O favored one."

Marrika crouched down and gazed levelly into Lorinda's eyes. They were wet, but did not look away.

"Why?" Lorinda asked. "Why are you doing this? What have I ever done to you?"

Marrika fingered the blade. It was sharp, honed to a keen edge. "One word: Pedric."

The younger woman frowned. "Pedric? But . . . I don't understand."

"He was mine, but he threw me away." The words hurt her to utter them, and she hissed them, softly, for Lorinda's ears alone. "And I want him to suffer for that. I want *you* to suffer for that!" Without another word, she swiped the hungry blade across the beautiful face. Lorinda cried out as the knife laid her cheek open. "Your beauty dies first, whore!" And Marrika spat into the girl's disfigured visage before yielding the knife to another.

She spared a glance for Kannil. His eyes were closed in ecstasy. He opened them, and gave her a smile. Marrika's breath caught.

The bastard was using his mind magic, linking himself to Lorinda, savoring her pain from two vantage points— his, witnessing the torture, and hers, experiencing it. Marrika hid her shudder of revulsion and turned away, holding out the knife. "Who will be next? Who will be next to inflict a blow for his freedom?"

"Me," said Freylis, shouldering his way through the crowd in an effort to reclaim the dignity he had lost. Without pausing he snatched up the knife and impaled it into Lorinda's right hand. The girl convulsed, her fingers splaying in reactionary agony but affixed firmly to the altar by both blade and bonds.

"Please," she whimpered.

"That's right, girl," crowed Marrika, "beg!"

The bloodlust spread through the crowd. The thought that they could so hurt another human being, with utter freedom and no reprisal, had a dark allure. The thieves were working past their initial revulsion, were starting to embrace Lorinda's fear and suffering. The girl sensed it, and her face reflected her horror.

Marrika drank it in like wine.

One by one they came to torture the innocent maiden, while Lorinda gasped and tried to twist away from them. Khem removed an ear. Clia stabbed her shoulder. Others inflicted different wounds. With each injury, the Blesser seemed to reach new heights of delight. But then something strange happened.

Lorinda managed to lift her head slightly, searching out Marrika. Her beauty was gone now, past any Healer's ability to salvage. Pedric, with his love for pretty things, would no doubt turn away in revulsion from her. But something shone in her eyes, a quiet integrity that unsettled Marrika. The girl's words distressed her even more.

"I served the goddess Love," rasped Lorinda. Jeers met this statement, but she continued, though the effort clearly was costing her. "Love teaches us . . . to be kind . . . to forgive."

"No," murmured the Blesser, a frown shadowing his face. "Don't spoil it . . ."

Lorinda swallowed blood, then pressed on. "For you to . . . to hurt me like this, to . . . to kill me . . . you must be in much torment, worse than any you could inflict on me. I . . . I pity you—all of you."

A snarl began in the back of Marrika's throat. Only dimly realizing what she was going to do, she surged forward and grasped the knife from someone's grasp. Springing at Lorinda, she struck. Blood fountained onto her hand.

At that precise instant, Kannil grabbed Marrika's free hand. The thief's vision shattered into a thousand pieces and she realized that Kannil, with his touch, had linked her to Lorinda. Images flashed through Marrika's mind even as agony trembled through her nerves.

Pedric, looking at her with love and fear of rejection;

Pedric's face achingly dear, beloved, beautiful. Marrika's own visage, cruel and unforgiving. Images of women and men she had never seen, but loved; Vandaris, gentle father; Love's temple; and the pain, the pain, the not understanding—why, why? What have I done? Gods, gods, please stop, stop—

—and the knife, above all, the knife, in the throat . . . cold . . . cold . . . dark . . .

The Blesser pushed her away just in time. Marrika stumbled backward, gasping, her hand going to throat and not truly believing it to be whole. Lungs heaving for air, shuddering with what she had just seen, a wave of remorse lifted Marrika for just an instant. *What have I done?* She moved toward the girl, half-formed thoughts of somehow halting the dreadful forces that she had set in motion flitting about her brain.

Lorinda spasmed once, then was still. It was too late.

At once sanity rushed back. The girl had been the price for the power Marrika had tasted, and a tool for revenge. Surely, that brief flash of regret had been the lingering traces of Lorinda's presence in her mind, nothing more. Marrika shot the Blesser a look of mingled disgust and horror. His face was flushed, his eyes dewy and radiant. What she had found disturbing was his delight. His tongue crept out to moisten his lips. She knew he would want more, having tasted this.

And Marrika would see to it that he got it.

"Vengeance is placated," said Kannil, his voice trembling. "He has blessed this mission, this woman. Let us calm ourselves and then break bread together, sealing the pact that we have made!"

Those assembled bowed their heads, forcing their breathing to slow, their pulses to calm. Kannil opened the circle and brought out bread and wine, which was gleefully accepted. No one gave a second thought to the body of the councilman's daughter who lay across the bloody altar.

"Lady Raven," said Khem, seating himself next to her as Marrika finished her first glass of wine, "you have called great power here tonight."

Her eyes narrowed. "Aye," she agreed. "And what is your point, Hound?"

He glanced about quickly, then spoke in low tones. "Your ally is a god, but sometimes, one needs human allies as well. Would you like an ally, Lady Raven—one of the most powerful men in all of Verold?"

Her heart skipped a beat. "Go on."

The King's word is law.

—traditional motto of Mhar

*All decisions must be approved by the governing body
of the council of Mhar, in consultation with His Majesty.*

—Charter of Governance, 1183

CHAPTER NINE

Deveren was about as angry as he had ever been in his
life. He slammed down the little hunting cup almost hard
enough to shatter the ceramic beast. "'The Fox gives Fox a
taste quite fine, /When out of his head you drink your
wine,'" he quoted through clenched teeth. "The first theft."

The thieves watched, sitting in a semicircle in Rabbit's
back room, their eyes round. Rarely had they seen Deveren
this agitated.

"'The hounds will chase, the hounds will tear/Your
flesh, unless their teeth you bear.'" Out of the sack came
three studded collars, which Deveren tossed on the floor
next to the cup. "Behold the 'teeth' of Vandaris's hounds.
And finally, the literal brush of Vandaris's 'Vixen'—the
final theft."

He did not drop this one, but held it clenched in his hand.

His hazel eyes scanned the crowd, searching for some twitch, some nervous tic, anything that would betray the thieves seated here as kidnappers and would-be murderers. He prayed he wouldn't find it. Damir had been certain that one of the thieves had been responsible for Lorinda's abduction—certain, as far as Deveren was concerned, without a shred of proof.

"Is there any among you who doubts that I have passed the test—that I am in truth your leader?"

There was silence for a long moment and then, unexpectedly, someone in the back began to clap. Others joined in until the sound rang through the little room. Discomfited, Deveren raised his hands, trying to quiet the crowd.

"Hurrah for Leader Fox!"

"Three Grand Thefts. We didn't think you'd do it!"

"Tell us, Fox, how did you manage them?"

"That's another story for another day," protested Deveren. He glanced over at Pedric worriedly.

Pedric was not doing well. Under Vervain's ministrations he had physically healed. Even the dreadful swelling of his nose was starting to go down now. But the Blesser could not heal Pedric's inner wounds. Only the safe return of Lorinda would do that, and with each hour that passed, Deveren grew less and less hopeful that such a thing would occur.

Feeling his friend's gaze upon him, Pedric raised his eyes. There was very little about him now that bespoke the debonair rake he used to be. He had not changed clothing since the incident two nights ago, nor had he bathed. His thick brown hair was wild and his face was pale, save for the huge bruises that encircled his eyes, the result of lack of sleep and the broken, healing nose. It was almost only by sheer force of will that Deveren had managed to get him to choke down some food. As soon as Vervain pronounced him well enough to rise, Pedric had gone to the Council Seat. Deveren presumed he was scouring the dark back streets and unsavory areas in search of the girl. But such

searches, including those performed by the city guards, had
yielded nothing.

Tonight, Healsdae, had been the first time Deveren had
been able to gather his thieves. He cleared his throat, and
with a silent prayer that they would listen, he began.

"This is my first instruction to you as your leader, and I
know it's not what you're expecting. I've got no plans for a
heist, no theories on where the biggest crowds will be for
pickpocketing come the Midsummer Festival. I'm asking—
telling—you to keep your eyes and ears open for news.

"Lisdae evening, Pedric here was viciously attacked and
his lady abducted from the maze in the Garden. The incident occurred sometime between Death's hour and Vengeance's hour. Pedric was set upon from behind and is
unable to identify his attackers. The woman who was abducted—" and here Deveren took a deep breath, "—was
Lorinda Vandaris, only child of the Head Councilman. No
doubt, you've heard about this before now. I can't imagine
that any of you could have missed the redoubling of security that's been going on the two days."

Murmurs of alarmed surprise greeted Deveren's statement. They had heard about the abduction, but clearly had
no idea that young Pedric, one of their own, had been so intimately involved. All of the faces showed concern; but to
Deveren's surprise and pleasure, some showed sympathy.

He attempted to lighten the mood a little. "Now, I'm certain that you'd hesitate to go to Vandaris or Jaranis with
any information." He smiled a little at the chuckling that
ensued. "Can't say that I'd blame you. But you—any of
you—can come to me if you've heard anything—anything
at all. Even," he added pointedly, "if it's bad news." Bear
had been notorious for blaming the messenger of bad tidings. Deveren was wise enough to realize that if he wanted
to use his thieves as an information-gathering system, he
needed to establish himself as an understanding leader.
Who would deliver bad tidings if a beating was certain to
ensue?

"To prove what I say," he continued, "I'm offering a reward to whoever can give me information leading to recovering Lorinda." He glanced at Pedric again, then went on. "Alive . . . or dead. A higher reward if she's alive."

"No one will be troubled by the law," said Pedric unexpectedly. "There will be no repercussions. And I'll add my purse to whatever Deveren's offering. Please," and his voice cracked ever so slightly, "help me to find her."

Deveren continued, giving a detailed account of what had happened that night and Lorinda's physical appearance. When he had finished, he listened to various comments and questions, and when all business had been attended to, the meeting degenerated into a social swirl.

He expected the worst when Marrika separated herself from Freylis and walked over to Pedric. The younger man, too, tensed. Marrika was a volatile woman. What was she up to?

She glanced over at Deveren, then addressed Pedric. "I'm sorry to hear of your loss," she said.

A muscle tightened in Pedric's jaw. "I'm sure you are," he said in a tone that indicated precisely the opposite.

"You don't believe me. I admit I was angry when we parted, but I certainly wouldn't be cruel enough to wish something like this on you." She touched his shoulder gently. "I *am* sorry," she repeated.

Pedric gazed into her eyes, then smiled slightly. "Thank you," he said. She squeezed his shoulder and walked away, slipping into Freylis's arms for a quick embrace before settling into her usual corner, taking out her carving knife, and beginning to work on a chunk of whalebone.

"Seems we may have judged Raven a touch harshly," said Deveren softly to Pedric. The youth shrugged.

"It doesn't matter. All that matters is finding Lorinda." He took a deep breath, seemed to rouse himself, and asked, "Why didn't you mention the attack on your life? Someone might have come forward with information."

Deveren laughed, a sound that had no humor in it. "With

this group—at least the way they are now—that would only be putting ideas in their heads. The ones who tried it will probably try it again. And the ones that didn't might think it would be a grand idea. No, I'll just keep my eyes and ears open."

"And hire a taster," said Pedric, with a trace of his old humor.

Deveren grinned.

The breeze was high on HoDesdae, but the weather was otherwise mild. Hair, capes, dresses, and hats were tousled by the wind but all the celebrants were in good humor. After all, today was a citywide holiday in Ilantha.

The death of the former Blesser of Love had been swift and unexpected. She was only in her forties, far too young, one might think, to have had a killing seizure that stopped her heart within minutes.The Healer who had been summoned had been able to do nothing, and she had died, ironically, on Healsdae. Fortunately, the Healer assured the grieving community, the Blesser's death had been quick and painless.

The city was plunged into mourning for a full day. But with the dawning of HoDesdae, mourning was cast aside. It was a new beginning, with a new Blesser of the best-loved goddess in Verold. The revelers who thronged the winding streets of the port city wore their most festive colors; the shopkeepers were quick to come up with items to commemorate the day, and taverns were crowded.

Probably the most pleased celebrant was the young king. He wondered if the gods would be angry at him for being so happy that one of their Blessers had died, but the nature of this ceremony demanded that he be present. And that got him out of Seacliff, and out, for a few brief moments, from under the thumb of Bhakir.

Oh, certainly the guards were still there, but there was at least the illusion of freedom as young King Castyll rode on his fine mount at the side of the youthful Tender. On such occasions, when the king was residing in that particular city, tradition demanded that he be the escort of the Blesser-to-be as he or she rode the "Long Mile" from the Holy House to the center of town. Sometimes it was, of course, longer than a mile; sometimes it was only a few feet. Nobody cared. The Long Mile it was called, and the Long Mile it would remain.

Castyll and his entourage, including Bhakir, had arrived at the door of Love's temple at dawn. A throng of citizens had followed, eager to witness the entire ceremony from beginning to end. Adara, the Tender who had been appointed to succeed the late Blesser, appeared at the door. Castyll, even in the midst of dark thoughts and longing for his freedom, couldn't help but notice how young and vulnerable she looked. She was only fourteen, younger even than he. But like him, Adara carried herself well, and the enormous responsibilities that came hand in hand with being the Blesser of Love in such a large city did not seem to rest awkwardly on her narrow shoulders.

Her hair was braided with wildflowers, and she wore not the light blue robe of a Blesser, but the simple white garment that marked her, for the moment, as a mere Tender. Her feet were bare, used to walking inside the Holy House and through Love's garden without protection.

She was not beautiful, but her smile was. He proffered his arm and Adara took it, letting him escort her to the unsaddled mare which awaited her. She mounted clumsily and her grip on the horse's mane was white-knuckled, but her face betrayed nothing of her fear. Castyll's heart went out to her. She was awfully young to have had this thrust upon her. But then, so had he been. His sympathy soured into a stab of self-pity as he thought that at least Adara's predecessor had died a natural death. The late Blesser of Love had not been helped along toward her meeting with the Dark Lady by a scheming counselor.

They did not speak overmuch. It would have been hard to chat pleasantly regardless, for the cries of the happy crowd drowned out any but the most full-throated declarations. Castyll tried to reassure the girl with smiles, and Adara returned them nervously.

At last the Long Mile was done. Castyll dismounted easily and reached to help the Tender slide down. She dug her fingers into his shoulders as she dismounted, and he felt her tremble. He squeezed her arm reassuringly, then the two of them, king and the god's earthly representative, walked forward to meet the highest-ranking Blesser of Love in Mhar.

All Blessers had a Protector or Protectress of their order, selected by a council of Blessers chosen at random throughout the whole country. The council traveled through the land, visiting every city, town, every castle and farmstead, meeting all the Blessers and basing their decision on these meetings and on personal testimony. It was as free from political maneuvering as such things could be—which is to say, not quite entirely free. Once chosen, the Protectress would sever all personal ties to her friends, family, and home. She would even be stripped of her name, henceforth be known only by her title. Her duties were many and varied, but the induction of new Blessers certainly was among the happiest.

Mhar's Protectress of Love was rail-thin, but stood straight as the young king, perhaps even straighter. Her long hair, gray as slate, hung unbound, strands dancing in the playful wind, and despite the solemnity of the occasion there was warmth in the old woman's eyes and seamed face. Her garb was a rich, bright blue and she wore a belt of golden chain. Standing beside her was Love's chosen animal—a small, skittish fawn. Encircling the little beast's throat was a golden chain that matched the Protectress's. A Tender not much older than Adara held the nervous creature in check, speaking to it softly and patting its smooth, dappled coat.

"Welcome, Adara, Tender of Love," said the Protectress in a husky voice that nonetheless carried well. "You come before Love's Protectress a girl, but you shall depart a woman."

Castyll watched the initiation along with the others, but his thoughts were not on the sacred rite he witnessed. He was thinking about the speech tucked into his belt; the speech that he was to give to all within earshot after young Adara became a full Blesser; the speech that he, Castyll, had not penned one single word of. Every syllable was Bhakir's, pushing forward the counselor's treasonous plans. In that document was amnesty for pirates, official countenancing of replacing good men with evil. It shook to the foundation everything Shahil had worked for—everything he had hoped that his son would carry on in his stead.

There was another speech—in Castyll's mind. He mentally reviewed it while the young Tender was undressed, bathed, anointed with oils, and reclad in the light blue robe of a fully vested Blesser. Her body was tanned and firm, only just beginning to fill out with womanly curves. There was little salaciousness in observing Adara nude. Everyone present knew that this was a deep ritual, and the majority behaved accordingly. The sight of the young Blesser's body made Castyll think only of Cimarys, and he wondered briefly what the young Princess of Byrn would look like standing naked in the sunshine.

The thought produced an instant physical reaction, and Castyll hastily returned his wandering thoughts to more pressing—even deadly—matters.

It was over. Laughing and crying, the new Blesser embraced the Protectress, then knelt to put her arms around the young deer. It bleated in protest and skipped backward, and all assembled laughed. Adara, Blesser of Love, rose and turned to Castyll, her eyes shining, with an odd mixture of pride and apprehension on her plain face.

"King Castyll," she began, stepping forward boldly, as was her right now to do—the Blessers obeyed the king, but being representatives of the gods, walked on almost equal footing with their liege—until she was only a foot or so away from him. "I am now a fully vested Blesser of Love. I invite you, before all assembled, to be the first to come to me to be taught in the ways of Love, so that you might better honor the goddess."

Castyll was momentarily taken aback, but almost at once he realized he should have expected this. Young men, especially the sons of nobles or others of high regard, were sometimes invited to lie with the Blesser of Love their first time. She would teach them how to honor the goddess through the movements of their bodies, in the sacred act of lovemaking. The son of the king certainly would have been asked. Shahil ought to have been the one to escort his son to the temple for this passage into manhood; instead, the boy had become a man not through the passion of a woman, but through the weight of an invisible crown upon his dark head.

But one thing or another had delayed the rite of passage, and now Castyll would go as a man to the temple of Love. Castyll did not for an instant think this was betraying the sincere love he bore Cimarys; and knew that she would not regard it so. The excitement that flooded him at the offer of this very young Blesser of Love was not sexual. Rather, he knew that, for one full night, he would not be under the eye of the guards. And one night would be enough to escape.

He bowed low. "Lady, you honor me. I shall come to Love's temple, and be taught in the ways of love." Adara's face shone with joy, and blushed with nervousness. A huge roar went up from the crowd, for the day that the king rode to Love's temple would be yet another holiday. Ilantha had not recently seen such happy times.

Castyll sobered somewhat as he realized what was next in the ceremony. Now it was time for him to take center stage, to step forward, and spread Bhakir's poison throughout the happy crowd.

He moved toward the raised dias, carrying the rolled-up parchment in his right hand. Then, deliberately, he caught the toes of his right foot behind his left and stumbled forward. To catch himself, the young king flung his arms wide, hurling the vile speech outward. His brief, whispered prayer was answered. The wind, as if it were a live thing sensing a new playpretty, caught the parchment and lifted it up high above the heads of the onlookers.

Feigning distress, Castyll cried, "My speech!" He kept his smile small and secret at the sight of the guards chasing after the dancing parchment as it dipped and skittered just out of their reach. Finally, a stronger gust than the others caught the four pages and bore them up high, till they were lost from sight.

"Oh, no!" cried Castyll in mock horror. "I—well, my people, you will now have the opportunity to see your king speak unrehearsed. I ask your indulgence." He gave a winning smile, and the crowd chuckled appreciatively. Castyll felt Bhakir's gaze boring holes into him, but he did not meet the counselor's eyes. He was doing it. The words he spoke today would be listened to by travelers, who would take the news to their own towns. Many of those here today were sailors; Castyll knew that this speech would reach even Byrn.

"I shall speak, then, from the heart," he began, "which is more appropriate to such an occasion than carefully scripted speeches. Today we are here to celebrate the goddess Love and those who serve her. We all serve her, whenever we think a good thought about our neighbor. We serve when we clothe and feed the poor. We serve when we treat our families with gentle words and a soft hand. And we serve," he said, watching the crowd's reaction intently, "when we take steps towards peaceful relations with other countries."

They were listening. Bhakir's face was outwardly composed, but Castyll knew that the counselor was furious. He continued.

"We have long had good relations with our neighbor to the north, Byrn. Many of us have friends or family there. And trade, particularly between Ilantha and Braedon, has never been better." He smiled, and said in a confiding tone, "I in particular have great need of Love's blessing, for as you all know, I am betrothed to Byrn's princess, the fair Cimarys. And dear Lady Adara, new Blesser, perhaps you will even preside over our vows soon!"

This, as he had hoped, produced an enthusiastic round of applause. Few things pleased the common folk better than tales of young royals in love.

"Therefore, I take this opportunity to officially state that I, and I hope all my people, are at peace with our neighbors. We fear no invasion, no threat to our wives or children. Trade is sound, and all make honest profits. Byrn is not populated with the cold elves, nor the evil Ghil—it is home to people just like us. And on this day of changes, the only change I advocate is that we move forward in the spirit of Love, in the spirit of understanding and harmony. You are my people, and I swear to you now—I shall always strive to protect and nurture you, just as the beloved goddess sustains us with her kindness. Thank you."

The applause was thunderous. Castyll grinned from ear to ear, but the grin faded as the guards and Bhakir swept up to usher him away from the scene of celebration. Bhakir, too, smiled and waved at the throng, but his grin reminded Castyll of the predatory smile of a mountain cat.

"What in the Nightlands were you doing?" growled Bhakir through his grimace of a smile.

Castyll feigned innocence. "I lost my speech, you saw what—"

"I saw you *drop* the speech, you little . . ." Bhakir composed himself with an effort. The guards now had closed in around the young king, and though he still stood taller than most of them they formed an effective barrier between him and the crowd. "Forgive me, Majesty. I am merely distressed that your . . . lack of grace at such a crucial moment resulted in such a poor speech. You mentioned none of the things we discussed."

Triumph flared in the youth. Bhakir wasn't ready—yet—to voice his true thoughts in front of the guards. Perhaps some of them were still loyal to the young king, after all. No, he hadn't mentioned the "things we discussed." Not one cursed word. "I'm sorry, Bhakir—I got flustered," Castyll lied. "I tried to think of something appropriate. Something to do with love."

"You said nothing of the appointment of Lord Zhael's appointment as Commander of the Navy," snapped Bhakir. "Nor did you mention the amnesty we have granted Captain Porbrough and his compatriots. Why didn't you remember to do *that* when you were speaking so eloquently of love and good relationships? Castyll, this is a seaport. If you don't inform people of changes in the navy immediately, they won't be as quick to accept them!"

Which was, of course, exactly what Castyll wanted. He hung his head, lest Bhakir see the rebellion in the dark Derlian eyes. "I'm sorry. I guess it was because I hadn't done either of those things myself that they just—I don't know—slipped my mind."

Bhakir tensed, and Castyll realized that he had perhaps gone too far. It was a dangerous, delicate game he and Bhakir played with one another. The moment either of them clearly admitted to the other that Castyll was a prisoner, the game would be over. Castyll knew that both stood to lose should that happen. Bhakir would lose an important figurehead, a mouthpiece beyond compare. Castyll was beloved by his people; Bhakir would have a much more difficult time putting his plans into effect without the young king's apparent approval. And Castyll—well, he'd lose what little semblance of freedom he had and, sooner rather than later, he'd lose his life.

His breath caught in his throat. He could not meet Bhakir's eyes.

"Perhaps then, my young majesty," purred Bhakir, "it is time to get you more directly involved."

Inwardly, Castyll shrank back. Bhakir's words were a threat—of closer guard, of harder, more direct manipulation. He began to wonder if, today, all he had done was to delay the inevitable. Suddenly the beauty had gone out of the day, as the young king of Mhar, ostensibly the most powerful man in the land, trudged with his armed escort back toward his prison.

*But take care when working with old wood, for if you
bend it too far, it will break.*

—Advice from master carpenter to apprentice

CHAPTER TEN

Castle Seacliff had been designed with escape from siege
in mind. The space below the castle was riddled with tunnels and little rooms where the royal family could be hidden—and where their enemies could be imprisoned. As he
descended into one of these dungeons, Bhakir's refrain was
simple: *At least the little bastard has no magic.*

That thought was the only thing that comforted him after
Castyll's outrageous performance earlier in the day. It had
looked like an accident, and admittedly Castyll couldn't
have counted that the wind would be so anxious to snatch
up a royal counselor's speech. But it was just too convenient. Bhakir suspected that if the warm summer zephyr
hadn't been so obliging, the boy would have ignored the
speech and done exactly what he had ended up doing. He'd
have come up with some excuse.

Castyll knew he was a prisoner, or at least suspected as much. Whatever else Shahil might have been, the late king of Mhar had not been stupid. Nor was his son, though Bhakir had hoped that simply because of his youth Castyll might be more pliable.

But today he had seen calculation in the boy's actions. He was starting to push, to test the limits, and soon he would become too hard to control.

Puffing with even the simple exertion of walking downstairs, Bhakir narrowed his eyes. But damn it, he still needed Castyll. The people's reaction to the king's speech today proved that. He'd just have to step up security around the youth, that was all there was to it. After Love's Blesser, ugly little thing, had had her way with him, it would be Castyll whom Bhakir would be visiting now, as well as Jemma. Enough of coddling the boy. Time to put him in the dungeon as the prisoner he was.

"Peace with Byrn," he muttered. "Pieces of Byrn, is more like it." The innocent-sounding speech had set Bhakir back several days. He'd have to contrive another official occasion, where Castyll could actually deliver the prepared speech.

Bhakir reached the foot of the stairs and paused to lean up against the cold stone wall, catching his breath. A soft moaning, emanating from the torture room, was sweet to Bhakir's ears. The two guards stationed outside the cell shrewdly averted their eyes from the sight of their master appearing less than perfect. When his breathing had slowed, Bhakir spoke to them.

"Any progress?" he asked.

They snapped to attention. "We believe so, sir. She broke down and begged for us to stop for the first time yesterday. You can hear her now."

"Indeed I do. That is good news. But has she agreed to cooperate?"

"No sir."

"Ah, well, that is unfortunate, but I'm sure it can be remedied. I've saved something special for her."

It had been ten days since he had first ordered her imprisoned; six days since the torture had begun. They had tried almost everything they could think of that would not injure her hands or her speech. Such delicacy in selection ruled out some of Bhakir's favorite tortures, such as the strappado. Hoisting Jemma up by her hands, bound behind her back, and then letting her drop would dislocate her shoulders, thus making arm movements difficult. And the water torture was perforce eliminated as an option as well. Forcing her to swallow a long length of rag and then yanking it back up—well, that could seriously injure her throat.

He nodded to the guards, and they opened the door. Bhakir swept inside. Over at the table, the torturer was busily cleaning bits of the old woman's flesh out of the clogged cat-o'-nine-tails. Jemma, barely recognizable, lay on the floor. She was bound hand and foot and was curled up in a tight ball, whimpering. Welts covered almost every inch of her body. If Bhakir hadn't known better, he'd have thought that the torturer had sliced her up with a knife.

The torturer rose immediately. Grandly, Bhakir waved him back, indicating he should finish his task. He strode over to the weeping heap that had once been a proud woman and kicked her soundly at the base of her spine.

Jemma screamed and flailed. Bhakir waited calmly for her cries to subside, then said, "All you need to do is cooperate. It's not that much to ask."

An incoherent mumbling was his response. He sighed. "This isn't working."

The torturer, a bulky man stripped to the waist, nodded. Sweat from his exertions gleamed on his torso. "I only hope my lord finds no fault with the methods."

"Good heavens, you've more than proved yourself on past occasions, Garith," Bhakir hastened to reassure him. "You're limited in this one, unfortunately. I can't give you the free rein to which you are accustomed. No, we just have to think of something else."

"How about a variation of pressing?" volunteered Garith, as they both stood gazing at the whimpering, bloody woman. Pressing was a particularly effective form of coercion. Victims were tied faceup and arched upwards, and one by one, stones were placed on their torso, eventually crushing them. "She has muttered about her joints. Anything I've done to them has produced very positive results. It would be very painful, but not necessarily destructive."

Bhakir nodded slowly. "I see what you mean. It sounds like a good suggestion. Here, let me assist you."

Jemma lifted her head as they approached, sensing a progression in her torment, and cried out, "Nay, my lords, have mercy! I am an old woman! Please!"

"Jemma," said Bhakir in a tired, firm voice, as if he were speaking to an errant child, "I have told you what you need to do if you wish to stop this. I'd much rather you cooperate. Garith's talents are very costly." The two men exchanged a chuckle.

The old Healer closed her eyes, sinking into herself. She fell silent.

Bhakir sighed. "As you wish, old woman." Garith jerked her into an upright seated position. She hissed through her teeth as the caked-over welts began to bleed anew, and shrieked as they pushed her bound ankles into her crotch. Working swiftly, Garith tied a short length of rope between ankles and wrists, so that her feet would not slip away from her body.

Wordlessly, the two men began putting stones on the woman's thin legs, forcing them down to the floor. At this, Jemma screamed aloud, a terrible, rasping cry of pure agony. The men exchanged hopeful glances and continued applying stones. Mercilessly, Jemma's thighs pressed toward the floor, tearing the ligaments that bound them to her hips and fanning the fire of her inflamed joints. She wailed constantly, seeming not even to draw breath.

"Will you do what I ask?" demanded Bhakir.

She opened her eyes. For a second, it was as though she didn't see him. "I Heal," was all she said.

Bhakir growled in angry frustration. Was the whole world trying to thwart him today? First Castyll, with his impromptu speeches and lies, and now this tiny, wasted woman with a body seemingly too frail to house her rebellious spirit. Unable to contain himself, he placed one booted foot on her knee and stamped down.

Her agony was rewarding. He turned to Garith. "The spider," he said shortly.

Garith frowned. "The injuries that causes are very severe," he reminded his lord. "She might not survive them. I suggest sending her back to her cell, letting her stiffen up in solitary confinement, and then resuming. That often works better than straight torture. Something about having the time to think clearheaded about what's to come often breaks them."

He spoke calmly, with the authority of a man who knew what he was talking about. Bhakir was certain he did.

"But I am running out of time," he replied. "I need her help soon. The boy will before long be of no use, and unless I have something special—" he broke off. He had the utmost confidence in Garith's trustworthiness. The two men had worked together in this capacity for years, in secret, and Garith had never yet betrayed him. But what Bhakir was planning was of great import, and he wished to trust no one, not even his torturer, with all of the facts.

"I am running out of time," he repeated. "She must cooperate soon or she is of no use to me."

Garith bowed. "You are my lord and commander, and I am sworn to obey you. But I think we might kill her."

"I'm willing to take the risk," snapped Bhakir. "Something about this particular method seems to break women swiftly."

"That is true enough," conceded Garith. "Many who

can withstand abuse to other parts of the body cannot deal with targeted attacks on their sex."

Bhakir suddenly had a dreadful mental picture of his maleness trapped within a cold, sharp-toothed device, and he suppressed a shudder. He know that he would talk in such a situation. He could only hope that Jemma would, too.

"Proceed," he said, banishing the mental image.

"As you will, my lord." Reluctantly, the torturer went to the stone wall and yanked the coverings off a previously unrevealed instrument. It appeared simple enough; nothing more than a series of bars, eight in all, affixed vertically to the wall with claws running along their lengths. Bhakir reached and yanked Jemma to her feet. She crumpled, her broken legs unable to support her, and he held her with one strong arm about her waist. With the other, he seized a clump of gray hair and yanked her head back, forcing her gaze upon the metal bars.

"This is the spider," he hissed in her ear. "This won't hurt your hands or your tongue, Healer. But this is specially designed for your sex. We'll hoist you and drag you along those eight claws. You are an old woman, but you are a woman still, and though your breasts have long since dried, I would think you'd still like to keep them intact."

Jemma did not respond. Bhakir tasted despair. Suppose the torture had unhinged her mind? He might as well toss her in the ocean right now, for all the good she would do him. He swore violently and began to half drag, half carry the injured old woman toward the torture instrument.

Garith waited, and together they lifted her, brought her unresisting, aged body up, placed her in the correct position. Cold metal came into contact with warm flesh.

Suddenly the limp body sprang to life. Jemma began to writhe and scream. "Mercy, lord! *Mercy!*"

Bhakir, caught up in his anger, almost missed the opportunity he had been waiting for. It was Garith who paused and said, "Milord, I haven't seen her like this. Ask her again."

Startled, Bhakir paused. Jemma's body was inches away from mutilation. "You wish me to stop?"

Incoherent with fear and pain, Jemma only nodded.

"Will you do as I ask? Will you help me?"

Her head lolled back, resembling a heavy blossom on a delicate stalk. Her eyes fixed on his. "One last time," she breathed, "I beg you, don't ask this of me."

Irritation roiled in Bhakir's brain, and he lifted her toward the spider again. "I care not if your withered old teats are shredded. Do you?"

She twisted in his grasp. "No, lord, no! I—gods save me!—I will do what you want, only spare me this!"

At once Garith took over, as professional now in his compassion as he was in his torture. He swung the broken, naked body into his arms and carried her gently to a corner, where he wrapped her in blankets that were there for just such an occasion.

"There, you see, Jemma?" he said gently, using her name for the first time. "All you had to do was cooperate." He glanced over at the counselor. "Tell the guards to bring hot, nourishing food, wine, and clothes suitable for her," he told Bhakir. "Give me a few hours to tend her hurts and she will do as you ask."

Bhakir wasn't so sure. He stalked over to the Healer and stared down at her. Her eyes were squeezed shut, and tears escaped from beneath her closed lids. They were not the strained sobs of a panicked, pain-filled prisoner. These were quiet tears, tears that mourned, not protested.

"The spider waits, if you change your mind," he told her.

She nodded, her eyes still closed. "Aye, lord, I know. I will not." Her voice was dead, empty, devoid of emotion. Her tongue crept out to lick dry lips. At the gesture, Garith was quick to ladle some water into her mouth. She gulped thirstily, then continued. "Listen . . . you must get me . . . these materials."

* * *

Bhakir could barely restrain himself. For the first time, he could truly see his plan coming together. He'd been able to maneuver here and there, such as working on Zhael's behalf and negotiating the treaty with Captain Cutter; and, of course, keeping a sharp eye and heavy hand on the troublesome king. But those were each separate pieces of a vast, complicated puzzle. Now, finally, Jemma was going to give him the tool to hamstring his enemies and emerge triumphant.

Garith had asked for a Healer, but Bhakir had deemed it too great a risk. The torturer would have to content himself with what healing he himself knew. Still, when Bhakir returned a few hours later bearing all the strange and mysterious items Jemma had requested, he was surprised at the change in the old woman.

She had been transferred to another, more comfortable cell, though this one was still subject to the dampness and vermin that were common to all the prison cells. But at least there was a small brazier now to cut the cold, and a bed that was adequate if not much more. Jemma was dressed and her wounds tended. She sat erect on the bed, her useless lower extremities covered with the blankets, and regarded Bhakir steadily as the guard opened the door to let him enter. The counselor realized with a start that if he had set out to break Jemma's spirit, he had failed. It was of no matter, he told himself; as long as she was willing to cooperate, she could keep her precious dignity.

"I have the items you requested," he said without preamble, indicating the bag he carried.

"You will have to be my assistant," she said with equal coolness. "Your torturer left me my hands and voice, but neither you nor he remembered that I must be able to walk to cast a circle."

Bhakir broke out in a cold sweat. Jemma was about to embark on a ritual that, he of all people know, called upon some of the darkest, most evil powers in existence. He had planned to reap the fruits of her labor, not assist her—and thus perhaps be subjected to danger. He licked thick lips with a moist tongue.

"I will assist where I can, but this is your ritual, Blesser."

Now she cringed, as if with his words he had hurt her as badly as Garith had with his instruments. "Do not call me by that title," she said. "By what I am about to do I am proving myself no Blesser—nor a Healer. I am Jemma. That was the name given me, and that is all I have left now. As for the limits of your assistance," and fire seemed to return to her, "it would be meet and right for you to suffer for the evil thing you demand. But I accept that this is my burden, my debt to the gods for the blasphemy I have agreed to perform."

Bhakir was, for once, at a loss for words. Instead, he plopped the bag on the straw and began emptying it. Though he was confused by the strange assortment Jemma had instructed he obtain, he had managed to get, through a variety of means, every item on her list. A map of Byrn. A sharp knife. A stoppered jug full of milk. A handful of wheat. A small, but fresh, cut of raw meat. A small ceramic bowl. A sack of ground bone powder. And an amazing amount of herbs and other bizarre items: hemlock, nightshade, bat's blood, sheep's fat, monk's hood, lily of the valley, soot, mugwort. A mortar and pestle, presumably for grinding the ingredients.

Jemma watched him in silence. At last she spoke. "You are mad," she said in a conversational tone, "to think the gods will let you curse an entire country of innocents."

Bhakir spared her a sharp glance. "I would not advise trying to undercut your efforts in this curse," he replied. "My mercy will depend on how well I am satisfied with what you produce."

"Then the gods save us all," she said softly. "Clear a space in the center of the floor. Place all the items inside it, and then set me down there."

He did as she instructed, pushing the scattered straw to

the sides of the room, then moving the strange items to the center. Even this little exertion was difficult for the obese man, and he was panting by the time he lumbered over to pick up Jemma. Fortunately, she was as light as a pile of twigs. Gently he set her down, then stood back. Sweat gleamed on his high forehead.

"Take the bowl and place some hot coals from the brazier inside it, along with a little straw to keep the flame alive." He obeyed, handing her the warm container. Carefully she set it aside, then reached for the herbs and other items. One by one they went into the pestle. She lifted her head. He stood ready to jump to her next command, excited by the fact that victory was so close at hand.

"Take the bone powder and make a circle, enclosing us both within."

He laughed at that. "I will make the circle, Healer, but I will seal it from the *outside*."

Her eyes narrowed. "What a coward you are, Bhakir."

"Ah, but a victorious coward, thanks to your efforts on my behalf." This close, he had no desire to be angry with the woman. She was, after all, doing his bidding, and if she tossed a few barbed comments his way, what did it hurt him?

"When Lady Death's spirit wolves come for you, I hope they tear your fat body to pieces." The hate in her voice gave him pause, but only for an instant. Holding the bag open with one hand, he spread the bone powder with the other, walking in a circle as Jemma worked to combine all her ingredients into a thick, greasy paste. He closed the circle, then sat on the bed, safely away, watching. Bhakir heard a skittering sound beneath him—the rats that so often found their way into the cells. Reconsidering his position, he drew both feet up onto the bed.

Jemma muttered to herself as she prepared the ointment, moving her long, thin fingers in complex patterns over the bowl. Then, using the two fingers of her right hand, she scooped out a small amount. Still chanting softly, she rubbed the ointment into the skin behind her ears, along her throat, under her arms and, grimacing, in the bends of her broken knees and useless feet. For several long moments she sat, her eyes closed, breathing slowly.

Bhakir became impatient. He was just about to speak when her eyes flew open. He gasped, instinctively drawing back.

The eyes that looked out of Jemma's face were not hers. They were completely black, with no trace of pupil or iris or white left. And they were as cold and unfeeling as that of a snake, or a rat. Her body began to convulse, and gibberish spilled out of her mouth.

Dear gods, Bhakir thought, *she's poisoned herself.* He watched, wondering what in the Nightlands he would do if this plan didn't work, when suddenly she seemed to recover herself.

Quickly, precisely, Jemma—or the thing that had assumed her body, Bhakir didn't know which—began to lay out the rest of the items. She spread out the map of Byrn, anchoring it with the containers of milk, wheat, water, and meat at each of the four corners.

Out of the corner of his eye, Bhakir caught movement in a dark corner of the room. His nerves strained taut, he whipped his head around, fearful that some sort of Nightlands Demon had been conjured by the Healer and now waited to pounce. But it was only a rat, scuttling about on some rodent business. Bhakir closed his eyes in relief, aware that his pulse was racing. He again turned his attention to Jemma.

"May the purity of water become as acid; may thirsts in Byrn never be quenched; what was used to cleanse, now pollutes."

As he watched, fascinated, Bhakir saw the clear water suddenly begin to cloud, as if Jemma had poured in ink from an unseen vessel. A shudder racked him. By the gods, it was happening!

"May the wholesomeness of meat become as filth; may

hungers in Byrn never be sated; what was used to nourish, now poisons."

She impaled the knife to its hilt in the fresh meat. The meat began to rot before Bhakir's eyes. Its stench floated out of the circle and threatened to make him vomit.

"May the goodness of the crops become as straw; may the fields be as barren as an old woman's womb; what was used to earn riches for the kingdom, now breaks its spirit."

As had the water and the meat, the wheat began to spoil. It dried out as if it had been suspended over hot coals, its berries blackened and useless. Bhakir could barely contain himself.

"May the breasts of the women of Byrn become as old bones; may the children perish, may the milk of human kindness sour; what was used to nurture a people, now betrays."

The jug of milk began to froth. Sour chunks floated to the surface as the milk spoiled from the power of Jemma's work. Now the old woman reached and gathered up the map, crumpling it in her hands.

"The land is cursed. The people are cursed. Their own natures shall rise up against them; their own land shall betray them. When this map has been destroyed, so shall the land it stands for be destroyed."

She moved to drop the crumpled parchment into the small, coal-filled bowl. Before she could do so, something small and black scuttled into the sacred circle, leaping gracefully over the lines of ground bone and landing squarely where it clearly wished to be—beside the putrid lump of rotting meat, upon which it began to feast.

Jemma drew back, then lashed out at the intrusive creature. Her hand sent it sprawling, knocking over the milk and water and scattering the kernels of wheat. Undaunted, it hissed at her and continued to feed.

Suddenly Jemma began to laugh—a robust, deep, rumbling sound that had no business issuing from the slender throat of an old woman. "So be it then!" she cried, and seized the rat. It squirmed and twisted in her grasp but she did not release it. Frantic, it bit her fingers; she ignored the bright blood that began to drip. Now the creature wanted nothing to do with the fouled meat and grains, but mercilessly Jemma crammed its writhing body into each item. "Be thou the vehicle!"

Suddenly the rat froze, its four little limbs and tail sticking straight out as if galvanized. Almost scornfully, Jemma released it, and it fell heavily onto the crumpled map of Byrn.

Bhakir watched, horrified. The curse had been interrupted by a foolish rat! His plans, his dreams . . . all for nothing. Clearly the rite had driven the old woman mad. He half rose, an angry protest on his lips, when what happened next ripped all thought of protest from him.

The rat began to grow.

As if inflated, it grew larger, until it was nearly the size of a cat, a small dog. Its coat moved like waving grain in a windswept field, moved as if it was crawling with an unholy life of its own. The color of the fur deepened from dark, dirty gray to an inky black. Its eyes brightened, as if suddenly filled with a glorious good health. It ceased struggling and sat up on its back legs. Bhakir was reminded of the one glimpse he had ever gotten of the Ghil, the dreadful, almost humanly intelligent creatures that were the plague of the northern parts of Byrn, as the unnaturally sized rat looked about, its ears flicking, its gaze observing.

Jemma gasped, then sagged, as if all the energy housed within her fragile frame had bled from her into the filthy beast. When she spoke, her voice was once again that of an old, tired woman.

"It is done. You have your curse. May you reap nothing but ill from it."

Bhakir stared, enthralled, his small, piggish gaze never leaving the rat, which now began to run the circumference of the circle. "But . . . the *rat*?"

"It has taken the curse into itself, and will spread it to all those it comes into contact with," explained Jemma heavily. She reached up a hand to brush her gray hair out of her face, and that hand trembled as if palsied. "It will take good and turn it to evil. It will take what is wholesome and turn it to poison." She watched the evil creature skittering about, its nose twitching. It reached out one clawed paw and tapped at the ground bone, then jumped back as if stung. Chittering angrily, it resumed its search for an exit.

Jemma began to rock back and forth, seemingly ignoring the agony that ripped through her broken lower body. "What was pleasure is pain; and bringing pain is pleasure." She closed her eyes and, incredibly, a smile spread across her face.

"Jemma," said Bhakir sharply, his eyes flicking from the rat to her. There was no response. "Jemma!"

She began to croon, and Bhakir recognized it as a child's lullaby. He could not rely on her further for aid.

That was just as well. He had what he wanted. He rose, and walked over to the rat. It fixed him with its beady eyes for an instant, then returned to its ceaseless pace.

Good. It was contained, for the moment, at least. Bhakir left, taking care that the guard locked the door securely behind him. He would need to acquire a special box to contain the rat; it wouldn't do for the curse that had cost him so much to escape. Jemma had used a sacred circle to contain the creature. Bhakir's mind was already working as he hastened up the stone staircase as fast as his enormous bulk would permit.

Behind him, in the locked door, Jemma did not notice his departure. She sat and rocked, singing softly to herself. But part of her still clung to sanity, and knew that there was only one way to escape this dark path upon which she had set her feet. She spared a glance toward the door, but did not see the guard looking in on her. Good. She said a silent prayer to Health, the cheerful, benevolent goddess whom she had just betrayed, and thanked the deity for causing Bhakir to make his exit so quickly. He would be pleased with what she had done. He would want her to do it again; use her goddess-given gifts to hurt and destroy other innocents somewhere else. But in his haste, he had overlooked one important thing—within the confines of the sacred circle, he had left Jemma with access to a knife.

Alone with the rat that bore the dark burden of a curse intended for an entire country, Jemma reached and gripped the dagger. Slowly, so as not to attract the beast's attention, she raised the dagger. She could do it; could kill the foul thing now, before it ever got to Byrn.

But as she moved, it stopped its movements. It sat up on its hind legs and fixed her with a steady, red gaze. It knew. Dear gods, it knew.

Crying out, she lunged for it, but the creature was quicker. Again she tried, and again it danced just out of reach. With her ruined legs, she would never be able to move fast enough to reach it, and it knew it. Safely out of reach, it seemed to taunt her.

She could not undo the damage she had done, but she could prevent further grief. It would work. Even if the guard saw what she had done, neither he nor anyone else would be able to violate the circle to stop her as long as she still lived. Still humming insanely, she now positioned the knife just below her ribs, its sharp point aimed for her heart. It would be swift. Time enough, then, for her to fall forward and press the knife deep inside.

Time enough for one old woman to die.

Many miles away, separated by land and by water, Vervain bolted wide awake. The tears were wet on her face, and her heart beat a rapid tattoo not of terror, but of apprehension.

"It has begun," whispered Vervain to the dark silence of her room.

When the rat is big and the cat is small,
then perhaps Puss won't come home.

—Byrnian proverb

CHAPTER ELEVEN

"Surely it is not much to ask," said Captain Porbrough, more widely known as Captain Cutter. The most hated pirate of the oceans seemed very little like a threat now as he sat across from Bhakir. He was not a big man, barely over five feet, and much softer and rounder than his reputation would have one believe. But he had eyes hard as flint, and a grim set to his mouth that promised he would brook no disobedience. Few survived unharmed who dared oppose him. His voice was nasal and grated on the ear, but Bhakir paid attention as if the man's voice was sweet as music.

He turned politely to his new head of the Mharian navy. "And what do you say, Commander?"

Lord Carroc Zhael, as tall and lean as Cutter was squat and soft, pursed his thin lips. He leaned back in his chair. "Well, we'd have to do it very carefully, that's for damned

sure," he said. "The safe harbors requested by Captain Porbrough—that's easy enough to manage. He's in the navy
now, with ships under his command. Every harbor is theo-
retically open to you, sir, and your men in His Majesty's
Navy."

"But the men who haven't joined—what of them?
They've served me well, and will continue to serve well,
provided that you grant my requests."

Those requests had been expected. The pirates that, till
now, had been plaguing the coasts of both Byrn and Mhar
had agreed to ally temporarily with Mhar in the attack that
Bhakir had been months planning. In exchange, they
wanted a few safe harbors in Mhar, and first pick of the
plundered city of Braedon. The former Bhakir had been
willing to grant, and Zhael seemed willing to agree as well.
But the latter . . . Bhakir took another sip of the fine Mharian wine as he watched the two men, so similar yet so different, interact.

"We could arrange a mass clemency, if your men agree
to serve the interests of the navy."

Cutter spluttered indignantly. "They are *pirates*, sir, *not*
members of His Majesty's . . ." Changing ideas in mid-
sentence, Cutter turned toward Bhakir. "Speaking of His
Majesty, when's the boy going to be brought into this? He
didn't seem too eager to sup with us this evening."

It was an understatement. The dinner with Castyll, Cutter, Zhael, and Bhakir had been little short of a disaster.
Castyll endured the event with poorly contained contempt
and hatred, often making subtle, biting comments that
Bhakir was able to counter only with the quickest wit. The
two men had been left seething by the time it was over and
Castyll "retired to his quarters."

"He won't be brought in at all," Bhakir replied sourly.
"I'm afraid Shahil's ghost still lingers, gods rot his soul."

Zhael frowned. "If he opposes us—"

"He won't," Bhakir assured the commander smoothly. "I
have him completely under my thumb, I promise you.

When I cease to be able to manipulate the youth as I choose—well, then, accidents do happen, don't they."

He raised his glass and, grinning, heard the two other men silently toasted Castyll's eventual—and no doubt tragic—demise. At that moment, one of the guards burst in. Bhakir frowned. "You were told not to disturb me," he said in a warning, rumbling voice.

The guard bowed obsequiously low. "Your great pardon, my lord, but there is news I felt you would wish to hear." When Bhakir did not answer, the man continued hesitantly, "News from Byrn, my lord."

At that, Bhakir rose. "Your pardon, gentlemen," he said to his guests, "but a good cook sees to all his dishes, lest any of them spoil for want of attention."

Zhael and Cutter chuckled appreciatively, and Cutter reached for the bottle. "You're pardoned, sir, but I suggest you return or else Zhael and I shall put an end to this delicious vintage you've provided."

"There's more where that came from," Bhakir replied gaily, and hastened out as quickly as he could without seeming to be in too much of a hurry.

In a small receiving room, one of Bhakir's finest spies paced back and forth, looking up anxiously as his lord entered. Bhakir waved the guard away, then greeted his servant.

"Khem, I had not expected to see you back so soon. I hope the news you bring me is good, not ill."

"Indeed it is, my lord," replied Khem, his small eyes gleaming. "I have found you a worthy group of allies."

"Excellent! Don't tell me you've convinced a councilman to turn traitor?"

Khem shook his head. Bhakir winced a little at the odor of the man. In his guise as a less savory member of Byrnian society, Khem was able to move unnoticed among the populace. It was clearly a fruitful venture, but unfortunate from a hygienic point of view.

"There is a splinter group of thieves in Braedon, sir. Normally this wouldn't be of much use, but their leader has allied with a Blesser of Vengeance."

Bhakir's eyebrow went up. The Blessers were powerful people indeed. "Go on."

"This Blesser," and Khem shook his head again, this time reaching for words. "He's not a well man, if you know what I mean."

"Sickly?"

"No, he's . . . I think he's but a step or two away from madness. He takes great pleasure in hurting things, sir. A few nights ago, we murdered a councilman's daughter for the leader's revenge. That Blesser—well, 'twas almost as pleasant for him as lying with the girl, sir."

"You weren't caught?"

"No, sir. This group—the leader's very smart, sir. Very intelligent. I spoke with her about supporting your cause—in a very roundabout way, of course—and she's very interested."

Bhakir could only gape. "Her? *She?*"

Khem looked uncomfortable, but did not flinch from his lord's displeasure. "Aye, milord. The leader of the splinter group is a woman. She hides behind a rough brute of a fellow, but not for much longer. The Blesser of Vengeance holds her in high regard—calls her Vengeance's Chosen. She's spent many years in Mhar herself, as a thief, so she is not a blind patriot to her country. I think we could use her. She has great goals, and I believe she is destined for bigger things than simple thievery."

Bhakir regarded Khem with a searching gaze. The man met his lord's eyes evenly. Khem was a good and trusted spy. He had proved his worth on more than one occasion, and Bhakir knew of no better judge of character. At length, the counselor sighed.

"Then you may go ahead and reveal what we have discussed. Ally yourself with this—what is her name?"

"Marrika."

"Marrika." A thought struck him, and Bhakir smiled.

"She is the Chosen of Vengeance, eh? Then I have a gift for the Chosen and her followers." He leaned forward conspiratorially. "A dark gift, for performing dark deeds. A gift that will bear the mark of the god himself. An appropriate gift for a group of thieves who would overthrow their betters. Khem, when you return to Byrn, you will take with you the first Mharian warrior to lay foot on Byrnian soil— my first soldier."

Khem's dark eyes were confused, but he knew better than to question. "As you wish, my lord."

Allika nestled in among her pile of rags and sighed contentedly. It had been a good day for eating. She'd stolen a whole loaf from the bakers, filched fruit from a market vendor, and been able to gather many pocketfuls of nuts when the crate had unexpectedly broken open as it was being loaded onto the pier.

It was too warm for a fire, and she lay back, cuddling Miss Lally. The early summer storms had come and gone, leaving the occasional wreckage of small vessels on the shoreline of Braedon like ruined skeletons. A few days ago, Allika had found one such boat, half buried in the sand, and had decided to make it her home for the time being. Every home she had was for the time being; it could change from day to day, sometimes hour to hour.

The dinghy, about eight feet long, lay on its side, providing a perfect shelter from the winds that blew in over the ocean. It was easy enough to find a few rags and blankets to further block what little chill reached the girl, and as for her personal possessions, they all fit in the small pouch that was constantly by her side. Now she huddled back, gazing out across the sea that was lit up with starlight and moonlight.

"Pretty, huh, Miss Lally?" she asked the doll.

"Mmm-hmmm!" agreed Miss Lally, using Allika's voice. The waves sounded a soothing song, and Allika felt her eyelids start to grow heavy. By force of will she kept them open. Today was Lisdae. Most ships left port on a Travsdae if they could help it; it was a "lucky" day for travel. It usually took three or four days for a ship to reach Braedon from the neighboring port of Ilantha; hence Lisdae usually meant a lot of activity on the dock.

Allika was a good pickpocket, but her primary coin was information. She was quiet, but she had sharp ears and eyes, and more often than not gleaned something by quietly slipping around the docks. So now, though she was warm and drowsy and her belly was stretched tight with good food for the first time in days, she forced herself to stay alert.

Her diligence was rewarded. A ship came into her view, and the moon was bright enough for her to determine that it flew the flag of the lion of Mhar.

As always, for an instant, the thought of the neighboring country hurt the girl. She had come from Mhar, and not so long ago, either; come to Braedon on just such a ship. The Death Ship, it would later be called. Allika's family—her parents and her two younger brothers—had decided to travel to Byrn. Allika's father was a strong man and hoped to find better employment as a soldier; Byrn needed men to fight the Ghil to the north. But there had come with Allika's family others, not so strong. The memory of one man, pale and sickly, stuck in the girl's mind.

Disease had broken out on the ship and spread like wildfire. Those afflicted had run high fevers and had terrible visions. Allika knew she would never forget the name: cloud sickness, so dubbed for the "clouding" of the mind. They had been forbidden to enter the port, lest the disease spread to Braedon.

For days the ship had sat in the waters, forbidden to dock, forbidden to leave. The food had run out. Allika had watched as, one by one, the dreadful sickness had claimed all the members of her family. Her only solace was Miss Lally, who never got sick.

When the Byrnians finally came, it was not to find and

help the survivors. It was to torch the ship and its victims—both living and dead. A terrified Allika, who had somehow been spared the ravages of the disease, had jumped overboard and swum to safety. Huddled on the sand, clutching her doll, she watched that night as the ship burned, lighting up the ocean with a dreadful crimson and golden glow. She had been the only survivor of the Death Ship, and as the long days turned into months and then years, became convinced that she was somehow "cursed." It was why she refused to live with any of the kinder-hearted thieves. She did not want ever again to bring sickness and death upon the heads of those whom she cared for ever again. Every time she saw a ship, for an instant, Allika saw not the true ship, but a burning ghost-ship as it sank slowly to the ocean depths; and she was reminded of how alone she and Miss Lally were—how alone they would always remain.

The ship from Mhar did not sail steadily up to the port, as was customary. This pricked Allika's curiosity. She crawled out from underneath her shelter, straightened, brushed sand from her buttocks and legs, and proceeded to make her way toward the port. She kept an eye on the ship as she walked through the soft sand, expertly sidestepping buried rocks, wood, and the occasional dead thing washed up from the depths.

"What do you think they're doing, Miss Lally?" she whispered to the doll. She held Miss Lally close, then placed the doll's mouth to her ear to hear the rag doll's "reply."

"Hmm, I don't know. But I bet we'll find out!"

She giggled a little to herself, then quieted as she drew closer to the pier and people. This late at night, no one noticed a small, silent shadow slip beneath the wooden pier.

Allika plopped down, sat Miss Lally in her lap, and waited with a patience that was almost unnatural in a child her age. But she had had to learn it, as she had had to learn many things over the last two and a half years, in order to survive.

After a time, another, softer sound was heard over the lull of the ocean. It was a rhythmic splashing noise, and Allika now saw that the big ship had dispatched a dinghy. It came closer, and the little girl could see that there were two men and some kind of crate in the smaller boat. At the same moment, she heard feet walking just above her. Sand, stirred up by the booted feet of the people above, sifted down to land in her short black hair. Silently, she tried to brush it out with one hand, listening intently.

"It's about damn time." The harsh, booming voice, loud even when its owner was trying to be quiet, was familiar to Allika. It was Wolf.

"Quiet," hissed another voice. That was Raven. Clearly, they were here to meet the little boat. Who was in it? What were they there for? Her curiosity now well and truly aroused, Allika got to her feet. Dragging Miss Lally behind her, she moved cautiously to the edge of the pier. If she moved just so, she could see up, catch a glimpse of her two fellow thieves.

The splashing was closer now. Allika strained to see who was in the boat, but the man saved her the effort.

"It's as I promised," came Hound's voice. Allika narrowed her eyes. What was Hound doing in a ship from Mhar? "A sign of good faith. Here—help me get it up onto the pier. And by all the gods, be careful. We don't want to drop it!"

There was much grunting and splashing as a box was heaved up from the boat onto the dock. Allika peered up, trying to catch a glimpse through the cracks in the boards. She stifled a grunt of pain as sand showered on her face, getting into her eyes. She knuckled the grit out of her watering eyes, listening hard.

Something made angry, chittering noises. Allika's curiosity grew. Some kind of animal? What in Verold was going on up there? The little girl followed the scraping and scratching sounds of the box being dragged the length of the pier. There was no more talking. Then, with a grunt,

Wolf and Hound hoisted the box and moved onto the main streets. Allika scrambled out from under the pier, losing her footing in the soft sand.

Keeping them in sight, she followed, a silent little shadow. The thieves were silent, wary. Hound and Raven kept glancing about furtively. Allika shrank back from the look on Raven's face, caught for a moment in the silvery moonlight. Something was happening to Raven. Allika had never liked her much to begin with, but now that dislike was growing, backed by a fear of something the child couldn't articulate. She licked dry lips, tasting sand, and knew that if Raven caught her spying on them like this, something very, *very* bad would happen to her.

Fortunately, now that they were entering the winding streets, there were more shadows in which the child could hide. She was able to move closer, get a good look at the crate, memorizing every feature. It seemed to be simple enough—a large wooden box. If it housed an animal, it would have to be something the size of a small dog. But why would Raven want to steal an animal?

For an instant, Allika's childish imagination concocted something exotic, like a baby mountain cat, or a fabulous creature out of legend. Perhaps this was the king's special pet, stolen in order to exact a bribe. And then another thought struck her, sobering her at once: The cries and noises could have issued from the throat of a kidnapped child—a child just like her.

Unconsciously Allika folded Miss Lally just a little bit tighter in her embrace.

The three thieves stopped over a sewer grate. Wolf and Hound carefully set down the box, handling it as if it contained something fragile and valuable. Then the two men set to work heaving aside the grate, while a clearly nervous Raven kept watch. Allika pressed her back against the stone wall of a building, hardly daring to breathe.

"This whole damn thing doesn't sit well with me," grumbled Wolf as he rose, panting.

"It doesn't have to," snapped Raven icily. "I am the Chosen. You serve me, Freylis, not the other way around."

Wolf growled. "Without your mad priest to protect you, bitch—" He moved forward menacingly. Allika whimpered, softly, her eyes going big with terror. She tried to make herself invisible, but could not tear her gaze from the scene.

Hound smoothly stepped between them. "Our fight is not with each other," he soothed. "Let's set the thing loose and be gone before we're discovered. If we waste time arguing, we may lose all!"

"Khem is right," said Raven. "Let's hurry up and get out of here."

Now the two men eased the crate forward, close to the opening of the sewer. Hound produced a metal tool of some sort and began to open the crate. At the final sound of tearing wood, the three leaped aside.

Nothing emerged.

Wolf peered down and swore. "Another damn box. What in the Nightlands is this, Khem, some kind of Mharian puzzle-game?"

"Security, I think," replied Hound absently. "I told you—this is quite the weapon."

"So you say. But how do we get the thing down there?" asked Wolf.

Hound flashed Wolf an angry look, but said nothing. Instead, he set to work disassembling the innocuous-looking crate. He tossed pieces of wood down into the sewer as they came loose. After a moment, Wolf joined in. Raven watched for a moment, then moved away. Tension radiated from her. She hunched her shoulders and tucked her hands under her arms as she glanced first one way, then the other.

"This is taking too much time," she hissed between clenched teeth. "I'm going to take a look around. You two are making enough noise to rouse the Nightlands King himself."

Wolf uttered a careless epithet, and Raven moved off. She sprinted down the alley, peered out, then returned.

Allika bit back a whimper. Now Raven was heading her way! Desperately the girl crouched back further, wishing there was a pile of refuse in which to hide. But there was nothing on this street, save the shadows themselves.

Raven moved closer with a steady pace.

"Got it," came Hound's voice laced with triumph.

Raven halted, wavered between continuing to investigate the length of the alley and returning to help her compatriots. If Raven moved another two yards down the street, Allika knew, she'd be close enough to penetrate the shadows that were Allika's only disguise.

After a moment that seemed like an eternity to the terrified girl, Raven whirled with a fluid movement and hastened back. Allika breathed again. She dared now to move a little, strain for a better view.

And gasped softly.

Inside the crate was a second box. It was as unlike the workaday crate as the sun at midday was to a dying ember. Allika guessed it was two feet long and over a foot wide. It was smooth wood, exquisitely carved and painted with symbols. None of them were familiar to Allika. It was clearly an item of value. The girl frowned and rubbed at her eyes. She must be more tired than she had thought, for it seemed to her the box was . . . glowing softly.

"I confess, Khem, I doubted," said Raven softly. "I doubt no more." She turned a beautiful smile on him and gripped his shoulder. He returned the grin. Wolf's frown deepened as he watched them, but he said nothing.

"I would not let it out now," said Hound. "Let's damage the box, and let it make its own way out."

"Good idea," said Raven. With his metal tool, Khem loosened the nails that held the front of the box closed. The creature inside—Allika was sure now that it was an animal, not a child—hissed and scrabbled at the confining wood, and the box rocked softly. All the thieves jumped back.

What was *in* that box? Something that was able to scare three grown-ups, that was for sure.

Hound stepped forward and loosened the wood a little bit more. The thing inside raged now, and even as far away as she was, Allika could hear it beginning to gnaw on the wood.

"That's good enough," said Raven. "Push it down."

They began to shove the ornate box toward the sewer hole. With a final push, it went over the edge. Allika heard it crack as it hit.

"Excellent," said Raven, peering down. "That shattered the box. It's sure to work its own way out now. Come on, let's—"

They froze. All of them, even Allika crouched unseen in the darkness, could hear the muted sound of voices heading in this direction.

"Guards," hissed Raven. "Let's go. *Now*."

Hound glanced back. "The grate . . ."

"Leave it. Let's *go*!"

They vanished into the shadows as if they had never been. All that was left to mark their presence was the open sewer hole cover.

Allika wasn't overly worried. If the guards happened upon her, she'd just start to cry and claim she was lost. They'd have pity on her and give her food and a warm place to sleep until the morning—by which time, of course, Allika would be long gone. She'd done it before, sometimes even on purpose. As long as the guards of Braedon didn't catch her with her little hand inside someone's pocket, she had discovered that could manipulate them as she chose.

But the booted footsteps and low talk died away without ever venturing down the alley. She waited a few moments longer, just to make sure that neither they nor the thieves were returning, then propped Miss Lally up on her bent knees.

"What do you think was in that box, Miss Lally?"

"Hm, I don't know, Allika. Let's be brave and find out! I bet Fox would want to know."

Her mind made up, Allika rose and walked softly over toward the open sewer entrance. Kneeling a safe distance away from the edge, she peered down.

The faint light of distant torches and moon's glow revealed nothing save some faint shapes. Allika frowned and scooted closer, angling her body so that she didn't block what light there was. Still nothing.

She plopped Miss Lally down near the edge, so that the doll could see, too, then stretched down on her stomach and edged forward an inch at a time, propelling her small body with toes and hands. Now her head was over the opening. Still, she could see nothing. Growing impatient, she also grew daring and leaned down, securing herself with her hands.

Something moved, and then two points of red light glittered up at her.

Startled, Allika gasped and flailed, trying to move back away from whatever was down there. One hand knocked into Miss Lally, and the little rag doll tumbled down, head over heels, to land with a soft *plop* in the sludgy water.

"Miss Lally!" cried Allika, heedless of the noise. She suddenly had a vision, of soft hands and a kind voice; a remembrance of a brand new Miss Lally, white and clean and unstained: *You must take good care of her, she's your baby*.

"Miss Lally," said Allika again, her voice a whimper now. Tears filled her eyes, dropped down twenty feet into the filthy water beneath. Miss Lally was made of light material; Allika had no trouble seeing her.

Again a movement, a flash of two red lights.

Allika sobbed brokenly. What was she going to do? Miss Lally was twenty feet below the surface, down there with that . . . whatever it was that Raven and Hound and Wolf had put there. But Allika couldn't just leave her. Miss Lally was her baby; she had to take good care of her.

She wiped her eyes with a dirty hand, forcing them to

clear. Taking a deep breath to steady herself, Allika whispered bravely, "I'm coming, Miss Lally."

The shaft that led down to the sewers was about three feet wide. Allika pulled off her ragged boots and swung her body around so that she would be descending feet first. Small, strong toes groped for crevices, protrusions, anything to ease her passage downward. Allika forced herself not to think of the *thing* down there in the dirt and dark, but only of Miss Lally. Slowly, she lowered herself, her small, soft mouth pursed in a grim line of concentration. The rocks were not smooth, and she was able to find purchase.

She was hanging by her hands now, and it took a great effort to move them down to the holds that had secured her feet. By leaning back, Allika was able to wedge herself in more securely and inch her way down.

She had already gone several feet. The rock was unforgiving and tore her already ragged clothing, left bruises and scrapes on her soft, pale skin. Allika paid it no attention. The main thing was getting down to Miss Lally, and finding her, and getting back to the docks where she could get out without running into that *thing* that was down there and—

The slippery walls turned traitor. Allika's feet shot out and she fell. There wasn't even time to scream before she landed, on her back, in six inches of filthy water and at least two soft, squishy inches of waste matter. The wind was knocked out of her and she gasped like a fish, splashing. Her shoulders and tailbone hurt, and as she flopped herself over and tried to stumble to her feet, her ankle shrieked in white-hot protest and she fell.

But Miss Lally was right there, smiling up at her with her faded, painted face. Allika's breath came back and she sobbed with joy as she seized her beloved toy, now soaked with filthy water. She sat in the sludgy water, clasping the doll tightly, completely oblivious to everything save her dear, sweet Miss Lally.

"I will take good care of you," she whispered fiercely.

Something moved in the dark, inches away. Memory returned and Allika's small body went taut.

The *thing*. It was still down here. It was down here with her in the darkness.

Again, she tried to rise. Her ankle wasn't broken, but it was twisted badly. Clutching the saturated toy, she managed to make it to her feet. Every instinct was crying out, telling her to run, but she couldn't run. Instead, she found a weapon—a length of nail-studded wood from the crate used to house the *thing*.

"Where are you?" she called, sounding as brave as she could. "You're not gonna hurt me or Miss Lally."

A soft splash came behind her. She whirled unsteadily, and yelped, horrified.

It sat in the square of light that came from the street above, barely a yard away from the little girl. The thing was a rat—enormous, as bit as a cat, *bigger*, and pitch black, save for its eyes, which burned in the dark like two hot coals. It was sitting up on its haunches, regarding her evenly. As she stared back, one ear twitched.

Then, with no warning and no sound, it sprang, leaping for the soft flesh of her face. Allika stumbled backward, swinging the nail-studded slat with all of her wiry, seven-year-old strength. It caught the rat in the side, and the creature squeaked in agony and rage. It came again, and this time managed to sink sharp yellow teeth into Allika's upper arm. She screamed and lashed out, slamming the wood on its head. The blow, though not as strong as an adult's, ought to have been enough to crush the thing's skull, but the rat darted away. As it vanished into the darkness, Allika saw something painted in white on its back.

It was two lines, one long, one shorter. The shorter line bisected the longer line about three quarters of the way down its length. The symbol was somehow familiar to Allika, but at the moment, in her pain and terror, she couldn't place it. For a moment she stood, panting, clutching the wooden slat like a club, her ears straining for a telltale splash that indicated the *thing* had returned to renew its attack. She heard nothing.

"Think we chased it away?" she asked Miss Lally.

"Sure do!" she said in a higher voice, speaking for the doll. "You're wonderful, Allika! I knew you'd come save me."

Turning, the little girl took a deep breath. She was almost a half a mile away from the port; a half mile from the nearest place where she could scramble out of the sewers as they opened into the sea. Low tide would be coming soon. If she didn't make it, she'd be trapped.

"Come on, Miss Lally. Let's go find Fox."

> *Unkind thoughts breed like rats in*
> *the darkness; but good thoughts grow like*
> *the oldest of trees.*
>
> —Mharian folk saying

CHAPTER TWELVE

Tap, tap, tap. Deveren tossed in his sleep. Kastara wanted him to get up for some reason, but the bed linens were so warm and comfortable . . .

Tap, tap. More insistent now. "Love, what is it?"

And with the sound of his own voice, soft and sleepy, he came fully awake and realized that it was not Kastara tapping on his shoulder, trying to rouse him; would never be Kastara, not ever again, and even as the grief resettled upon his heart he was fully alert.

Tap, tap, tap!

Something was rattling on the glass panes of his solar window with a regularity that put the thief leader instantly on his guard. This was no random clatter of tree limbs in the wind, and the memory of his attempted murder flashed starkly in his mind.

Moving in silence, Deveren pushed aside the curtains that shrouded his bed and glanced about. There was no one in the room with him. He reached for the knife he kept beneath the bed and swung his legs out onto the floor. His feet sank into the thick sheepskin.

Tap, tap, rattle.

That was it. Someone was outside, throwing stones up against the window, trying to get his attention. While this deduction brought some relief, Deveren did not drop his guard. It could yet be a decoy. Naked, Deveren moved toward the window and cautiously peered out. He closed his eyes as his relief was complete.

Allika stood on the ground beneath, her ubiquitous doll clutched in one hand. She was in the process of gathering more stones, and Deveren saw that one little hand was clenched around a rock that was significantly larger than the pebbles she had tossed up hitherto. The child was clearly growing impatient.

She pulled her hand back as if to toss the stone when she saw his face. Her own was a pale blur in the moonlight, but when Deveren waved, signaling that he had noticed her, she waved back. Quickly she disappeared into the shadows, moving toward the library, where she would not be seen.

Deveren lit a lamp from the fire that had burned to embers in the bedroom. He quickly shrugged into breeches and a fur robe, stepped into slippers, and rapidly descended the stone stairs. As he hurried past the dining room, he paused long enough to grab a peach for the little girl, then continued to the library.

She was there, outside, crouched up against the wall. As he entered, she turned to the window. Her face was not the lively, cheerful visage he was used to seeing; rather she reminded him of a small, forlorn little ghost.

Quickly Deveren opened the window and helped the little girl inside. His hand closed on her arm, trying to maneuver her, and she uttered a sharp, pained ejaculation and jerked out of his grasp. Surprised, Deveren glanced down—

and gasped himself at the ugly wound on the child's soft flesh.

"Sit down," he said, "and let's take care of this first thing."

"Here, let me," came Damir's voice. Deveren's head whipped around and he saw, to his annoyance, that his brother stood in the doorway. Like Deveren, Damir was only partially dressed, but he was clearly awake and alert. He moved to the little girl, who ducked away from him, burying her face against Deveren's thigh.

"Come on, Little Squirrel," Deveren soothed, patting her dark head. "My brother won't hurt you. You can trust him like you trust me." He glared at Damir. "Can't she?"

Damir's eyes glinted with amusement, but his voice was sober. "Certainly you can. Here, let me see." He waited, and finally Allika, after glancing from one brother to the other, slowly stuck out her arm.

Deveren winced as he took a good look at the wound. It was a nasty gash, and the flesh around the wound was red and painful. Damir probed it gingerly with long, gentle fingers, but even that delicate touch prompted the girl to yelp "Ow!" and twist away. "What happened to your arm, sweeting?" Deveren asked softly, stroking the girl's dark hair.

"Rat bit me," she replied in a low voice. "*Big* rat."

Damir and Deveren exchanged glances. It couldn't have been a rat; the bite was far too large for that. And yet, Deveren thought to himself as he regarded the injury in the lamp's glow, it did look as if it had been made by the teeth of a rodent.

An idea came to him that made him stagger. "Little Squirrel—where did this happen?"

"In the sewer. I dropped Miss Lally."

"Are you sure it wasn't a Ghil?" The Ghil were sometimes called "giant rats." They were far more intelligent than regular rats, and far larger—they stood five feet tall when they rose on their hind legs. The Ghil certainly did have rodentlike teeth. But for her to have found a Ghil in the sewer system of Braedon was unthinkable.

Allika now frowned impatiently at him. "I know what Ghil are, and I know what a rat is. This was a big rat. Wolf and Raven and Hound set him loose." Her frown mutated into a sly grin. She reached with her good arm into her clothes, scratched busily. "Want to know more?"

Deveren rubbed at his eyes, startled to hear the names of three of his thieves in connection with a giant rat. Damir rose and with a jerk of his head indicated that he wished to speak with Deveren alone.

"We're going to get some water and bandages for that . . . that bite," Deveren reassured Allika. "In the meantime, have one of these."

He placed the soft, fragrant peach into the child's small hand. Allika sniffed it and grinned, biting into the juicy fruit eagerly. With her mouth full she pointed at her ankle and said, "Foot hurts, too."

Deveren nodded acknowledgement and followed Damir outside the library, closing the heavy oak door softly.

Damir spoke first. "She's clearly hurt herself somehow and is making up a story to justify coming to you for help," Damir stated.

Deveren shook his head. "No, I don't think so. Allika's imagination has, up till now, anyway, confined itself to Miss Lally. Her doll," he added for Damir's benefit. "Whenever she makes a report she's usually very accurate. She's actually one of my more trusted observers."

Damir seemed skeptical, but pushed it no further. "Then what do you make of this, if she is telling the truth?"

"I won't know till I've heard it all. You get the water and cloths, I'll go find some coins. She does expect to be paid for her information, you know."

A few minutes later, the two brothers returned to the library. Allika had finished the peach, and its sticky juices covered her mouth, chin, and dress. But she was smiling,

and deigned to let Damir tend her wound and her twisted
ankle while she told Deveren her story.

The leader of the thieves of Braedon listened intently.
Enough of it rang true for him to swallow the rest. The
landing of the boat by night, the ordinary box housing an
extraordinary box, and, most convincing of all, the bitter
barbs between the thieves. Allika recounted the dialogue
verbatim.

But it raised as many questions as it answered. What was
in the second, glowing box? What did the symbols mean?
How could a rat be a weapon? Who was the mad Priest that
Freylis had mentioned so derisively, and what had Marrika
been chosen for?

An idea came to him. "Allika, I know you can't read, but
can you remember exactly what those symbols were?"

The child, stuffing herself with a crusty slice of bread
thickly covered with butter, nodded. Deveren hastened to
fetch several pieces of parchment and writing implements.
He placed the parchment, quill, and ink in front of the girl.

"Can you draw them for me, Little Squirrel?" he asked.

She scratched herself thoughtfully, her gaze soft, recalling the images, then nodded. Damir had finished tending
her wound, and her arm was now swathed in clean, soft
cloth. Her ankle had been soothed with cold water and was
also bound to give it support. Allika reached for the quill
and, looking shy and embarrassed, tried to draw with it. It
blotted and scritched.

Allika's dark brows drew together in a frown. Angrily,
she crumpled the spoiled parchment, flung the quill aside,
and dipped a forefinger in the ink. Deveren was surprised.
Allika was generally a mild tempered, sweet little girl—if a
bit on the impish side. He'd never seen such a display of irritation from her before. But then again, if her story was
true—and Deveren didn't doubt it—she'd had a rough,
long, frightening night.

Allika stuck her tongue out to aid her concentration. Beneath her small fingers, designs came to life.

"Now, sweeting, what are these?" asked Deveren, crouching down beside her.

"These are the things that were on the box," said Allika. "And it was glowing, too."

Swirls and dots, arcs and circles. Deveren didn't recognize him, but across the table from him his brother's face grew pale.

What in the Nightlands is going on? Deveren felt an icy finger of apprehension trace its way up his spine and he shivered.

"Very good, honey," he approved. "Do you want another slice of bread?"

"No," said Allika shortly, flashing him an annoyed glance. "I *want* to finish my *drawing*."

Deveren said nothing. She completed the symbols and sat back. "Those were on the box," she said. "And this was on the rat. It was done on its back in white paint." Softly, she added, more to herself than the Larath brothers, "It had red eyes."

She dipped her finger in the ink again—by now the digit was stained completely black—and traced a long, single line horizontally across the page. She examined her work, then filled the line out a little bit. Again she inked her finger and drew a second, shorter line about three quarters of the way through the first.

Even Deveren knew what that one was. He glanced over and saw comprehension in Damir's eyes.

The Sword of Vengeance. The mark of the god.

Allika had finished. She wiped her inky finger on her dress and announced, "Now I want some more bread." Busily she scratched her scalp. *The poor thing's probably crawling with vermin after spending a night in the sewers,* Deveren thought to himself.

"Would you like to stay here for the night?" he invited her, knowing she would reject the offer.

As he predicted, she shook her dark head. "No. I got a place to stay tonight."

He sent her on her way loaded down with bread, dried meats, and dried, sugared fruit. She exited the way she had come, climbing out the window, glancing around to see if she was being watched, then slipping into the shadows.

Deveren closed the window, locked it, and drew the shades. He turned to face Damir. "You reacted to the symbols that were on the box," he said, wasting no time. "What were they?"

Damir shook his head, gathering his thoughts. "I was convinced the child was lying," he said softly, "but when she drew these . . ." He tapped the sketch with a long, thin forefinger. Deveren slipped into a chair beside his brother, and the two of them stared at the designs.

"These are wards," Damir continued. "And not your ordinary, workaday wards, either. Nor was the box of the common sort, from what she described. It was built to order, and warded heavily. Something very dangerous and very evil was inside it, Deveren." He raised his eyes to meet his brother's. "Something that could indeed be called a weapon."

Deveren felt a strange tightness in his chest at the thought of brave little Allika, alone in a dark sewer, battling this . . . creature . . . with only a toy for comfort. "Is Allika going to be all right? That bite—"

"—should heal up just fine," Damir reassured him. "That's what sits ill with me about this whole thing. Something that dark and powerful—it should have overcome her at once."

"But what do Freylis, Marrika, and Khem have to do with something like this? I know them all, Damir, and while I'd not trust a one of them with my back turned, I find it hard to believe that they've mastered this sort of magic."

"I suspect they haven't. Allika describes the box as coming from somewhere else—probably a bribe of power to come or some such thing."

Deveren smiled a little. "So now you're trusting her information, eh?"

"I know a good spy when I see one, little brother," Damir replied.

"Well, it wouldn't surprise me at all to find out that Freylis was the one behind my attempted murder. But a giant rat loose in the sewers? It doesn't make any sense to me."

"You do not have all the pieces of the puzzle."

"Well, one piece I intend to get," stated Deveren, "and that is the pelt of that damned rat. If it's skulking about in the sewers, then it's a danger to my thieves. I'm going to put out orders for it to be destroyed."

It sounded so feeble. But it was the only thing he could do.

The second rite was over.

The corpse lay across the bloodied altar, the shell of what had once been an old man, now stiff and cold. They had found him begging in the streets; an easier abduction than Lorinda's, but, as far as Marrika was concerned, not quite as satisfying.

Kannil, though, fairly radiated joy. The thieves sat now in his temple, feasting on the food he had prepared for them. Marrika observed them—"her" thieves—with pride and excitement. She sat in a place of honor, her newly donned robes of black bringing out the blue-black sheen of her thick hair, the sparkle of her brown eyes.

She had been inducted as Vengeance's Chosen, in a private ceremony with the Blesser earlier that evening. Kannil now provided for all her needs. She would never have to prowl the streets again, save for her own amusement; never know the press of a lover's body against hers, save when she chose. She bit into a chunk of mutton, delicately wiped the grease from her face, and smiled to herself.

When the feasting was done, she rose. All eyes were upon her. Even Freylis, now, was afraid of her. She walked past her thieves, making and holding eye contact with each one, before she spoke.

"'Unkind thoughts breed like rats in the darkness,'" she quoted. "That's an old folk saying from Mhar. Many of you have heard it, for relationships between Mhar and Byrn have been good these days. Very good," she repeated for emphasis, her gaze lingering on Khem's scarred countenance. He smiled.

"As the Chosen of Vengeance, I have found favor with certain elements in Mhar. And what favors come to me," and she spread her arms magnanimously, "I share with you, my loyal thieves. Greatness is coming our way—great riches, power. If all goes well, no one in this room may have to steal by cover of night again. By midsummer, we may be able to take what we want!

"Vengeance has heard the prayers of Kannil, and has been pleased with the sacrifices. He has sent us a blessing, by way of certain people in Mhar. In the sewers beneath the city," she said, regarding them evenly, "our vengeance on the rich and sanctimonious of this city—this *country!*—is waiting. That old folk saying has been given life. There now lurks in the sewers a rat—not an ordinary creature, but a gift from Vengeance himself!"

She was losing them. Looks of puzzlement crept across their faces. Some were incredulous. Marrika continued, speaking quickly.

"It bears a great curse that will be laid upon this land. And it will breed, so the curse may travel. It is the size of a cat—nay, a dog!—coal black, with eyes red as flame."

"I have seen it," said Khem, rising as the assembled crowd began to murmur. "I bore it from Mhar, locked in a box with protective runes to keep its evil confined. But now it is loose, and working for our ends."

Clia couldn't hold back. "A curse? Then pray, what keeps us from being stricken? Curses are dangerous things to tamper with, My Lady Chosen!" Her accented words dripped sarcasm, and Marrika flushed.

"I have been told how the curse works. It is very simple—almost deceptively so. But it will not affect us. Do you wish to hear, or would you rather continue to insult your leader? You are all in too deep; the blood is up to your eyes in a red tide. Betray me now and you will all certainly die!"

That got their attention. Every person in this room had been party to deliberate murder not once, but twice. Clia did not say anything more, and dropped her gaze. Marrika waited, but the room was again silent.

"If unkind thoughts do breed like rats in the darkness," she said, "then what of a rat whose curse is to cause unkind thoughts? That is its purpose, and those who resist the desire shall be driven mad. Deeds such as we have performed here tonight will give pleasure. Denying the urges, performing so-called 'good' deeds—that will cause pain. Dreadful, sickening, crippling pain, until the sufferer inevitably yields to the desire to hurt, to kill. And then will come release—but for many, it will come too late."

She began walking again, searching for the words to explain a concept that was as hard to grasp, even for her, as quicksilver. "Soon, little hurts will not be enough. Soon, those afflicted will want more pain, more cruelty—and these weaklings will not be able to stay sane, knowing what they have done and will do!"

She whirled, all fire and intensity now. "We are immune to such contortions of the will, for we already embrace the darkness! Behold what we have done!" Marrika pointed triumphantly to the dead man, slain by them all. "How, then, can we be disturbed by wanting more? There is no conflict that will tear us apart inside. Ah, but the guards, the councilmen, the Blessers of other faiths," and she sneered, "they will be ripped apart. When a Healer's hands shine red with blood she herself has spilled, then how can she stay sane? When a guard, sworn to protect and serve, rips apart a child for the slightest transgression—why, then, madness is the only escape.

"And when this curse has run its course, there will be no one left to stand against us. No one who does not see the world the way we do. No one who would have the strength of will to refuse conquest by our friends, our allies who have given us this great blessing. *Now* do you understand?"

They did. The thieves laughed and whooped. When the celebration had sobered a bit, Marrika continued.

"How fast a rat breeds," she purred. "The curse has begun, is certain to have claimed victims already. We should give it some time to take firm hold—say, about two weeks. The curse should reach its height just in time for the Midsummer Festival—the day when Braedon will least expect an attack."

Applause broke out. Marrika laughed, taking it as her due, and halfheartedly tried to calm them. "But we must prepare. Midsummer Festival has always been a good time for us. There are many travelers in town with heavy purses. Much ale is poured, and those who drink deep may wake up the poorer for it. But this year it will be special. We have many things to do before we will be ready to take full advantage of this great gift from the god. Each of you will be assigned tasks. Of this, I will speak later. Enjoy the fruits of your labors."

The meeting thus adjourned, as it were, the thieves began to leave—quietly, by ones and twos. Marrika walked up to Khem. She felt Freylis's eyes on her, but ignored him. He was nothing to her now but muscle for her cause. Khem rose, smiling.

"You were magnificent," he said softly.

She answered his smile by enfolding him in a hot embrace, kissing him deeply. Khem was far more interesting a lover than Freylis could ever be, and he had served—and was continuing to serve—her well.

"You please me," she murmured, "in *all* things." They laughed quietly, together, and then she sobered. "I have been speaking with Blesser Kannil. I have a very important job for you to perform during the Festival. I can trust no one else with it. And," she added, slipping her hand between his legs, "I have another important job for you to perform tonight."

Again the lovers laughed softly. Out of the corner of her eye, Marrika saw Freylis stalk off into the night. She spared a moment from her passion to enjoy her victory over the big man, then returned her attention to Khem's kisses.

I change but in death.

—meaning of the bay leaf

CHAPTER THIRTEEN

Darshirin's form was sleek and graceful, his movements subtle and yet powerful enough to propel him swiftly through the water. It was not yet dawn, though a slight lightening of the horizon would have proclaimed the morning's approach, had the aquatic creature bothered to look. But Darshirin was intimately familiar with the darkling depths of the oceans, and did not need eyes to "see."

A flick of his powerful hind flukes sent him rushing forward a few feet above the sandy bottom of the harbor. Small clouds of swirling sand rose from the movement, then floated softly back downward. He emitted sounds; high squeaks and whistles, little clicks and chirps. He had tried to explain this method of "seeing" with his ears to Damir, but intelligent as the mortal was, and though he had the ability to hear and return some of the ocean's songs, Damir hadn't quite been able to understand.

He did not need to. Darshirin and his kind understood; knew that sometimes song was the most powerful of all the gifts granted to the ocean's inhabitants by the One Who Makes. With his eyes, Darshirin could not see at all in this darkness. But with his vocal vision, he could have counted the number of shells on the sandy bottom, navigated his way through the sturdy beams of wood sunk deep to support Braedon's docks. He passed unharmed beneath the hulls of ships.

The only things that he could not see this way, he recalled with a momentary flash of anger and pain, were the nets used by humans. He had learned to be careful around such things. He had taught himself to distinguish fishing vessels from cargo ships, and gave the former a wide berth. Darshirin certainly did not blame the humans for fishing; fish were delicious food! But neither did he wish to be caught a second time in the frightening strands that lifted him up out of the sheltering sea.

Sounds were emitted; images returned. Broken shards of wood that had once been mighty seagoing vessels, washed up on the sands and in the shallow waters. Fish, and bits of floating items that Darshirin knew as human refuse, coming in from the sewer systems. He was not concerned. The ocean was powerful with a strength that mortals could not comprehend. It would take the filth that the humans spewed into it and make of the insult a gift; food for the ground-feeders and drifting seaweed. The ocean would wear it down, until it was part of the sea itself and no longer an earthly intrusion onto the green and blue depths.

Darshirin paused. His expression did not waver, for in this form his mouth was fixed in a permanent grin. But his heart began to beat painfully. He emitted the high sounds again, and the picture returned. It did not, could not lie.

Something was caught in the sewer mouth, hung up on piles of refuse and trash. Something that someone had intended to wash out to sea and vanish without a trace. Something that had thwarted that someone's intention by not doing so. Something very sad indeed.

Slowly, reluctantly, Darshirin swam closer. The picture in his mind grew more detailed, and horror swelled inside the gentle creature.

It was a human body, female. Probably the poor girl Darshirin had been dispatched to help locate; the councilman's daughter Lorinda Vandaris. He would need to look upon her in daylight, with his human eyes, to distinguish the finer points that would identify her, but he feared he had been successful in his mission.

He wished he had not. Darshirin had swum the oceans for centuries, and was not unfamiliar with human corpses. He had seen far too many sea-swollen, rotting bodies of drowned men for that. He had even been witness to a barbaric burning of a vessel in Braedon's port; had watched sorrowfully as charred bodies clogged the harbor until the merciful ocean had gone about its business and washed them out to sea. But this . . .

Lorinda, if it was she, had been horribly mutilated. She was lacking many features that Darshirin knew to be common to humans, and the bloated body bore innumerable cuts and slashes. Darshirin darted about, overcome with his horror and revulsion. To do this to one another—he had known humans were barbaric, but . . .

He recalled what Damir had told him of Lorinda. *There is a girl who has been stolen from her people. . . . She is tall, fair as we of the land reckon beauty, and full of laughter*. The revolting shape before him could not be reckoned beautiful in anyone's eyes. And Darshirin was glad she had known laughter once, for she had not died with it.

His heart ached in sympathy. Though she was a human, she had clearly been of good heart, or else Damir would not have said so. Not even the evil should end up like this; and that someone who was as kind and mirthful as Lorinda should be found so, hurt Darshirin deeply.

He could not help himself. Those of the ocean kept their love and sympathy for themselves, and though it was not strictly forbidden, did not share it with the land dwellers. But Lorinda . . . poor Lorinda. Darshirin closed his eyes and began to sing. He sang, in a voice that could not be heard by ears, of her beauty, and gentleness of nature. He sang of her brutal murder and tragic end. He sang, that those in the oceans might know of and lament the passing of something true and good.

And as far as Darshirin knew, it was the first time since the oceans began to teem with life that the song of the sea had been sung to mourn one whose face was raised to the sun, and whose feet trod upon dry soil.

It was almost dusk by the time Damir reached the meeting place. For a moment, the diplomat allowed himself the luxury of enjoying the incredible beauty of a sunset over the ocean, something he was not often able to witness. The sun was a magnificent, swollen orb of orange-red. The sky itself was a rainbow of fiery hues, ranging from indigo to purple to yellow. Far above the horizon, the bolder, brighter stars were already beginning to appear. The ocean itself seemed to be bleeding, turning a rich variety of shades that mirrored the dying sun.

Damir shook himself out of his reverie. There was a great deal on his mind, and he hoped that tonight, Darshirin would have news for him. He did not permit himself to hope that the news would be good.

Just as the sun dipped below the horizon, a dolphin leaped and splashed down. Damir tethered his mare to the weathered tree, patted her absently, and made his way down to the shore. This time he had no trouble navigating the rocks and rough terrain, as he was properly dressed for just such activities.

Again Darshirin broke the surface, but this time he was much closer and in his human form. And as the sea-being walked slowly out of the water onto the shore, Damir saw that he bore a dreadful burden.

"Ah, no, please, no," Damir whispered futilely to himself. But he could not escape the truth.

Darshirin's bluish-hued face reflected his own grief, and he carried the burden of the dead and barely recognizable Lorinda with as much gentleness as he might bear a newborn to its mother's arms.

"I have found her," he said softly. "And it hurts my heart to have done so."

Carefully Darshirin knelt on the beach, where the sand was still soft and rocks did not yet encroach into the ocean. He laid the body down tenderly, stroking the ruined face of the once beautiful girl with a gentle, webbed hand.

Damir knelt too, forcing his own sorrow aside and replacing it with shrewd observation. Lorinda had been dead for several days—probably the full week that she had been missing. Damir estimated that she had met her dreadful fate on the same night she was abducted. He made allowances for the immersion in salt water and decomposition, and tried to distinguish what had happened to her while she was alive.

His stomach turned over when he realized that in all likelihood the mutilations had been performed on a living body. Dear gods. Who—what—was loose in Braedon, that would do this to an innocent young girl?

"Do you know who might have done this?" asked Darshirin, echoing Damir's thoughts.

Damir shook his head grimly. "Not yet. But we will. This is . . . an abomination. Darshirin, you must believe that we're not all like this."

Darshirin smiled ruefully. His emerald eyes sparkled with unshed tears. "I thought you were all without compassion, until I met you and Jemma. I know better now. But there is a darkness among your people, my friend, that stains the whole. At least the shark in the ocean gets no pleasure from his feeding; and at least those that he devours help him in turn to live. This," and the sea-being gestured helplessly at the bloated corpse, "this, I cannot understand. And I do not wish to."

Dismissing the subject, he gazed at Damir. "I come bearing more bad news, I fear. I have not had contact with Jemma in many days."

"When was your last contact?"

Darshirin thought. "Fifteen, as you land dwellers measure your days."

Damir closed his eyes. Things were just getting worse and worse. "Any word at all?"

"None. I reported that she has made contact with Castyll, as you recall, but I have heard nothing since. She does not come to the ocean anymore, and I do not think it is because she does not wish to. There is an increased presence of Mharian guards along the docks."

"Somehow that doesn't surprise me," said Damir. "Thank you, Darshirin. Your information and help have been invaluable. I think, though, it is time for me to become more active in this little scenario. I must journey to Mhar myself."

They talked for a few moments longer as Damir explained his plan. Darshirin listened, nodded. "It is past time that I returned to the ocean," he reprimanded Damir softly at length. He rubbed his forearm, which was beginning to dry out.

"Of course. I shouldn't have kept you so long."

Darshirin glanced down at Lorinda's body. "What will you do with her?"

Damir again knelt beside Lorinda. He closed his eyes and muttered an incantation. Light began to glow from his palm, and he moved his hand gently over Lorinda's body, covering every part of her. Beneath his radiant hand, Lorinda's body changed. When he was finished, she looked healthy and whole, as if she was just asleep and would awaken soon to look at the world again through laughing eyes.

"That was kind of you," said Darshirin. "Those who love her would not wish to see her as we have."

Damir knew that Darshirin, being related to the elven clans, could see through the illusion, as if the whole Lorinda was painted on gauze and laid over the real body like a shroud. "It's the least I can do. Would that we could have brought her safely home."

"She will not be forgotten," said Darshirin quite unexpectedly. "I have sung for her, Damir, and now all the ocean knows of her loss."

The admission startled Damir. Moved, he reached to clasp Darshirin's shoulder. Gently, the sea-being laid his own hand—slippery, moist, webbed, and warmly comforting—on Damir's own. Then he turned and slipped into the ocean. Damir did not see him again.

He took a deep breath. Death was no stranger to him. He had even seen corpses mangled almost as badly as Lorinda's was. But few of those were people he had known; fewer still, people he had liked. Gently, he picked up the body, selfishly grateful for the mind magic that allowed him to, at least partially, fool himself as well as others.

Deveren's mare was skittish at the smell of death, and pranced nervously as Damir approached. Not for the first time, Damir wished he could use his mind magic on animals. But they were less—or perhaps, Damir mused drily, more—intelligent than humans and their minds could not be so easily manipulated. For several long minutes, Damir used soothing words to try to calm the agitated creature. At last, her soft brown eyes still rolling in fear, she permitted him to strap Lorinda's corpse to her saddle.

It would be a long walk, Damir thought, but at least this time he had brought his cloak. And it would give him time to plan.

Alone with his brother in the fine dining room, Deveren stared into his goblet, not seeing the distorted reflection of his unhappy face in the glossy red surface of the wine.

Lorinda . . . dead. Not just dead, murdered. And not just murdered—butchered. His heart hurt just thinking about it; ached with sympathy for the loving father and the devoted paramour of the girl; and cried out, most of all, for his own wife, killed in a similar, if not quite so brutal, manner.

He listened without comment as Damir coolly told the story of how he had found the girl washed up on the beach when he had left earlier to take a long ride. How he had cast a spell over the damaged corpse and walked beside the mare for many miles to bring it home to Vandaris. How he had not told the grieving parent just how badly his only child had been mutilated. How Pedric had sat and stared numbly, his eyes dry, his voice mute.

"What in the Nightlands," said Deveren at last, wetting his throat with the ruby liquor, "is happening? Silence from Mhar. Lorinda—gods, an innocent if there ever was one—murdered. An attempt on my life, and some kind of ratlike thing crawling about in Braedon's sewers." He raised sad eyes to his brother, who had no solace to offer.

"I don't know," said Damir softly. He rose, and in passing laid a strong hand on Deveren's shoulder, gripping it tightly in mute sympathy. Damir went to the sideboard and poured himself a drink. He sipped it for a long minute. Deveren watched him dully.

"I want to find out, though," Damir said at last. "And I intend to."

Deveren frowned. "What do you mean?"

Damir turned to face him. "I've decided to go to Mhar. In disguise. Too many things are happening for this to be just a run of bad luck, Deveren. My whole career has been based on an ability to determine what is merely bizarre coincidence and what's got some sort of plan behind it. And this thing reeks of Mharian interference. To be more precise, Bhakir's interference."

Deveren leaned back in his chair, studying his older sibling. "What makes you so sure?"

Damir smiled slightly, his thin lips curving upward. "Oh, I have my ways."

Deveren shook his head. "It's too dangerous. Send one of your, er, 'ways' to do the job."

"Can't. Dev, think for a minute." Damir sat down and gazed at his brother intently. "If I have my spies, then you have to know that Bhakir has his. Word surely has gone out that I'm here. For all we know, all this could be connected with him trying to get at me."

"I wouldn't flatter yourself. After all . . ." Deveren broke off suddenly and took a gulp of wine.

"After all," Damir finished in a soft, compassionate voice, "my spies couldn't find the killer of your Kastara."

Deveren shot his brother an angry look. "I hate it when you do that!"

"It's not that difficult. Dev, I know this has to be bringing back painful memories. And I did use all my sources to try to find out who'd killed her. But Kastara's murder was an accident. She wasn't the target. It was clearly a theft gone wrong—horribly wrong. But that's all it was. Lorinda's murder has an element of anger about it, of—of ritual, if you will."

"Why didn't you tell Vandaris that?"

"If you'd seen the body, you'd understand. There's nothing his policing efforts could do. Enough for him to know that she was murdered—enough for Pedric, too."

Deveren leaned forward. "Show me."

Damir seemed surprised. "I really don't think—"

"Show me. If you're going to go into Mhar and probably get killed over this, I want to know what you know!"

Damir hesitated. Deveren met his gaze evenly. He had to know. At last, Damir nodded. Wordlessly, he rose and re-seated himself next to Deveren. As he placed his fingers on his brother's temples, Damir said half-jokingly, "You know the routine."

Deveren did. He closed his eyes and opened his mind to the delicate probing of his brother's magic.

Though his eyes were closed, he could see clearly, through Damir's eyes. He saw the beautiful, limp body of Lorinda in her father's arms. There was a single wound, if the bloodstain between her breasts was any indication. Damir had been honest about her death, at least—Vandaris knew she had been murdered.

Before his eyes, the scene shifted. Suddenly he was on a beach at twilight, staring down at the same corpse. The illusion melted away, like wax from a candle flame, and Deveren stifled a gasp.

Dear gods. Who—no, whatever did this could hardly be called human, could they—what sort of monster had done this to a young girl? Nearly every inch of skin on the young woman had been cut. Her features—they were barely recognizable. And, Damir's "voice" whispered in his mind, she had been alive when they had done this.

Deveren jerked away. He stared at Damir, his breathing quickened, and he blinked away the horrified tears of compassion that had sprung to his hazel eyes.

Damir's face was sad, sympathetic. "Now do you see?"

Shuddering, Deveren wiped at his eyes. He nodded. Yes. Now he could see why Damir had gentled Lorinda's death for those who had loved her. It would have killed old Vandaris and driven poor young Pedric mad.

"Something is behind all this, I'm convinced of it," Damir continued. "And I have to go to Mhar myself. I can't risk anyone else. The only reason I'm even telling you is, I need someone to keep up the pretense that I haven't gone."

"What? How am I supposed to do that? Make a scare-the-crow and prop him up in the window?"

"It should only be for a few days. You can tell people I'm ill, or have gone on a sightseeing trip. I will leave tomorrow—that's Healsdae. If I'm not back by Loesdae, you'll have to come up with something." He hesitated, then added softly, "I fear for the young king. You should know that I'm planning to bring him back with me if I can."

Deveren buried his face in his hands. "From the cook pot to the kindling, Damir. Dear gods."

"If Bhakir knows I'm gone, he will look for me on Mharian soil. You've got to make sure that doesn't happen. I leave the methods," and here Damir, damn him, actually *laughed*, "to your lively imagination. Good heavens, Dev, if you can perform three Grand Thefts and not get caught, goodness knows what that fertile brain of yours will concoct when faced with a real challenge."

Deveren swore violently.

Castyll stared dully at the mound of herbs that lay where he had placed them. They were rotting; no human hand had disturbed them.

He had come to the garden nearly every day; and nearly every day had placed a "message" for Jemma. Castyll had left such herbs as fennel and thyme, indicating he was keeping his courage up. Then rosemary, for remembrance, and rue—"to set free." Finally, just yesterday, he had left a handful of bay leaves. Their message: "I change but in death."

He was convinced that Jemma could no longer come to the garden. And that meant but one thing—that somehow Bhakir had found out about their correspondence.

Castyll plucked a sprig of mint and continued on his daily walk. He felt the presence of the guards behind him, and wondered if he would ever be able to walk in freedom again. The dinner five nights ago was, the young Mharian king was convinced, the beginning of the end. The power of men such as Porbrough, Zhael, and Bhakir seemed to be growing by the hour. He would have one chance to escape; to try to hide among his people and somehow rally their support.

He laughed without mirth as his booted feet trod the little paths through the flowering garden. How could he go unrecognized? Who would he contact? It was more than likely that he would be recaptured within hours, even if he did manage to make an unnoticed escape.

I change but in death. Castyll recalled the phrase associated with the bay leaf, and knew that he could pursue no other course. If he turned coward now—if he went back to Seacliff after his night with the Blesser of Love—he knew Bhakir would drop the facade. It was getting too deep. Only imprisonment—true imprisonment—or death awaited him if he remained. He would no doubt be killed immediately if he were recaptured, but at least for a few hours he would have lived up to the expectations of his father and tried to do what was right. And perhaps his death might make a martyr out of him. Perhaps people would realize what was going on before it was too late; before the net closed in around them.

It was a fool's dream and Castyll knew it. But even with that knowledge heavy on his head and heart, his spirits lightened as he thought about the day, five days hence, when he would ride to the temple of Love. It would be a highly public journey, but a highly private night.

It was a chance. And as King Castyll strode, a prisoner, through the garden that ought to have been his, trailed by guards who should have been willing to die for him, Castyll knew that the chance was more than worth it.

Though the body shall crumble to dust, know ye that
the spirit lingers on, and shall take flight from the earthly
prison, and shall serve the gods as it strives for
the great Light.

— excerpt from traditional Byrnian burial ritual

CHAPTER FOURTEEN

It was too little to be noticed, at first.

All across the city, Braedonians were finding that their sleep did not refresh them as much; that their spouses were much more irritating to be around than they used; that the merchants cheated in the quality of their goods; that the drunks in the streets were more obnoxious than hitherto. They also discovered that tempers soared more quickly, that tavern brawls were bloodier—and that this was much to their liking.

It was right, wasn't it, to strike a man who had insulted you? To beat your wife when she displeased you? Children were supposed to obey, weren't they, if they didn't want to make their hardworking parents angry? And if one's heart felt more at ease when one had wounded another, through scathing words or an aptly placed blow, well then, that was merely a sign that one had done what was right.

Wasn't it?

Of course it was.

The day itself seemed to mock the solemn and tragic ceremony. It was another typical summer day—bright blue skies, with only a hint of wispy clouds, a warm, strong sun, and a breeze that came in off the ocean to cool what might have been an uncomfortable heat.

The public crier had begun his melancholy task at dawn. He had walked through the streets of Braedon, announcing Lorinda's death and the time and place of the burial. Deveren had had warning, thanks to Damir, and when he rose he dressed in black. A messenger had come from the Councilman's Seat shortly after the crier's voice had faded. Lord Vandaris wished Damir to be one of the pallbearers. Both Larath brothers were invited to march in the procession.

Damir had brought no black clothes, and those he had perforce borrowed from Deveren hung loosely on his slender frame. Now Deveren waited with the throng of black-clad mourners outside the Councilman's Seat. He knew what was transpiring within. Health's Blesser—Vervain, wasn't it?—would be working side by side with Death's Blesser to prepare the body. Together, the representatives of the gods of Health and Death would be briefly united in their tasks. They would bathe the torn body with scented water; anoint it with balsam and ointments. They would sew Lorinda first into a linen shroud, then into a deerskin. They would lay her in the wooden coffin, on a bed of moss and scented herbs.

Deveren did not envy them their sad task.

He squinted up at the sun; it was midmorning now. How could such a day be so beautiful? He returned his attention to the massive doors. As custom demanded, they were draped with black fabric.

Then, with no warning, the doors swung open. The

Blessers were first. They came in order of their deity's age; Love first, the eldest of all. She was a middle-aged woman with streaks of white in her dark hair. She was clad not in the more usual, arm-revealing tunic typical to her rank, but in a heavy gown.

Following the Blesser of Love was Light's Blesser, an elderly gentleman also clad more formally than usual. Third was Vervain, clad in heavy red robes, her hair completely covered by her formal wimple and her eyes encircled by dark smudges. She caught Deveren's eye and nodded slightly in recognition. He nodded back. Then came Traveler's Blesser, a young man who seemed to have trouble moderating his healthy stride to the solemn walk the occasion warranted.

Death's Blesser was next. Deveren was confused at first. He had seen Death's Blesser on the night of his Grand Thefts, when she had given him that odd warning that had, perhaps, later saved his life. That woman had been young and very beautiful, though rather alarming. This woman, though dressed in the formal black robes that marked her as a Blesser of her deity, was much older. *And much less attractive*, Deveren thought to himself, hoping the observation wasn't offensive to the goddess. What was going on? Perhaps Braedon's Blesser was ill today and they had asked one of the neighboring towns to send their Blesser as a substitute.

Next in line were the earthly representatives of Hope/Despair. This twinned-natured god was perhaps the hardest for mortals to comprehend. Health, Death, Love—all were concepts easily grasped. But the strange, contradictory nature of Hope/Despair was unsettling. How eagerly they had all hoped Lorinda would be found alive and unharmed; how bitterly they had despaired at the sight of the corpse, gentled though the sight had been by Damir's compassionate mind magic. Since the divine being Hope/Despair had two faces, s/he had two representatives. The adult Blesser who assumed the aspect of Despair was a woman, and the

youthful innocence of the boy Hope could only be con-
veyed by a lad whose years were few. Because of this,
Hope/Despair was the only divinity who allowed children,
who were normally merely Tenders to other gods, to be as
valued as adult Blessers. The woman seemed to be too
beautiful to represent Despair, but the Tender could almost
have stepped out of a painting, so perfectly did his sweet
face seem to embody Hope.

Bringing up the rear of the line of Blessers was Vengeance's Blesser. He was a slight, small man, and moved
with quick, jerky movements. Deveren could not see his
face; it was hidden in the shadow of the black cowl. Despite the warmth of the day, a shudder passed through Deveren. Both the thought of Vengeance and the sight of his
twitchy little Blesser were unnerving.

The murmurs of sympathy escalated into sobs and wails.
Lorinda's coffin, closed and draped with black cloth,
emerged. It was borne on a pall, and the four men who had
the grim burden of taking the once beautiful maiden to her
final resting place were a fragile-looking Vandaris, a gray-
faced Pedric, a solemn Damir, and a stricken Telian Jaranis,
the captain of the guardsman who had failed to protect an
innocent or even discover her killer. For a moment, Jaranis
met Deveren's eyes, then he glanced away quickly.

It was too close, too much like that horrible night seven
years ago. For just a moment Deveren was there, shouldering the weight of his dead wife's coffin, his face no doubt
as gray as Pedric's, his eyes as haunted.

Deveren was not aware that his fists clenched and his
mouth thinned. He had a group of thieves at his command.
Somehow they would find the killer. Somehow. He could
not stand by and hold his head up knowing two beloved
women had gone to their deaths while their killers walked
free.

Now the mourners were in line, carrying candles. Deveren was not surprised to see that many of his thieves were
among them. He knew it was not for love of Lorinda,

though it might have been in sympathy for Pedric, one of their own. Most likely it was because traditionally, candle-bearing mourners could earn alms at the funerals of wealthy families. Deveren couldn't find it in his heart to begrudge them; he knew how hard life was for some of them.

Deveren fell in line, one of many in a sea of black. He kept his emotions carefully in check, for he knew if he wept it would not be just for Lorinda; and if tears started for Kastara in such an environment, Deveren did not know if he could stop them.

They walked down the cobbled streets of the wealthy parts of town, then the line of mourners turned and headed up into the mountains. Once, several decades ago, the dead had been buried closer to town, down in a meadow not far from the ocean. But when a terrible storm had come, it had left in its wake the macabre sight of dozens of corpses floating in the harbor. So Braedon's cemetery had been moved farther away from such calamities. The dead deserved to rest in peace.

Now the cemetery, fenced in by a low wall of stones, was in sight. The gate stood open, and the procession turned in to it. Ahead, Deveren caught sight of Vervain's vivid red garb as the Blessers went to the grave that had been prepared earlier that morning.

The procession came to a halt. Deveren threaded his way through the crowd. Vandaris would want to see him there. He stood, the sun beating down upon his uncovered head, as the coffin was gently lowered into the grave. The smell of flowers and clean, newly dug earth reached Deveren's nostrils. It was a dreadfully incongruous scent.

The wind rose, and it snatched away the Blessers' words as each one of them spoke in turn. Deveren strained, but could only catch phrases: "Pure light," "courage," "family have strength to endure," and other phrases that were meant to comfort but more often than not sounded hollow and weak.

Deveren knew that the theory regarding life after death
was that the spirits of the dead served the gods in various
ways, until they had achieved enough purity to pass into
immaculate, holy light. It was a pretty idea, and Deveren
was certain that the majority of people believed it. But he
did not. Perhaps if Kastara had not died so violently and
unnaturally, he might have been more willing to listen to
tradition and let her go. But she had not, and Deveren had
no comfort in the thought of his beloved as pure, holy light.

He let them drone on and turned his attention to the four
men who had borne Lorinda here. Jaranis clearly felt responsible for the death, and seemed ill at ease next to Vandaris. Damir had struck the perfect pose between grief and
composure. It was utterly typical of the diplomat, Deveren
thought. Vandaris seemed as if he had aged a decade. He'd
always been on the heavy side, his face round and jovial in
leisure, reassuringly solid in his role as councilman. Now
the excess pounds seemed to be literally weighing him
down. Surely he had not stooped quite so much before. And
there were hollows in his pasty cheeks despite the double
chin. Lorinda had been his only child.

Pedric seemed to be the hardest hit by the dreadful turn
of events. He, too, had aged. One would have to look hard
to find the handsome, rakish youth beneath that solemn,
stricken face. Deveren feared that one might not find it
again. He seemed ill at ease, fidgeting as the Blessers continued their seemingly eternal litanies and scratching himself nervously. There was something in his pain-filled eyes
that Deveren did not like, not at all. Something that seemed
too familiar—cold anger.

At last it was over. Vandaris stepped forward and tossed
in a handful of earth. It landed with a dull *thump* on the coffin. Deveren felt a lump rise in his throat. Of all that had
transpired, that dreadful thump on the coffin was the worst,
the saddest. It was so final; so real.

The grave diggers took over now, shoveling clods of dirt
onto the coffin. Vandaris walked away, his footing unsure.

He was surrounded by well-wishers. Jaranis left the scene at once, several of his guardsmen falling in behind him as he briskly strode back down toward the city. Deveren knew that for him, solace lay in action—in trying to track down and punish the murderers.

Damir made his way over toward Deveren. "Lovely ceremony," said Deveren dutifully.

"It was a farce," said Damir, totally unexpectedly.

Deveren did a double-take at his brother. "What?"

"Beautiful words, beautiful weather, polite condolences—bah!" Damir did not let his carefully composed expression change, and his voice was pitched soft. His scandalous words were for his brother's ears only. "That girl died badly, Dev. As badly as it is possible for a human being to die. What was called for here was righteous anger and justice, not the same ceremony one uses for an old woman who dies in her sleep."

Despite the sorrow that hung on his heart, Deveren found himself grinning a little. Strangers would discount it, and even friends of the pair didn't always believe it, but Deveren and Damir were far more alike than they were different.

He glanced around, trying to find Pedric. The youth had wandered away from the well-meaning but no doubt intrusive mourners. Deveren spotted him alone, leaning up against a tree. He was rubbing his temples as if his head hurt. "I'm going to talk to Pedric," he told Damir. The older man nodded.

Deveren walked slowly across the flower-starred meadow, making his way between the stones that covered the dead. Pedric glanced up as he approached, then back down to the ground. He did not speak.

"Pedric," began Deveren, "you know how sorry I am."

Pedric snorted, and the look that he shot his friend had real hatred in it. "Pretty words won't bring her back."

"No," Deveren readily agreed. They stood for a time in awkward silence. "Pedric . . . believe me, I know how you feel."

The younger man's response was a blistering oath. He wheeled, turning on Deveren, his fists clenched. "How in the Nightlands would—oh." Some of the anger faded, but not much. "I guess you're the one person here who *would* understand, come to that."

Suddenly he shuddered and a small sound of pain escaped him. Worried, Deveren reached to steady his friend. "Pedric, are you all right? You're probably exhausted. Here, let's get you away from this crowd. I've got some wine at home, we can go and talk and—"

"That's your answer to everything, isn't it, *Fox*?" The word was spat, like an epithet. "Talk, talk, talk, let's all play nice, be good little thievey-weeveys. Well, I'm not going to play nice. I want whoever killed her and I want to rip him apart with my bare hands! You once felt as I do, but you let it go. You let life just suck the hurt right out of you. You go home to your fine house, and you drink your fine wine, and you watch your fine plays, and you spin fine little schemes for turning your thieves into kind-hearted do-gooders."

Pedric was raging now. His bloodshot eyes were wild and flecks of saliva flew from his lips. His voice was rising, and Deveren grew alarmed. If someone overheard . . .

"Lorinda wouldn't want you—"

"To the Nightlands with Lorinda! She's dead, Deveren, *dead*, and the dead are nothing but dirt. There's no purity in *rot*. Gods, Dev, couldn't you smell her as we brought the coffin by? She's gone, and there's nothing left of her now but decaying flesh and a memory, and the hope that I can somehow do to her killers what they did to her. So you can just take your wine and your talk and leave me alone!"

He stalked off, head held high, every line of his slim but muscular form radiating anger. Deveren watched him go, absolutely stunned. He had never seen Pedric like this before. Grief he had expected, and anger, but not the poisonous vitriol and contempt that had spewed from Pedric.

The reaction set in and Deveren began to shake. He felt

as though Pedric had physically assaulted him with his words. Dear gods, the boy must be dying inside to have spoken like that.

"Give him a little time to think and room to be alone with his pain," said Damir's soft voice behind Deveren.

Deveren started. "Damn it, I wish you'd quit doing that."

Damir smiled briefly, then sobered. "I'm going to have to leave very shortly. I've been coughing this morning and doing my best to appear as if I'm going to get very ill. It's up to you to keep that appearance going."

Deveren searched his brother's eyes. "I don't like this, Damir. I don't like it at all."

"You don't have to like it," replied Damir. "You just have to agree to keep up the illusion that I'm resting in your house." At once, he leaned away and coughed loudly, raspily. Deveren thought to himself that had not Damir pursued the path of a diplomat, he'd have made an excellent thespian.

Castyll could not contain his excitement. Freedom was just a few hours away. He laughed as he rode the beautiful white horse down the main road of Ilantha, waving to the enthusiastic throngs who had turned out to see their young king walk the path to true manhood.

He was clad symbolically in white, down to the beautiful leather boots that had been made specifically for the occasion. The guards who rode attendance had exchanged their somber uniforms for bright tunics, and their horses all had colored ribbons braided in their manes. Even Bhakir had supplemented his sky-blue robes with a lively crimson and gold sash. The entire company looked more like they were going to a festival than to a holy rite. But then again, this rite was something out of the ordinary.

As usual, Bhakir was never more than a yard away from him. The counselor sat astride a large bay gelding. Castyll felt his disapproval.

"You're in a jovial mood, my good King Castyll," said Bhakir.

Castyll didn't take his eyes off his subjects. He didn't want to spoil the mood by looking at Bhakir. "And why shouldn't I be?" he replied gaily. "I'm a healthy young man going off to learn the secrets of love."

Bhakir snorted. "She's hardly qualified to teach you anything."

"Doesn't matter. She is the Blesser of Love. It's her right."

"She's not beautiful."

"She doesn't have to be." At once, Castyll realized he had misspoken. He had meant that physical beauty had no part to play in the holy rite between Blesser and initiate. Instead, Bhakir clearly interpreted the words to have a cruder meaning, and he laughed nastily.

"All cats are gray in the dark, eh, lad?"

The king's good spirits soured. Bhakir managed to sully everything he was part of. Castyll did not let his ire show, however. Instead, forcing himself to reply on Bhakir's level, he replied, "Indeed."

Again Bhakir laughed, and turned around in the saddle, sharing the coarse joke with the guards riding attendance. They laughed along with their master. Castyll swallowed his anger and his natural instinct to come to the defense of the shy young Adara. Instead, he rejoiced in the fact that he had lulled Bhakir into a false sense of security. If he thought that Castyll was riding eagerly toward a long night of rutting, then Bhakir would not be expecting an escape attempt.

Up ahead, he glimpsed the temple of Love. Here in a major port city, it was not as rustic as men's memories tended to paint it. In the smaller towns and countrysides, the temple would often be surrounded by trees, or in the center of an uncultivated meadow. Necessity required that a city dwelling forgo such a setting, but the actual building itself still spoke of the uncomplicated goddess it represented.

The building was a simple, single-story stone house. There was a garden; Love's temple always had a garden, but instead of a vast, fruit-laden orchard, this one was small and simple. It was crowded with flowers in the front, and Castyll knew that there was a small plot of land in the rear. Flat stones formed a path from the street up through the simple garden to the door.

On the overlarge wooden door was a carving of Love—a young girl, naked, bedecked with flowers and laying a small hand on a fawn. Castyll dismounted. The crowd had gone quiet. Had things progressed as they ought, Castyll thought bitterly, he would be coming as a prince, not a king. Shahil would be there, asking the questions and answering them, performing the part of a father leading a son to manhood. Bhakir had proposed taking this role, but for once Castyll had given full reign to his feelings and shot down that idea as if it were a quail he was hunting.

Alone, then, the young king approached. He stepped forward and respectfully kissed the image of Love, then knocked on the door. After a moment, one of the Blesser's Tenders, a girl not much younger than the youthful Blesser herself, opened the door. She was as awkward as Adara herself had been just a few days ago, but she stood arrow-straight and her voice didn't tremble. The Tender wore a simple white gown, belted with a length of rope, and her feet were bare.

"Who comes to the Temple of Love?"

"I, Castyll Alhaidri Shahil Derlian, knock on Love's door," the young man replied, complying with the ritual. He did not use his title. He came now as a supplicant, not a king.

"What seek you, Castyll Derlian, within these walls?"

"I seek Love's Blesser."

"What would you have with her, Castyll Derlian?"

"I would be taught in the ways of Love, that I might better honor the goddess."

The Tender nodded. "It pleases Love. Enter in." She

stepped aside and allowed the young king to pass into the coolness of the house. "Castyll Derlian, you have come as a boy to Love's Temple. By this time tomorrow, Love shall have made you a man."

Cheers broke out among the crowd. Castyll waved to his people, met Bhakir's eyes for a long moment, and then Love's Tender closed the door.

She indicated a table in the center of the room. It was laden with simple foodstuffs—bread and cheese, meat, fruit, wine. "Please, Castyll. Sit down. Take refreshment after your journey."

"I thank you, Tender, but I must speak with the Blesser as soon as—"

"Within these walls," said the young girl with more dignity than her years would indicate, "you do not reign. Whatever you may be to the world outside, here you are but a humble subject of the goddess, like any other man. The Blesser will come to you at the time of her choosing. You cannot order her about at your whim."

Castyll raised his eyebrows. He was not offended, but he was slightly taken aback. He recovered quickly. "Your pardon, good Tender. I meant no offense. Certainly I will partake of the good food you have provided."

He wasn't hungry—in fact, his stomach was turning somersaults—but he sat down on the wooden bench at the table regardless. The Tender, satisfied that Castyll was going to abide by the rules, slipped quietly away. He poured himself a goblet of wine and drank, glancing around.

The windows and the door to the garden in the back stood wide open, letting a breeze circulate through the house. The fire was unlit, but the remains of one sullied the otherwise clean hearth. There were no rushes on the floor; rather thick woven rugs. As he continued to observe, a small cat wandered in from the garden. It paused, regarded Castyll, then slowly, regally approached him. It rubbed its smooth head against his leg, and Castyll heard the rumblings of a purr. He bent and petted the creature.

"Well, if you meet with Timmar's approval, then you are welcome indeed." It was Adara, of course. She had followed the beast in from the garden and now leaned against the doorway. Castyll was pleasantly surprised at what ten days as Blesser had done to the shy young girl he had seen invested.

She stood straighter now, and her movements were more composed and fluid. While she was still sadly plain, there was a dignity about her that cloaked her rough features with a beauty all its own. He smiled and bowed.

"Lady, you do me honor."

She met his smile, then her own faltered. Suddenly both young people realized the full awkwardness of the situation. Here they were, both virgins; one a king, the other a priestess. They were both young for the weight of their stations, and neither could rely on the other for a mature head and years of experience to steer them through this uncomfortable period.

Castyll was the first to recover. He strode swiftly to the Blesser, gathered the slim girl in his arms, and nuzzled at her ear. But what he said were not honeyed words of romance.

"Are you loyal to your king?" he murmured.

Adara was thoroughly confused. Her arms crept up to embrace him as she replied softly, "Of course I am. That is why . . ."

"Then I must ask you to do something very dangerous," continued Castyll, continuing the charade of seduction lest a curious, giggling Tender was watching. "Is your bedchamber secure from prying eyes and ears?"

Love's Blesser pulled away, her hands on his chest, pushing him back slightly. "Yes," she said, a bit louder this time. "My room is private. We need have no fear of being observed at our pleasures."

Her hand dropped to his. Smiling coyly, though Castyll could see apprehension in her eyes, she led him through the door to her own bedchamber. When they were inside, she leaned on the door and turned, questions on her lips.

Castyll held up a warning finger. Carefully, he began to inspect the room. The bed, large enough for two and covered with soft blankets, had no canopies. No one could hide there. He checked Adara's wardrobe and finally peered outside, glancing about repeatedly before closing the shutters. Moving purposefully, he seized Adara's upper arms and gently but firmly steered her toward the bed.

She began to laugh. "Usually it is the Blesser who does the seducing, but . . ."

He laid a finger on her lips. Still pitching his voice soft, he began to speak.

"Things are not as they seem. I am a prisoner in my own castle. My counselor Bhakir murdered my father and he plans to murder me as well. He has cut me off from any official sources. He has dissolved the betrothal between myself and the princess of Byrn. I am nothing but his puppet. I believe he plans to make war on innocents, and I believe that after tonight I'll see nothing but the walls of a prison cell."

Her eyes widened. He removed his finger and she said softly, "But Your Majesty—how could this happen and we your people not know?"

"There is much that the people do not know," replied Castyll, his face grim. "But you must believe me. If I am ever to be a true king to my people I must escape tonight. It is my only hope."

He sat back, letting her absorb what he had told her. She seemed stunned. Finally he said, still whispering, "I need your help."

"What . . . what can I do?"

"You can help me escape. I cannot lie to you. If they find you here tomorrow and me gone, they will interrogate you. Your only chance is to come with me. I know there are people who are still loyal to me. It's my hope that I can find them and rally them to my cause. They do not know," he said sadly. "Even some of my closest men think me happily here in Ilantha for the summer."

Adara edged back, unaware that she was putting the down pillow between herself and the young king. "But . . . I have my duty as a Blesser. I cannot abandon my Tenders. They are unsettled enough already, with the death of the previous Blesser. To lose me so soon . . ."

Castyll realized with a growing sense of horror that he had made an enormous mistake. Adara would not willingly betray him, but he should have tried to escape without involving her. Far better to have lain with her as was expected and have left like a thief in the night. Now it was too late. She would be subjected to mind-reading, he felt certain. And very few mortals, certainly not a person with no magical training, could resist that. She would therefore betray him in the end anyway, if she did not come with him.

"I'm sorry," he breathed. "I'm so sorry. I should never have done this to you. It's only . . ." What? Only that he missed speaking heart to heart with someone? That he was weary of guarding his true plans? That he yearned for someone to say *it's all right, you're doing the right thing, I understand*?

She gazed at him for a long moment, then reached to touch his face. "How horrible this must be for you. I cannot imagine . . . Of course I will help. I serve Love, and part of our training is to know and understand our own hearts. My heart wants to help, even if that means abandoning my duties. My Tenders will be confused and hurt, but I will serve my goddess best this way."

A lump rose in Castyll's throat and he hugged her tightly. "Thank you," he whispered. "No harm will come to you. I give you my word."

"Speak not so," she warned, "for you tempt the gods when you do."

He nodded, acknowledging the truth of what she said. Castyll took a deep breath. "It would be best to wait until after dark," he said. "I know there will be guards posted."

Adara's brows drew together angrily. "Not around the temple of Love!" she said indignantly. "It would be a blasphemy!"

Castyll nodded sadly. "These are men who have no sense of honor." He watched her reaction, knowing that this, more than anything had yet said, brought home to her the depths to which his captors would sink.

She glanced down at her hands clenched around the pillow, and deliberately disentangled them. She straightened, and jutted her chin slightly forward. "You came for a purpose other than flight," she reminded him.

Suddenly, Castyll's mouth went dry. He felt shy and awkward, and judging by the flush in Adara's cheeks, she did as well. "True," he managed.

Her mouth opened, her small pink tongue creeping out to moisten suddenly dry lips. "Nightfall . . . is a long time away."

Castyll's heart began to race. No, Adara was no beauty like his beloved Cimarys. But she was brave, like Cimmy, and kind. And she was the Blesser of Love. To not lie with her tonight would be an insult. Besides, Castyll found that he was more than ready for her. Their gazes locked and he moved toward her over the soft bed.

"A very long time," he agreed. He gently pressed his lips to hers, felt the soft swell of her small breasts as she arched up toward him.

And for a time, all thoughts of flight were banished from their minds.

Castyll started awake much later. The room was completely dark. His jerky movements awakened Adara, who awoke with a gasp. "Castyll?"

"Shh, I'm sorry. I didn't remember where I was for a moment." She moved toward him, her skin soft as silk, her warm nakedness inviting him back to sleep—or sport. He placed a kiss on her hand and slid out of the bed. "It is time we were gone."

He groped about for his clothes as she rose to light the

lamps. She moved gracefully, without embarrassment, as the lights revealed her nakedness to his eyes. Seeing her thus brought the image of Cimarys to his mind, and suddenly tears clouded his vision. He wiped at his eyes. At once Adara was there.

"What is it?" she asked, concerned.

He took a steadying breath. "It's just . . . forgive me, Adara. But lying with you only makes me want my Cimarys all the more. I miss her so much."

He had thought he would hurt her with the words, but instead Adara flung her arms about his neck. "Oh, Castyll, thank you!" Tears were in her own eyes. "This was my first . . . I was afraid I couldn't . . ." Seeing his confusion, she replied, "A Blesser hopes that the man she has initiated into lovemaking will take that skill to his own bed, share it with his beloved to their mutual joy. I am so happy that you are even more in love with your Byrnian princess after being with me!"

He grinned back at her and kissed her soundly on the lips. "Then know, dear Adara—that when your king lies with his queen, we will both think of you . . . and thank you. But we must hurry. I know not the hour."

Adara dressed quickly. "I have nothing but my Blesser's robes," she said apologetically.

"Do you have a cloak?" She nodded. "Then wrap yourself in that. Be quiet—I'm going to take a look around first."

He went to the door, opened it and peered out. It was dark in the main room of the temple. But he couldn't just walk out. Castyll went to the window and gently opened the shutters.

And stared, shocked, into the hooded features of a man waiting outside the window.

What has a thousand faces, a hundred voices,
the conscience of a cur, and the purse of a beggar?
A thespian.

—traditional Byrnian riddle

CHAPTER FIFTEEN

Swift as a thought, the dark-clad stranger seized both of Castyll's arms just as the king curled his hands into fists. *Friend! Friend!* came a cry, but not in Castyll's ears. It hammered in his brain with a truth that could not be denied. Even as his eyes recognized the face inside the cowl as a familiar one, the young king had already opened his hands.

"Good gods!" breathed Castyll. "Damir! What in the name of—"

"Trying to assist you with what you were obviously planning," replied the Byrnian ambassador as he climbed swiftly in through the window. He bowed toward the startled Blesser. "My apologies, my lady."

"Castyll . . . who . . .?" Adara's voice was faint as she glanced from youth to man.

"He is a friend." Castyll flashed Damir a relieved grin.

"A very welcome friend, at the moment. But Damir . . . how did you know what I was thinking? Where I was?"

"Your Majesty, when the king goes to become a man under the ministrations of the Blesser of Love, it's hardly a state secret. As for your state of mind—I've known you for some time now, and none of the recent behavior of your country's politics jibes with what I know of its king. But we must hurry. I have several men waiting in the garden area."

Castyll stared, open-mouthed. "But . . . there must be guards everywhere!"

Damir raised an eyebrow, and his thin lips curved into a slight smile. "I have several very good men," he amended. "We have not been noticed. Nor shall we be. My Lady Blesser," and again he turned to the young woman, "I'm sorry you had to get involved in all this."

Adara stuck her chin up in a gesture Castyll was coming to recognize. "I know what is right."

"It's my fault," said Castyll. "I should have tried to steal away without compromising her."

"I'm willing to go," insisted Adara.

"But you do not have to," said Damir. "Not if you trust me. I have mind magic," he added, seeing the confusion on her face. "I can make you forget what has happened—plant a false memory in its place. This way, when Bhakir brings someone in to mind-read you, you will have nothing to fear. You will be utterly innocent, and able to continue with your duties as Blesser."

"Can you really do that, Damir?" asked Castyll, somewhat dubious.

Damir nodded. "And more—if the lady will let me. She can help us, if she will, by following certain instructions not known to her that I will implant. But we must hurry. Every minute we linger increases the risk. Are you willing, lady?" Adara gnawed her lower lip, glancing from one to the other. Taking a deep breath, she nodded. "Excellent," said Damir. "Now, come, sit down on the bed, and close your eyes."

She did as she was bid. Damir seated himself next to her and placed the fingers of his right hand against her temple. His expression was composed, almost blank, but as Castyll watched, various emotions flitted about Damir's angular face. At one point, the older man's lips curved into a happy smile. Knowing that Damir was reading the Blesser's thoughts—and guessing at what the Blesser was recalling—Castyll blushed.

"Now," said Damir softly to Adara, "let us go back. Castyll never spoke to you of his plans. You talked for a bit, then completed the holy ritual. Then you slept in the king's arms. You will awake refreshed when the morning comes, and you will be as startled as anyone else that he has gone. Do you understand?"

Beneath her closed lids, Adara's eyes flickered back and forth. "Yes," she said softly.

"Now, Castyll," said Damir, his eyes still closed, "do you yet have men loyal to you?"

"Yes," replied the king swiftly. "I hope most of them. Bhakir has been careful to keep my imprisonment a secret. I think most of the guards back at Castle Derlian in Jarmair are loyal to me."

"That is hope speaking," reprimanded Damir. "Tell me who you *know* to be loyal to you unto death."

Castyll licked his lips thinking hard. *Unto death* . . . "My seneschal. Lord Maren."

"And who reports to him that you trust?"

"The Captain of the Guards—Kester."

Damir nodded and leaned over toward Adara again, whispering softly into her ear. Castyll couldn't quite catch the words this time, but it did not matter. Beyond all hope, Damir had come to help him escape.

Damir finished, and gently eased the girl back into her bed. "Help me remove her clothing," he said. When Castyll hesitated, overcome with a bout of shyness, the older man said sternly, "If we want this to work, she can't be found fully dressed in a traveling cloak, now can she?"

Castyll wordlessly conceded the logic of that, and together they removed Adara's clothes. The young king brought the blanket up to her chin, kissed the girl's forehead, and whispered softly, "I will remember." He straightened, and this time the redness on his face was from excitement, not embarrassment. "Let's go."

They extinguished the lamps and Damir went first. He looked around, then quietly eased himself out the window into the flower beds beneath. He helped Castyll out, wincing as Castyll loudly banged a knee against the wooden sill. At Damir's gesture, Castyll froze.

No sound. They had not been spotted. As his eyes adjusted to the dim night lighting, Castyll was able to see Bhakir's guards. Two were out here, one of whom was clearly asleep at his post. The other was facing away from the house. Castyll suspected there were more in the front of the building. Anger flared in him again, but he pushed it aside.

His eyes attuned to the night now, he found he could also make out three of Damir's men. One sat comfortably in a large tree, a bow with a nocked arrow at the ready in case they were discovered. Other than his dark clothes and the soot smeared on his face, the man made little effort to hide himself. Another black-clad man waited by the stone wall. There were no weapons visible, but Castyll suspected the man was well armed indeed. A third man waited with—of all things—horses at the ready.

Castyll frowned in annoyance. "Your men may be good, but they do a damned poor job of hiding themselves," he whispered to Damir.

Damir shot him a look that Castyll couldn't readily decipher. He opened his mouth, was about to say something when a sudden yowl split the night.

It was Timmar, the temple's cat, and all she was doing was performing her duty of keeping the rats at bay. But one of the vermin had clearly managed to get in a good bite before Timmar's sharp claws ended its life, and Timmar was not a creature to suffer in silence.

The drowsing guard started awake while the one on patrol whirled. Castyll's heart climbed into his throat. Timmar and her dead rat were but a yard to his left. The man was staring right at him and Damir!

Panic seized the young man. He began to run toward the waiting horses. Damir grunted softly and reached out to grasp him. "No!" hissed the older man, but it was too late.

The guard began to run in their direction. Suddenly he stumbled and pitched forward. A slender black arrow protruded from his back. The guard who had been sleeping was now on his feet, looking around drowsily. He opened his mouth, perhaps to cry out a warning to his fellow guardsmen, and again an arrow sang through the air. The second of Bhakir's guards toppled, the arrow, fired by Damir's man in the tree, piercing his throat.

By now Damir had seized Castyll, twisted the young king's arm around in a painful grip and covered his mouth with one hand. "Silence!" hissed Damir, his lips brushing Castyll's ear. "I had worked mind magic on Bhakir's guards. We were all invisible to their eyes. They would not have seen us had you not bolted. Be silent, and all may yet be well."

Castyll nodded to indicate that he understood. Damir released him. They stood still as statues, Castyll trying to make even his breathing as quiet as he could, waiting for the sound of the other guards to come rushing back, demanding what was wrong.

But they did not come. The murders of the two men had been done in silence. The yowl of a temple cat was nothing unusual; and the remaining guards had been too far away to hear Castyll's frightened footfalls.

Castyll felt the panicky tension ebb away, and he sagged in Damir's grip. He had never witnessed murder before, and it horrified him. No matter that it had been done to save his life; no matter that the men now dead were in the pay of the hated Bhakir. No matter. Two men who had once been alive were now stiffening on the grass outside of Love's temple, and Castyll could not help but be repulsed.

Damir's grip was strong and comforting. "I know. The first time you see it . . ." his voice trailed off and he did not complete the thought. "Come. We cannot hope to hide the fact that you had help escaping, not now, but we can make good that escape."

Moving as silently as they could, Damir and Castyll hastened toward the waiting horses—and freedom.

Six days.

Six frustrating, lie-filled, anxious, and above all long, days. Days in which Deveren was certain that someone would send a Healer to attend the ill Damir. Days in which he dreaded that he would suddenly run out of falsehoods. Days in which he just knew, as certainly as the sun rose in the east, that he had said something untoward that would alert some stealthy spy that Damir was not home in bed suffering from a bad case of the sneezes, but was on Mharian soil and off to rescue the young king.

Six very difficult days.

The only bright spot in this dreadful time was the simple note that had been left with one of the servants: *The cats have caught the rat, and sent it to the gods.* The strange, huge, dangerous creature that had lurked in Braedon's sewers had been captured, killed, and burned by some of this thieves; he did not yet know who. That was a huge relief, though not as huge a relief as Damir's safe return would be.

Deveren had been obliged to attend the final performance of *The Queen of All*, though public appearances generally led to unwanted questions about his "poor sick brother." But Deveren could not refuse to show up; that would draw even more unwanted attention. Although the night was beautiful—clear and balmy, with a thousand stars glittering in the indigo sky—and the play was fine, Deveren

Larath hunched in his seat at the amphitheater and watched the show with no enjoyment whatsoever.

Pedric was not in attendance. Deveren hadn't seen him since that dreadful day of Lorinda's funeral. It was unlike the young man not to attend a closing performance, but Deveren couldn't blame him. This was the show he had seen with his beloved on the night she was slain. Pedric probably couldn't bear watching it now. Still, Deveren worried about the youth.

A soft sob next to him brought his attention back to the stage. Ah, yes, this was the scene that always brought tears to the eye. The dreadful Elf-King, played so skillfully by Kyle Kierdan, was using his unnatural charms to trick the Queen of the title. Despite the fact that he had watched this play and this scene at least a dozen times during rehearsals and performances, Deveren found himself leaning forward, engrossed.

Kierdan was tall and slim; too tall for a real elf-king, if the legends were to be believed. But he moved with an uncanny grace, and his voice was smooth as honey. The poor Queen would have had to be more than mortal to resist such charms. And before she realized it, she had voiced her darkest desires—to murder, with her own hands, her enemy's children.

A sudden flash! Deveren blinked, and when his eyes had adjusted he saw that the Elf-King had two children with him. They wore hoods and cloaks, and the Queen rushed at them with a dagger, brutally killing the young things.

Deveren felt a chill. Playacting, yes; the blood was fake and the children would take their pleased bows at the curtain call. But it was hard to watch, nonetheless. Harder yet when the Elf-King crowed gleefully that the Queen had murdered her own children, taking evil delight in yanking off the hoods of the dead little boy and girl.

Deveren heard sobs throughout the audience, and smiled. What a show. That Kyle Kierdan—he was magnificent. Deveren watched the rest of the play, and stood along with the rest of the audience to applaud the hardworking actors. Kierdan received the loudest applause. And as always, to distance himself from the role of such an evil being, he removed the fair-haired wig and pointed imitation ears before he bowed.

Deveren smothered a grin. Poor Kyle. He was sensitive about that thinning hair of his, almost as sensitive as Damir was about his.

His grin faded as the thought registered. Suddenly Deveren was very glad indeed that he had chosen to come tonight.

An hour later, after Kyle Kierdan had been plied with drink and fine food at one of the better establishments in town, Deveren took a deep breath, said a silent prayer, and stated the reason for the meeting.

"I want to buy out your contract with the troupe."

Kyle choked on the mouthful of roasted salmon with wine sauce. Deveren glanced around quickly, hoping the actor's coughing would not attract undue attention. Kyle recovered himself, wiped at his streaming eyes, and took a drink of wine. His face was angry but composed.

"May I ask why? I daresay that my performance as the Elf-King has made your purse the heavier, Lord Larath. There have been no complaints about my conduct off the stage, and—"

"It is precisely your skill as an actor that I need," Deveren interjected. "Keep your voice down, please."

Kyle's eyes narrowed. "Your pardon, my lord, but I don't understand."

"Let me try this again. I want to terminate your contract with the troupe because I wish to hire you for another performance."

Kyle cheered up considerably and dove into the braised greens with renewed gusto. "Well, that's quite different then, your lordship."

Deveren regarded him intently. He had the same basic build as Damir; the same receding hairline; even the same

color eyes. The face was not quite right, but the right actor
could do wonders with makeup. If he was kept at a distance . . .

"It's a very unusual assignment. You won't be able to
discuss it with anyone, either during the, er, performance or
at any time afterward. And after you are finished, I must
ask you to leave Braedon for a few months." He leaned
over the oak table, looked Kyle in the eye. "I will make it
worth your while."

Kyle leaned forward, until their noses were only inches
apart. "How much worth my while?"

"I'll match every copper you earned for the entire run of
The Queen of All. And give you a bonus if you do the job
right."

The actor's thin eyebrows shot up, but otherwise, he did
not react. "How long a run?"

"Three, four days. Perhaps a week."

"Good gods, Lord Larath . . . what kind of a job is this?"

"Finish your meal. I don't want to attract attention." As
Kyle returned to his salmon, Deveren glanced about surrep-
titiously. No one was paying them any heed. "It's just a
lark, really—a joke. You know my good brother, Lord
Damir Larath?"

"I've met him, yes. What about him?"

"He's going to be gone for a few days. He's been ill;
thinks getting out of the city for a while will help him recover. We were talking last night; he was saying how much
the good people of Braedon will miss him." Deveren was
well into his own role now, completely at ease spinning the
falsehood. "I of course replied that he could fall into the
ocean and not be missed. We had a slight wager on it."

"Can't have been too slight," murmured Kyle.

"All right—not slight at all. It's one of those silly things
brothers do." Deveren smiled his most disarming grin. Kyle
smiled back and poured himself another goblet of wine.
Clearly, he suspected nothing. "At any rate, I'd like for you
to impersonate him while he's away. That way, if no one

thinks he's gone, no one can miss him. And I win my wager."

"Your pardon, sir, but . . . I haven't really had a chance to study the man. And I don't think I resemble him that much."

"Kyle, I've seen how you can transform yourself into any character you want. And you look enough like him that I think we can manage it. Come, man, have you no sense of adventure?"

"Well . . . your brother won't be angry with me?"

"Oh, he'll be hopping mad, all right, but with me, not with you. Damir generally knows who's to blame for what."

"It *is* tempting. . . . Oh, very well."

"Wonderful! Do you know where I live, Kyle?"

"Aye, milord."

"Then order yourself a sweetcake to end your meal and tonight, after Death's hour has tolled, come to my house. Take care that no one sees you. I have my brother's clothes and other things that—"

"Come back here, you little rat!" The innkeeper's voice was loud and thunderous with anger. Deveren turned to see what all the commotion was about. Even as the innkeeper continued to yell, a shrill, high voice rose in wordless counterpoint. Deveren was just in time to see the flash of a black dress, bare feet and, for just the briefest instant, the faded face of an old rag doll.

He scattered a handful of coins on the table as he rose, saying hastily to Kyle, "This should pay for the meal. Keep the rest." Before the startled actor could reply, Deveren was threading his way through the clutter of tables and benches, trying to reach the child before the angry innkeeper did.

He was too late. Allika had not been swift enough and the heavyset man had her by the arm. She squalled and twisted, her face red as a pomegranate with fury. The innkeeper's heavy hand crashed down on her small face.

"Damned little vermin-ridden thief," the man grunted,

his eyes bright and his own face flushed with excitement. "I'll teach you to steal from my kitchen, gods help me I will!"

Deveren lunged forward and seized the man's meaty arm, preventing a second blow from landing on Allika's already swollen cheek. Growling, the man turned to Deveren, his teeth clenched in raw fury. The anger faded as he recognized Lord Larath. Allika, though, continued to scream.

"What in the Nightlands is going on?" yelped Deveren.

"This—brat—was stealing from my kitchen. Gone and eaten nearly half a chicken pasty by the time I'd caught her!"

Allika paused long enough to fill her lungs with air, then continued shrieking. Deveren was confounded by her behavior. If she'd wanted to steal, she'd have done so and not gotten caught. And he'd never seen her carrying on like this, wailing and screaming . . .

"Here," he said to the innkeeper. "Let me recompense you for your trouble and take the child away."

The innkeeper's eyes narrowed in suspicion. "Do you know this brat, Lord Larath?" He had to speak loudly to be heard over the din of the screeching little girl.

"No," lied Deveren, "but if she stole your food and not your money, I'm sure she's just hungry. I will take care of it," he emphasized, dropping a heavy silver coin into the man's beefy palm. The innkeeper's expression turned from suspicion to greedy pleasure.

"That you will, sir," he agreed. He let go of Allika's arm. At once, like a rabbit flushed from its lair, Allika bolted for the door. The only reason Deveren was able to catch her was that he had longer legs. His hand closed on her arm and Allika stumbled, starting to scream again.

Now Deveren saw why. The wound he and Damir had bound only, what, eight days ago, was oozing and ugly. Even in the dim torchlight from the inn, he could see that there were dark tendrils winding up and down her small, pale limb. Her head lolled back on her shoulders and her eyes were squeezed shut. The dreadful sound she was emit-ting would have woken the dead.

"Allika!" Deveren gripped her shoulder and shook her hard. The dark eyes snapped open and for the first time that evening she seemed to recognize him.

"F-fox?" she whispered.

"Yes, honey, it's me," he replied. "What's wrong?"

She blinked, as if dazed. "I don't . . ." Suddenly she gasped and doubled over, clutching her stomach as if she were in excruciating pain. "Oh . . ." she moaned.

"That does it," said Deveren. "I'm taking you to a Healer."

Her head whipped up and there was a feral look on her face. Her little teeth were bared in a grimace. *"No!"*

She fought him like a mountain cat, but his superior strength won over. Finally Deveren slung the struggling girl over his shoulder and, unnamed fear welling inside him, strode swiftly toward the temple of Health.

Heart of a doe,
Voice of a lark,
Breast of a dove,
Hands of a Healer.

—Byrnian saying, "The Virtues of Woman"

CHAPTER SIXTEEN

Despite Deveren's best efforts, Allika's cries of protest preceded them as they approached Health's temple. By the time Deveren, one-handed, managed to wrestle the waist-high gate open and enter the area that served as a small garden, the lights had been lit in the temple and Vervain stood silhouetted in the doorway.

"I never seem to see you but in a crisis," she said lightly, as she swept forward to meet him. "I didn't know you had a daughter, Lord Larath. What is her name?"

"I don't. Deveren, please. Her name is Allika, though at this moment her name ought to be Miss Needs-A-Spanking." Allika's shrill cries had managed to find that special resonance and volume that engendered real irritation, fond though Deveren was of the child.

"Oh," replied the Blesser, "no child ever needs a spank-

ing, do they, Allika?" The little girl was on the ground now,
though still held in Deveren's secure grip. She glared first
at the Healer, then up at Deveren.

"Want to spank Fox for holding me like that," she
snarled.

Deveren's heart spasmed. He found Vervain looking at
him strangely, her eyes wide, one slim hand reaching up to
her throat. His gaze locked with hers. He searched frantically for a lie, anything to explain why Allika called him
"Fox," but his tongue cleaved to his throat. Why should he
be so alarmed? Fox could simply be an affectionate nickname, not the alias of the leader of the thieves of Braedon.
Yet he stood, guiltily silent.

"Fox," Vervain breathed at last. "Sweet Health. Come in,
the both of you."

"Miss Lally doesn't want to go in," sulked Allika.

"Miss Lally has no choice in the matter if Miss Lally
doesn't want her little rag head ripped off."

Allika stared at him, latching on to the undercurrent of
annoyance beneath the teasing words, and began to bawl.

Deveren picked her up hastily and hurried inside. The
scents alone would have marked this a place of health. It
was . . . clean. Wholesome. Deveren recognized several
smells—fresh and drying herbs and flowers, mostly. But
there was something else, something fresh and calming that
he couldn't quite name. Rushes crunched beneath his feet,
giving off their own gentle fragrance as he walked. The
stone cottage was bare, almost severe in its lack of orna-
mentation. But the table upon which Vervain indicated Allika should be placed was covered with soft blankets, and
the bench at which Deveren seated himself was comfortable and well made. Something was heating over the hearth
fire. Deveren sniffed. That was what was emitted the gen-
eral smell of cleanliness.

Vervain immediately spied the injury and gently touched
the girl's arm. Allika winced and drew back. "Allika, you
must let me examine you, or else I won't know how to

make the pain go away," reprimanded Vervain in a gentle but stern voice.

Allika looked at her, then ducked her head. "Sorry." Instantly she clutched her abdomen and curled up on the table like a shrimp, wailing in agony. Deveren was by her side at once, trying to get the girl to uncurl.

"What happened?" Vervain moved to the heating cauldron and took a pair of tongs from the mantel. While Deveren replied, she fished out a hot, dripping cloth from the herbed water.

"Eight days ago she got bitten by a rat." To tell, or not to tell? Vervain might think him mad . . . but she needed to know. Something told Deveren that not all of Allika's sickness was due to the simple pain of an infected rodent bite. "I have reason to believe that the rat wasn't an ordinary creature. Something . . ." gods, it sounded so foolish, ". . . something evil."

Vervain shot him a look, but he couldn't decipher it. "Go on."

"My brother and I cleaned the wound and put salve on it. It should have been fine." He glanced down at the little girl. Sweat shone on her pale face, all scrunched up with agony now. Her breathing was rapid and shallow. Unable to help himself, he smoothed her black hair. Allika . . .

"Clearly, it wasn't. Allika, give me your arm." The girl refused, and Deveren had to hold her down while Vervain wrapped the steaming cloth about the ugly wound. "Why do you think it was evil?"

"According to Allika, it was in a box with symbols of warding on it before it was let loose in the sewer. It was twice as large as a normal rat and had the Sword of Vengeance painted on its back. It . . ."

Vervain's eyes were enormous. Her full lips trembled. "What . . . what is her name?" she asked.

"I told you, Allika."

"No. You are Fox. What is her name?" Vervain's voice

was tense, as if it was having trouble escaping from a throat that was squeezed tight with apprehension.

"I don't—"

Across the whimpering girl's body, Vervain grasped Deveren's wrist in a grip that hurt. "Do not lie to me, Deveren. This is more important than you know. What is her name—Crow? Raven? Squirrel? Blackbird?"

Deveren stared open-mouthed. "She . . . I call her Little Squirrel. But how did you know?"

Her hands crept up to her mouth and her eyes squeezed shut against tears. "Vervain . . ." said Deveren helplessly. First Allika acting strangely, now Vervain.

"I had a dream. A vision," she said at last, attempting to compose herself. "It featured a fox, a little chattering squirrel, and other animals—including a rat. The dream went on to depict the statue of Health weeping tears of blood. The head toppled to the floor, still weeping. It was . . . horrible. I knew that something dreadful was going to happen, but I didn't know what. Still, I began to prepare—lay aside special herbs, spend more hours resting and in meditation. Now you have come, Fox, with the Little Squirrel. And your enemy is a rat sent by Vengeance."

Deveren's legs felt weak. He groped for the bench and sat heavily. "She's different," he said, more to himself than to Vervain. "She used to be such a sweet little girl. Full of mischief, yes, but not of spite. Now she's angry, and hostile, and . . . oh, Vervain, I barely recognize her." He looked up at Vervain's tear-streaked face. "Can you help her?" he asked, his voice soft and pleading. "Her life is difficult enough as it is."

"And why is that, Deveren?" asked Vervain with equal softness, as though she already knew.

"She's a thief," he replied, his gaze locked with hers. "And so am I." The words came effortlessly, simply. And Vervain merely nodded her understanding.

"I will do what I can. But I am afraid your chattering Little Squirrel may be a harbinger of something terrible—

something beyond even a Healer's ability to heal. Remove the cauldron and stoke the fire."

Deveren did as he was told. Using a cloth, he lifted the heavy cauldron off the direct flames, smiling despite the desperateness of the situation as the wonderful fragrance teased his nostrils. He placed two more logs on the low-burning fire and poked it till it sparked and began to crackle. Meanwhile, Vervain undressed the child. Deveren turned to see if he could help.

Allika was like a mad thing, fighting the Healer every inch of the way. "I hate you!" she screamed, and catching sight of Deveren, snarled, "I hate you too, Fox!"

The words were like a blow. Deveren gasped softly. Vervain saw his distress and said, "She is not rational, Deveren. Pay no heed. It is the sickness in her speaking. Come help me get these things off her." As the two of them wrestled with Allika's filthy clothes, reduced finally to literally tearing them off the struggling child, Deveren saw that she was covered with tiny bites. Small insects scurried for the darkness as the warm, concealing clothes were lifted away.

"Poor little thing, she's absolutely crawling with . . ." the Healer's voice broke off. "Dear gods. Deveren, burn these. Every scrap of clothing that's touched her. We'll have to burn the blankets, too, and perhaps our own clothes."

Deveren didn't understand, but he recognized the Healer's absolute authority in this matter and did not question. He immediately tossed the filthy rags onto the fire. They began to smoke and an oily, unpleasant scent crept into the room.

"Don't burn me!" Allika's shriek of terror ripped Deveren's heart.

"No, child, just your clothes," assured Vervain. "Now we're going to clean you up—make you fresh again, hmmm?"

Allika began to cry. Not the vexed, petulant wails that Deveren had heard before earlier tonight, but deep, heart-wrenching sobs. Deveren held her down, gazing at her white, naked body covered with sores where she'd scratched herself raw. Vervain took another cloth from the pot and began to wash Allika. "Thank Health that my Tenders are home with their families." She spared Deveren a glance. "I was expecting something to happen tonight, you see. And I didn't want my little Tenders caught up in it."

The filth had been washed off Allika's body now, but the little red bites remained. Vervain excused herself and hastened out into the garden. Deveren continued to hold Allika, wiping away the tears that seemed endless. Vervain returned, carrying a basket laden with a small, weedlike plant. She began busily to crush the plant, rubbing Allika's body with it.

"What's that?" Deveren asked.

"Vervain. It should calm her." She spared a glance for Deveren, and smiled a little. "I come from a long, unbroken line of Healers. My mother named us after healing herbs. I was lucky. My sisters are Agrimony and Chamomile."

Deveren laughed, and the Healer's smile grew. Their eyes met, and suddenly Deveren realized that for the first time he was seeing the Healer without her severe red wimple. Her hair was a rich, warm brown, and tumbled down her shoulders and back. There was a little gray winding its way through the thick curls, but there was no hint of aging on the open, warm face and kind eyes. She was, he realized, beautiful.

Allika's hitching breath brought his attention back to the matter at hand. She did seem to be calming down somewhat. Vervain's . . . vervain . . . would appear to have the desired effect. He stroked her wet cheek.

"Now I must try to Heal her. Deveren, many times I deal with things I do not understand. This is one of those times." Her voice and mien were calm, almost tranquil. Deveren marveled at it. "If she has picked up a disease from Vengeance, the attempt to Heal her may kill us both. You need to know that before I begin. If something happens, you must somehow get Lord Vandaris and the council to agree to a quarantine. If it is so powerful that I cannot contain or cure it, then we must protect the rest of the country from contamination. Do you understand?"

Her words were almost like a physical blow. He'd simply assumed that Vervain would be able to take care of Allika. With a sinking realization, Deveren felt like someone who had set out to cross the ocean in a small dinghy, and only now, with land out of sight, fully realized the danger.

"Yes. I understand." His own voice betrayed him. Spontaneously, he reached out his hand to her. She took it, squeezed it tightly. Then, taking a deep breath, she sat down on a stool next to the bed, closed her eyes, and placed her hands on Allika's chest.

Healing.

It was a simple word, really. A simple concept. And often, it was her bone-deep comprehension of the utter simplicity of the act that enabled Vervain to accomplish what some called "miracles." She did not dare hope for a miracle tonight.

Her hands felt the chilliness of Allika's damp flesh. She spread her fingers; reached deeper, for the warmth of the small organ that pumped life. She murmured a brief prayer: *Lady Health, guide me to accomplish your healing.*

Her hands suddenly felt hot. The healing energy had responded to her call—a good sign. Heartened, Vervain directed the heat inward, into the chilled child's soul.

And gasped.

Her healing energy slammed up against an icy blockage. She recognized some of it—the natural fear of the sick or injured. That, she knew how to penetrate. But there was something else, something cold and dark and deadly. Its chill began to seep into her own hands, trying to turn the tables on her Healing.

She frowned, eyes still closed. No. She could not let it. Again the healing energy welled, came to her call, and again she sent it forward. She felt the child beneath her hands jump at the attack of heat, writhe, trying to break

contact. Then Allika ceased flailing. Vervain suspected
Deveren had stepped in, helped quiet the girl. Thank Health
for him. He was steadier than most she had known.

This time Vervain burst through the blockage, and it was
as if she found herself adrift in a raging river. Her breath
caught, froze, and she forced herself to breathe as she was
mentally buffeted by *something* that had its talons in the
child. Briefly, Vervain had an image of twisting; of something being turned inside out. And again the darkness
brushed her healing warmth. This time, Vervain knew what
it was, and the thought alarmed her.

Not disease. Curse.

It was the perfect opposite of all she had been taught.
Dimly, she recalled learning how to summon such things in
order to know how to dispel them. Tears formed beneath
her closed lids. She recalled Jemma teaching . . . what?
Gods, it was so long ago, she had been barely ten years old!
Hard to recall, now that everything depended on her
memory . . .

Yes. A third time Vervain called for the great power of
Healing. This time, she remembered what to do.

She surrendered.

Surrendered herself and Allika utterly to the power of
evil that raged within the girl's spirit. Felt the cold seize her
own heart, felt the mammoth hate that seemed far too large
to be housed in the tiny body of a seven-year-old child turn
eagerly upon this new, sweet prey. Vervain saw her own
thoughts and memories being twisted, tainted, as the curse
tried to corrupt her as it had Allika. But it failed. She was a
Blesser of Health, and the goddess's claim upon her loyalty
and spirit stood firm against the buffeting of the curse. Angrily it receded, renewing its attack upon the more vulnerable little girl. Vervain felt herself drowning in the dark,
black cold . . .

. . . and a fourth time called forth the red warmth of
Healing. She remembered how to direct it. It scattered the
bearer (*bearers, thousands of them*) of the dark curse with

the force of a rechanneled river. Vervain began to pant with exhaustion, dimly felt sweat gather at her hairline, trickle down the back of her neck. Her body began to quiver. No . . . no, she had to stay strong, had to keep fighting!

The power was ebbing, cooling. She reached for it a fifth time, something she had never done before, and found no trace of the gift left. Her own strength of will had to do. Vervain gritted her teeth and continued fighting, and at last the black darkness ebbed, went away, like a shadow before a growing light.

She opened her eyes. Allika lay quietly, as exhausted by the struggle as she was. Vervain realized she was trembling. Deveren went to her, steadied her with strong arms on her shoulders.

"What . . . is it all right?"

She couldn't speak, only nodded. Gods, she was tired. Vervain licked her lips and pointed feebly to a pitcher on the sideboard. "Some water . . . please . . ."

Deveren leaped up and poured her a goblet, sloshing the water on her red dress as he handed it to her. His hazel eyes were concerned. Vervain gulped greedily. Never had water tasted so sweet. She sighed, waited for her racing heart to still, then spoke.

"Allika was cursed," she said. Deveren gasped, then glanced back up at the girl who was sleeping soundly. "I was able to cure her, do not worry. It was spread by the rat . . . or, rather, by the rat's own vermin."

"The fleas," breathed Deveren. "I had the rat killed, but . . ."

"Exactly. The fleas have no doubt spread." She took a deep breath, drank some more water, and continued. "I had to surrender to the curse in order to defeat it. Deveren, this is . . . I can hardly even articulate it. It . . . it likes darkness. It likes to make people do evil things. They will thrive on cruelty. Goodness, kind deeds—that weakens the victims, makes them hurt. Did you notice every time Allika cooper-

ated, seemed sorry for what she had done, she was stricken
with pain?"

Deveren nodded.

"It's like the bite of a snake. To cure, one must fight
back with an antidote crafted with the same poison. To cure
this curse, one must be made utterly evil, cease fighting it,
in order to defeat it. It is called the Law of Similarities. Do
you follow me?"

This time, Deveren shook his head. Her heart went out to
him. Poor man. For all that he was a self-confessed thief, he
had a good soul. And all of this had shaken him pro-
foundly—as well it might. "In essence, then, Allika and I
surrendered completely to evil—and then I was able to fight
back, to pull her out along with me." She wiped a hand
across her brow, greasy with sweat. "We almost didn't
make it."

Deveren reached for her hand, squeezed it. "You look
exhausted."

"I am."

He voiced the question she was thinking but did not dare
articulate. "Vervain . . . if one healing does this to you . . .
how can you expect to cure a whole city?"

She closed her eyes, opened them. "I can't. Not with
heart magic alone. But there may be something else . . .
perhaps I can come up with an herbal substitute. I have
been able to do that on occasion for people who are too ill
to come to me themselves, or too far away for a Healer to
reach." She forestalled Deveren's exclamation of relief
with a wave of a weary hand. "It won't be easy. And truthfully, I am not hopeful. Even if I am successful, it will take
time to create . . . and the victims must be cured one by
one."

Her body ached. She rubbed her stiff neck absently as
she added soberly, "And such a struggle of the soul . . . the
cure could even be fatal to some."

They sat for a few moments, weighted down with the
new, dreadful knowledge, the only sound the rhythmic

breathing of the slumbering child and the crackling of the fire. At last Vervain struggled to her feet. "We must finish burning the clothing. Then Allika must be bathed."

At the sound of her name, the child roused, groped sleepily. "Where's Miss Lally?" she asked, stifling a yawn.

"Here she is, honey," Deveren replied swiftly, reaching to pick up the rag doll from the floor where she had fallen during Allika's struggles.

"No!" Vervain's voice was sharp.

"But . . . ?" Deveren was confused. Allika sat up, sensing trouble.

"The doll is as contaminated as her clothing. Perhaps more so," replied Vervain. "I'm sorry, Allika. But . . ." she glanced helplessly over at Deveren. "We have to burn her."

"B-burn her?" Allika's lower lip trembled. "But you can't! She's my baby! I have to take good care of her!"

The tone in her voice was different. Vervain noticed it immediately. This was not the wild Allika, enjoying being spiteful. These were the words of a hurt child, crying out for the thing she loved. If Deveren was right, and she was a thief, familial love must not be easy for her to come by.

But even as Vervain gazed at the doll, she saw vermin crawling over its faded, painted face. It had to be destroyed.

"Allika," she said gently as Deveren still clutched the doll, "Remember how sick you were just now?" The girl nodded, her eyes brimming with tears. "Well, Miss Lally's sick, too. But I can't heal her. And unless we put her in the fire, she'll make you sick again."

"But . . . Miss Lally's never got sick. Not even . . ." Allika gasped. "I made her sick! I made her sick! I make *everyone* sick, and then they have to get burned, just like on the ship!" She buried her face in her hands and sobbed.

"Dear gods," said Vervain, her face going white. "She must have been on the Death Ship." What a dreadful thing that had been. She had fought to be permitted to go aboard, to try to Heal the sick, but had been denied.

"But there were no survivors," said Deveren.

"That we knew of," amended Vervain. "Allika, do you think you killed all those people? Made them sick?"

The little girl nodded wretchedly. Vervain's heart went out to her. "Oh, honey, you had nothing to do with that. And Miss Lally didn't get sick because of you, either."

"But . . . I saw them burn . . ." She turned brimming eyes toward Vervain. "I don't want to make you or Fox sick."

"You won't," Deveren replied swiftly. "We'll be just fine."

"But . . ." Allika paused, wiped an arm across her streaming nose, and said softly, "Miss Lally makes me brave. She got me through that night when the, the black-soot men came, and when I found the rat . . ."

Deveren picked up Allika, blankets and all, and sat down with her in his lap. "Allika, you've got it backwards. *You* made *Miss Lally* brave. And now you have to make her brave enough to go into the fire so that she won't make you sick again."

Allika's eyes searched Deveren's. Vervain watched them both closely. Neither spoke for a long time, but neither had to. She wondered if Deveren could see the aching need for love in the child's small face; wondered if he realized how his own softened and brightened when he was with the little girl. Somehow, sadly, she doubted it.

At last, Allika spoke, with a voice as small as the littlest breeze. "Hold her up, please, Fox."

Deveren did so, taking care that the girl did not come in direct contact with the soiled, ratty doll. Allika gulped.

"Miss Lally," she said, "you're going to have to go into the fire."

"But Allika," she said again, pitching her voice high, "I don't want to."

"I don't either," sobbed the girl in her own voice, "but Fox says you're sick. And it's the only way we can both get better."

"Oh," came the higher voice of Miss Lally. "Remember what I said to you that night? They can't hurt me!"

"I love you, Miss Lally." The voice was a whisper. Allika buried her head in Deveren's chest, fighting back tears. "You can put her in the fire now, Fox. It's all right."

Gently, Deveren leaned forward, keeping a firm grip on Allika as he tossed the rag doll into the flames. It caught at once, and Miss Lally seemed to writhe as she was blackened and consumed. Allika didn't watch. She clung to Deveren as if he were life itself, and the nobleman's arms went around her to hug her just as tightly.

Vervain turned her eyes toward the burning toy, but in her mind's eye, she saw the burning Death Ship that Allika had escaped. She said a silent prayer to her goddess that she would be able to find a cure, and soon, else all of Braedon—perhaps all of Byrn—would only find purification through the leaping orange tongues of flame.

She may be no beauty, no goddess is she,
And all of her charms can be had for a fee;
But although her body can be bought and sold,
She's surely a whore with a heart of pure gold.

—Byrnian drinking song, *The Whore with*
a Heart of Gold

CHAPTER SEVENTEEN

Castyll had no idea that the majority of the people he ruled smelled quite so bad. The odor of unwashed bodies vied with the reek of meat that had turned, the choking smoke of dozens of pipes and, most unpleasant of all to the young king's innocent nose, the cloying, almost overwhelming perfumes that the prostitutes used to disguise their lack of hygiene.

Castyll had never been in better spirits.

He had to nearly shout to be heard over the hubbub of laughter, chatter, and off-key music that filled the "house." "I hardly picture you being at home among such company," he said to Damir.

The other man smiled slightly. "I'm able to blend in where I must," he replied. "As are my men," he added with a smile. The men who had helped Castyll escape had ac-

companied them, and presently, with their lewd talk and
loud laughter, the formerly silent killers were indistinguish-
able from the regulars.

"Are all these women spies?" Castyll asked, looking
from one painted face to another. Some of the women were
in various stages of undress, as their clients examined what
they'd be paying for, and Castyll felt a blush creeping up
his cheeks. He hastily returned his attention to his friend.

"Every last one, gods bless them. A few are professionals and turned their, er, hands to this as readily as posing as
lost nobility in a king's court. Others were working here
before and proved to be easily bought."

"Are they . . . can you trust them? And what about the
men who . . . their . . ."

"Their clients?" finished Damir, chuckling a little. "I
think it's rather clear that they are not interested in espionage at the moment; and even if they were, they are too
far away to hear our conversation. All the whores are loyal
to me—and therefore to you. This is probably the safest
place in Your Majesty's entire kingdom." He raised his
frothing mug of beer in a salute.

Grinning, Castyll lifted his own mug and took a sip of
the bitter brew. Like the smells of the place, the taste of the
beer was crude and unrefined. But oh, it was a taste of true
freedom for the first time in what seemed like years.

"Now tell me what has happened," Damir requested, settling back to listen.

Castyll lowered his eyes for a moment, then began. He recounted Shahil's "accidental" death. The deaths and demo-
tions of many who were loyal to the late king. The sudden
disappearance of Jemma without warning. The traditional
summer holiday in Ilantha that had become a prison term.
His attempt at thwarting Bhakir with the speech a few days
ago, and the lucky breeze that had so obligingly snatched
the scripted speech from Castyll's slack grasp. Bhakir's
sudden, seemingly unfounded confidence of recent days.
Castyll's conviction that there were yet many who were

loyal to him, who did not see in Bhakir the monster that lurked beneath the surface. And finally, his own deep suspicion that, if he did not escape now, he never would.

Damir listened without comment, nodding now and then. Finally, when Castyll had finished, he said, "I have come to offer you asylum. My men and I can spirit you away from here by the time Bhakir knows to begin looking for you. The king of Byrn has offered his support and his army to back it up. And," Damir leaned forward, a slight smile on his thin lips, "Cimarys eagerly awaits a chance to see you again."

A lump rose in Castyll's throat. "The letter I sent—she was not hurt by it?"

"None of us believed you wrote it of your own free will. Cimarys has kept her faith in you."

Suddenly Castyll reached across the table and grasped Damir's hand hard. "Thank the gods. Knowing that she still believes in me gives me the strength to do what I feel I must. Damir . . . I thank you and your country for your offer of aid. But if I left, it would send the wrong message to my people. It would leave Bhakir utterly in power with no one to stand against him, no one to protect those who still follow me. You know how he twists things around with that cursed clever tongue of his. If I abandon my country now, he will have poisoned the people against me by the time I could return. No. I must remain here, and strike soon. He will not expect that."

Damir allowed himself another of his small, cryptic smiles. "I suspected as much. That's why I told the Blesser what I did."

"And that is?"

"After she has been interrogated with someone who can read her thoughts—and you know and I know Bhakir will locate someone who can—she will be left alone. A few hours later, Adara will have a desire to visit her sister Blesser in Jarmair. She will travel to the capital and find herself at Castle Derlian. She will ask for either Maren or

Kester, and, because of her position, her request for an audience will be granted. Once she verifies that she is speaking to Maren or Kester *alone*, her memory of her night with you will come back to her—and those whom you trust will finally know your true plight."

Castyll suppressed a desire to whoop aloud with joy. Damir continued with the plan he had "outlined" to the unaware Adara, and Castyll's delight grew. When Damir had finished, Castyll could practically feel the weight of an earned crown sitting atop his brow. Damir wet his throat with the cheap ale and said something that took his drinking companion totally by surprise.

"And in the meantime, we can work on your magic skills."

Castyll blinked. If it were anyone other than Damir—Damir, who had just proved his friendship and worth a hundred times over—he would have thought the comment an insulting jibe. He replied stiffly, "I have no magical skills. The Derlian line of wizard-kings died with my father."

Damir shook his head. "Oh, no, Your Majesty."

"But . . . damn it, night after night I have sat and tried to light the cursed candle in my bedchamber. I failed the Test with the bracers as a child, and I've never exhibited any talent whatsoever."

"Did it ever occur to you that you might be trying too hard?"

Castyll did not reply, but apparently his uncomprehending stare was answer enough. Damir continued. "I've seen this before—not connected with magic, but with marksmanship, for instance, or other skills. Sometimes, one can try too hard, and the very pressure of the effort undercuts any hope of success." He leaned forward and spoke quietly, but very intently, so that Castyll could not possibly misunderstand.

"You spoke of the breeze that so conveniently tore the speech out of your hands, when you wished not to have to deliver it."

"Well, yes, but—"

"I have seen many things in my life. I have grown to be highly suspicious of coincidences. I believe that you *called* that breeze. You were not thinking, 'if only a gust of wind, blowing at a certain speed and strength, would come right here and be of sufficient force to snatch away this speech.' You merely wanted to find an excuse to deliver your own message. And you made that excuse."

The hair along Castyll's forearms began to prickle. "Damir, you are dangling my dearest hope in front of my eyes. I hope you're not toying with me."

"I would not do such a thing."

"No," Castyll said slowly. "No, you wouldn't. I . . . I hardly dared to hope any more."

"Dare, Your Majesty. Dare."

The examiner sighed, removed his fingers from the young woman's temples, and told his master what he knew he did not wish to hear.

"She's telling the truth, milord. When she woke up, he was gone. She really does have no idea where he might be."

Bhakir smothered his anger. Cursed little royal brat. He should have killed the young pup when he had the chance. Accidents happened, after all.

The two little Tenders, huddled close to one another, watched with round eyes. They, too, had been subjected to an examination; they, too, had been exonerated. Now they stared, silent, at their mistress and the big, black-bearded man who had come to see her.

"You must be a very deep sleeper, Blesser," Bhakir said in a voice that sounded perfectly sincere to those who did not know him well. "Two of my guardsmen lie dead in your garden. Yet you did not waken."

The skinny little Blesser shrank back still further. "I did not know. I shall pray for them and their families. Is Castyll—why would he do such a thing?" She seemed gen-

uinely confused, and Bhakir reluctantly dismissed the idea
that she was a collaborator. Women, other than Healers,
had no magic. There was no way Adara could have "lied"
to his mind-reader.

"I fear that our good king may have been kidnapped," he
said gravely. Adara's hands flew to her mouth in horror.
"That was why I had guards stationed about your Holy
House—though I know that it is against custom to do so.
Byrn . . ." He sighed and shook his dark head helplessly.
"They pose as our allies, but my dear young Blesser, I must
tell you that they are no friends to Mhar. I have long feared
that such a catastrophe would occur. But to think that even
Byrnians would so blaspheme as to kidnap a king from a
Holy House!"

"If this is indeed what happened," murmured Adara,
"then their souls are lost in truth. Your Grace, please—if
you have word of Castyll, let me know. I would see him
safe."

"As would I, dear lady." He bowed as low as the huge
bulk about his midsection would permit. "My men and I
shall leave you in peace now. Thank you for cooperating
with us."

He led the way out into the bright, midmorning sunshine.
With an effort, he heaved himself into his saddle, his mind
working furiously. He slowly motioned for the two guards
to ride at his side and the mind-reader to bring up the rear,
and the four horses clopped down the cobblestone way toward the palace.

To the guard on his left, Bhakir said softly, "Keep an eye
on the girl. Follow me until we are well out of sight, then
slip off the horse and double back."

"Certainly, milord, but may I ask your suspicions? The
girl knows nothing."

"No, but Castyll may try to reach her—turn her to his
cause. If he returns, I want someone there to capture him.
It's doubtful, but right now I will not take any risk. Keep
the Blesser in your sight at all times, understood?"

"Aye, sir."

To the guard on his right, Bhakir said, "Ride up ahead. I want every road sealed off, every ship that docks at the Ilantha port inspected."

"Quietly, sir, or publicly?"

"*Very* publicly. Put the word out that he's been kidnapped by Byrnians. Put a reward out for any sightings. If he shows his head anywhere, I want someone to report it. And if he disappears without a trace, well, we can turn that to our advantage as well. What bothers me most about this is, he had help." His eyes narrowed, thoughtful. "What do our spies say about Damir Larath? I was suspicious of his coming so close to our borders in the first place."

"He is still in Braedon, milord. He was apparently ill, but has recovered."

"You're certain?"

"He was spotted just a day ago at a public ceremony, milord."

Bhakir swore. "I would have been willing to wager he was involved directly in this—it's just the sort of thing I'd expect from him. Too clean. But I suppose not. Indirectly, though . . ." His voice trailed off. Castyll might already be well on his way to Byrn. Time, then, to take the hunt to Braedon, and watch for him there. And, mused the counselor to himself, if the young king of Mhar were indeed in Braedon, then in a very few days, Bhakir's worries would be over.

"My lord Bhakir!" The voice was youthful, strong, the voice of one used to being obeyed. Bhakir stiffened, then turned slowly in the saddle to see who had hailed him.

Striding up boldly to him and his guards was the Blesser of Vengeance. "We have business, you and I." The face turned up to Bhakir was handsome, with thick black brows and a strong mouth. Anger snapped in the dark eyes.

Bhakir looked around uneasily. Several people had paused to look at the unusual sight. Mentally, Bhakir cursed the man a thousand times, then smiled ingratiatingly. "Greetings, Blesser. And what business might that be?"

The Blesser had reached him now. His arms were folded and he stared at the mounted counselor. "The business of blasphemy."

Bhakir felt a chill. "I'm sure I don't know what you mean."

"My god has revealed to me that you are taking his name in vain. That you are doing something of which he does not approve. You may tread men beneath your heel, my lord, but you defy a god at your dreadful peril. Especially when that god is the mighty and implacable Vengeance."

Bhakir looked concerned. "If I have offended, then I ask forgiveness and to be shown what it is that I have done wrong. Blesser, will you come to Seacliff tonight and pray with me?"

The man's tense face relaxed somewhat. "Well," he said, slightly mollified, "I am bound by my oaths to help those who ask for it. Very well. I will be there at sunset. But don't think that false piety will spare the Sword of Vengeance," he added.

"Of course not," replied Bhakir. "Truly, I would atone for whatever sins I may have committed. May I expect you at sunset?"

The Blesser's eyes searched Bhakir's face, then he nodded. Bhakir inclined his head, then gently squeezed his mount, continuing the ride. He said nothing to his guards, and after a moment, the one on the right rode ahead while the one on his left slowed, then circled back, per their lord's instructions. The mind-reader kicked his mount and came to ride alongside Bhakir. The counselor remained silent. There was no way of knowing what the Blesser really knew. Not yet.

But come sunset, Bhakir would have Garith use his "methods of persuasion" on the man. And then, when they had learned all there was to learn, Bhakir would order the

Blesser killed. He'd gone too far to let one loose-tongued, arrogant Priest ruin it all.

Alone with her young Tenders, the Blesser of Love brushed out her long hair thoughtfully. Things were very unsettled, Adara mused to herself. Perhaps she needed some advice from another.

"I think I will go visit Love's Blesser in Jarmair," she said to her Tenders. "Can you ready my things for the trip?"

Deveren drummed his fingers on the table. He had no interest in the fine food before him, but he absently watched Kyle eat heartily.

The resemblance truly was uncanny. With the wig, putty nose and other makeup tricks, Kyle was almost a mirror image of Damir. He had most of the gestures down and had captured Damir's precise manner of speaking. If Deveren closed his eyes slightly, it could indeed almost be Damir across from him at the table. Kyle had even managed to fool the servants by keeping out of their way as much as possible. When he did come in contact with them, it was usually only at meals—times when the servants' attention was occupied by the food and the serving of it, not in looking closely at their master's brother.

The first two public appearances—token things, really— had gone off without a hitch. Fortunately there had been no parties, nothing involving people who knew Damir well and would have a chance to speak with Kyle at length and up close. If only Damir would return in time for the Midsummer Festival, all would be well.

Traditionally, Braedon's Midsummer Festival was a time of good-natured cheer and banter. Deveren, though, had now been with the thieves long enough to know that it was also a prime opportunity for crime. But even the thieves of Braedon seemed to get into the joyful spirit of things. He knew of no violent crimes that had been perpetrated during the event over the past years. A great many thefts, yes, but no murders or even attacks.

This year, he mused darkly, staring into his goblet of wine, could well be different. There had been one attempt on his life. There ought to be more. The very lack of a second attempt at murder had Deveren unsettled. There could only be one reason—he was no longer deemed a threat. And *that* was actually even a more frightening thought. It meant that whoever had tried to kill him now felt it was no longer necessary to remove him—that the would-be killer had found another means to his goal.

The rat.

Deveren suppressed a shudder. If one of his thieves was trafficking in that sort of dark magic, then Deveren knew he was right to be afraid.

Who was it? Freylis? Khem, who had kept to himself and whom Deveren didn't know well? Someone else?

He took a gulp of the wine. It didn't help.

"Your pardon, Lord Larath," came the voice of Millia, the cook's young daughter. "But . . . there's someone come to see you."

"Who is it?" asked Deveren, tensing.

The girl frowned. "It's . . . it's a child, sir." Deveren smothered a grin at the slightly superior tone of voice. Millia was a child herself, a mere ten years of age. "She says she comes from the Blesser of Health with news."

Hope flooded through Deveren. "Very good, Millia. Send her in to the library and I'll speak with her there. No doubt," he added for the benefit of Millia, Kyle, and other ears which might be listening, "she brings a cure for those nasty headaches I've been having."

A few moments later, Millia showed Allika to the library. It was all Deveren could do not to gape openly at the change wrought by just two days in the Blesser's charge.

She was clothed in a simple but clean brown dress, probably loaned from one of Vervain's tenders. Her face was clean, showing Deveren for the first time how white and pink her skin was. Her short-cropped black hair had been combed into obedience, and gleamed. On her feet were small brown boots, and her back was straight. Her eyes sparkled with delight and she rushed into Deveren's arms, hugging him.

"Don't I look pretty?" she crowed immodestly.

"Little Squirrel, you look beautiful," he told her truthfully, planting a kiss on shiny black hair that smelled of herbs and sunlight.

She grinned, and it warmed Deveren's heart to see the impish sparkle in her eyes again. He'd feared that her laughter and sense of play had burned to ashes along with her beloved doll, but clearly that was not the case. "Vervain has been taking good care of you."

"She's nice," agreed Allika readily. "She's tired, though. She stays up late and gets up early. Got black circles round her eyes."

"I don't doubt it," said Deveren.

"But she says to tell you that she's got good news. She says," and Allika thought carefully before continuing, "she says, 'Tell Deveren that I believe I have perfected the tinc—tincture—but I will need to test it on someone. Ask Deveren if he knows of anyone who would be willing to undergo such a test. I don't think it will be harmful, even if it doesn't work.' That's what she said."

And Deveren was certain it was, word for word. He was silent for a moment, thinking. Allika waited patiently. Deveren again marveled at the sight of her, remembering the angry, violent, squalling creature he had lugged by sheer physical force to the Healer's temple; recalled her rage, her pain when she tried to apologize—

Suddenly Deveren's thoughts flashed back to that dreadful day of Lorinda's funeral. He saw again Pedric standing in front of him, screaming angrily, froth on his lips and hate in his eyes. The poisonous, cruel words sounded again in his ears.

To the Nightlands with Lorinda! She's dead, Deveren,

dead, and the dead are nothing but dirt. There's no purity in rot. Gods, Dev, couldn't you smell her as we brought the coffin by? . . . There's nothing left of her now but decaying flesh . . . and the hope that I can somehow do to her killers what they did to her. So you can just take your wine and your talk and leave me alone!

He remembered with growing horror how Pedric had at first gentled at Deveren's sympathy, then doubled over in pain to emerge twice as bitter. And he remembered the youth fidgeting and scratching . . .

Deveren had been blinded by the memory of his own aching loss. He had thought Pedric merely suffering from grief and the natural anger at the violent crime. Now he realized that something far darker and dreadfully unnatural had been at work.

"Dear gods," he said softly. Poor Pedric . . .

"What?" asked Allika anxiously.

"Nothing you need to worry about, sweeting. Go back to Vervain and tell her I will be there tonight with . . . with someone to test her tincture."

It was with a lie that Deveren coaxed Pedric into the streets and out of his drunken isolation. A lie that Pedric believed because he wanted to believe it; believed because the curse that raged through him believed that everyone was as filled with hatred as he was.

I know who murdered Lorinda, Deveren had said. *I know where we can find them. And I will help you kill them.*

A feral light had come into Pedric's aged-looking, unshaved face; illuminated his haunted eyes, red-rimmed with drink and sleepless nights.

Yes, he had answered. *Let us kill them.* Words that Deveren had never thought to hear emerge from Pedric's cultured throat. And off they had gone, into the quiet darkness of the night. Pedric had laughed wildly, eager for blood and revenge. It was only the knowledge that Pedric was not truly responsible for his thoughts and actions that kept Deveren's heart from breaking for his friend.

They made their way through the city, and Pedric slowed as Deveren led him to the temple of Health. He stopped in front of the little gate and turned to stare suspiciously at Deveren.

"At Health's temple?" he asked, incredulous.

Please let this work, Deveren said to himself. Aloud, he said, "They are injured. They will be easy prey." He stretched his mouth into a smile. "We can subdue them with our bare hands."

That temptation proved to be too much for Pedric. He smiled himself, and inwardly Deveren drew back from the simple evil in that smile. *How close we all are to evil*, he thought. *How terribly, dreadfully close*. "Come," he said, inviting Pedric to go in front of him.

He waited until Pedric had opened the door to the temple proper before bringing his hands down hard on the back of the young man's head. Pedric groaned and fell forward.

At once Vervain was there with a light. "Get him on the table!" she cried.

Pedric was not unconscious, and fought as Deveren tried to shove him onto the table. Again Deveren dealt him a hard blow, this time to the temple. The younger man stumbled and Deveren managed to get him onto the table. "Hurry!" he called to Vervain. "I won't be able to hold him!"

Swiftly, efficiently, Vervain was there. Deveren crawled onto the table himself, trying to pin the writhing young man down with legs, arms, elbows, anything that would work. The heel of Pedric's hand came up and smashed Deveren in the mouth. Deveren tasted blood, but did not loose his grip. Vervain poured a swallow of her herbal tincture into Pedric's snarling mouth, saying as she did so, "Take care, Deveren! It will make him worse before it makes him well!"

What was she talking about? Deveren thought wildly.

Pedric gulped, choked, coughed, finally swallowed. Like the shadow of a hawk falling across a frozen, terrified hare, Deveren saw something dark pass across Pedric's fine features. His eyes seemed almost to be glowing with evil, and Deveren wildly recalled Allika's comments about the rat's red eyes. With a bellow, Pedric got his arms free and clamped his hands about Deveren's neck. Deveren's eyes flew wide and his own hands reached to his throat, trying to pry loose powerful fingers that were slowly squeezing the life out of him.

Pedric's mouth was open, spewing obscenities. Vervain maneuvered about the struggling men and managed to slosh another mouthful into the wild younger man.

The pressure about Deveren's throat suddenly disappeared. Coughing and gagging, Deveren lurched backward, almost falling off the table. He breathed in great gulps of sweet air, massaging his bruised neck and gazing at Pedric.

The young nobleman was pale and sweating. His chest rose and fell as he himself sought air. But, thank the gods, that dreadful crimson glare was gone from his eyes, and his face had lost its unnatural tension. Already the grim lines of hate and anger were fading.

"Dev," he said slowly, "Dev . . . I tried to *kill* you."

Hoarsely, Deveren replied, still rubbing his aching throat, "And you damn near succeeded."

Confused, Pedric blinked, looking about stupidly. "There were people—Deveren, you were taking me to murder someone! What in the Nightlands—"

"Not the Nightlands," interrupted Vervain smoothly, handing steaming mugs of fragrant liquid to both men. "Something all the darker for it happening right here. Drink this. It will calm you."

As he sipped the hot herbal tea, Deveren silently marveled at the cool strength of the woman. She seemed completely unruffled by what had transpired. As he drank, she glanced over at him with a raised eyebrow. He indicated that she might proceed. His throat hurt too much for him to talk right now.

As Pedric and Deveren sat quietly, Vervain explained what she and Deveren had discovered about the curse. Pedric's eyes grew wider and sadder. When the Healer had finished, he glanced over at Deveren, looking like a whipped cur.

"I'm sorry I said what I did . . . at the funeral."

"I thought you were merely grieving. I knew what you were going through—or, at least, I thought I did," said Deveren. His voice was back to normal, thanks to Vervain's tea.

"Oh, I hurt," said Pedric, his face grim. "I still ache for her. And if I ever did find the murderers, I'm not sure what I'd do. But to say those things to you—and attack you . . . !"

Deveren waved it aside. "Let's just say you weren't your normal self."

Pedric smiled a little—a very little—at that. Then the smile faded. "But if what you say is true . . . then nearly everyone in Braedon must be affected by now."

The Healer nodded grimly. She was in full vestments. The red wimple hid her glorious brown hair. The open, friendly woman Deveren had seen with Allika a few nights ago was hidden by weariness and calm efficiency. "The tincture worked, but it will be tricky to apply. Do you remember what I said to you when I healed Allika, Deveren? That she first had to surrender, be made completely evil, before she could be restored?"

Deveren nodded, drained his mug, and went to the steaming pot by the fire for a second serving. As he passed Pedric, the younger man held out his cup wordlessly. He, too, could stand another dose of the calming brew.

"Well, the herbal remedy mimics that. There must be two doses. The first replicates the surrender to the darkness. The second restores wholeness. That was why I warned you that Pedric would get worse before he got better."

A sudden, dreadful thought occurred to Deveren. "What

about a recurrence? Does this cure someone permanently or
temporarily?"

Vervain now allowed herself a tired but proud smile. "It
is a permanent cure. I gave Allika a dose earlier today, before I sent her over to you. If she had not been cured, it
would have made her angry and cruel again. But it had no
effect—other than to make her stick out her tongue and
protest that it tasted bad."

Deveren laughed. His heart began to lift. With a permanent cure that could be spread to the public at large—his
face fell.

"But how do we get everyone to drink it?"

Vervain rubbed her bloodshot eyes. "That, my dear
friend Deveren, is the question of the hour." Her voice softened. "I do not need to drink the tincture. I will not succumb to the sickness; I know I can fight it alone. That is
part of my gift of Healing. Allika is cured. Pedric is cured.
But, Deveren . . ." Her voice trailed off.

Deveren felt something cold clench his stomach. "But . . .
I haven't displayed any symptoms. I took precautions—
even burned my clothes like you suggested. I'm not sick."

"No," Vervain agreed. "But think. You met Allika right
after she had been bitten by the rat. You bore her over here.
You led Pedric here. Deveren, you may not be manifesting
symptoms yet, but all I know about the spread of disease
tells me that you either are infected now or shortly will be."

"You . . . you want me to drink that? As a precaution?"

She nodded, slowly, implacably.

Deveren sat silently. A Healer could not force him to
obey her suggestions, when she did not know for a certainty that disease would result. That was part of her creed.
And Pedric was not going to insist, either. They left the
decision up to Deveren. He thought about what, exactly,
it would mean—to become evil. Ah, gods, he didn't want
this . . .

. . . and then he thought of Allika, and Pedric, raging and
out of control. Better to choose the moment than have it

thrust upon him. Abruptly, his decision made, Deveren snatched the bottle from the table and swallowed a huge mouthful.

Vervain rose, crying, "Pedric, hold him!" At the same moment, Pedric, alarm spreading across his handsome face, moved to grasp Deveren.

But he was too late.

The mixture was not the bitter draft Deveren had expected. It was honey-sweet, slipping easily down his throat. Instantly, Deveren felt wonderful. The worry for his brother slipped from his mind. He moved easily out of Pedric's clumsy reach, almost dancing free. Ah, Pedric.

"Sorry, friend. Should have left you as you were. It's a lot more fun."

He directed his gaze at Vervain, who drew back before it, her eyes wide. She was a pretty piece. Needed to get rid of those bulky robes. Deveren was certain that underneath all those red garments was a body that would thrill a man in bed. He'd show her what a real man was like. And she'd like it. Or if she didn't, no matter. Murder held the same release and pleasure as copulation. He instinctively knew it.

Again Pedric tried to grab him. This time, Deveren landed a solid punch to the younger man's face. "Ah, ah, ah," he chastised as Pedric staggered back. He spared another glance for the Healer. "Not now, pretty thing. I'll come back for you when you're least expecting me. But here's a little something to whet your appetite."

He strode over to Vervain and roughly pulled her to him. She struggled in his arms. "That's it, fight me," Deveren growled. He bent his head, his tongue licking her face like an animal's as she cried out and attempted to turn her face away. Oh, to be able to take her right here, right now . . .

"No!" cried Pedric. Deveren felt strong hands on his arm, spinning him around. Vervain stumbled backward. Out of the corner of his eye he saw her reach for the tincture.

Deveren turned on Pedric and saw that his former friend

had drawn his dagger. He'd had enough of this youth's meddling. He charged and Pedric fell before the onslaught of pure fury, whirling to unexpectedly attack the youth and pinning him on the floor with a knee on his throat.

"Try to pull a knife on me, will you? It'll be harder to do that when you don't have any fingers, won't it?" He savagely opened Pedric's hand, and the blade clattered to the floor. Deveren forced the hand flat, spreading the fingers, and prepared to use the dagger to slice off Pedric's fingers one by one.

"*Kastara!*"

The word, barely a whisper issuing from Pedric's throat, halted Deveren, blade poised above Pedric's little finger, penetrating the hot dreams of lust and violence. *Kastara. Beloved.* A deep love battled with the newly aroused evil. And then pain, pain so intense he had never tasted its like, hit him like the fist of an angry god. All the strength went out of him and he rolled off Pedric, clutching his stomach and squealing like a rabbit with the agony.

At once he felt fingers pinching his nose shut. Another hand forced open his mouth, poured a liquid into it. He had to swallow or choke to death.

This time it was bitter, harsh and acidic, and burned his throat as he gulped it down. There was a sudden ache as the evil that had flooded him receded. He blinked, coughed, then slowly sat up.

Pedric had scooted away, rubbing his throat. Vervain, too, had stepped out of immediate reach. Both were eying him warily. Hot shame rushed over Deveren as he recalled what had just happened. What to say? What to do? How could he possibly apologize? And the one thing that lingered, that frightened him the most, was that somehow he was aware that what had just washed over him was not insanity. He had merely become the Deveren that might have been, had there been no love, no goodness, no light to brush his life in the previous thirty-four years.

There was a beast within everyone, and Deveren had

looked it in the face. His expression of horror and contrition must have reassured them, for they relaxed as they watched him.

Pedric smiled shakily. "Welcome back," he said quietly.

*And Parin took the Sword of Vengeance, and for seven
days and seven nights, the river ran red with blood.*

      —Mharian folktale, *The Seven Deeds of Parin*

CHAPTER EIGHTEEN

Castyll had been able to sleep only for a few hours; a
short nap in a whore's scented bed. Both he and Damir
knew that speed was of the essence. By the time midmorning came, Bhakir would have already put word out about
Castyll's disappearance. He would be closing roads,
searching ships, and it would be increasingly dangerous to
be en route to Jarmair. But only in Jarmair would Castyll be
able to gather armed men to fight for him; and only with
armed men could he hope to defeat Bhakir.

So Castyll, Damir, and his loyal men were on their way
as dawn lightened the horizon. With relatively little effort—or so it seemed to the young king—Damir had put an
illusion on Castyll that disguised his features so that he
would not be recognized. At one point, traveling along a
little-used road that led out of Ilantha, Castyll had glanced

down at the major road and seen a large group of armed men heading for the port city. He'd shuddered, and thanked whatever god was responsible for sending Damir to Mhar.

They talked of magic, to pass the long hours on horseback over difficult terrain. Damir seemed certain that Castyll had indeed inherited the ability to use magic, and that the only thing stopping Castyll was his own trepidation. That night, when they made a camp devoid of fire for warmth or cooking meat—Damir had deemed it too dangerous—the older man had gently probed the young king's mind, seeking confirmation of what he expected.

He smiled as his fingers left Castyll's temples. "It is there, locked away, as a miser might hoard his treasure. I fear it is far too deeply rooted in your mind for you to locate it on your own. It might take weeks of searching, but I could guide you."

"Will you, Damir? Will you be my tutor?"

Damir chuckled. His face was dim in the starlight. "Let us recapture your kingdom first, Your Majesty. Then we will be free to contemplate tutoring and other such happy activities."

They moved on before dawn of the following morning. Castyll ached from such long hours in the saddle, but reminded himself that had he been forced to walk the distance, he'd have long since been captured.

He had desperately wanted to ride into the capital city openly, with his royal standard snapping in the breeze, waving to the people he was certain were still loyal. Damir had immediately quashed the idea. "Assassins," he had said simply. "The humblest peasant could be one of Bhakir's men in disguise. We will proceed carefully. There is always the chance that my plan might not have worked."

"Do your plans have a history of not working, Damir?"

"Not often."

"They call you the Problem Solver. Did you know that?"

Damir laughed. "So I have heard, Your Majesty."

By the end of that long day, Castyll's royal bottom was

aching and his legs screamed for rest. But Jarmair was within sight, and even from this place up in the hills he could see the castle that had been his home since the day he was born.

"Castle Derlian," he said softly. "Oh, Damir. We're almost there."

On Damir's instructions, they waited for full night. Then, after all the men, including Castyll, had armored up and checked their weapons, they rode slowly into the quiet farmlands that surrounded Castle Derlian, keeping well away from the darkened houses. Damir's men closed ranks about the king, while Damir rode, sometimes scouting ahead, sometimes circling behind. Castyll guessed that Byrn's finest ambassador was using his formidable mind magic, trying to sense danger. It was all very reassuring.

At last, they came within sight of the mammoth gates of Castle Derlian. Damir kneed his horse and approached Castyll and the circle of men. "We go no further without reassurance that we're not walking into a trap," he stated bluntly.

"What do you suggest?" queried Castyll.

"We send in a decoy." Damir's bright eyes roamed over the faces of his men, and it was to them that he addressed his next words. "I'll cast an illusion on one of you. You will go forward and demand entrance. You will appear to be the king—alone, unarmed. If they attack the decoy, then the rest of us flee. If they take the false king inside, we wait till we hear a report and if not, then—"

"What?" cried Castyll, aghast. "You'd send a man to walk into a trap?"

"With His Majesty's pardon," spoke up one of the men, "we have all faced death many times before. That is our duty. Any one of us would consider it an honor to die protecting you and obeying our own king's orders."

"No." Castyll shook his dark head. "I won't allow it."

Damir sighed in exasperation. "Majesty—"

"You are under orders to obey me as if I were your own king, yes?" asked Castyll, knowing the answer.

"Aye, but it would behoove you to listen to someone with my experience."

"I have, Damir, and I know you know what you're doing. But—this is my kingship we're talking about. I should be the one walking into a trap, if there is one. Let us compromise. I will agree to send a man up as a decoy. But if they attack him—me—then we fight. And if they want to take him into the castle, we ride up and reveal the deception."

"Your Majesty," replied Damir with more than a touch of exasperation, "what if I'm right and you are walking willingly to your death?"

Castyll weighed his words carefully before he spoke. "It is my firm belief that this castle is manned with people loyal to me. That they have no idea of the evil Bhakir has been perpetrating. If that's true, and if your plan has worked, then we are walking toward the final victory, the restoration of my kingdom. If it's not true—if there is no one inside those stone walls who remains loyal to me— then there is no one within these borders whom I can trust. And the kingdom is lost beyond recapture. The Derlian line will have come to an end, and I will go down fighting to uphold the honor of those who have died before me."

He turned in the saddle to look at the men who had risked so much for him already. "I'm not your king. This is not your fight. If need be I will go forward alone, and take my chances. Come with me of your own will, if you choose. But I will not order you forward, nor will I allow Damir to do so."

Damir frowned terribly. Castyll knew he was angry, but he didn't care. He knew in his heart that was making the right decision.

"Very well," said Damir. "I will go with you, Your Majesty."

"And I," said the man to Damir's right. "And I," said another. In swift succession, Castyll faced six men who had pledged to fight or die with him. Tears stung his eyes; he blinked them away.

"We shall not fail," he said.

A few moments later, a man wearing Castyll's body and face ran up the cobblestone road that led to the castle walls. Castyll, safe for the moment in the shadows cast by Damir's magic, marvelled at the depth of the man's skill. The decoy looked exactly like the young king. He appeared to have no armor or weapons, though Castyll knew he was in reality well equipped with both. His heart hammered rapidly as the false Castyll hammered on the huge wooden doors.

"Who comes?" came the challenge from above.

The decoy tossed back the hood of his cloak, revealing his face plainly in the torchlight.

"It is I, your king!" he cried. Castyll silently shook his head. Damir had even gotten the voice right. "I have escaped and have come to where men are still loyal to me!"

"Majesty! We were told to expect you!"

At once Castyll heard the grinding, mechanical sound of the portcullis being raised. A moment later, the doors of the keep were opened, and "Castyll" was surrounded by men wearing the royal livery who immediately knelt to their liege. There was no attempt to usher the "king" in, either quietly or by force.

Castyll couldn't suppress a smile of triumph as he shot a glance at Damir. The Byrnian's face was inscrutable, but he replied, "It would appear that you were correct, Majesty."

Taking a deep breath, Castyll squeezed his mount forward, riding into sight from the concealing shadows. "Right pleased I am to see that the men of Castle Derlian have not forgotten their liege—even though they have mistaken him!"

The guards, confused, glanced from one "king" to the other. With an unobtrusive wave of his hand, Damir dispelled the illusion.

"A necessary precaution in these troubled times," said Castyll by way of apology, as the man the guards had taken for their king resumed his true appearance. "You were told to expect me. Might I ask by whom?"

"Why, by Lord Maren and Lord Kester. They had word from a source they would not name that all was not well with you and that you had to come by stealth to the castle that is your birthright," replied the man who was clearly in charge of the night's watch. Castyll nodded. Neither Maren nor Kester would have said anything that would have put Adara in any danger. "My lord Maren awaits your appearance in the main hall. He has news for you."

"Then let us not keep my loyal seneschal waiting!" said Castyll. He would have cantered forward eagerly into the courtyard had not the five men who had so carefully guarded him up till this moment closed in around him again. Even now, it would appear, Damir was suspicious. No doubt the diplomat's caution had been wise, but surely there was nothing to fear now. Nonetheless, Castyll did not protest the extra precaution.

Escorted by the castle guards, Castyll, Damir, and the five soldiers rode into the courtyard and dismounted. No sooner had Castyll's booted feet hit the dirt than he once again found himself in the center of the armed Byrnian men. He tried to catch Damir's eye to quietly express his annoyance, but Damir was not paying him any attention. His quick hazel eyes flitted about, searching for any threat to the young king he served.

Most of the castle was asleep at this hour. The tramping of booted feet across the stone floor of Castle Derlian was the only sound. There were no questions for Castyll; nor should there have been. Whatever the soldiers of the keep needed to know, they would be told by their commander. Enough to know that their king had returned, that the seneschal waited for an audience with His Majesty. Castyll's joy grew with every familiar turn, every tapestry, every piece of furniture, every well-known sight and sound of his birthplace.

The guards stopped at the entrance to the main feast hall. Their commander banged on the door and slowly the two massive doors heaved inward. The room was not fully illuminated. The candles on the massive stag-antler chandeliers were not lit, but a few torches burned in their sconces toward the end of the hall. In the dim lighting, much of the place remained shadowed, including the galleries above their heads that would, in happier times, have housed minstrels. The ornate tapestries, twenty in all, that covered the bare stone might have been plain cloth for all the detail the faint lighting revealed. Fat candles glowed on the huge center table that could seat twenty-four. Three others paralleled it, but there was no activity at these tables. At the head of the center table, his head bent over his books, sat Castyll's seneschal, Lord Maren. He glanced up, and a slow smile of delight spread across his face as he rose to greet his liege.

Maren was an old man. He had served Shahil for twenty-odd years, and had not been young when that position had been granted to him. He had a hawk's bill of a nose, watery brown eyes, and several teeth missing. But he stood straight despite the burden of the years that sat upon him, and his mind was as sharp as a knight's blade. Castyll was very fond of Maren, and the sight of him there, waiting patiently, was the final proof the young king needed that all would, finally, be well.

Maren was flanked by two younger men whom Castyll did not recognize, but who wore the traditional mantles of scholars. He assumed they were Maren's scribes.

"My king!" cried Maren, moving from his chair toward the door.

"My old friend," replied Castyll, his voice deepening with warm affection. He shouldered his way past the Byrnian guards and moved forward, his hand reaching out to grasp his seneschal's.

From behind, he heard Damir's voice. "Castyll, no! It's a—"

And then Castyll knew what it was. His smile froze on his face like a death's grin as suddenly, from the seemingly empty gallery above their heads, dozens of men sprang to life. They leaped from their places of concealment and leveled crossbows at the small group of men who pressed tighter around Castyll. The Byrnians and Castyll drew their own swords as doors flew open and more armed men charged in. Damir had moved as well, not to draw a weapon, but to begin casting a spell. Quick as lightning, one of the guards had him, yanking the diplomat's arms behind his body and pressing a blade to his throat.

Sweat trickled down Castyll's face as he glanced frantically about, his shocked gaze encountering nothing but hard faces, swords pledged to the use of his enemy. There was no friend among any of the guards that stood here. But there was no attack—not yet. Damir's men shielded Castyll with their bodies and readied swords as the disloyal guards of Castle Derlian waited, drawing out the moment with unbearable tension.

"Maren!" Castyll cried, brokenly. "How could you betray me?"

The old seneschal fixed him with a smile that was not his own, yet somehow familiar. And then, before the young king's horrified, revolted gaze, Maren's features melted, reformed. His slim frame seemed to swell and bloat, and then it was Bhakir standing at the head of the table.

"You tried such an illusion earlier. They work very well, don't they?"

"Bhakir," breathed Castyll. His stomach clenched.

"It is over, little king."

The tense seconds ticked by. "How?" said Castyll at last, furious that his voice broke on the single word.

Bhakir smiled evilly and made a gesture. A guard emerged from a corridor, holding a young woman roughly by the arm.

Castyll's heart sank. It was Adara. She had betrayed them. But then why was she being handled so brusquely? Why was there fear on her plain features? And then, even before Bhakir began to speak, the young king guessed at the truth.

"Castyll, I'm sorry—" Adara began. The guard struck her with his mailed fist as casually as if she were a disobedient hound. Her head jerked to the side with the force of the blow. Castyll instinctively moved toward her. At once there was a clattering sound as every guard in the room moved a step toward him. Two dozen weapons were poised, ready to slay him at a word.

"I had your homely Blesser followed." Castyll closed his eyes in pain. "I presume it was Damir whose clever idea it was to plant a suggestion in her dull little brain. I assumed you were in Braedon, Damir. How thoughtful of you to come to me. It was easy enough to determine what your plans were by whom the Blesser spoke with."

"Maren," Castyll managed. "Kester. You killed them, didn't you, you son of a—"

"Castyll, I am shocked that you would think such a thing." The mock horror in Bhakir's voice was an insult itself. "I'd never risk incurring public outcry like that. No, I merely reassigned them to other stations. Very distant stations, I might add. And sent some of my own men to make sure they stayed in line. And your Blesser—well, if one suggestion worked so well, then it is ease itself to give her another. She'll have no memory of this encounter by the time I'm done with her."

Unable to help himself, Castyll glanced back at Adara. Tears filled her eyes, ran down her cheeks. She might be the earthly representative of the best-loved deity in Verold, but right now, she was utterly helpless. Just as he was.

"And so, stone by stone, my little king's tower of dreams is toppled." Bhakir's voice was silky. He was enjoying every second of this. Castyll spat. He was too far away to reach anyone, but the gesture made him feel better.

Bhakir's heavy brows narrowed. "You are a foolish hot-head, just like your father," he growled.

"You murdered him!"

"Aye, I did. And too simple a deed it was. As simple as murdering you right now. You've made it so easy for me, Castyll. By stealing out of the Blesser's temple and conveniently disappearing, you've practically done the deed for me. Almost disappointing, I must say. I was content with things as they were. Content to pull your strings and watch you dance."

Outrage thrummed through the young king's veins. The sticky sweat of anger popped out on his brow, beneath his arms. He had thought he hated Bhakir before, but this—it dimmed his sight and hearing, made his heart swell with an abhorrence and loathing that almost overwhelmed him. Unbeknownst to him, a low growl of sheer white-hot fury began deep in his throat. His world suddenly narrowed to one thing—the image of the fat, hateful man who had deliberately, piece by piece, destroyed Castyll's world.

"But you have forced my hand," Bhakin continued. "Your Blesser's memory will be wiped as clean as the sand when the tide comes in. You will die within moments, by my hand. And don't think I won't relish every second of it. But first," and he smiled, that terrible, falsely jovial, despised smile, "you will watch your friend die before you."

Out of the corner of his eye, Castyll caught a movement. It was Damir, his hands pinned painfully behind him, a sharp sword at his throat, being propelled toward the center of the room with ungentle pricks from a spear. He stumbled forward, falling and unable to catch himself with his tied hands. The sword was never more than an inch away from his neck.

How could this be happening? Damir was a powerful wizard. Castyll had seen his mind magic—

—and then he realized. Bhakir also knew of Damir's skills. He would have warned his men not to trust their eyes until they had Damir secured. With his hands straining against the rope and a sword ready to pierce the soft flesh of his throat, the great Byrnian ambassador was effectively bound and gagged.

Castyll knew what he had said to the Byrnians earlier, about dying with glory, fighting to restore his kingdom. That if there was no one here who was loyal to him, then he might as well be dead. But he had never truly believed failure to be possible. Of course Damir's message would get through; of course the men would be loyal to him.

Bhakir. In the end, always, it was Bhakir. And now Damir would pay the dreadful price first. Damir, who had risked all to help a king of a foreign land. Damir, whose advice had been sound, who had been right all along. Damir, who foolishly believed that Castyll Derlian had magic.

Bhakir watched the boy's face greedily. Then he nodded to the man who stood over Damir. The man lifted his sword.

"No!" The word was ripped from Castyll's throat, a cry of utter despair and rage. At that moment, he seemed to hear a voice speaking from inside his head.

I am the Second who comes, to right a dreadful wrong. Wield you the Sword of Vengeance.

And all at once it was as if a veil had been lifted from Castyll's eyes. His blood sang and his body arched with the force of his emotions. He focused all his being on the silver blade of the sword as the guard lifted it to its height. There was a sharp *crack* and the guard toppled backward, screaming. The sword began to melt, turning first red, and then white hot, then losing its shape altogether as the molten steel flowed down over the man's hand and arm.

Immediately afterward Castyll heard the whiz of dozens of crossbow bolts being unleashed. Power surging through him like a savage tide, he spun on his heels. His eyes narrowed with outrage. He saw the tiny bolts, and with a wave of his hand thought: fire. Instantaneously, every last bolt

exploded into a small ball of flame, flaring and then burning to harmless cinders.

More, thought Castyll. *I want more.*

His completely unexpected use of magic had galvanized
Bhakir's soldiers. The clang of steel now rang through the
hall, and Castyll thought of the swords, the dozen or more
swords now being used on Damir's brave noblemen who
had pledged their lives to serve him.

Sheath them!

And each sword of the enemy suddenly writhed like a
fish. They sprang loose, sheathing themselves in the
wooden doors, in the stone walls, in the bodies of the men
who wielded them.

"An illusion!" Castyll heard the frantic cry dimly
through the blood that thudded in his ears. With narrowed
eyes, he turned his attention to Bhakir, who suddenly
looked a great deal less sure of himself than he had a scant
few seconds earlier.

"No illusion," Castyll growled. "The Sword of Vengeance!"

Castyll shoved his right hand forward, splaying the fingers hard. A ball of blue fire formed in his flat palm. It
screamed past Bhakir, igniting his robes. The fat counselor
cried out, futilely trying to extinguish the flames.

No. Not enough. Not enough for what you've done.

He stretched out both hands, clenched the fingers closed,
and then yanked them back. Bhakir screamed, a high,
falsetto shriek, as blood spurted from the sudden hole in his
chest.

There was a distance of some three yards between them.

Grinning fiercely, Castyll squeezed Bhakir's heart to
bloody pulp between his strong fingers. Now unseen hands
reached and grabbed bits of the dying man. Flesh and blood
flew as Castyll, delighting in the carnage, ripped Bhakir
apart without even touching him.

Take care. My Sword cuts both ways.

The red haze of bloodlust lifted. Castyll suddenly felt

bile rise in his throat. There was nothing remaining of Bhakir but a bloody pile of tiny lumps of flesh being ripped into still smaller pieces. He gasped, staggered forward a few steps, and fell to his knees. The terrible shredding ceased.

He felt a hand on his shoulder and jerked away, glancing up wildly. Castyll calmed a little when he realized it was Damir. The older man helped the king to his feet, but said nothing. Castyll glanced about, still panting. The guards who had minutes before been ready to slaughter him stared back. Their leader had been destroyed. Their weapons had melted in their very hands. They waited, for orders from their new liege—or death.

Castyll's throat hurt. Probably he'd been screaming his throat raw and not realizing it. He swallowed a few times, then spoke.

"Before you were Bhakir's men, you were my father's men," he rasped. "I don't know what Bhakir used to turn you against the Derlian line. Money, or promises of power, or fear. It doesn't matter. The line has run true—I now know, and you bear witness that I have the magical skills of my father, and his father before him." He straightened, pulled away from the supporting arm of Damir. His words rang like bells through the suddenly silent hall.

"I am Castyll Derlian, rightful king of Mhar. You are a body without a head, men without a leader. Serve your king, or await his punishment. Choose!"

For a long moment, no one moved. Then, one by one, the guards dropped to their knees. A wave of movement crested along the galleries as the archers dropped their weapons and made obeisance. A smile touched the youth's mouth. Gods, he was weary; so weary. And terrified by what had lain, latent and silent, in the depths of his soul to be awakened by . . . what? His own desperate need and desire? Castyll suspected more than that.

I am the Second who comes, to right a dreadful wrong.
Wield you the Sword of Vengeance.

Something, someone, had granted the young king access to his magical talent. He shuddered at the thought of the strange voice. He would need to speak of this to Damir at some point. Squaring his shoulders, he turned to his friend.

"I had no idea of the power of such magic. I didn't mean . . ." No. He would not start out the first moments of his true reign with a lie. He turned to gaze speculatively at the tattered pile of bloody flesh that had been Bhakir. "No. I did mean to do that. And I do not regret it."

"Your Majesty," came a voice. It belonged to a man whom Castyll did not know, but whom he had seen often in Bhakir's presence. The man had been one of the "scribes" standing near the false Maren. He looked frightened but resolute.

"Speak," said Castyll.

"Bhakir has already dispatched the Mharian navy, under Zhael's command, to Byrn. They will sail in partnership with Captain Porbrough's fleet."

"The pirates," breathed Damir.

"Aye, sir. For the moment, there is amnesty."

"What are their orders?" barked Castyll, striding over to the thin, ascetic man. He towered over the scribe, who shrank back, then continued in a voice that shook.

"B-Bhakir seemed to think that by the night of Braedon's Midsummer Festival, the city would be in chaos. Said he had made plans to ensure it. The fleet's instructions were to attack at Death's hour. He said—" and the man swallowed hard, "—none shall be spared."

"Good gods!" cried Damir. "Castyll, they will take Braedon completely unprepared!"

"We've got to stop them," said Castyll. He was feeling drained by the use of his newly discovered magic. He wanted nothing better than to lie down and sleep for a few hours, then rise and eat a hearty meal. But he did not have that luxury. His first act as king of Mhar must be to prevent his allies from slaughter by his own fleet—for Byrn's safety and Mhar's own. "There must be a few ships still left in the harbor that we can send in pursuit!"

"And I," said Damir with grim satisfaction, "have a friend who may prove to be very helpful indeed."

Summer is here, the breezes are sweet;
And ripening fruits are ready to eat.
Travel, ye serf, ye servant and thane,
To Braedon's Midsummer, where idiots reign.

—Byrnian folk ballad

CHAPTER NINETEEN

At last it had come—Midsummer Festival. A time of joyful revelry, humor, and mirth. Many would be the richer for this favorite holiday, for sales were always good; and many more would end up poorer and perhaps wiser. The preparations had been many and varied. Apprentices had worked longer hours than usual, scurrying to and fro to obey their masters as procrastination took its bitter toll. The city itself never looked better than on the dawning of Midsummer Festival—although by the next day's dawn, one often wondered if there had been any point to all the hard work, as Braedon looked much worse immediately after the revelers had retired for the night than it ever looked before.

During the day, with the sun smiling hotly in a cloudless sky, the booths and other makeshift buildings located between the stretches of farmland and the city proper had been crammed to overflowing. Merchants had come from all over the country, and even from Mhar, to sell exotic foods, wines, spices, and bolts of cloth, from warm wool to airy silks to heavy, ornate brocades. Other items, too, could be had if one had the coins—knives, leather shoes, jewels, whalebone carvings.

Deveren had wandered through the crowd, after having left strict orders for "Damir" to stay home. Kyle would have to make an appearance tonight as part of the parade. That was quite enough for Deveren's nerves. At least after tonight, the "season" would be over, and Kyle wouldn't have to make quite so many public appearances. Damir had picked the worst possible time to disappear, and Deveren hoped desperately that all was well with his brother.

Deveren had listened carefully to the various conversations that bubbled about him and had heard nothing of note. There had been no violence perpetrated save for the occasional, and expected, complaint of a "lost" pouch of coins. Now the day had had enough of Braedon's festival, and the sun sank quietly over the ocean to the west. But the lengthening shadows did not discourage the happy throngs that moved easily from fields to streets.

Many of the merchants were still open, hawking their wares from smaller booths in the town. But now most of the activities would take place inside taverns. If the tavern keepers were wise, they'd have taken care to clean their dice and stock up their supplies of ales and wines. Tavern brawls over such things were bad for business.

Business of another sort, too, was being conducted inside the taverns and on the streets. Dozens of women immodestly bared arms, ankles, and generous portions of bosom as they strolled about, a smile at the ready. Like rubies, brocades, or beer, they too could be bought if one had the coins.

In other words, this Midsummer Festival looked to be shaping up like any other.

One thing that Deveren definitely didn't like was the

conspicuous absence of most of his thieves. Where were they? He'd been everywhere today and hadn't encountered anyone but Rabbit, who was innocuously engrossed in the harmless activity of selling his wares, and Pedric, arguing good-naturedly over the price of a bolt of brocade. Allika would be with Vervain. But where was Freylis? Clia? Marrika? Khem, and all the others? Perhaps they were lying low during the day, resting; saving their energy for the night's activities. Perhaps. But Deveren suspected something worse.

If there were an attempt to be made on his life, it would be tonight; and if there were any time for the curse borne by the rat's cadre of vermin to spread like wildfire, it would be in this crowd.

The sun had set fully now. He shouldered his way through the crowd to get a good view of the Parade. It wasn't an easy task, for the Parade was one of the most popular events of the whole festival. For one day a year, the Council and any visiting dignitaries were at the "mercy" of the commoners. It was all highly symbolic and completely safe. The Councilmen would march in a procession, hands (not very securely) tied behind their backs as the people teased them (good-naturedly). A Byrnian commoner would be selected at random to be Master of Mischief who would "rule" over the Council for the duration of the (brief) ceremony.

It was touted as a harmless outlet for any frustrations the people of Braedon might have with their leadership. And more than once, good-hearted Vandaris had heard something shouted as jest that he recognized as a real complaint, which he had later brought up at a council meeting. Guards were thick as flies in a slaughterhouse; should anything get out of hand, it would be stopped before it had really begun. Deveren could not recall any incident occurring at the Parade in the thirty-four years that he had lived in Braedon. Still, he mused; still . . .

A roar went up. The Parade was beginning. Deveren

craned his neck, trying to see over the crowd in the dim lighting provided by lamps and torches along the street.

"Oh, no," he groaned softly.

"Damir," the visiting ambassador, led the procession. Kyle skipped stupidly down the street, his hands tied behind his back. A parti-colored, garishly hued cap with more feathers than Deveren had ever seen on a real, living bird was perched atop his dark head, and the idiot grin he was wearing pleased the crowd no end. Behind him, wearing a face that had been painted on and did not entirely hide the tired, worn expression, was Vandaris. He still wore black, in mourning for his dead daughter.

A slight tug on his hand caused Deveren to glance down. It was Allika. She grinned up at him. Was she here for the Parade, or did she have news from Vervain? Deveren had just opened his mouth to ask her when a gleeful roar of approval made him glance forward, just in time to see "Damir" execute a flip in the air, only to sprawl helplessly in a pile of horse dung. Friendly hands helped him up, but deliberately didn't bother cleaning him off. Deveren thought curses. Kyle was certainly going to give himself away if he wasn't more careful.

But he softened his mental rebuke almost instantly. Kyle was having the first real fun he'd had in days. He was an actor performing before an adoring throng; finally in his own element. He didn't have to feign dignity, not in the Parade. He could relax and play a little. Who was Deveren to deny him that meager comfort? And certainly the real Damir wouldn't have pleased the crowd quite so much. Deveren smiled a little at the thought of his dignified brother with horse manure on his well-tailored clothes.

Another tug on his hand, more insistent. A second time Deveren bent to listen to the girl, and a second time the spontaneous roar from the crowd drowned out anything she might have needed to say.

"Hail to the Master!" came a cry that was picked up and repeated. "Hail to the Master!"

The crowd rippled, moved to let this year's Master of Mischief enter. Deveren couldn't quite see who it was, as the figure was on the short side and the traditional heavy fur robes—the contrast between the hot weather and the heavy robes was meant to point up the foolishness of the whole thing—turned his shape into a large, furry, brown lump.

Then the Master of Mischief turned. He was smiling and waving the customary Rod of Ridicule gaily, but Deveren's heart turned to ice within his chest.

It was Khem.

The selection was random. Anybody who wasn't in a high position in the local or national government and who didn't own land was eligible to be chosen for the role of Master of Mischief. But Khem—a thief who had been spotted by Allika in the act of helping to bring a curse upon Braedon—here, now, in this position . . . The hairs along Deveren's arms crawled and he rubbed them unconsciously. Like his brother, Deveren Larath had seen too much to believe in coincidence.

"O-ho, what do we have here?" said Khem, peering at the bound diplomats. His scarred face crinkled into a smile.

"Oh, Mischief Master, sir, we be humble folkses, we does," drawled "Damir." "Does that not be right, mates?" He craned his neck to look at the rest of the councilmen, grinning. They mumbled appropriate responses.

"Humble folkses, eh?" mused Khem, drumming his fingers against his chin. "Hmmm. Here, catch!" And he threw his Rod of Ridicule at Damir.

The blue-and-red painted staff caught Kyle's temple. The actor gasped, then pretended to swoon.

"This'll bring him around!" another man cried, pouring his beer in Kyle's face. "Damir" merely opened his mouth and swallowed the amber liquid. Another point scored; the crowd applauded. Deveren had to admit, the actor was handling his audience perfectly.

"But is it not a crime to drink an' pass out in the streets?"

queried a young woman that Deveren recognized as one of
the barmaids at Jankiss's tavern. Her words brought a wave
of laughter, for if they had been true, approximately two-
thirds of Braedon's population would presently be in the
stocks.

"Why, so it is!" Khem exclaimed. He whirled and pointed
directly at a surprised Captain Jaranis. "Place that miscreant
in the stocks!"

Jaranis seemed totally taken aback. Then he winced, as
from some inner twinge of pain, and stepped over to Kyle.
"In you go, you lawbreaker you!"

Deveren suddenly found it hard to breathe. *Not Telian . . .*

He noticed a trace of worry on Damir's—Kyle's—face,
and winked, hoping desperately the performer would see
him. The last thing Deveren needed right now was for Kyle
to panic, even though Deveren was beginning to think that
there was a damn good reason for panic. The stocks bound
a criminal's hands and feet. For a short time, it wouldn't
hurt, but after a while it became agony. And there was
something terribly frightening, at least to Deveren, about
being so helpless.

Allika's tug on his hand almost made Deveren stumble. He
bent a third time. She stood on her toes, made a cup of her
hands, and said into his ear, "Vervain says she's got enough
tincture to distribute! What would you like me to do?"

Deveren did not reply at once. He watched two of Jaranis's
men untie Kyle's hands and lead him to the stocks, located
on a raised dais in the middle of the street. He had just
opened his mouth to answer the girl when a piece of rotting
fruit sailed through the air and splattered in Kyle's face.

Deveren tensed. *That* had never happened before.

There was a stunned silence, then someone guffawed. Nervous laughter rippled through the crowd, and as more fruit
and vegetables followed, it relaxed into more comfortable
mirth. Khem scampered onto the scaffolding, turning a cart-
wheel that went awry as he got tangled up in his long robes.

"Master of Mischief!" came a cry from the crowd. "Rhyme us! Rhyme us!"

A swell of approval greeted this suggestion. The Rhyme was a pivotal part of the festival, where the Master had to make up nonsensical verses on the spot. The Hound grinned.

"Hmm, hmm . . ." And then he smiled, put his hands behind him, and cleared his throat.

> An honorable fellow is Deveren,
> Lord Larath is always endeavorin'
> To clean up the street
> Which would be quite the feat
> Save his own neck he seems to be severin'.

The crowd murmured, confused. They didn't get the joke, but some of them laughed a little anyway. Khem stared right at Deveren, his lips curved in a knowing smile. It was a threat, plain and simple, and Deveren stared back. Almost, it seemed, he could count the minutes left to him. He leaned down with unnatural calmness and said to Allika, "Go find Pedric. We'll need his help."

She nodded, then slipped away, vanishing amid the sea of legs. Meanwhile, Khem had found another victim for his wit. He turned back to Jaranis, pointed at him, and intoned:

> Of guardsmen, Jaranis is master.
> Wrong-doers are fast, but he's faster.
> But who harks to rules
> When they run with the fools?
> Tonight could bring utter disaster.

There was no laughter this time. Something was definitely going on. With a little jump, the Master of Mischief turned to the imprisoned actor:

> A diplomat of great renown,
> Damir finds his world upside down!

Here bound in the stocks,
He's a target for rocks,
And aid shall not come from this town!

He executed a flip, and disappeared into the crowd.
Then, to Deveren's horror, a fist-sized stone slammed
against the stocks.

"No!" he shrieked. He headed at once toward the dais.
Almost immediately a shower of stones pelted the trapped
Kyle. The actor cried out, clenching his fists reflexively
and trying to duck his head. Deveren had never known so
many people could be in one place. Wherever he tried to
push through, he seemed to meet with resistance. And then,
his horror escalating, he realized he wasn't imagining it.
People *were* deliberately moving in his way, preventing
him from reaching "Damir." Growling angrily, Deveren
began to punch his way through.

One rock shattered Kyle's nose, and blood cascaded
down. Another caught him in the eye. Deveren wasn't even
aware of his own voice screaming out futile protests.

Suddenly he hit the earth hard. A heavyset, obviously
poor older man pummelled him violently. "Filthy bastard!"
he cried. "Damn rich nobles like you take it all . . ." The
man was hauled off of Deveren by a guardsman, who in
turn had to defend himself as the man attacked him, crying, "You're supposed to protect us . . . damn city isn't
safe. . . ."

Deveren struggled to his feet, almost falling as bodies
slammed into him. It had become a full-fledged riot now.
He stumbled and fell again. Fear shot through him as he
clawed his way upright. If he fell again, he might not get up.

He could hear Kyle's sobbing. At last he was there. Fighting the press of bodies all around him, Deveren struggled
onto the platform, getting first one leg up and then the other.
He struggled to his feet and lowered his head, ramming the
guardsman who challenged him. With an "oof!" the man
stumbled backward, falling into the maddened crowd and

disappearing from Deveren's view—but not before Deveren had managed to seize the key ring from the man's pouch.

Blocking the rain of stones with his own body, he hurried to free Kyle. The actor's face was like so much raw meat now. Blood streamed freely and there were huge, almost fist-sized lumps on his head. Deveren could even see shards of broken bone. He gasped as a stone landed squarely on his spine, sending waves of pain quivering through his body. He inserted the key, turned it, and pushed up the stocks that bound the actor's arms. Deveren gathered the limp form in his arms.

He feared he was too late. One eye stared up at him sightlessly; the other was swollen shut by an enormous purple bruise. If the actor survived, Deveren suspected he would be blind. Then Kyle's chest hitched, slightly. He was still alive. Deveren had to get him to Vervain.

Biting back his anger, and aware that the stones had stopped being hurled at him, Deveren stood up. Lost in their own vented rage, the rioters had forgotten about him and "Damir." Their targets now were one another. Deveren scanned the crowd for a possible friendly face and a chance to escape.

Out of the corner of his eye, he saw Vandaris struggling toward him. Compassion and caring was on the old man's face, not in the least obscured by the ridiculous painted grin. Deveren was moved. Suddenly, as if Vandaris's feet had been cut out from underneath him, he fell, to be swallowed up by the manic crowd. The last thing Deveren saw of him was horror as his hands reached to clutch his abdomen, as if he were in terrible pain.

No! mourned Deveren. *Not Vandaris, too . . .*

"Dev!" The word was shouted, but even so, Deveren barely heard it over the shrieks of the maddened revelers. Pedric, with Allika perched on his shoulders out of the way of trampling feet, stood at the foot of the dais. "I've got about four dozen doses of the tincture with me right now. Is Damir all right?"

"I'm going to take him to Vervain," Deveren yelled back. He moved over toward the younger thief, threw himself on his stomach, and spoke urgently into the young man's ear.

"Vandaris is sick," he said. Pedric groaned in sympathy. "I saw him go down right over there. He was trying to help—it got him right away. Get him—take him to Rabbit's. Make him take the tincture. Then work with him—we need to dose the guards and then we'll have a prayer of getting this under control, at least a little. I'll get more doses when I see Vervain, and try to catch up with you. Understand?"

Pedric nodded. Allika did too, her little face sober and comprehending. Impulsively, Deveren reached out and fluffed her short hair. She smiled, just a little. Then they were gone.

For just a moment, Deveren watched the insane crowd. They were ripping one another to bits. Gods, did they stand any kind of a chance against this madness? Two thieves, an exhausted Healer, and a little girl. He closed his eyes briefly, but refused to surrender to despair. He would fight this. He would fight this with everything he had in him, down to the last drop of blood. He had to believe there was some way to win, to bring Braedon's people back to their senses. Because if he did not believe it, then the last candle would have gone out indeed, the last hope would be exhausted, and the world would fall to chaos and insanity.

He returned to Kyle and lifted the injured man as gently as he could, then scanned the crowd for the place of safest passage.

Far from the scenes of wanton violence, Marrika sat on the beach near the Braedon port. By the moonlight, she whittled a chunk of whalebone, humming tunelessly.

She had been where the action was, about four hours ago. She had seen the crowds go mad; had watched Khem orchestrate the murder of Damir Larath with pride and satisfaction. Deveren's murder, too, would come tonight. He who had thought to lead the thieves. Thieves who had turned to her, instead.

All things came to her now.

Scritch, scritch. The carving took shape beneath her skilled fingers.

Now the night belonged to the organized. The infiltration had begun. The murders were no longer random, but carefully calculated, as professionals took control of the town. Some of them were from Mhar. But some were her own people.

Scritch, scritch. It was clear now what she was carving. The moonlight glinted on the white bone. A skull grinned back at her. Gently, she kissed the smooth white surface, then continued.

There came a brief flicker of light, almost subtle enough to be missed. Marrika rose, absently brushing sand from her buttocks. Her gaze focused, concentrated.

The signal came again. It was time.

Gleefully Marrika picked up the dark lantern and flashed the signal to the ships approaching, mere faint shapes on the horizon.

The answering signal came again, and Marrika's heart began to beat faster. They were coming. Khem had not lied. They were really coming! The approaching Mharian navy and their pirate friends would meet with no resistance. The guards had been among the first to succumb to the curse.

She shivered in the night air, and hugged herself, jumping up and down with delight. At last, she would fully come into her own. Master of thieves, master—no, damn it, *mistress*—of Braedon, maybe all of Byrn.

She glanced down at the skull she still held clutched in one hand. Softly, she whispered to it, "Soon it will be Deveren's."

Your horse is strong beneath you,
Your heart is brave and bold,
So ride, O ride, brave Deveren
Before the night is old,
Ride hard and strong and swiftly,
For in your hands resides
The fate of every Byrnian
And Mharian besides.

—Chorus, Byrnian ballad, *Deveren's Ride*

CHAPTER TWENTY

Deveren had had nightmares in which he ran as fast as he could, exerting every muscle, fighting to make progress, and never seemed to be able to move a single step. He felt as if he were trapped now in one of those nightmares. The crowd was thick, and both Deveren and the injured man he bore received more blows. Deveren was jostled back and forth, sometimes losing his direction altogether. He fought back panic. He was one of a few sane people still left in the town, and he knew he needed to use that coolness to his advantage—or die, trampled and torn to bits by the rabid mob.

Kyle grew heavier and heavier a weight with each passing moment. Deveren's muscles trembled with exhaustion, but he stubbornly clung to his precious burden. Finally the crowd thinned just a little and he was able to make progress.

And when he at last spotted the temple of Health, with its lamps burning in the window and a sense of peace about it sharply at odds with the lunacy running rampant through the streets, Deveren almost sobbed with relief.

He couldn't manage the gate while carrying Kyle. "Vervain!" he cried out.

The door flew open and the Healer rushed out, immediately assessing the situation and opening the gate for Deveren. "We've got to get him inside," gasped Deveren. "He's been badly hurt . . . that crazy mob . . ."

Vervain again moved ahead, opening the door and permitting Deveren to enter. He laid the body on the table. Coming up behind him, Vervain gasped in soft sympathy.

"Your brother . . . oh, Deveren, I'm sorry."

"No, it's not. No time to explain. You've got to help him!"

But this time, instead of moving quickly to aid, Vervain merely regarded Deveren with great sorrow in her eyes. "Deveren . . . I'm sorry, but there's nothing I can do for him. It's too late. He must have died some time ago."

Disbelieving, Deveren bent over the actor. In the warm glow of lamplight, he saw the truth in what the Blesser had said.

"Ah, no," he whispered in futile protest. "No, no, no . . ." When had Kyle died? How long had he been carrying a corpse? Could he have saved the actor had he pushed harder, run faster? He closed his eyes in misery.

"He's dead because of me," Deveren said softly. "He's an actor. I hired him to impersonate my brother. They killed Kyle, thinking he was Damir. It's my fault." He felt the gentle touch of the Healer's hand on his shoulder, turning him around, away from the sight of the dead man.

"And part of you is rejoicing, that it wasn't your brother," said Vervain. He looked at her, shocked.

"Didn't know Healers could read minds," he said with a trace of sarcasm.

She smiled, ignoring the barb that had sprung from pain.

"I am a Healer. That means I know people very well. It's all right, Deveren. It was Kyle's time. Death comes when she will, and not even Healers may challenge her."

Deveren laughed, a short, harsh, angry bark. He turned back to Kyle and closed the single unseeing eye gently. "The performance of a lifetime, my friend. Forgive me."

He took a deep breath and composed himself. "I understand that you've made several batches of the tincture," he said, changing the subject.

Vervain nodded. "Can't you smell it?" Now that she mentioned it, Deveren realized the little temple was redolent with some sort of strong odor. It wasn't unpleasant, but it was certainly powerful. "I've got my two Tenders busy bottling it when it cools. Pedric has come by and taken several doses."

Deveren nodded. "Yes, I sent him by here. And I assume you'd like me to take some as well."

A slow, strange smile spread over Vervain's face. "No. I have another task for you tonight, Deveren Larath—a task that was set for you by Health herself, if you are willing."

Utterly confused, Deveren managed, "What are you talking about?"

The smile grew. Vervain's face almost glowed, as with an inner light, and her eyes were luminous. "I have had a vision," she said softly. She reached and took Deveren's hand in hers, gazing at it, gently stroking the fine hairs on the back. "My own task is clear. There is no one else who can make the tincture, and there are many who will find their way to the temple tonight to be cured. This is how I shall serve. But there are powerful forces on the move on this dark night—more powerful than we dared suspect." She lifted her eyes to his, and her voice trembled with awe as she spoke. "We were arrogant to think that the gods would not intervene when mankind has so blasphemed. Health herself would help us set things right, and she is not alone. Deveren—she wishes you to be her avatar."

Deveren could only stare, his gaze locked with the Healer's. "But . . . how? I'm . . . Vervain, I'm not even the right sex to be a Healer!"

At that, the Blesser of Health chuckled softly. "Do you think so trivial a thing matters to a goddess?"

"What . . . how . . ."

"That does not matter. Will you accept the task? For tonight, will you be Health's Chosen—the only man who has ever been granted the gift of heart magic? You have been a key part of this ever since the outset. Now you have a chance to help stop it."

Her eyes pleaded with him to say yes. Fear welled inside him. He had had a glimpse of the sort of person he could have been—Vervain had seen it, felt it. How could she think for a moment that he would possibly be acceptable to a goddess? The strain must have addled her wits.

Still, he knew he could not tell her no. Mutely, he held out the other hand to her.

And gasped.

The moment her fingers made contact with both hands, Deveren felt an unnatural heat emanating from her. It was as if he had opened his palms to a blazing hearth. First it warmed, and then it grew hot, hotter. He did not pull away, but he gritted his teeth against the pain.

I am the Third who comes. Wield you the touch of Health.

The voice was inside his head. It was soft, strong, feminine. But it was most definitely not Vervain's. At that instant, the heat lessened and seemed to move to his chest, swelling, filling every crevice of it with a warmth that was more than physical. He ached with the pains of the world now, it seemed; his compassion for the injured, the sick, made him sob aloud. Tears filled his eyes.

Abruptly, it lessened, became tolerable. He gazed down at his hands in wonder. They glowed with a soft, barely perceptible radiance. Vervain removed her own hands, and when he glanced up, blinking rapidly to clear his vision, he saw that her eyes were wet as well. He looked at her, and

he could sense—almost see—the exhaustion emanating
from her. Without realizing what he did, he lifted his right
hand and placed it between her breasts. The glow around
his hand increased, and he felt it leap from his hand to her
heart. She inhaled swiftly, closing her eyes, and the weariness and fear fled before the healing of a goddess. Smiling,
blinking back tears, she touched his face gently, then stepped
back.

"Go, Deveren. Go . . . and Heal."

Vandaris wondered why he was dreaming of herbs.

The scents wafted through the scenario of the dream—or
rather nightmare. Damir's face was being pounded to a
bloody pulp. In the background were the cries of the Nightlands. Vandaris moved forward, anxious to help . . .

. . . and the pain, the pain, oh gods the agony of it . . .
like a knife, a spear, a firebrand, shooting through his chest
and gut. No one to help. No one to even break his fall as he
hurtled toward the cobblestones, and his arms refused to
move to catch himself. He fell heavily, striking his head.
And there he lay as consciousness disappeared, breathing
in the scents of herbs in the middle of a sweaty mass of
humanity, wondering why in the name of all the gods he
couldn't seem to do something, anything, to stave off the
encroaching madness of a world turned upside down.

He became aware of something cool and wet on his forehead, easing the pain. Vandaris realized that he lay not on
cold cobblestones, but on something else—a wooden floor?
He opened his eyes and saw the reason for the overwhelming scent of herbs; hundreds of them seemed to point directly down at him from the rafters.

"He's waking up," came a nervous voice.

"Good," said another. Suddenly Pedric's face came into
Vandaris's view. "Lord Vandaris? I apologize for the ropes,
but they really are necessary."

And it was only then that Vandaris realized he was bound
hand and foot.

Suddenly a wave of hot fury swept through the councilman. With the anger came energy that banished pain. He roared in outrage and struggled with the strength of a man half his age, shredding the flesh about his wrists but succeeding only in tightening the knots.

"Help me get him down, Griel!" cried Pedric, leaping on the writhing body.

Griel ventured close, then backed away, wringing his hands. "He's awfully violent, Pedric, I don't know that I can—oh!"

Vandaris kicked out at the skinny older man, who jumped out of the way just in time. He growled at Pedric and rolled suddenly, pinning the youth beneath his bulky frame. Pedric gasped for air, and Vandaris grinned wickedly.

The voice inside him that protested, that mourned the viciousness with which Vandaris defended himself, was small and faint. But it could still be heard.

And as suddenly as it had come, the senseless rage evaporated, leaving pain in its wake. Whimpering, Vandaris ceased to fight and Pedric scrambled out from beneath him.

"Thanks a lot, Griel," he gasped.

Griel had the grace to look embarrassed. "Maybe we should explain it to him, rather than forcing it on him. It worked for me. I listened to you."

"And came after me with a poker before I subdued you," Pedric reminded him.

Vandaris heard it all through the pain. "Do you . . ." he gasped, then tried again. "Can you stop the pain, P-Pedric? Do you know what's going on?"

"I do," said Pedric urgently. "Braedon has been visited by a curse. Nearly everyone's infected. It saps the strength and causes pain when a person thinks about doing something kind, something good. And it lends energy when one has an evil thought, a thought of violence and cunning. It will wear down your resistance until, in the end, you surrender to it—and then it will probably be the death of you."

"I would never embrace evil!" cried Vandaris in protest,

only to clutch his chest as his heart thudded with a painful unnaturalness.

"There, you see?" said Pedric. "Just now you were willing to kill us, when you learned you were bound. Didn't it make you feel better when you fought?"

Vandaris could only stare. Shame flooded him, and hard on the heels of that emotion was pain. "Yes," he confessed. "But how can this curse be stopped?"

"You must trust us," said Griel. "Pedric here has two doses of the same elixir. The first draft will cause you to become totally, completely evil. A second draft will restore you to your normal state of mind, but you'll be rendered immune to the curse. I didn't believe him at first. Thought it a lot of silly nonsense until it worked on me. Healers didn't use to dabble in herb lore, you know. That was my business. Let them use their skills and me use mine, I say."

Pedric raised a hand and the older man fell silent. "We can force you, Lord Vandaris," said Pedric. "I don't want to, but I will if I have to."

Vandaris regarded him steadily, then nodded. Looking relieved, Pedric lifted the older man's head and positioned the uncorked bottle to his lips. "Sit on his heels," he instructed the apothecary.

"Goodness, Pedric, I'm an old man!" protested Vandaris.

"Yes," said Pedric tactlessly, "but I know what this can do to someone. I know what it did to me." Reluctantly, the apothecary positioned himself delicately across Vandaris's ankles.

"Remember," said Pedric as he tilted the bottle, "two swallows, not just one."

Vandaris gulped down a mouthful, and with a suddenness that startled Pedric, who ought to have been expecting it, he screamed in fury and struck the youth's hand with his forehead. The bottle tumbled from Pedric's fingers, spilling across Vandaris's black clothing.

Pedric swore loudly and fumbled for another bottle. His face paled. "That was the last one!"

Vandaris kicked and the apothecary tumbled back. A second well-placed kick made him curl up in a ball, groaning. Pedric tried to hold him down, but Vandaris would have none of it. He squirmed like a madman, for suddenly the thought of drinking a second dose seemed to him to be the worst punishment some cruel god could inflict on a hapless mortal.

He barely looked up when the door slammed open, but he heard the shocked cry of Pedric.

"Deveren, your hands!"

Deveren couldn't take the time to explain. He assessed the situation at a glance and sprang forward. His radiant hands reached, not to hurt, but to heal, and he touched Vandaris's broad chest.

Light flooded from him into the dark corners of Vandaris's corrupted spirit, gently chasing away the demons that lurked as a child might brush away a fluffy bit of milkweed. There was nothing that could harm Deveren when he ventured into the dark places tonight, and it was with real joy that he reached for and grasped Vandaris's evil and shaped it into light.

Heal. Be warm. Be comforted.

His strong fingers, glowing with an unearthly radiance, turned sorrow into joy, pain into pleasure. And it gave Deveren joy in the doing as well. He touched something in Vandaris's mind that was still crouching, whimpering, like an injured beast. Tears stung Deveren's eyes as he realized it was the old man's love for his daughter. Deveren longed to touch it, heal that wound as well, but something wise beyond his ken whispered that such was not for him. Vandaris would need to heal himself of that particular pain.

Gently, reluctantly almost, Deveren withdrew. He rocked back on his heels, as full of energy now as when he had begun. Vandaris gazed up at him.

The whole encounter had taken only a few seconds.

"Good gods, what did you do?" whispered Pedric, his eyes glued to Deveren's still-glowing hands.

"A gift from our Lady Health herself," said Deveren with quiet reverence. "For tonight, I am as she is. I can Heal." His eyes met Pedric's and he smiled. Gently he brushed his fingers across the younger man's furrowed brow, erasing the pain and fear and exhaustion. He moved toward Griel— Rabbit—who only now was beginning to recover from the kick Vandaris had dealt him, and took away his pain as well.

The three men stared at him, and Deveren began to grow uncomfortable. "It's still me," he said, almost defensively.

"Are you sure?" quavered Rabbit.

Deveren rolled his eyes in exasperation. "Last time I looked, it was. Now listen, you three. You are now immune to the curse's effect. Rabbit, go to Vervain. With your knowledge of herbs, you can probably be a great help to her in creating more of the tincture. Otter, I've got about four-teen more bottles in the pack on Flamedancer. You and Vandaris have to split them. You go and find the rest of our people and make sure they take the doses."

"But Dev—it's because of them that this damn curse is even here!" protested Pedric.

Deveren didn't waver. "You weren't part of that. Rabbit isn't part of that. I think you know who we can trust, Pedric. Find them; heal them. When they're cured, send them to the temple of Health. They in turn can distribute the tincture. Vandaris, you need to find Telian Jaranis, the rest of the council—anyone in law enforcement. We need those people on our side. Vervain will be working through the night, making more of the stuff. Any questions?"

"Yes," said Vandaris, his gray brows drawing together. "Why do you refer to 'our people' and call Griel and Pedric by animal names?"

Deveren's mouth went dry. "Um . . . it's nothing, really. Private nicknames."

"You don't lie very well, Lord Larath," replied the Head Councilman coolly.

"It doesn't matter!" Deveren exploded. "Good gods, the world is going mad out there!"

"You are right," conceded Vandaris. "Now is not the time. But Deveren, I'm starting to put a few things together. We'll have to have a long talk about this when all this chaos is over."

"If you and I are alive by dawn," agreed Deveren grimly, "then we'll talk. In the meantime, gentlemen, the people of Braedon need our help."

The four men hurried out of Rabbit's shop to their various tasks. Deveren paused, pressed a hand to his mount's head. The gelding snorted, suddenly full of energy. Flamedancer would be able to go at full speed for the rest of the night.

He swung himself into the saddle and glanced around, heartsick. The crowds had been here earlier. Doors were broken. Filth had been written on walls. Most of the shops had been robbed, and sometimes the shopkeepers had not escaped with their lives. The smell of fire was in the air along with the tang of the salt sea, and a dim orange glow in the distance had nothing to do with a setting sun.

He glanced down at his hands, and his heart lifted slightly. With a single touch, he could bring healing and sanity to the cursed of this town he so loved. With only the gentlest of squeezes, Flamedancer leaped forward.

Later, ballads would be written about the deed, of how one man, blessed by a goddess, had ridden through the longest night in Braedon's history. Deveren would be lifted to the ranks of hero. Long after he had turned to dust, his name would echo in taverns and feast halls, by firesides and on the road. But as he thundered through streets lit only by fires and moonlight, reaching down to grasp a hand curled into a fist, touch a brow streaming with sweat and blood, Deveren Larath's thoughts were not of future glory and immortalization in song. He did not think of the dozens, perhaps hundreds of people whom he would, by the grace of Health, pull back from the edge of madness tonight.

It was each individual that mattered, each touch that counted.

His thoughts were firmly in the present, rooted in each minute as if it were the last he would live. He felt as though he memorized every face whose expression went from hate to compassion, from confusion to clarity. In the space of a few seconds, he knew them all, and he brought hope where there was none.

And he would later count it a mercy that, as he raced through the night on a fire-hued horse, he did not know that the Mharian and pirate fleet was sailing into the Braedon harbor.

One foe of yours is human,
One foe of yours is not.
And everyone you love most dear
In their dark web is caught:
Your brother fights for freedom,
At perhaps a bloody cost,
But it's here in these dark streets tonight
That the war is won or lost.

—First verse, Byrnian ballad, *Deveren's Ride*

CHAPTER TWENTY-ONE

The night wore on, and, for the first time since Vervain's touch had enabled him to be a vessel for Health, Deveren began to despair.

Gods, there were so many of them. So very many. He could not possibly reach all of them tonight. Though he felt no physical exhaustion, his initial joy was tempered by simple fact. Many had tried to take Flamedancer from him; he had always been able to make physical contact with the would-be horse thief before it was too late, but each time it startled him.

He had worked his way through the merchant's area and was braving the throngs clustered around the square when the attack came. Deveren knew, even as the figure came crashing down on him, dragging him off a terrified Flamedancer, that he ought to have been expecting this. He hit the street hard, and heard Flamedancer neighing frantically. He opened his mouth to scream at the horse, send it away from these insane people who would do him harm, but a fist landed in his mouth.

Automatically, Deveren clamped both hands around his attacker's wrist—and stared right into the furious face of Freylis.

His healing touch had no effect, and Deveren realized with horror that it was because Freylis was not contaminated with the curse. He was at this moment, and always had been, a simple, angry, dangerous brute, and no Healer, not even the divine one, could remedy that.

So it was Freylis, then, who had tried to kill him. He must have enlisted the aid of someone far more resourceful, for the whalebone-needle trap had been clever indeed. Deveren did not even try to fight. His hands, tonight, were meant to help, not kill. He would not so blaspheme them.

Snarling, Freylis spat in Deveren's face. Spittle mingled with the blood from Deveren's mouth and trickled down his face. Freylis called Deveren something dreadfully emasculating and laughed. "Won't even fight me, will you? I'd rip you apart, you bastard, if she didn't want you alive."

That jolted Deveren. *She?*

More familiar faces swam out of the crowd, each one stabbing Deveren's heart with a fresh pain of betrayal. Khem, still clad in the overly warm garb of the Master of Mischief. Clia, her flamboyant dress stained with blood and filth. More and more of his thieves materialized, all grinning hatefully as they roughly bound him hand and foot. He offered no resistance, for there was no purpose. Deveren, at least, would go to meet his fate knowing that he had saved a few souls from a dreadful destiny.

Freylis slung him over his shoulder and began to trot, jolting Deveren with each step. Others followed behind, jeering and laughing at their "leader" in such a state. Deveren craned his neck, morbidly curious, in an attempt to see where they were headed. They raced past the Godstower, which had not rung all evening (gods, were even the Blessers ill with this dreadful curse?) and it was only after the door slammed in his face that Deveren realized where they were.

In the temple of Vengeance.

He was thrown to the floor and the bonds on his feet cut. A voice reached his ears; a voice he knew well.

"I want you to walk to your death, *Leader Fox*!"

It was Marrika. Khem jerked Deveren to his feet, turned him around to face the Raven.

He barely recognized her. Gone was the sullen woman wearing form-fitting men's clothing and a constant expression of repressed anger. She stood in what was clearly a place of honor beside a slight man whose long, thin hands fiddled nervously with the tassels on his belt. Both wore floor-length robes of black cloth, but whereas the man's face was hooded, Marrika's was proudly bare for all to see. Her face was tranquil in its certain victory, and her hair tumbled about her shoulders in blue-black glory. Deveren had never before thought her quite so beautiful—or dangerous.

"Raven," he whispered.

"Not Raven, not anymore," she replied. "I am the Chosen of Vengeance!"

He continued to stare at her. She was almost otherworldly here in the enclosed, small building. The light from dozens of candles danced across her features, lending them an unreal appearance. Beyond what the candles illuminated, the darkness waited, hungry.

"You have come to me tonight, as part of the pact with Vengeance," Marrika continued. "All things come to me, in time. I have power, and followers, and now you, Deveren Larath, and soon the city, perhaps the whole country, shall be mine!"

"You're mad," Deveren breathed, but Marrika shook her head. And he realized with an even deeper loathing and horror that she was right. She was utterly, completely sane.

"Oh, how I have waited for this," she purred, walking around him and sizing him up from head to toe. There was a movement, and she extended a hand to him, palm up. "Recognize this?"

Deveren did. It was a white sliver of bone—twin to the one that had almost cost him his life just a few weeks ago. He didn't reply; he didn't need to. The shock on his face was answer enough for Marrika, who chuckled throatily.

"I thought you would. Whittling is a skill I picked up from my Mharian sailor lover. And the trap—which really ought to have claimed even you, clever Fox—was something I learned from the thieves in Mhar." She continued walking around him, her fingers trailing lightly, teasingly, over his back and buttocks. Deveren glanced around, meeting the gazes of men, women, and even children who, until now, he had thought were "his" thieves.

"My destiny does seem to be tied up with you, Deveren," Marrika continued, completing her circle and stopping to face him from inches away. "In Mhar, I learned things that have brought me to this place, this rank. And it was because of you that I fled to Mhar, some seven years ago."

Deveren waited, tense. The way her eyes glowed, she had some dreadful news to impart.

"I was so young then, a mere sixteen. Agile and quick, yes. But wise? Well, not really. You see, someone older than I would have realized that the house of the nobleman I planned to rob wasn't empty. Someone more experienced would have been able to complete the robbery without waking the pregnant woman asleep in the bed upstairs."

Deveren couldn't breathe. He felt suddenly icy cold, and not even the heat of his Healer's hands could warm him. Blood drained from his face and for a moment his vision swam. His knees trembled, then gave way, and he found himself kneeling on the hard-packed earthen floor, staring mutely up at the beautiful young woman who had so ruthlessly butchered his beloved wife.

She laughed, drinking in his pain, then squatted down to his level and yanked his chin up. "She begged, you know."

Tears filled Deveren's eyes, but her fingers dug into his jaw. The pain from his injured mouth shot through him. He couldn't turn away.

"Begged more for the life of her child than for herself. Very noble. But she'd seen me—could identify me—and, well, I admit I panicked. I was on my way to Mhar by ship in the first mate's bed before you even got home, Deveren Larath. And I slept very well."

Marrika straightened, nodded to someone. At once, Khem and Freylis seized Deveren's arms and hauled him to his feet. Their ungentle hands shoved him forward. Deveren, still reeling from the dreadful knowledge with which Marrika had stabbed him, only dimly noticed the incomplete circle of white on the earth, took note of the wooden platform encrusted with something dark and thick. It was only as they tossed him down in front of it that the smell reached Deveren's nostrils and the rest of the pieces of the dark puzzle came together.

The altar was crusted with old, dried blood. And a chunk of long, dark hair—human hair, not the fur of a mute beast—had gotten snagged in a crack.

"Lorinda!" Deveren cried brokenly, jerking backward. The image of the murdered girl vied with the recollection of his wife in his mind. Damir's words floated back to him: *Kastara's murder was an accident. . . . It was clearly a theft gone wrong—horribly wrong. . . . Lorinda's murder has an element of anger about it, of—of ritual, if you will.*

It had been a ritual. An abominable, vile ritual of darkness that made gorge rise in Deveren's throat. "Lorinda . . . you murdered her too! To become the Chosen!"

"Ah, now that it is too late, you see," laughed Marrika. Again she gestured. Khem grabbed Deveren's arms, jerked them forward—and gasped at the gentle glow radiating from his hands.

"What the . . ." Now all the thieves could see plainly, and

a cry of fear rose from them. They shrank back, their lust for blood suddenly expunged by fear for their own safety.

"No," whispered the man Deveren took to be the Blesser of Vengeance. His face was pale as parchment and he trembled. "No, we must not harm him!"

"Watch what you say to me, Kannil," warned Marrika, her throaty voice carrying a warning. He turned to her, his eyes wide with terror.

"He bears the mark of Health! Look at his hands!" A sob broke from him and he seemed to shrink about a foot. "She knows," he whispered. "Dear gods, she knows, and she is angry with what we have done . . . with what I have done, and felt, and thought . . ."

He stared wildly around at the thieves, his face gleaming with the sweat of sheer terror. "Don't you see? Health knows that we have blasphemed! She knows that Vengeance had nothing to do with this, nothing, and she has given this man the power to tame the evils we have loosed. . . ."

Without another word the Blesser rushed forward, his shaking fingers working to undo the knots that cut deeply into Deveren's wrists. "Lady Health, forgive me, forgi—"

His eyes widened. Deveren stared back. Then the Blesser gasped, and a thin stream of crimson trickled from suddenly bloodless lips. He slumped forward on his own altar of darkness, and Deveren, shrinking backward, saw that a slim dagger protruded from his back. Deveren turned his shocked gaze upon Marrika, who only now was withdrawing her hand from the extended position of hurling the knife.

"It's a trick, isn't it, Fox," she snarled. In some dim part of his mind, Deveren wondered how he could have thought her beautiful a few moments ago. "You, you painted your hands with something, or you got someone to cast an illusion on you, didn't you? Well, it may have fooled Kannil, but it doesn't fool me!"

She sprang forward and wrenched the knife from the

dead man's back. Her eyes flashed in the candlelight as she growled and moved toward Deveren.

He watched her, transfixed. Pain and grief and horror racked him, but not anger, not hate. He was incapable of those emotions tonight, as incapable of feeling them as he was of lifting his blessed hands to strike back. He could only stare, observing with an odd detachment the folds of her garb as they slipped back from the lifting arm, the slim strength of that arm, the grimace of mingled hatred and joy on the finely chiseled, tanned face . . .

A howl shattered the moment. It was not the cry of an angry dog, or the anguished wail of a person in pain. Those, Deveren had already heard tonight; heard, identified, and dismissed.

This sound shivered along the air, cutting it like a knife. It was long and keen and piercing, with something eerie behind it. It was the howl of a wolf—but what in the name of all the gods was a wolf doing here? The hairs along every inch of Deveren's body lifted in a primal response to the sound.

Marrika's blow froze as she, too, responded to the eerie noise. She whirled, angry at the interruption, but there was fear on her face now, too—fear that Deveren had never seen there before.

The temperature of the room dropped like a stone.

Laughter, as eerie and unnatural as the wolf's howl, filled the room. Standing in the doorway, at least a dozen wolves at her feet, was the Blesser of Death who had so mysteriously come to Deveren on the night of his Grand Thefts. Her long white hair whipped wildly about her almost alabaster features, though there was no wind. She lifted her pale arms, one of which bore the jeweled rosewood staff, and cried, "Taste you the kiss of Death!"

And then Deveren knew that it had not been merely the Blesser of Death who had save his life that night.

Many things happened at once.

The wolves began to shimmer. Their forms shifted, became translucent, reshaped. Abruptly, where the wolves had stood were the shapes of women; women who had no color to their faces or hair; women that one could see through if one tried. They were as different as any woman in shape and form, but they all had weapons of silver and steel that glinted in the flickering orange-yellow light, and that steel was echoed in their hard faces.

Thinking he must have gone mad, Deveren recognized among their number the slender form of Lorinda Vandaris—and the petite, but no less beautiful, image of his long-dead Kastara.

He cried out, an aching sound of mingled despair and hope, before the women descended on the terrified thieves. It was a pitiful battle. The ghosts of the dead could not be injured, but their shining blades could and did decimate their foes. Most of the thieves were too frightened to even fight back. The spectral blades wielded by Death's army left no wounds on the flesh, but those who felt the blows shuddered and died as if stricken by a mortal blow from a corporeal sword.

As they slew those they had come for, one by one, the women returned to their wolf shapes and crouched by the still-twitching bodies. Deveren watched, riveted, as something bright yellow separated itself from the dying men and women. The wolves yipped happily, their tails wagging, and leaped, open-mouthed, to devour the fleeing spirits.

They feed on souls, Deveren realized. *Lady Death's spirit-wolves feed on human souls!*

He felt something cool and damp brush his hands, and whipped his head around. A huge lump rose in his throat. There was no fear, only joy.

"Kastara," he managed.

The specter's incorporeal hands released the heavily knotted ropes from Deveren's hands. He stared up into the face of his beloved. The pert, pointed chin, the full lips, the look of love in the ghostly eyes. She was exactly as he remembered—no, not exactly. Her rounded belly was flat now, flat and taut as it was on their wedding night . . .

"You've come for me," he whispered.

She shook her head, her transparent hair floating with the gesture. "No, my love." Her voice was soft, still Kastara's voice, but not human, not anymore. "You can see me because of the gift Death's sister has given you. I have come to say farewell."

She smiled at him, then began to drift away, her attention already returning to her duty—that of collecting souls for her mistress.

Deveren couldn't bear it. His hand, glowing with Health's own power, shot out to seize the ghost. He expected it to be a futile gesture, and assumed his hands would close on nothingness. Instead, to his shocked joy, he clasped a human wrist.

Kastara gasped and stared at him. Where his hand gripped her, the milky translucence had solidified. Her hand was completely human—and alive.

"No!" she cried, struggling.

Deveren stared at her hand. The human tint started to spread, tracing a languorous way up. Now Kastara's flesh was solid almost to her elbow. He realized dizzily what had happened. For all intents and purposes, he had the hands of Health tonight. And Health alone, of all the seven gods, had the power to bring back the dead.

Elation flooded him, and he grasped her other wrist. This, too, flushed a warm, living hue.

"Deveren, no, my love, you don't understand!" Kastara fought him like a wild thing. "It was my time! Let me go, if you love me—let me go to the Light!"

She blurred in his sight, and for a horrible instant Deveren thought she was escaping him. Then he realized it was only his own tears that clouded his vision. She was mortal now almost to the shoulders.

"Love, love!" he cried brokenly. "I am nothing without

you! What is there, who is there left for me to love? Marrika took even our baby when she took you!"

Up to the chest now. Suddenly, Kastara ceased struggling. Comprehension and an aching compassion spread over her face. "Beloved, there are many who yet need you here—who need the love that fills your heart, as I once did. And as for your child—you have found her already. Go and be with them, Deveren, while life is yet yours to enjoy, to drink of, to savor. But I am not of this world anymore; I cannot dwell here, mortal though you would have me be. Let me go, if ever you loved me. Let me continue my journey to the Light!"

Tears coursed down Deveren's face. Kastara was almost completely mortal now. If the transformation was allowed to continue, she would be alive, warm, in his arms, as she ought to have been.

But even as he clung desperately to this thought, he realized how selfish it was. The Blessers had been right after all. The ghost-wolves of Death were not evil, any more than their mistress was. They were not slaves; they served Death willingly, doing what must be done and earning their passage on to the Light.

He was past words; past the ability to let her know how he had loved her, how bleak life had been without her. Tears spilling down his ashen cheeks, Deveren in silence did the single most difficult thing he had ever done, would ever do, in his life.

He let her go.

At that moment, he felt a hand—a real, solid, human hand—clamp down on his shoulder and spin him around. He stared up into Marrika's face as she lifted her hand, clenched tight around the dagger, to complete what she had begun. A roar came from behind him, and he saw Marrika's face change to absolute terror as a white, wolf-shaped wraith leaped upon her. Both Deveren and Marrika were knocked to the floor. Deveren scrambled up and back, just in time to see the wolf that had been Kastara a few seconds earlier clamp her powerful jaws down on Marrika's throat. The white muzzle disappeared for an instant, buried in Marrika's neck, though to Deveren's eye the Raven's throat appeared utterly whole. Then the spirit-wolf tugged, pulling loose the bright flash that was dying woman's soul, which she swallowed.

"Honored among men are you twice this night," came a soft voice. Startled, Deveren tore his gaze from the feasting wolf to see Lady Death herself standing beside him. "First by the touch of my sister, then to bear witness to my spirit-wolves."

She knelt and stroked his cheek. He was surprised to feel that her hand was warm, not cold, as he had expected. Leaning forward, she brushed his forehead with petal-soft lips.

"It was not your time that night, nor this one. I was the First to come, to stand against the blasphemy and the evil that were loosed; and I shall be the last to leave. Those that have died here were destined to die tonight. You are not among them. But the next time that Death kisses thee," she whispered, "thou shalt come with her."

She straightened, and turned to the phantom pack. "Come. There are other souls to feast upon ere dawn lightens the skies!"

Howling, the wolves fled, racing out into the madness of the Midsummer Night, their feet leaving no trace of their passage. And their mistress followed, a darker shape against the darkness of the night.

For a long time, Deveren simply sat, leaning against the bloodied altar and trying to comprehend the miracles to which he had been witness. At last, he stumbled to his feet. Absently, he rubbed his injured jaw. The pain disappeared, as he would have expected had he been thinking more clearly.

The candles were burning low now, but somehow it didn't seem quite as dark outside as it had been before. His eyes fixed on the still-open door, Deveren made his shambling

way over the dead that littered the floor. He leaned against
the door for a moment, letting his eyes adjust.

The fires of last night seemed to have either burned
themselves out or had been extinguished. Yet there was
definitely a lightness about the night that told him that
dawn, while not yet here, was on its way.

The streets were curiously deserted of the living. The
dead, though, lay where they had fallen. Indeed, Lady
Death's wolves had had a feast tonight . . .

The clatter of horse's hooves on cobblestone roused him
from his trancelike contemplation. He glanced up to see
Pedric, perched on Flamedancer, barrelling down on him.
The young man pulled on the gelding's reins and Flamedancer slowed to a stop.

"Deveren! Thank the gods you're all right. Come with
me—there's something you must see!"

Obligingly, still moving as one in a dream, Deveren
mounted behind Pedric. The young man turned the horse's
head around and headed back down the street, down
Ocean's View toward the port. It was definitely getting
lighter. They rounded a bend in the street and suddenly
Deveren found himself staring at the open ocean. Hundreds
of others were there as well; those who had fought the
curse and won to stand, now, shoulder to shoulder, enraptured by what they witnessed.

A tremendous battle was taking place against a gray sky.
Deveren couldn't even count the number of ships in the
port, though he realized that most of them were Mharian
vessels. He knew the lion of Mhar as well as anybody, and
nearly every ship in the harbor flew it. The vessels that did
not flew a flag that was solid black.

"Good gods," he whispered softly. "An invasion?"

"I'm not so sure," said Pedric. "They seem to be fighting
among themselves. Look."

And sure enough, just as Deveren watched, the sails of
one of the ships went up in a burst of orange flame, providing even more light to see by for the shocked onlookers

clustered around the port. "But how could that happen? A fire just doesn't start that fast!" exclaimed Pedric.

Suddenly Deveren realized who it must be. "Damir," he said, his voice trembling with joy.

"Dev . . . but wasn't Damir . . . ?"

"It's a long story. Oh, thank gods, he's alive! Don't you see?" Deveren leaned past Pedric and pointed. "That's His Majesty's own ship, right there. It's got his personal standard. King Castyll himself has come to help save Braedon!"

He would have said more, save that a spectacle that even Deveren was totally unprepared for silenced the cheering throngs. The ocean rippled, and without further warning a huge whale cleared the surface. It thrust itself high in the air, landing with a mighty splash near one of the ships not allied with the king's fleet. A tremendous wave rocked the ship, but it did not capsize. Then, incredibly, a second whale—a *third*—also leaped into the air. The ship could not stand against that and it overturned.

And was it . . . could that be *sharks* who found the flailing seamen and dragged them down? And *gulls* that dove, shrieking, at those who still lived?

The ocean churned. *More whales?* wondered Deveren wildly, but the sudden rapid pounding of his heart told him that something far more miraculous was about to occur.

From the depths emerged a creature that Deveren had never seen outside of fanciful paintings. It was enormous, far longer than any five ships put together. As its massive head broke the surface, the creature, long tongue flickering and sharp teeth bared, rose . . . and rose . . .

Then it leaped, diving across the ship as easily as a deer might clear a tangle of brush. A length of sinuous, shimmering scales followed it. It emerged to repeat the movement, encompassing the hapless vessel within its crushing coils. The ship didn't have a prayer. Even this far away, Deveren and Pedric could hear the sound it made as the creature cracked the mighty ship to useless spars.

"Dear gods," breathed Pedric. His eyes were wide with wonder. "Dear gods."

Riveted, Deveren leaped off Flamedancer. He scrambled to the top of a tavern for a better view. As he watched, hardly daring to breathe, the remaining enemy vessels ran down their flags. For a long, tense moment, they flew nothing at all. And then, just as the sun cleared the horizon, the enemy ran up another flag. The dawn's light turned the white flag of surrender to a bright, glowing pink. A huge cheer went up among the crowd.

The ocean's creatures, summoned at this hour of need, disappeared as if they had never been. And Deveren, standing alone atop a rundown shanty of a tavern, felt his hands flare with divine heat, one last time, and then, with the tranquillity and inevitability of a sunset at the end of a hot day, softly cool.

He stumbled. The exhaustion and the tension that Health's gift had kept at bay all through the nightmarish ordeal descended now, full force. He was utterly depleted. He was famished. And most of all, he felt achingly empty and alone. Deveren had not realized how Health's gift had bound him to others through the act of Healing. He had been not one man, but many. Every person he had touched had become a part of him for this one brief, miraculous time.

Now he was more alone than he had ever been in his life. Despite himself, a sob of mourning left his lips.

No.

Not alone. Kastara had reminded him. He had been part of a miracle tonight, the only man every permitted Health's glory. He had had a chance that all people long for—to see his departed love a final time, to know beyond a doubt, with a certainty not granted to even the most faithful, that she was at peace. Her words sounded again in his ear, as he suspected they would for the rest of his life: *Beloved, there are many who yet need you here—who need the love that fills your heart, as I once did. And as for your child—you have found her already. Go and be with them, Deveren, while life is yet yours to enjoy, to drink of, to savor.*

Her words about his "child"—what did she mean by that? With a suddenness that dizzied him, he realized that it didn't matter. He *did* know who his child was . . . if the girl would have him. Whether she was his lost child in another body or merely a little girl whole unto herself, it didn't matter. And he hoped, with an earnestness that hurt, that he was right about who one of the "others" might be.

He was still tired. He was still ravenous and aching with the trials of the long night that had been. But that night was over, and Deveren's heart was freer than it ever had been.

He leaped down from the roof and found his footing. And then Deveren Larath began to run, his burning muscles protesting but obeying as he raced toward the square, toward Health's temple and toward his future—bound up with that of a little girl, whose name he cried out as he approached:

"Allika!"

EPILOGUE

A week had passed since Midsummer Night, and Braedon was beginning to show tentative signs of normalcy. The quarantine imposed by the City Council had eliminated the threat of a pandemic. Many still dealt with the grim task of gathering up the dead where they had fallen and loading the corpses onto what was called, with a trace of black humor, the Deathride. They would be taken out of the city limits and burned, to lessen any chance of the curse spreading. The resulting bonfire, visible from Braedon, kept the night skies from ever becoming fully dark. And when a cruel wind blew, ashes from the dead would fall like gray snow on the town.

But even in the somber aftermath, there were bright glimmers of hope. More had survived the disaster than could have been expected. As each person was healed, he had come, taken an armload of bottles of the tincture, and gone forth to heal many others. Once cured, Braedon's citizens rallied further to help those less fortunate. Nobles, perhaps recalling what the curse had done to them when they suffered in its grip, opened their homes to provide temporary shelter for those whose dwellings had been burned during the height of the curse's rampage. Those who were hungry came to the Councilman's Seat, where hot soup and bread awaited them. Vervain found herself with no shortage of willing, if unskilled, hands to distribute the tincture to those who were still alive but unhealed.

Many of these volunteers, thought Deveren Larath to himself with a trace of justifiable pride, were his own thieves. The knowledge pleased him. Those who had intentionally followed the darker paths carved out by Marrika and Freylis had not survived that night. The thieves who remained were more inclined to listen to Deveren's ideas, to be aware of something a little larger than their own needs. Deveren's dream of honor among thieves seemed to be coming true, after all.

He lay back in the cooling grass, staring up at the blue sky. The wind, today, was kind, and there were no solemn reminders of the disaster visible at present. The only clouds were large, fluffy ones; natural and harmless. On a whim, Deveren plucked a sprig of grass and chewed on it, as he had when he was a youth.

He'd been surprised to learn that it was largely Castyll's doing that had thwarted the attack on Braedon. Damir admitted to helping, but would not say exactly how. "I must have some secrets, even from my brother," he quipped. But Castyll in private had later confided to Deveren that Damir had friends in the ocean's depths, who had come and given their aid in a most marvelous fashion.

Deveren liked Castyll, who for the time being was an honored guest in Lord Larath's modest home. He was young, yes, and oh so terribly earnest. But he was genuine in his love of his people and his fondness for the Byrnians.

And he was clearly devoted to Princess Cimarys. There were rumors of a united kingdom—a new country. Deveren idly wondered what the flag would be. Mhar had a lion; Byrn had an eagle. Maybe they'd make a griffin to represent this new realm.

He heard a squeal of laughter, followed by a puppy's yipping bark. His lips smiled around the sprig of grass in his mouth. The laughter of his daughter was the sweetest sound in the world to him now. Allika had wept and readily agreed to an official adoption, and had fallen in love with the little brachet Deveren had bought her to be a new companion in Miss Lally's stead. The child had named the little bitch Miss Lally, stating confidently that Miss Lally hadn't ever really died and that she would always be there, guarding Allika.

After what Deveren had experienced on that night of nights a short week ago, he was in no position to argue.

"Liest thou there, thou summer youth, /Contemplating life and truth?" came a voice tremulous with suppressed mirth.

Deveren bolted upright, brushing sheepishly at the weeds in his hair. Grinning, Vervain sank down beside him. She brought her knees up to her chin and hugged them, her eyes shining. Her scarlet garb contrasted vividly with the green grass and blue skies.

"I didn't know you read bad poetry," said Deveren, blushing a little at having been found in such an undignified position. The current trend among those with too much money and time was to idolize the innocent farmer, not taking into account the backbreaking realities of the "simple country life."

Vervain grimaced mockingly. "Some things one just can't avoid," she said with an exaggerated sigh.

Silence stretched between them. Deveren had spoken with Vervain about what he had experienced during his "ride," a feat that many of the local bards had seized upon as perfect ballad material. Deveren had even heard a few, and had begun to fear that he'd be subjected to various versions of *Deveren's Ride* for the rest of his life. It was all rather embarrassing. He had told Vervain about Kastara's spirit, about Death's manifestation. But he had said nothing about Kastara's words to him—not yet.

To break the uncomfortable silence, Deveren said, "How did you know where to find me?"

Vervain smiled gently. "Your brother told me that you come here about this time every day, since Midsummer Night."

"Here" was Kastara's grave. Deveren had never been able to bring himself to visit his dead wife's final resting place before. It had been too painful. Now, Kastara's passing bore no pain at all. He *knew* she was all right, and hoped that perhaps, when her work for her mistress was done, she might quietly come visit him here, now and again.

He smiled a little. "You must think me a poor father, bringing Allika to play in a place like this."

"Not at all." Imitating him, Vervain lay back in the grass, her arms folded behind her head. "Cemeteries don't have to be frightening. They're very peaceful. Especially when they ring with the laughter of a happy little girl." She turned her head and smiled at him, lifting one hand to shade her eyes from the sun's glare.

Allika scampered up to them at that moment. She was a tiny whirlwind. She paused to briefly kiss Deveren's forehead with a loud *smack*, repeated the gesture with Vervain, and then ran off again. The fat little puppy at her heels barked and jumped at her as she leaped up into the branches of an old, gnarled tree.

"She keeps begging me to allow her to wear boy's clothes to play in," sighed Deveren. "I may have to surrender." Allika was now hanging from the branches by her knees. The pretty dress Deveren had bought her, covered with dirt and grass stains, flopped over her head.

"Be grateful she's healthy and happy, Deveren. It's what all parents pray for."

Taking a deep breath, Deveren turned to look at her. "When I lost Kastara and our baby, I thought I'd lost everything. I wanted very little else from life but to be a husband and a father. Have you ever longed for a family, Vervain?"

"I am a Blesser. Such is denied to us while we serve the goddess."

Deveren's heart sank. He turned away quickly, fearful that she would see his expression and interpret it correctly. Apparently, though, he was not quick enough.

Vervain sat up, placing a soft hand on his arm. "You, alone of all men in Verold, know what it means to serve Health. You know what a duty it is."

Deveren nodded. He did know, but the knowing did not help ease his growing unhappiness.

"As long as I hear Health calling me to serve her, I am oath-bound to commit myself to no lesser being," the Healer continued. "But," and she squeezed his arm, coaxing him to face her, "there will come a day when the call will not come. And on that day, I will lay aside my scarlet robes of a Blesser and become merely a Healer—a woman free to give her hand where her heart has already gone."

Surprise and pleasure jolted Deveren. He gazed at her, hardly daring to believe his ears. Vervain's smile grew. He was seized with a longing to lean over and kiss her, but hesitated, wondering if such a desire was, at this point in their lives, right or wrong. He remembered their last such encounter and shame flooded him.

"Vervain," he stammered, "when you gave me the tincture . . ." He couldn't even say it. She reached up a gentle hand to brush his cheek.

"You succumbed to evil, as I knew you would—as you had to if the cure were to work. That was not the Deveren I love, kissing me. This is."

She leaned forward, pressing her lips, as scarlet and soft as her Blesser's robes, to his.

And oh, it was right.

*   *   *

The small gathering at Deveren's that night was not quite merry. Not yet. But it was a celebration, for at dawn the next day the quarantine would be lifted.

Castyll, Damir, Pedric, and Vandaris were in attendance. The feast was too large to feed six people; Deveren had planned it that way. Some of Braedon's hungry would be fed with what Deveren's gathering did not consume.

Deveren didn't do much talking. Instead, he observed. Castyll was fitting more and more into his father's shoes every day. Damir, his task in Braedon completed, would leave with the king to ride to Kasselton early in the morrow. Deveren knew that Damir was more than eager to see his family again. Vandaris had aged, but he was starting to get a little of his humor back, as was Pedric. Both men, young and old, no longer wore solely black clothing, though neither yet sported vibrant colors.

There was only one uncomfortable moment in the meal, when Vandaris, with a strange gleam in his eye, said, "I was talking with young Pedric here about your group—or should I perhaps call him Otter?"

Deveren had just brought a goblet of wine to his lips and almost choked. He forced himself to swallow. "And?" he pressed.

"I was very angry indeed."

Visions of the stocks, or prison, or perhaps the gallows appeared before Deveren's eyes. With a shadow of his old wicked grin, Pedric said, "Oh, yes. That we would form a hunting group and not invite Vandaris angered our good head councilman considerably."

"And how playful, to use animal names for a hunting party," said Vandaris, draining his own glass. "Perhaps this coming autumn I shall be able to join you in your, er, *fox* hunting." Slowly, Vandaris winked.

Relief made Deveren weak. He knew the explanation Pedric had offered was utterly false, and he was certain that Vandaris knew it, too. But as long as the head councilman pretended to be satisfied, it was enough for Deveren. He managed a weak smile.

Much later, Vandaris had gone home and the young king had retired. Pedric, Deveren, and Damir sat alone, finishing a bottle of extremely potent and extremely fine Mharian liquor.

"I'm going to miss you when you leave tomorrow," Deveren said honestly to his brother.

"And I you. We do not often get to see each other. And," he added, "now might be a good time to say farewell to Pedric, too."

Startled, Deveren glanced at Pedric. "You're leaving, too?"

"Guilty as charged," said Pedric, sipping his drink. "There's little here for me in Braedon, Dev, other than you and the thieves. And that's not quite enough to counter . . . counter the memories. Not yet. Your good brother has offered me a position where I can put my skills and talents to good use."

"A position?" Both Pedric and Damir stared at him. Deveren waved his hand. "Oh. One of *those* positions. I'm sure you'll be very useful to my brother, Pedric." He frowned into his glass, then made up his mind. "I hadn't wanted to tell you this, not yet. But since you're leaving . . ."

He drained his glass to work up the nerve, then began. "I told you about that night . . . about almost being killed by the thieves."

Pedric nodded, his brow furrowed. "Go on."

"Well, you saw enough that night to believe in miracles, I think. We all did. I . . . because I had been blessed by Health, I had the gift to see . . . ghosts."

He met Pedric's eyes. The young man stiffened. "Lady Death came that night. It seems the Blessers were right, much as we scoffed at them. I saw the dead come and take the souls of the dying. I saw Kastara, Pedric . . . and I saw Lorinda."

Pedric's breath caught. His hand tightened on the goblet,

shattered the fragile glass. Red blood mixed with red alcohol but Pedric didn't even notice.

"You're lying," whispered Pedric.

Deveren's eyes were sad, compassionate. "I'm not," he said quietly in a voice so sincere it could not be doubted.

"Why you?" cried Pedric. "Damn it, why did you get to see Kastara and I couldn't see Lorinda? Just see her for a moment, to know she was all right . . . !"

"Well," stammered Deveren, recalling the chaos that had swirled around him that night, "she was very busy at the time."

Horrified, he clapped his hand over his mouth. He'd been a little the worse—or better—for the alcohol and the words had just slipped out. They were true, as far as they went, but so flip, so thoughtless . . . !

"Pedric, I'm sorry, I . . ."

The young man buried his face in his hands. His shoulders shook. Deveren, stabbed with a thousand knives of remorse, rose and went to his friend, meaning to comfort. Then Pedric turned his handsome face up to Deveren's. Deveren realized with a jolt that the young man was not sobbing—he was laughing!

Then Damir began to chuckle. Finally Deveren, too, relaxed into laughter. "Oh, Dev," sighed Pedric at last, knuckling tears of mingled mirth and pain from his eyes, "I imagine she was busy indeed." He sighed heavily and wrapped a linen napkin over his bleeding hand. "I'll miss her till the day I die. Oh, I'll be all right. But she was beautiful, and wise, and kind, and I'll always regret not being able to have her in my life." He turned to his friend and said sincerely, "I'm glad you saw her. I wish it could have been me, but . . . I'm glad to know that there's more to death, after all, then rotting in the earth somewhere."

He rose. "I'll take the napkin, if I may. Sorry about your goblet, Dev."

Deveren saw him to the door. For a moment they stood, then wordlessly reached and embraced each other. Pedric grinned, looking almost like his old self again, punched Deveren playfully in the shoulder, then left. Deveren's heart lifted as the sound of Pedric's whistling reached his ears.

He closed the door. "You've got a good man there, Damir," he said to his brother. "I hope you take care of him. Don't let him run any unnecessary risks."

"Risk is always necessary in that job," replied Damir. "But not in other governmental positions. Deveren, let me ask you something. During this whole dreadful affair, you behaved magnificently. You covered my absence perfectly—"

"—at the cost of an innocent life. I don't call that perfect."

Damir sobered. "I understand, and I share your regret. But you saved my life by doing so. And therefore, Castyll's life was saved. And then, you gave the great gift of healing to hundreds on a night when most men ran screaming through the streets. You've done your kingdom a service beyond belief, my brother. When Byrn and Mhar unite, King Castyll will have need of such a subject. You'd make a fine diplomat."

Deveren shook his head. He thought of Allika, asleep upstairs; of Vervain, warm and soft against him earlier that afternoon. He thought of the kindness in the faces of his thieves, of the things they could do for themselves and the city.

"No, brother. I thank you, but I'm a thief, not a king's man."

Damir chuckled. "Say what you will, Dev. But for a brief time, you were both."

N. LEE WOOD

"An impressive first novel."
  —New York Times Book Review

"Wood delivers fast-paced adventure in a hybrid sci-fi/spy thriller that also connects on a personal level."
    —Publishers Weekly

"Persuasive double-dealing and paranoia...a highly encouraging science fiction/thriller debut." **—Kirkus Reviews**

An Ace Trade Paperback
_0-441-00298-6/$12.00

Look for **FARADAY'S ORPHANS**

Coming in June 1997

L
O
O
K
I
N
G

FOR ◆ THE
MAHDI

VISIT THE PUTNAM BERKLEY BOOKSTORE CAFÉ ON THE INTERNET:
http://www.berkley.com

Payable in U.S. funds. No cash accepted. Postage & handling: $1.75 for one book, 75¢ for each additional. Maximum postage $5.50. Prices, postage and handling charges may change without notice. Visa, Amex, MasterCard call 1-800-788-6262, ext. 1, or fax 1-201-933-2316; refer to ad #718

Or, check above books **Bill my:** ☐ Visa ☐ MasterCard ☐ Amex _____ (expires)
and send this order form to:
The Berkley Publishing Group Card# _____
                  ($10 minimum)
P.O. Box 12289, Dept. B Daytime Phone # _____
Newark, NJ 07101-5289 Signature _____
Please allow 4-6 weeks for delivery. **Or enclosed is my:** ☐ check ☐ money order
Foreign and Canadian delivery 8-12 weeks.

Ship to:

Name _____ Book Total $ _____
Address _____ Applicable Sales Tax $ _____
                  (NY, NJ, PA, CA, GST Can.)
City _____ Postage & Handling $ _____
State/ZIP _____ Total Amount Due $ _____

Bill to: Name _____

Address _____ City _____
State/ZIP _____

PUTNAM $\cancel{p}$ BERKLEY

online

Your Internet gateway to a virtual
environment with hundreds of
entertaining and enlightening books
from the Putnam Berkley Group.

While you're there visit the PB Café and
order-up the latest buzz on the best
authors and books around—Tom Clancy,
Patricia Cornwell, W.E.B. Griffin,
Nora Roberts, William Gibson,
Robin Cook, Brian Jacques, Jan Brett,
Catherine Coulter and many more!

Putnam Berkley Online is located at
http://www.putnam.com

• •

PB PLUG

Once a month we serve up the dish on the
latest science fiction, fantasy, and horror
titles currently on sale. Plus you'll get
interviews of your favorite authors, trivia,
a top ten list, and so much more
fun it's shameless.

Check out PB Plug at http://www.pbplug.com

• •